CHANGING NATURE

BOOK THREE
THE IMMORTAL DESCENDANTS

APRIL WHITE

ENTERTAINMENT

The Immortal Descendants Series

Marking Time
Tempting Fate
Changing Nature
Waging War
Cheating Death

Edited by Angela Houle
Cover design by Penny Reid
Cover images by Shutterstock
Quotes from *The Name of the Wind*
used with permission from Patrick Rothfuss

ISBN 978-0-9885368-4-5
Library of Congress control number: 2015901007
First American edition, January, 2015

"It's like everyone tells a story about themselves inside their own head. Always. All the time. That story makes you what you are. We build ourselves out of that story."

– Patrick Rothfuss
The Name of the Wind

Author's Foreword

As in both *Marking Time* and *Tempting Fate*, several plot points in *Changing Nature* are based on actual historical events. I discovered some fascinating things that happened in medieval times, but not all of them occurred during the year in which I've set this time travel story. I've taken some liberties with dates – one specific event actually happened twenty-one years after it takes place in my story, another was committed during the decade following the events in this book, and a building I describe wasn't actually built until later in the same century. I'm being vague because I don't want to spoil anything for those of you who, like me, enjoy surprises, but there are some fact-checkers among my readers (I know this because I'm one, too), so I'm warning you in advance. If you look up a thing or two while you're reading, don't do it by date.

I didn't go crazy re-arranging history – well, at least not more so than usual – but please read the note at the back of the book if you'd like to know when things truly happened. This history is really interesting, and I appreciate your indulgence as I adjust things to suit my needs.

LONDON RUN

The view from the top of Salt Tower was magnificent. It was a corner tower in the ancient fortress of the Tower of London, which held court around me like an aging warrior that had only just laid down its sword. The Tower Bridge in front of my seat on the parapet wore the colors of its July sunset like a summer dress, with flickering lights for its sparkly jewels.

I had jewels on the brain. Professor Ravindra Singh, my mentor at the Tower complex, had been all over the news last week for *his* discovery of the "Armada Pearls," the exquisite six-strand black pearl necklace Queen Elizabeth I had worn in the *Armada Portrait*. The media had jumped on the story, and I grinned at the delight on Professor Singh's face as he talked about the pearls to the swarm of reporters hounding our office every day since they were pulled from the secret stash in the sub-crypt of St. John's Chapel. The Tudor crown that my friend Ringo and I had found there in 1554 was, of course, long gone. Elizabeth I had handed it down to her heir, and so on, until 1649 when Oliver Cromwell had ordered it melted down along with nearly all the other crown jewels.

But the black pearls had survived, and it may or may not have been my suggestion to Elizabeth to hide them that saved the spectacular jewels from the fate of the other royal treasures. Even if I couldn't take credit for that out loud – because seriously, who would believe I'd met Elizabeth Tudor, or that such a thing as time travel even existed – *I* knew, and that was enough.

I stood up, dusted off my black jeans, pulled the hood of my favorite Ugly Kid sweatshirt up over my head to hide my long braid, and started down the outside of the tower. The handholds on Salt Tower were decent, and it would probably only take a couple minutes to descend.

Or less if I slipped.

But I'd been scaling these towers since I got a historical research internship with Professor Singh, and the game I played with Archer to keep my commute entertaining was *Find Me*. Since Archer was a Vampire with some extra badassery in the skills department, the game was way better than traditional hide-and-seek. He couldn't rise until sunset, so I'd wait on top of one of the towers until the sun hit the horizon. And then it was time to play.

He was never sure which section of the Tower I'd choose for my escape route, or, if he didn't catch me outside the walls, which bridge I'd use to cross the Thames. The first person to hit a chair at Bishop Cleary's dinner table was the winner. Loser had to do dishes. Since Archer didn't actually eat with me and the jeans-wearing, silver-maned bishop who had become our friend, it wasn't really fair. But whoever said life was fair?

I touched down outside Salt Tower and took off at full speed toward the Tower Bridge. The route seemed straightforward enough, but involved a tree-climb, a roof-jump, and a drop down to the walkway along the bank of the Thames. By the time I got under Tower Bridge Road and up the stairs to street level, I was feeling pretty confident I'd left Archer looking for my dust back at the Tower.

It was almost nine o'clock at night – summers in England were brutal on Archer's waking schedule – so traffic on the Tower Bridge was fairly light, and I let my pace fall back into something less freakish. Foot traffic was almost non-existent, which was why the faint sound of rubber soles hitting the pavement behind me put my half-Shifter senses on high alert.

When my guts started twisting in the way Monger-proximity brings on, those Shifter senses started searching for an escape route. I didn't look behind me. I didn't need to. The Descendants of War were bad news in every sense of the word, and the only Monger I knew who didn't automatically hunt me on sight was Tom Landers, a mixed-blood like me. He was also probably dead by now, so call me a conclusion-jumper, but it was a safe bet it wasn't Tom on my tail.

I broke into a full sprint. That the footsteps behind me did too was no surprise. It *was* a surprise that they were gaining on me. I wasn't a sprinter, but not many people could keep up when I free-ran. My problem was that this wasn't free-running. This was just running. And I was going to lose.

The first support tower was coming up, and I knew that urban obstacles were going to be my best shot at getting out of whatever steaming pile of poo I was tap-dancing in. I darted across the road, and the sudden change of direction bought me a half second, just long enough to shove my way into the door at the bottom of the tower. I was up the first round of stairs before the door slammed open below me, and I knew I had to push hard to make it up to the scenic walkway first.

I spotted a dark head of hair below me on the staircase as I sprinted up the steps. His maleness and steroidal hugeness were confirmed, and not in a comforting way. He was also taking the steps two at a time and gaining on me.

Which meant the Monger-induced nausea was, too.

This wasn't going to end well for me unless I got really lucky or spectacularly creative. And since I had no control over luck, I made a split decision to go with my instincts. At the walkway level, high above the Thames, I saw a trapdoor above me that led to what I assumed was the upper exterior of the bridge structure. I remembered my Pixie friend Olivia once told me she'd gone across the bridge on top of the walkway, so this was as creative as it got.

I shoved against the trap door and it gave way. I didn't think Steroid-Boy could miss the fact that I'd disappeared from the staircase, but hopefully he'd have a little trouble with the size of the trap door. I was tall, too, but I didn't have shoulders like the fricking Hulk.

My breath hitched in my chest as I started up a ladder into the blackness above me. I tried to slow the gasping down so I didn't hyperventilate, and I was very glad Archer and I had been free-running every night after work, so I didn't actually resemble the flopping fish I sounded like. He'd also been teaching me the finer points of sword-fighting in our makeshift gym on the roof of Guy's Chapel. Not that I had access to a sword at the moment nor the inclination to use one on Steroid-Boy, but waving a sword around was hard work, and my arm strength was showing the benefits as I hauled myself up the ladder.

I still hadn't heard Steroid-Boy open the trap door below me, and I wondered if maybe I had actually given him the slip. Wait, no … there it was. The trap door. And a Steroid-Boy-sized grunt as he shoved his unseemly amounts of muscle through the opening.

I hit the ceiling and felt around the seams of another trap door above me. There was the latch, and I knew the minute I opened it I'd become a giant silhouetted target in the lights on the bridge structure. So, it was time for a diversion.

I did a speedy pocket-pat-down and realized the one thing I could stand to lose was my mini Maglite. So I took a breath, braced my shoulder against the trap door, and whipped it down on Steroid-Boy's head.

"THUNK" is a very satisfying sound when coming from the skull of the Neanderthal chasing me. I flung open the upper trap door, hauled myself out, and slammed it shut behind me. I crouched down on top of it for good measure while I took stock of my surroundings.

Okay, wow. This view was seriously spectacular. A tiny part of my brain that wasn't occupied with my immediate safety knew I'd be bringing Archer up here for a midnight picnic. Or, you know, sword-fight. But the fight or flight instinct had kicked in hard, and I knew my sprint across the top of the Tower Bridge had to buy me enough of an advantage to get down through the next tower and back out to the street before Steroid-Boy could catch me.

There was a wind coming off the Thames so I stayed low and took my center of gravity down close to the structure. When I was

4

about halfway across, a sudden gust nearly took me off my feet. Heart pounding, I dropped to my knees to stay balanced, and a flicker of movement behind me grabbed my attention. Steroid-Boy had flung open the trap door and was staring straight at me.

I spared him exactly one second of shocked silence before I did the most ridiculous thing I've ever done. I stuck my tongue out at him.

Yup, that's right. I was officially twelve.

Actually, my eighteenth birthday was in less than a week, but if I didn't get moving, I wouldn't see it. I jumped back to my feet, keeping low, and ran the rest of the way across the roof of the walkway. In that one second, I had seen such intense malevolence in his eyes that I knew which Family he came from. And despite his dark hair and scary glare, he reminded me very strongly of my delightful former roommate, Raven. Not that that proved anything, but if Steroid-Boy happened to be Raven's older brother, he wouldn't be bothered by little things like rules, laws, and fair play, especially considering I'd doinked him on the head with a Maglite.

If Raven was less-than-affectionately known as The Crow, I thought Steroid-Boy could be re-dubbed Dodo, after the big, clumsy paragons of intelligence who had managed to get themselves wiped out by humans. The way he was trying to cross the top of the bridge, at full height and speed, I put his odds of extinction at about fifty/fifty. Another big gust of wind came up just as I had crouched down to lift the other trap door, and I saw Dodo waver and almost lose his balance. He dropped to his knees and held onto the edge with a white-knuckled grip. I thought I caught a look of desperation on his face as I dropped down to the ladder inside, and I actually considered going back to help him across.

For about a second.

And then I got over it.

I knew I had maybe ninety seconds to make it down the ladder and through the lower trap door before Dodo hit the other side, and I didn't waste any more time on things like a pesky conscience.

5

This time I was faster, and I made it through the bottom trap door without hearing the other one open above me.

Maybe I'd gotten lucky after all.

I didn't bother with the stairs, just vaulted the railing and went landing to landing. That bought me another two minutes. I had almost hit the realm of self-congratulation when I got to the street-level door – and it was locked.

No!

And then I yelled it. "NOOOO!" I pounded on the metal door and yelled with every last ounce of breath. "Somebody let me out!"

I shot a quick glance above me and saw Dodo drop down from the trap door to the staircase. I had about three minutes left before he hit the bottom stair, and all I could think was, why did I stick my tongue out?

I faltered for one second. Then pounded harder. "Please! Someone open the door!"

The gnawing Monger-induced nausea was starting to hit full volume again when the door was wrenched open, and I was yanked outside. My fist was still raised to pound the door, and I almost slugged Archer in the face.

Archer! Thank God! He took one look past me to the big Monger vaulting the last of the steps, slammed the door shut behind me, and then twisted the metal handle so that it jammed in place.

He grabbed my hand and we ran.

It was a pure parkour run to get to Guy's Chapel at King's College – the most direct possible route at top speed, either over, under, or through any barrier between us and safety. Archer and I didn't waste breath on words; that would come later. Unlike the game we played every night, there was nothing fun about this. Grim reality had intruded into our world again, and I was pissed. I'd had exactly one month of a relatively normal, somewhat peaceful life since school had gotten out for the summer. I'd been staying in Bishop Cleary's guest room while I worked for Professor Singh at the Tower during the week, and spending weekends back at Elian Manor with my mom and Millicent. Archer slept in the priest hole under the Guy's Chapel altar while I was at work, and hung out with me after dark until I passed out around one or two a.m. Fortunately, Professor Singh was a forgiving boss and accepted my 11am-7pm shift without question.

When we got to Guy's Chapel, Archer pulled me into the courtyard across the street, out of sight of the front door. He held me close to him so he could whisper in my ear. "Did you feel anyone behind us?"

He meant the flu-like nausea that Monger-proximity induced, which he called my "spidey sense." I shook my head. "Not since the bridge."

"They were posted all the way around the Tower. The east towers were unguarded, so I knew that was the one who followed you."

I was angry. "Why now? They've left us alone all summer. What would they have done, kidnap me? For what?"

A car drove by, and Archer pulled me deeper into the shadows. It didn't slow down, but he scanned the street carefully, put his finger to his lips, and gestured for us to run across the street. I nodded, and then took a breath to open up all my senses. Nope, nothing predatory out there that I could feel; Monger, or otherwise. I squeezed his hand, and then we took off.

We made it to the side entrance and in the door with no movement from anything but us on the street. Archer threw the bar across the door behind us, and we made our way into Bishop Cleary's private kitchen.

A pot sat covered on the stove with half a loaf of crusty French bread on the cutting board next to it. Archer perched on the edge of his chair while I served myself a bowl of what smelled like curried vegetable soup, cut a big chunk off the bread, and sat down across from him.

He watched me eat in silence, and I was glad my hand was steady with the spoon. "The guy looked like a Rothchild. Like

Raven, only dark-haired and huge." I tore off a piece of bread and dipped before I finally met Archer's eyes.

His fingers were steepled, and he had relaxed enough to lean his elbows on the table while he considered what I said. Then he nodded. "There is an older brother, and I believe he's been working as a mercenary at the oil refineries in Nigeria."

"Awesome." Sarcasm dripped from my tone. "He would have caught me if I hadn't gone into the support tower of the bridge. He was faster than me on the straight away."

"The others I saw around the Tower of London were also trained. They intended to take you tonight."

"You're on their list, too. They must've known that if they found me, they would probably get you, too."

A grim smile played on his lips. "Not that I mind being a package deal with you, but if they had weapons, they weren't obvious. And an unarmed man would find it difficult to take me."

The soup was good and exactly what I needed to refuel after the energy burn of the night. "The view on top of Tower Bridge is really pretty." Nothing like being the queen of non-sequiturs.

Archer looked at me sharply. "You mean the walkway?"

I shook my head. "I mean the top. It's how I got ahead of Dodo. His center of gravity was too high for the wind up there." I watched Archer carefully.

He took a breath, then the corner of his mouth quirked up. "Dodo?"

Relief surged through me. He wasn't going to question my judgment or make me feel like a kid with a disapproving parent. But I buried it quickly with a casual shrug. "I caught the resemblance to Raven when he tried to go across the bridge at full height. He just looked like a big, dumb, about-to-be-extinct Dodo bird."

There was amusement in his eyes. "You'll have to take me up there some time."

I grinned. "Too bad the wind's so strong. Sword-fighting across the top of the bridge would be epic."

He suppressed a smile. "Too bad."

I cleared my bowl and washed my dishes, then put away the rest of the soup and washed out that pot too. Archer wrapped up the rest of the bread, and the domesticity of the scene struck me as strange and precious because it was so normal. And normal was definitely odd in our world where the Descendants of War were hunting mixed-bloods like me and had license to kill Vampires like Archer on sight.

"Speaking of sword-fighting, I want the katana tonight."

This time he actually did smile. "Confident enough in your martial arts to take me on with a katana?"

I threw the dish towel at him. "Are you?"

Bishop Cleary was the only full-time resident at Guy's Chapel, and the attics had long since been emptied of anything but dust and a family of finches that had made a nest under the eaves. He gave us permission to use it as a make-shift gym, and sometimes even came upstairs to watch us train. Tonight he was at some big ecclesiastical meeting, so he'd probably stop in when he got home.

I always trained in the same clothes I wore in real life – basically just jeans, boots, and t-shirts. In my world, the hand-to-hand combat had been real, and I never got a chance to say, "Hold on, time out. Excuse me while I go change into sweats so I can fight you." In fact, the last time I had to actively defend myself from a sword, I'd been wearing a sixteenth-century dress that weighed a ton, and the sword was being wielded by a Monger/Vampire named Bishop Wilder, who had been as much out of his Victorian time as I had been out of my modern one. He'd traveled to 1554 to make sure Elizabeth Tudor died in the Tower of London before she became queen, which he hoped would give him access to the blood of one of the greatest Seers of all time. Seers are the Descendants of Fate, and their skills range from basic fortune-telling to full-blown prophecies. Archer had Seer blood in him, which was why when Bishop Wilder bit him back in 1888, the mutated porphyria infection turned him into a Vampire instead of killing him outright like it would a regular, non-Descendant human.

9

I was descended from both Time and Nature – my mother, Claire Elian, is a Clocker, and my dad, Will Shaw, was a Shifter Lion. I can't Shift, but I do have hereditary feline skills that work really well when I'm free-running, or when someone's coming at me with a Japanese samurai sword like the katana in Archer's hands.

I leapt backwards and held my own sword in front of me with both hands on the hilt. Katanas are two-handed swords, and Archer had taught me the seven basic moves to use depending on where my opponent had left himself open.

My problem was that Archer was fast, so whatever was open, wasn't for long.

"The top two inches of the blade are where you should aim all your power when you slash, Saira. It gives you the distance you need for a good swing and allows the sharpest part of the blade to be the focus." Archer's skill with various weapons was impressive, though he said he'd always preferred blades to guns. With a knife or a sword, a person had to really mean to hurt or kill their opponent, which usually meant that running away hadn't been an option. With a gun, people could kill by complete accident, and that didn't sit well with his code about life and death. We joked about Vampire morality, but for him it was serious business. In spite of needing blood to survive, or maybe because of it, he had never taken anyone's life for granted.

My nerves jangled with the predator instinct that made me more agile than usual. Maybe I just anticipated his moves, or maybe the adrenaline from my fight or flight earlier had woken some new skills in me, but after forty-five minutes we were both grinning, and I was dripping with sweat.

"Nice. You're getting stronger," Archer said.

"I noticed it when I was climbing earlier. You're not so bad yourself, Vampire."

He took my katana and wiped it down carefully with a soft cloth before storing them both in a hard-sided case. For the past month, since I'd asked him for sword-fighting lessons, Archer had been acquiring pairs of all these different kinds of weapons to teach

10

me. Fencing with rapiers was the hardest since they required so much finesse, and broadswords were tough because they were so freaking heavy. I liked the very cool-looking scimitars, and katanas were totally badass, but my favorites to fight with were daggers.

Archer had given me throwing lessons, and we had a target set up at one end of the attic. While he was putting away the katanas, I picked up my two favorite daggers, a matched pair with silk-wrapped handles and hard steel blades, and chose a spot across the room from the target. I stood with my feet about shoulder-width apart and took aim.

I could feel that the first dagger was going to be off as it left my hand, and it hit the wall just under the target. Archer had been a patient teacher with me though, so I didn't give in to frustration. I just took a breath, re-set my shoulders, and threw.

The second dagger hit dead center on the target.

"Did you feel the difference in your throw?" Archer had been studying me, and my happy grin must have been infectious because his eyes lit up with pride.

"The way my fingers let go. The second throw was all at once."

He nodded. "Perfect." He pulled a piece of fabric, about five inches wide and about six feet long, from one of the weapons cases. "Grab the daggers and come here. I'll show you how to conceal them on your body."

I stood in front of him and let him wrap the fabric around me like a tight vest. He slotted a dagger under each arm and then checked the fit. "You could wear this under a loose shirt and the blades would be safe, even while you run."

I studied my reflection in a long mirror that stood in one corner. It looked simple, and even when I swung my arms to test it, the daggers stayed secure. "It's perfect. And low-tech enough that I can do it anywhere."

Archer appeared in the mirror behind me and turned me to face him. Very carefully he removed each dagger and set it down on the table. My eyes were locked on his face as he took his time unwrapping the sash from around my body. His touch was gentle, and his gaze sent shivers down my spine. When the fabric was open, he used it to pull me toward him.

"Thank you for outrunning the Monger." His whisper was like a caress against my hair.

"Thank you for getting me out of there." The deep blue of his eyes was mesmerizing, and I smiled when his glance went to my mouth.

Right before he kissed me.

"Eh, hem. I'm so sorry. I thought you'd still be training."

I grinned against Archer's mouth and pulled back from him to see Bishop Cleary standing in the doorway at the top of the attic stairs. "No worries. We were just wrapping up."

Our friend, the current bishop at Guy's Chapel, King's College, was trying unsuccessfully to hide his own smile. "Right, then. I'll meet you in the study?"

"Be down in a minute." I snuck another quick kiss in as Bishop Cleary turned to leave, and then backed up to pull my hoodie back on over my damp t-shirt before I got cold. Archer grabbed my hood and pulled me in for another, longer kiss before he reluctantly let go, and we went downstairs.

The fire was lit in Bishop Cleary's study, and I curled up in my favorite Danish modern chair across from his desk. Archer's hand brushed my shoulder as he passed me to sit in the other one.

"So, you know I was at a bishops' meeting."

"Right. What's new in the church business?" Bishop Cleary was used to my irreverence, so I knew I wouldn't offend him, but his expression stayed serious.

"Obviously I can't disclose the private affairs of the Church of England, but something came up tonight that may have some bearing on the situation with War's Descendants."

I stared at Bishop Cleary. "Mongers are getting mainstream attention?"

"They may have nothing whatsoever to do with what's being reported in every district in the city, but I thought you should know what the parish priests are concerned about." He paused, then

12

inhaled. "In the last week, over forty people have disappeared. Not all in London, so Scotland Yard doesn't seem to have picked up on the pattern quite yet, but the priests are hearing about it from frightened families of the missing."

Archer leaned forward. "Why do you think the Mongers are involved, Pat?"

Bishop Cleary regarded him steadily. "Because I recognize some of the Family names from your genealogy."

MISSING

The names Bishop Cleary had heard from the priests spanned the Descendant Families – all but the Mongers. There was a Rowen and a Mulroy from the Shifter clans, a Kardos, Foss, and Constantine from the Seers, and even a Kelly and an Eddowes from the old Clocker Families. There were many more names, of course, but because Archer had compiled the Immortal Descendants genealogy back in 1888, none of the more recent Family names were known to us.

"Do the missing people have anything in common? I mean, besides a relationship to Immortal Descendants?"

Bishop Cleary shook his head. "Nothing I could really put together from the reports. Some are young, a few are middle-aged, and only four of them are elderly. Their families said they had all left their home or workplace and just never made it to their destination."

A cold chill ran through me, and Archer and I stared at each other. "Was I supposed to be added to that list tonight?"

Bishop Cleary suddenly leaned across his desk. "What happened, Saira?"

I filled him in on my escape from the Monger, with Archer adding his observances about the array of thugs waiting outside the Tower. For me, apparently. The more I talked about it, the more likely it sounded that the night's events were supposed to have been an ambush. I suppose I should have been flattered that a gang of Mongers was sent after me, though if the whole gang had actually chased me, I wouldn't have made it.

Our friend looked grim. "I don't like it, Saira. Obviously, between the two of you, you're as safe as one could hope without hiding you away in an attic somewhere."

My gut tightened. Anne Frank I was not.

"However, of immediate concern is why are these people being taken, and what will happen to them?"

I looked at Archer. "I think maybe we need to talk to someone on the Descendants' Council, either Millicent or the Armans. Find out what they know." He nodded, and I turned to Bishop Cleary. "I guess I'm going to call in sick tomorrow, which is a bummer because with all the publicity about the Armada Pearls, other missing jewel mysteries are starting to come in from the academics."

Archer looked thoughtful. "I imagine it's the publicity that brought you to the Mongers' attention again. I'm sure you've been photographed in the background in Ravi's office. In any case, it's probably best to avoid the Tower for a few days."

I grimaced. "Why do I suddenly feel like the prisoner who can't get *in* the Tower of London?" I stood up and went around the desk to kiss Bishop Cleary on the cheek. "Thank you for everything. I hope we can be back next week, but I have a feeling I may have to stay low until we figure out what the Mongers are up to."

"You are always welcome here – both of you. If there's ever anything I can do to help, you have only to ask."

Archer shook Bishop Cleary's hand, and I ran upstairs to quickly throw some things into a backpack. I didn't want to be gone too long, but my wishes didn't seem to have too much to do with my reality when it came to Mongers.

Archer met me outside and we sprinted down the alley to a parking garage where he kept his Aston Martin. I loved that car, and he let me drive it whenever our journeys took us outside London. I was his look-out tonight though, and within fifteen minutes we were out of the city and speeding toward Elian Manor.

When it was clear we weren't being followed, I let myself relax back into the deep leather seat. "Have you Seen anything about any of this?"

He shook his head. "I haven't had visions of any kind in several weeks."

The only visions I knew he had were the ones I'd Seen by touching him, usually when we were asleep. We hadn't slept next to each other since 1554, when we were hiding out in the Tower of London trying to save Elizabeth Tudor from Bishop Wilder's bloodthirsty plot. Now, when I was in London, it was out of respect for Bishop Cleary that we stayed out of my room, and the weekends at Elian Manor were spent surrounded by people. Besides Lady Millicent Elian, my cousin many times removed and the current Head of the Clocker Family, my mom, Claire, and all the staff who kept the massive place running, we usually hung out with Mr. Shaw who, in addition to being in love with my mother, was helping us research possible points in history to look for Bishop Wilder.

Maybe tonight, since they weren't expecting us at Elian Manor, we'd be able to sneak in and curl up for a nap together.

Archer's voice drew me out of my fantasies of sleep. "If these missing persons incidents are, indeed, the work of Mongers, could they be escalating their mixed-blood moratorium policy? Or, even worse, are they perhaps a consequence of a ripple or split in time?"

I clutched my head. "Oh, God! I don't even want to imagine that Wilder could be messing around with history again." The last time he did that, there was a ripple effect in our modern time which altered the power structure of the Monger Families. It also turned the Head of the Seer Family, Camille Arman, against me when she thought I stole a Family heirloom. Her twin children, Adam and Ava, were my friends, and even with the accusations their mother leveled against me, they stayed on my side. The odd thing was that when Archer, Ringo, and I stopped Wilder from changing history, everything in our modern time went back to normal. And no one but us remembered that it had ever been anything different.

16

"I guess we'll need to start poking around Monger business to see if anything has changed." Archer sounded as frustrated as I felt.

"Changed from what? Who's to say we know what's normal? And temporal physics? Not my best subject."

"I don't know. You seem better qualified than most at this point." Archer's voice had a calming effect on me.

"Not better than my pain-in-the-butt cousin, Doran. But he doesn't count because his only job in life is to frustrate the hell out of me. I might start carrying daggers just so I can use him for quick-reflex target practice whenever he Clocks into a room."

That snarky statement earned a bark of laughter from Archer. Doran wasn't his favorite person either, although the information he'd parceled out in little bite-sized morsels had been incredibly useful as I learned the rules for time travel. But it was never enough and just made me greedy to know more.

"What do you really know about Doran?"

The question surprised me. "I don't know. Miss Simpson showed me a St. Brigid's School yearbook from the seventies that had him in it. She's the one who said he was a cousin, I think. And he's definitely a Clocker, though my mom's never met him. Actually, come to think of it, you're the only other person I know besides Miss Simpson and me who has seen him."

"I'm thinking a little investigating into your *cousin* might be in order."

I waved a dismissive hand. "Have at it."

The headlights were the only illumination on the single lane road we'd turned down, and the massive trees along the drive stood like ancient sentinels above us. "Park near the stables so we don't wake anyone up." It was after midnight, and the big manor house that came into view was dark. Archer cut the engine even before coasting to a stop, and we moved with tagger stealth around the grounds. Millicent's big gray cat stared at me from the eaves of the stables, and I whispered a greeting to him.

"Hey, Cat."

"He doesn't have a name?"

"Not that anyone's told me."

Archer held his hand up, and Cat came forward to receive his homage, rubbing his sides along Archer's knuckles and purring loudly enough to wake the sleepers inside the manor house. I stared. I'd never seen Cat do more than squint at anyone before leaning down to clean his bits.

"I didn't know you liked cats."

Archer looked over at me with a smirk. "Really … Shifter?"

Guh. I never felt feline unless I was running, but the way Archer's eyes slid over me, I suddenly felt like rubbing myself over his knuckles too.

Quickly switching tracks on that train of thought, I reached into the back seat for my backpack, slung it over my shoulder, and after a last look at the very playful smirk still dancing on Archer's face, I skulked off toward the house.

Archer's silent chuckle followed me as we made our way to the kitchen door. I knew the heavy wooden bar would be locking it from the inside, but the root cellar just outside had a trap door to the laundry room I'd discovered on one of my explorations of the massive house. When I pulled the old iron ring, the heavy metal door lifted without a squeak. Someone must have oiled the hinges recently, which was weird, since the root cellar hadn't been used for regular storage in years.

I motioned Archer to silence and carefully set my backpack on the ground outside the root cellar. I used hand signals to let him know I'd drop in without light. He nodded and indicated he'd be right behind me.

I listened with all the predator senses I had, but heard and felt nothing. I wasn't sure why my spidey sense was telling me something was strange, but I'd learned to pay attention to my instincts. And with Archer's super-speed and strength behind me, I was fairly confident I wasn't being stupid.

The drop to the dirt floor of the root cellar was less than ten feet, so I opted for speed instead of stealth, just in case anything needed surprising down there. My eyes adjusted quickly to the dark, and I took two steps forward so Archer could drop in behind me.

We both froze and let the silence of the root cellar fill our senses. Something small and likely furry skittered away in a far corner, but that wasn't the kind of creature we were listening for.

"It's empty." My whisper was more of a breath, but I knew Archer heard me. I reached for the mini Maglite I had restocked my back pocket with and aimed the business-end into my hand before clicking it on. Gradually I allowed the light to fill the space around us. I had expected it to be empty except for a couple of boxes stacked against a far wall and a built-in shelf under the ladder. But things were different.

"Someone's been here." I was still whispering, and Archer knelt down to look at the tarp that had been spread out on the dirt floor. There was a sleeping bag, pillow, battery-powered lamp, jug of water, package of cookies, and a magazine tossed in a jumble on the tarp. Archer turned on the lamp, and it illuminated nearly the whole space. He picked up a magazine and showed it to me. A classic bikers-n-babes garbage rag full of plastic girls spilling out of tiny triangle bikinis.

"The spine hasn't been cracked, and the battery on the lamp is fresh. I'd say whoever it is hasn't stayed here yet."

"Think it's one of Millicent's staff?" I asked.

"No." Archer was examining the sleeping bag. "This is the kind of gear they issue to paramilitary forces."

I stared at him. "And you know that because ...?"

"I might have been one once."

That was a conversation for a non-whisper situation. "Do you think this was back-up in case they didn't get us in London?"

"I don't think this is about me. There'd be more than one kit if they were planning to take both of us. No, Saira. This is about you."

"That's annoying."

Archer was fighting a smile at my sarcasm, which I loved. He had put the caveman back in the cave when it came to my safety, and I appreciated having a partner instead of a dad. Mr. Shaw was enough surrogate dad for a lifetime.

"I think I might need to wake someone up about this." There were so many reasons I was reluctant to do that. Most things look much less dire in daylight, for one.

"Don't," Archer said. "I'll stay out here tonight. Whoever is planning to camp out here will come either tonight or tomorrow night, since you've been spending weekends here. I'll wake the house if I need to. You should sleep and tell Millicent in the morning."

It was the smart plan, though a part of me still wished for my curl-up-and-nap one. "Okay, I'll get everyone together in the study tomorrow evening so we can figure out what to do about this, and in the meantime, I'll find out what Millicent and maybe the Armans know about Descendant snatchers."

Archer pulled me in for a kiss that made my toes curl. Then he slipped me some steel.

"Wait, what?" I pulled back to realize he had placed my two favorite daggers in my hand.

"I'd been resisting the idea of arming you in your bed, but now I think you should keep these under your pillow."

I grinned, savoring the weight of the daggers in my hand. "Means you can't sneak in."

"No, I just have to be faster than you."

"Yeah, good luck with that."

Archer laughed, kissed me again lightly, and sent me through the trap door into the house.

Sleep came quickly and was dreamless in the bedroom I used when I was at Elian Manor. I hadn't been asleep for long, when the light glowing in the room that had been my mom's when she was young told me I might still get breakfast.

I spent most of the week living out of a backpack, so it was nice to change out of my uniform of black jeans and hoodies. I branched out into low-slung red skinny cords, and when I paired them with a plain V-neck t-shirt and the long chain with the black, tear-drop pearl pendant Elizabeth Tudor had given me, I was positively dressed up.

As I'd hoped, the breakfast things were still out. It was almost like staying in a really fancy hotel, right down to the very proper lady holding court at one end of the table.

"Good morning, Millicent."

She looked up in surprise. "Saira. I wasn't aware you had come in. When did you arrive?"

"Late last night. Is my mom up yet?"

"She's gone out to the garden, I believe."

I didn't want to tell the same story twice, and although Millicent and I had hit a sort of neutral ground in our battle for control over me, I preferred to have my mom at my back whenever possible when I dealt with her.

"Are you around today?" I knew my casual sloppiness with the English language chapped her, but she managed not to wince.

"I have an appointment in the village this afternoon, but yes, otherwise, I will be at the manor."

"Good. I'm going to help Mom finish whatever she's doing because I need to talk to you both."

Millicent regarded me for a long moment. Part of me wondered if I had suddenly grown pink hair, but the other part was content to sip my coffee and let her have her examination.

"I'll join you, then. We can talk in the garden."

Huh. Wasn't expecting that.

Millicent swept from the breakfast room, and a mousy maid scurried in to clear her tea cup and plate. "Hey, Hazel?" She looked up, maybe surprised I knew her name. "Has anyone on the staff seen someone skulking around the grounds?"

She looked frightened. "Oh no, Miss. Lady Millicent wouldn't allow it, Miss."

I sighed. No matter what Millicent and her staff thought, she couldn't control the world with sheer force of will, indomitable though it may be. "Okay, could you just ask around?"

"Of course, Miss." Hazel dipped a curtsey before scurrying from the room.

I slugged my coffee and grabbed a croissant off the sideboard as I went out.

The day was already sunny, and my mom's face was invisible under her big English gardener's hat. It's why she had perfect skin and still looked like she was in her thirties. For that matter, unless she started Clocking again, she'd always look like this. We Clockers don't age unless we are in our native time, and this wasn't hers. My mom had been born in 1850, a fact I only just discovered last year when she went missing in 1888. My dad was also from that time, but he had died in a cellar collapse under Bethlem Hospital for the Insane, otherwise known as Bedlam, during my mom's rescue from Jack the Ripper. I was the last Clocker on the Elian Family tree because Millicent never had kids, and my mom's time-jump forward put her in the twentieth century for my birth. So despite the fact that I theoretically should have been born in 1871 and the Clocker line would have continued from my descendants, a couple potential generations were skipped when this became my native time.

"Good morning," I said to the hat.

My mom looked up, startled. "Oh, Saira! You scared me."

I knelt down to move her bucket closer and started gathering up all the weeds she'd already pulled. Mom's face broke into a grin and she kissed my cheek. "What a pleasant surprise. You took the day off of work?"

I sat back on my heels. "Sort of. I needed to get out of London."

The smile fled her face and concern immediately flooded her eyes. "What happened?"

Just then Millicent entered the walled garden, and my mom eyes widened. She stood up and dusted off. "Millicent. What a surprise to see you here."

"Saira said she needed to speak to both of us." Millicent pulled on a pair of dainty leather gardening gloves and knelt down to continue weeding the patch Mom had been working on. My mom and I stared at each other with twin expressions of shock, and I knelt to join them.

"I was followed from work by a Monger. A big one that Archer thinks might be Raven Rothchild's older brother. He came after me, but I managed to get away."

It was easier to talk when we were all working side by side because I could concentrate on my hands instead of their faces. I didn't have to see the surprise to know it was there.

"Devereux was with you?" It was hard not to bristle at Millicent's arch tone, but I knew it was just her breeding to sound cold and indifferent.

"At the end. He helped me get away."

"Well, you can't go back to London."

I looked Millicent in the eyes and took a deep breath to control my temper. "While I appreciate your concern, I don't respond well to being given orders." I included my mom in my gaze. "Archer and I came here last night because a lot of people have gone missing in the past week. People with Family names."

I was watching Millicent carefully, but her expression gave away nothing. My mom sat back and watched me. "You think the disappearances are linked to the attempt on you?"

"I don't know why Descendants are being snatched, or even if they are Descendants. But Archer said it was a full-on attempt at grabbing me. He saw Mongers at every entrance to the Tower, and the one who went after me has paramilitary training. Also," I turned to Millicent, "we found a stake-out set up in the root cellar last night. Archer spent the night outside watching it. Since he didn't wake us up, apparently no one came to use it."

Millicent's eyes narrowed dangerously. "Here? At Elian Manor?"

"Yes, here. We think it was set up as a base for snatching me when I came home this weekend. Archer said the kit is all paramilitary issue, and he expects it to be manned tonight."

Millicent huffed. "Well, this is just outrageous. I'll have Jeeves dismantle it immediately." She started to stand, but the sharpness of my tone stopped her.

"No. The best way we have of figuring this out is to take whoever comes and question them. Worst case we can bring them up in front of the Descendants' Council and put pressure on the Mongers to back off."

"And if Devereux can't capture him?"

I shot her a look with a poison dart attached. "If he shows, we'll take him. What I want to know from you is if you have heard anything in the council about what the Mongers are up to?"

Her expression froze into a neutral mask again. "Nothing more than the usual bluster from Markham."

"So, Markham Rothchild is still the Head?"

She looked startled. "Of course he is, though there seems to be some question of who will succeed him."

"Why, is he going somewhere?"

"Markham is younger than I. Nonetheless, his daughter is claiming rights for herself, and her husband seems to think the position should pass to him."

I stared. "The Rothbitch wants to be Head?"

"Saira!" My mom sounded a little horrified at the name.

I smirked. "Come on, Mom. You know she deserves it." I turned back to Millicent. "Could the power struggle have something to do with the snatchers?"

"I'm sure I wouldn't know."

"Well, who would?" I was challenging her with my tone, and she didn't like it. Her eyes narrowed as she stood to go.

"The Descendants' Council is a governing body, Saira, not a police force."

I stood to face her, and for the first time noticed that I actually towered over her. Being 5'10" definitely had its advantages. "Right. You guys just let the Mongers police us." She said nothing for a moment, then swept from the garden in a way that would have worked brilliantly with long skirts a hundred years ago. Mom shook her head as she watched Millicent go.

"Do you think she knows anything?" I asked.

My mom studied me from under the brim of her hat, and then wiped a hair out of her eyes with a sigh. "Millicent Elian believes the world should be a certain way, and she will twist her own corner of it to suit herself with very little regard for what's actually

24

true. It's one of her particular talents. Another one is convincing others to believe her version of the truth."

"Or bullying them into it."

A half-smile quirked her mouth. "Well, she can try …"

"What do *you* think, Mom?"

"Tell me more about the missing people."

I filled her in on what Bishop Cleary had reported from the priests. It wasn't enough to base any real theories on though, so we went into the manor and pulled out her laptop to check whatever news reports we could find. A couple of hours of internet searches later, we had a list of thirty names that had been publicly reported. The other ten may have only been reported to the priests.

Millicent had gone out, and my mom didn't recognize more than the few older Family names, so we called the Armans and got ourselves invited to tea.

My mom had never been to the Arman's stunning Georgian townhouse before, and I gave her a quick rundown of its history. The house had originally belonged to Archer's father, Lord Devereux, and Archer had sold it to Camille's great grandmother. Maybe because of that, Camille had always treated Archer with a kind of respect that very few other Descendants gave known Vampires.

"Hi, Earnest." The Armans' butler gave Jeeves a run for his money in the spit-shine department.

Earnest inclined his head toward us regally. "Miss Elian, Lady Elian."

My mom hurried to correct him. "Oh, no. I'm not Lady Elian. That title belongs to my … to Millicent." She had been about to say "great-niece," which required a much longer explanation than Earnest probably cared about, so instead, my mom just smiled and held out her hand. "I'm Claire. It's nice to meet you, Earnest."

Earnest covered his surprise with perfect manners. "I'll show you the way in. Follow me, please."

Ava was with her parents in the living room, and when she saw me she jumped off the couch and gave me a huge hug. "I saw the Armada Pearls splashed all over the telly. Tell me all about finding them. It was you, of course, who told them where to look?"

Ava's mother, Camille, turned from greeting my mom and hit me with the full wattage of her smile. "Oh yes, Saira. Tell us about the pearls. Are they as gorgeous as they appeared in the *Armada Portrait?*"

A feather could have knocked me over. Camille Arman, whose picture was probably under the Wikipedia entry for "elegance," looked like a four-year-old with her first Barbie. So I told them everything – from mentioning to Elizabeth that she might want to consider hiding the pearls she'd eventually buy from her cousin, Mary, Queen of Scots, to poking around in the sub-crypt and discovering that the old hiding place hadn't been opened since the seventeenth century.

Ava had already seen the black tear-drop pearl pendant Elizabeth had given me, but her mother hadn't, and I had the sense I'd somehow climbed in her estimation because I wore and treasured it.

There was a commotion in the hall that brought the jewelry conversation to a screeching halt. Then Adam burst into the room with his girlfriend, Alex, on his heels. He ignored the rest of us and walked straight up to his mother.

"Alex's cousin disappeared."

CLAIMED

Camille stared at her son, appalled – mostly at his lack of manners, I thought. "Disappeared in front of you, or in general? Adam, please say hello to our guests. Alex, dear, you look distraught. Sit before you fall."

Adam seemed to finally notice my mom, but he didn't see me until Alex gave me a kiss on both cheeks in greeting. He almost looked relieved, which seemed odd, until he directed his next statement to me. "Alex's cousin is mixed. Her dad was Marcus Rowen, a Shifter Elk, and her mum was from one of the lesser-known Seer families."

"Most people didn't even associate my aunt with Seers. They just thought she was ungifted." Alex spoke to Camille, but she hadn't left my side and I turned to her.

"Your cousin's last name is Rowen?"

She nodded. "Daisy Rowen."

"I heard about her." Alex looked startled, and I turned to Camille and her husband, James, who sat silently by his wife's side. "The parish priests from areas around London met last night. They told the bishops that forty people have disappeared in the past week, and it turns out that many of them have Family names."

The Armans all looked shocked, but Camille recovered first. "How did you come by this information?"

I opened my mouth to speak, but no words came out. I'd never told the Armans that Bishop Cleary knew about the Immortal Descendants, and I wasn't sure how they'd feel about it. My mom stepped in and saved me though.

"We heard about the disappearances, and then Saira and I spent the past several hours on the computer tracking down names." She pulled a sheet of paper out of her purse and handed it to Camille. "As you can see, all of our Families have been affected – even mine, which seems so unlikely given the scarcity of Clockers these days."

Camille scanned the list. "There are no Monger Family names on this list."

"Exactly."

"That doesn't necessarily mean anything." James Arman was always the diplomat, and I knew he was watching Camille's back, because Monger involvement would mean she'd have to take it to the council.

"Except that the Mongers are most likely the ones doing the snatching."

Camille gave me a measured look. "That's a very big accusation to make, Saira."

I shot the same look right back at her. "It would be if they hadn't tried to take me last night, too."

Maybe because I'd been expecting suspicion and disbelief, Camille's look of immediate horror was a surprise. "Oh, my dear. Please, everyone, let's sit so we can discuss this. Ava, darling, ring Earnest. I think we're going to need something a little stronger than tea."

Alex quickly squeezed my hand before taking a seat next to Adam on one of the sofas. Mom and I each sat in an armchair, and the Armans sat across from us on the other sofa. When everyone was settled, I gave them the Cliffs Notes version of the previous night's events.

"Saira has been a Monger target for months," my mom continued after I had finished. "But the fact that Alexandra's cousin is mixed would certainly beg one to wonder if the missing people weren't targeted because of their parentage." I guess my mom had always been diplomatic; I'd just never really noticed how effective it could be. No one got twisted up or defensive when she spoke. It was worth the mental note, filed under the "how not to piss people off" category of my brain. It wasn't a category I usually gave much thought to, sadly.

Camille's gaze went to me. "And Mr. Devereux's genealogy is still in his possession?" There was a twinge of accusation in her tone, and I knew how much it chapped her that Archer hadn't given her the book when we'd stolen it back from the Mongers a couple of months before.

"Yes. But it hasn't been updated since 1888, so it wouldn't be a good resource for finding mixed-bloods now."

"It is a resource, nonetheless."

I met her gaze without flinching. "The genealogy is safe."

"Have you heard anything from the Mongers at council, Camille?" My mom was pretty masterful and redirecting the conversation, and I thought she'd make a great Clocker Head. If she had stayed in her native time the job would have been hers, and probably still could be. At this point I wasn't sure Millicent would give up the job, even though my mom was technically the most senior member of the Elian Family.

"Nothing specific. But I intend to call a special council meeting on Monday. If the Descendants of War have, indeed, taken it upon themselves to address the situation of mixed-bloods in this manner, it must be stopped."

"Why is being mixed-blood even a situation?" I couldn't help it. I was the stir-stick in the pot every time, and I could feel the collective breath-holding in the room. For once, I didn't get the full weight of Camille's gaze. She turned it to my mom.

"I realize it's quite rude to ask this of you, Claire, and of course you can tell me to piss off if you like." That earned a grin from Adam and twin looks of shock on Ava's and my faces. "Is it true that Saira's father was a Shifter?"

My mother answered quietly, but with steel in her voice. "My husband was next in line to head the Shifter clan, yes."

"My God," I suddenly blurted. I'd never really put it together before. "Two Family Heads married to each other? They must've been crapping their pants at the idea of so much power concentration."

My mother winced at my language choice, but nodded. "It had occurred to us that *if* the Families were able to get past the illegality of our union, one of us would have had to step down ."

"Do you think that's why the council in 1871 went so ballistic on you guys? Because if you wanted to, you could have tied up the council on any issue you didn't agree with."

My mom looked suddenly fierce. "The motivation at the heart of most conflict, Saira, is fear. I believe the Descendants of War have one appreciable skill – the ability to take and keep power. Anything which threatens that is eliminated, be it a union between two other Families or the unaccountable combination of skills with which the offspring of such a union would be endowed. They also have a unique ability to persuade. For some inexplicable reason, Mongers have been able to convince otherwise intelligent people that wrong is right, discrimination is appropriate, and division is unifying. It is among the most frightening and dangerous of their abilities."

And on the heels of that delightful depiction of Mongers, she stood to go. "Camille, James, thank you for hearing us out. I don't envy you the conversations at council, but I appreciate that you're willing to have them. I can't say the same for Millicent, at least not with any certainty. And sadly, Bob Shaw's Family name still carries absolutely no weight with the Shifter clan Head, so I can't guarantee that support either. I'm afraid Saira and I have come to you with a problem and no solution."

Camille stood and gave my mom a quick kiss on each cheek. "It's time the continuation of the mixed-blood moratorium became a dialogue rather than an edict. Thank you for bringing it to us, and for your confidence. Our discretion is absolute."

"I understand and appreciate that, if only until the laws against mixed-bloods have changed."

My mom had just publically declared herself a breaker of Descendant law. It was bold and dangerous, and I'd do whatever I could to keep her safe.

I hugged my friends goodbye, and Ava said she'd drag them all out to the country to visit me soon. Adam walked us out to my mom's car.

"Devereux's with you?"

"Yeah, of course."

"Make sure you take care of each other, then."

I smiled. "That's what we do."

Mr. Shaw had made a habit of coming out to Elian Manor around dinner time on weekends so he could spend time with Mom and then do some research work with us after dark when Archer was up. We had pretty much taken over the library, and I had set myself up at an old, dark wood table with legs that twisted around each other. It was a totally masculine piece of furniture except for the unexpected elegance of its legs, and it felt like a table I'd want to own. Mr. Shaw always worked at the massive boardroom table that dominated the room, and Archer usually just sat wherever his stack of books ended up.

The three of us had worked like that for the past month of weekends, poring over all the histories and genealogies we could find in the old manor house. One thing about Clockers, we knew our history, and we had the literature to back it up. We'd been searching for the powerful Shifters in history, since we were pretty sure that was the next blood Wilder needed to collect. There was also the chance of finding his name in the historical record. It was the biggest needle-in-the-haystack search I'd ever done, especially since I kept getting distracted by all the Shifters I stumbled across in the Family books. I had no idea that William Wallace, of Scottish "Freedom!" fame had been a Bear Shifter and was distantly related to Mr. Shaw. And Hannibal used elephants to cross the Alps because he *was* an Elephant.

So, after a very lively dinner conversation about whether there were more Shifters or Mongers among the great warriors in history, I left Mr. Shaw and my mom to walk in the garden while I went to the library.

Which is where Doran found me.

"The real history never makes the books; you do know that, right?"

I always pictured a world traveler in my head when I heard Doran's voice. Laid back, don't-need-more-than-a-passport-in-the-pocket-and-a-credit-card kind of guy. I didn't look up from my book when I answered.

"Considering the stories are usually told by the victor, it's always going to be a little one-sided."

"Oh, but even more interesting is what doesn't make the books at all. Or was there, and then isn't."

Enigmatic and infuriating. I finally looked up and met Doran's eyes. In contrast to his laid-back voice, he was dressed in a very stylish, very expensive jeans and sport coat combination. He looked like he had just stepped off a runway, but the good looks were lost on me when all I wanted to do was yell at him to get to the point, because clearly he had one. So instead, I smiled sweetly and spoke in my most saccharine voice. "Hello, Doran. It's been awhile."

He grinned, like he knew what it cost me to be civil to him and was hugely entertained by my effort. "You were busy. I didn't want to get in your way or distract you from, you know …"

"From keeping the time stream intact? Gee, thanks for the help. Winging it with history isn't my idea of a great time."

Doran dismissed my growly-ness with a wave of his hand. "Maybe not, but it's always an education. And you did fine. Well, except for losing one to the skill-collector."

It took me a second to realize the "one" he was talking about was Tom, and the skill-collector was Wilder, who grabbed Tom just before he Clocked out of 1554. It felt like a gut-punch, and I wasn't prepared to still feel so much pain where Tom Landers was concerned. I struggled to get my verbal feet back under me.

"Skill-collector. An interesting term."

"It is actually interesting that each skill becomes stronger when he collects them. I can't say I expected that, although I'm not surprised. The mixes have always been much more entertaining than pure strains."

32

No matter how much Doran wound me up, there was always something vital smeared around under his words.

"So that's why I can Clock off the default range? Because I'm mixed?"

He shrugged, unconcerned. "I assume so. And since you brought it up, you may want to consider that defaults are useful when one is on the run and carrying a passenger."

"You mean Wilder, right? You think he just did a simple one-ring jump?"

His eyes sparkled like he was holding back the punchline on a very funny joke. "Well, that would be telling, wouldn't it?" He turned to go, and I was seriously considering leaping onto his back like a wild thing and making him tell me more when he paused, then pulled a piece of paper out of the inside pocket of his jacket. He tossed it on the library table and met my glare, the twinkle in his own eyes curiously gone. "For you. Because you care about such things."

I made the mistake of looking at the paper instead of keeping my eyes locked on him, because, of course, he was gone when I looked up again. Damn! I hated when he did that.

The paper he'd left was old and seemed to have been torn out of some kind of notebook. The handwriting was cramped and the ink was faded, but I had spent long hours deciphering Victorian handwriting and immediately recognized this as a kind of logbook. My eyes were trying to find something to land on in the tight handwriting, and suddenly a name jumped out at me: *Jonathan Starkey to be remanded to Newgate on July 20th, 1889.*

Jonathan Starkey was Ringo's real name.

What the hell was Newgate? Because being remanded anywhere did not sound good. I did a quick Google search and then sucked in a horrified breath.

Newgate Prison.

"Crap!"

"What?" Archer was just coming in the door and my eyes met his wildly.

"They're putting Ringo in prison."

Archer's expression looked like mine must have as I handed him the torn paper. He scanned it quickly. "It's a court clerk's log. Where did you get this?"

"Fricking Doran. 'Because you care about such things,' he said."

"I can't go." Archer's voice came out a little strangled. I hadn't even thought that far ahead, although if I had, I would have already drawn a spiral right there on the library table.

"Go where?" Mr. Shaw and my mom had just entered the room, and they could probably sense the tension coursing through it.

I took a breath to slow my heartbeat down, and then told them everything Doran had just said. "I have to go get him." I had no choice, and no idea how to break my friend out of whatever holding cell they had him in. The prospect of another trip to Victorian times was totally daunting.

"I'll go with you." Mr. Shaw's deep voice startled me out of whatever plan was trying to form in my head.

"No, Bob. You stay here and work with Archer to search for Wilder in 1429. I'll go with Saira."

My jaw would have hit the table if it hadn't been hinged. My mom was offering to Clock with me? But wait … something … "1429. That's a one-ring jump back from 1554? That's when Henry Grayson – the Clocker kid I met at St. Brigid's - was going. He called it his mission and said his birthday was foretold as a 'triumphant day for England' or something like that. It stuck in my head because he was so proud to go."

"You told me you thought Doran had sent you to St. Brigid's on purpose." Archer's voice was low and thoughtful.

"Yeah, he did." I screwed my eyes shut and rubbed them. "Have I said how much I hate him yet?"

Archer smiled grimly and pulled me into his arms. "We'll look at the history books for events around the simple jumps, and see if it's anything more than a coincidence that you met someone going to 1429 when we might be looking for Wilder there. How will you get Ringo out?"

I shook my head. "I don't know. I'll find Charlie, I guess, and go from there."

My mom's voice was thoughtful. "This logbook is from Old Bailey. I know that building. It's where the Descendants' Council used to meet and where my husband was captured."

I gasped. The council massacre. My mom's expression was strained, and I knew what this whole conversation was costing her.

"There's a spiral there." Her voice was bleak even though the words were electric. "I can get us there with the necklace."

"But …" there were so many things spinning around my head I couldn't grasp just one to say coherently.

Archer picked up the logbook entry. "This is dated July 19th, 1889. He will have been sentenced that day, so you can take him from there."

I turned to my mother. "Are you sure, Mom?" I searched her eyes and found them full of love – and fear. She touched my cheek with a shaking hand.

"I'm sure."

The closets at Elian Manor were like the St. Brigid's attics, only better because they didn't smell like mothballs and wet wool. Within an hour my mom and I were downstairs dressed in Victorian period clothing. She had on a finely woven, wine-colored wool dress, and I wore men's trousers and a top coat. Sanda, Millicent's housekeeper, who is a Hobbit even though she's descended from the Picts, wanted to put me in a dress, but surprisingly, my mom was on my side.

"I would wear trousers, too, if I looked more like a man and less like a cross-dresser in them. Men had all the rights and the freedoms, and if I'm with a man, no one will even give me a second look."

Sanda grumbled, but not about the unseemliness, like I assumed. Her beef was that there were so many beautiful dresses in the manor house that weren't being worn. I promised her I'd bring Ava and her niece Olivia over for an afternoon to play dress-up, and as ridiculous as it sounded when I said it, I thought it might actually be fun.

I debated banding my daggers to my lower legs, but realized I'd probably lose them if I had to run. So instead I wrapped a piece of cotton cloth around my waist, under my shirt, and was able to secure them in the layers of it. Now that I had them, I couldn't imagine going unarmed.

When Mom and I got back downstairs, Archer was outside on watch for any lurkers on the property. Millicent stood with Mr. Shaw, glaring at him like he'd just offended her in the worst possible way. When she saw us, it was clear we were the offenders.

"I don't know what you two think you're doing in those ridiculous clothes. You're not going anywhere tonight, either of you. And certainly not on an ill-conceived rescue mission for a nineteenth-century street urchin."

I took a breath to launch a missile strike, but my mom beat me to it. Her expression was thunderous, and frankly, I couldn't imagine where she found all the rage she unleashed in one of those calm, cold, scary voices that do way more damage than yelling ever could.

"Millicent Elian. As charming as it is that you believe you have any say over what my daughter does, you and I both know that she is her own woman and has been for some time. And as for your attempts to dictate to me, it has gone on long enough. You've done an adequate job heading our Family for several decades; however, I believe it is time for a change in leadership. When I return from 1889, I'll be taking over as Head of the Clocker Families. If you find you cannot live with that, I will expect you to find another place to reside as well. Otherwise, I'm happy to continue sharing my home with you."

Oh. My. God! Apparently my mother had been abducted by aliens who surgically implanted a rod of steel in her spine. I almost clapped. Except all the color had drained from Millicent's face, and I seriously thought she was going to pass out. I must have unconsciously moved closer to her to catch her if she fell, because she suddenly recoiled.

"Don't touch me!"

I flinched from the venom in her voice, but when she took a step toward the door and stumbled, I moved to her side and held her arm. "Do you want to sit, or should I take you to your rooms?"

Millicent didn't look at me. Her eyes were only for my mother. "They're not my rooms, are they?"

The thunder disappeared from my mom's expression as quickly as it had come. She looked tired. "Of course they are, Millicent. I'll come to you in the morning, and we'll talk. Bob, could you see Millicent to her rooms, please?"

Mr. Shaw hadn't moved a muscle since we entered the room, but my mom's request seemed to jolt him back into himself. He moved to Millicent's side and took her other arm, letting her lean on him as she walked stiffly from the room.

When we were alone in the library, I stared at the woman I thought I'd known for almost eighteen years. She looked sad, but stronger than I'd ever seen her.

"You okay, Mom?"

She took a shaky breath. "I suppose I will be."

"Are you sure you're up for this?"

Claire Elian looked me in the eyes. "If I don't do this now, Saira, I'm afraid I'll never Clock again. The fear is paralyzing, and I will not let it control me." She took a breath. "It's time."

OLD BAILEY – JULY, 1889

The Elian Manor Clocker spiral didn't have its own special room or even its own painting like the one in the Clocker Tower at St. Brigid's School. The spiral was in the walled garden that Millicent had allowed to stay overgrown and untended, and which my mom had reclaimed as her own when we moved in seven months ago.

Archer materialized from the shadows as we emerged from the house. He moved silently and spoke in a quiet voice. "Is everything okay?"

"It will be when we can get Ringo out."

"You have your daggers?"

"I think I'd feel naked without them."

He grinned at me, his eyes glinting dangerously in the moonlight. "And now I have that image to torture me tonight. Thank you."

My mom had opened the garden door and was waiting for me to join her. "I'll time our return trip so we still have some night."

He kissed me. "Just be safe, Saira. And bring him with you." His fingers found the braid I'd tucked down the back of the coat. "The trousers suit you, by the way."

"Thanks." I blew him a kiss, and my mom closed the garden door behind us.

The spiral was carved into the stone wall overhung with vines at the back of the garden. I hadn't known it was there until I Clocked back here with my mom when she was dying from blood loss. I hadn't used it since then.

I swept the vines to the side as Mom put the clock necklace on. It was an older, choker style, and it suited her long Victorian dress. She exhaled, then looked at me. "Shall we?"

I had never been to the Descendants' Council room and my mom had, so she was the one directing our travel. I let her trace the spirals while I held her other hand. The edges of the spiral began to glow, and the hum that went with the feeling of being stretched like a rubber band was somehow diluted through my mom instead of centered in my own head. When we finally slipped *between*, it was as though the nothingness echoed around me instead of focusing through me, and except for the nausea, I didn't have any of the weakness I normally felt when someone else hitched a ride. When we got to the other side, though, my mom was wrecked.

She dropped to her knees, gasping for air, and I gripped her hand. "Mom? Are you okay?"

Eyes clenched shut, breathing heavy, pulse slamming in her throat. She finally looked at me. "It's only been like that once before." The words seemed hard to speak. "When you were born."

"It gets worse the more people who hitch a ride."

She shuddered. "I don't want to do that again."

"You don't have to. I can get us home from here."

I helped her to her feet and then looked around the room we'd Clocked into. It was a big space with elaborately carved decorations in unexpected niches, adorning columns, and hiding in the plaster moldings. All the chiseled shapes were simple and almost tribal, with strong angles and sweeping swirls. It was beautiful and austere, and the room looked like it belonged in a temple in ancient Greece rather than in a public court building in the middle of London. A massive piece of veined black marble, roughly round but with unfinished edges, sat on a pedestal in the middle of the room. Twenty people could easily have sat around the stone table, and might have, if there had been any chairs. I looked behind me and realized the wall was divided into five panels. The center one was carved with a Clocker spiral, and the others had simple shapes that I realized had been echoed in the decorative carvings around the room: an oak tree, a trident, a stylized sword and shield, and an eye.

"What is this place?"

My mom had caught her breath and sounded more normal. "We're under Old Bailey. Most people have forgotten this room even exists, and those who know guard our secrets with their lives."

"This is where the council meets?"

Mom studied the room. "I don't believe they've used it since … that night." Her voice caught on the last two words, and I reached out to squeeze her hand. "Anyway, this room is gone. They rebuilt Old Bailey near the turn of the century, and the new council room is much less ornate."

"How do we get upstairs?"

She showed me a door I hadn't seen at first. It led out to a small, dark staircase and another door, equally well concealed, under a staircase, which we climbed. We exited into a corridor behind one of the long galleries, and I could see a court in session in a room nearby.

Mom walked straight up to a guard and said in her best posh accent, "In which room is Timothy Dalby the clerk?"

"Courtroom two, ma'am."

"And that is …?"

"Straight down the gallery and to yer left, ma'am."

"Thank you."

I was impressed with her confidence, and then I realized this was her time. These were her people, and they spoke in her accent. I had fallen a step behind and quickly caught up to her.

"I love when you get all bossy, Mom."

She smiled up at me. "I'll remind you of that sometime."

We had arrived at courtroom two and tucked into the back to listen. It seemed to be a petty crimes court, and the judge was determined to teach every one of them -- from the old man who skipped out on his bar tab, to the little kid caught stealing jam from the fruit cart-- that crime does not pay. Faces fell and groans of horror echoed through the room every time he sentenced someone to Newgate Prison. A guy about Ringo's age was "remanded to Newgate immediately" for striking his employer, and I whispered into my mom's ear that I'd be right back.

I slipped out of the courtroom and leaned against the wall of the gallery as the bailiffs marched the guy out of the room, one on each side, holding his arms. When they turned a corner I raced to follow them, and caught a glimpse just as they led the condemned man through a door and down a different staircase than the one that led to the Descendants' Council room. I waited a breath, and then trailed them down the stairs. The bailiffs were talking amongst themselves about what they'd be ordering for dinner at the pub as if the guy wasn't being marched to his grim fate between them, and their voices took on a hollow echo as they traveled farther away from where I stood hidden.

It wasn't until I reached the bottom of the steps that I could see the full length of the tunnel they'd gone down. It must cross the road between Old Bailey and Newgate Prison, and instead of a solid roof, it had what looked like a heavy metal grate overhead. The whole effect was like being led through an underground birdcage, and I knew there was no way Ringo and I could get out of there if he got this far.

Whatever I did had to happen in the courtroom.

I made it back into my seat next to Mom just as they were bringing in the next round of defendants. The fourth one in line was Ringo.

He looked tired, and skinnier than I'd last seen him. His clothes were torn and filthy, which made him look guilty just because he was such a mess. But unlike everyone else he came in with, his eyes were alive, and he started scanning the room the minute he walked in.

When he found what he was looking for his face lit up in a bright smile, and I strained to see who had captured his attention like that.

Charlie stood with her back against the wall near the other entrance, and her worried gaze was locked onto Ringo's happy one. He gave her a wink along with the grin, and it relaxed her just a fraction, until her gaze traveled to the bailiff at the front of the line. Her whole body tensed up, and I followed the direction her eyes had gone.

41

The bailiff was taller than the average man in the courtroom and beefy across the chest. His face was in profile, but I could see a hawkish nose and sharp eyes under his hat. I'd been feeling slightly sick since we entered the big room full of people and figured there were Mongers among them, but based on Charlie's reaction, I'd bet money the bailiff was something not of this world.

Charlie was an Otherworld seer, a skill that might have had something to do with the little bit of Clocker blood in her, but maybe not. Miss Simpson said she knew of one other person who could see through the human disguises Otherworlders used to get by, but this was a rare skill among Immortal Descendants.

So, Charlie was here, and based on Ringo's reaction to seeing her, I didn't think he'd be too willing to leave her behind. He also hadn't seen me yet, so I was going to have to trust that he'd know why I was here when he did. The group of accused was seated in a separate area that reminded me of a jury box in modern courtrooms. There was a low railing running around them, with a bailiff posted on each side. The hawkish Otherworld bailiff was on the side between Ringo and the door, which I mentally added to the obstacle list along with bailiffs at every exit and the courtroom crowded with onlookers. Above the plaintiff box was a second floor gallery for even more observers that ran all the way around the room. It gave the big space a theater-in-the-round vibe, with the judges and lawyers center stage. But the thing that started the wheels spinning in my head were three big metal chandeliers hanging from long chains down past the upper gallery to light up the room below.

Hawk called the court to order with a graveled voice that boomed over the sound of the rabble. I quickly turned to my mom and outlined a bare plan. I didn't give her too many details about my part in things, but I pointed out Charlie, and she nodded her agreement to her role and then quickly left the courtroom. A moment later she slipped in the other door and drew next to Charlie. They almost looked like they could be related, with the same ash-colored hair, slight build, and delicate features. The long dresses may have had something to do with their similarities, but I

42

thought another look at Archer's genealogy could be interesting. My mom leaned close to Charlie's ear and whispered. Charlie jerked back instinctively, her eyes widening in surprise. But then she got a closer look at my mom. She might have remembered her from before, or it might just have been what she said, but soon Charlie was nodding seriously.

The judge called his first case, and Hawk stepped up to shove the prisoner to the front of the box. Okay, useful information. And it meant I had only two more prisoners to make my move. I stood to leave the courtroom and caught Charlie's eye. She smiled shyly at me, and I gave her a quick grin back. Mom tugged her arm, and Charlie shot Ringo a last look before they slipped out of the courtroom.

The stairs to the second level gallery weren't in this room, but between the railings and the wall panels, there were good handholds all the way up.

The first prisoner was sentenced to five years in Newgate Prison and a collective rumble went up around the court. Hawk stepped forward to escort him to two bailiffs who waited to walk him down to the birdcage tunnel. I tensed, and the moment the two extra bailiffs left the room, I leapt.

My jump to the top of the gallery railing inspired a gasp from people seated around me. Going up the wall was the winner though - that move caused a couple of screams from the gallery, and suddenly I had the room's attention.

The only eyes I cared about, though, were Ringo's.

And the look on his face was like a floodlight had just been flipped on behind his grin. I jerked my head toward the door and then concentrated on the climb. The gasps and shrieks of the onlookers had drawn the attention of Hawk and the other bailiffs, and two of them were trying to climb after me. Silly rabbits, tricks are for kids. I hauled myself up over the second floor railing, and people went flying backwards to escape me. Hawk was still in the prisoners' box barking orders at the other bailiffs, and Ringo was edging around behind him out of sight. Good. Just one more big attention-grabber and he could get out.

I climbed up to the top of the upper level railing and counted on the fact that everyone behind me had fled and I wouldn't get pushed off. Then I took a deep breath, and jumped.

The bottom of the curving metal on the heavy chandelier was just like monkey bars, and I hit it perfectly. Screams below me had reached fire-in-a-theater pitch, and I saw Ringo dart behind Hawk and run for the courtroom door. People were fleeing the room as if I were explosive, which was making it tough for him to escape, but I knew he'd get there. He was scrappy like that.

I was going to have to revise my own escape plan, since the two exits I knew about were jammed.

One of the bailiffs had hauled himself up to the second floor railing, and I allowed myself one second of admiration for his skill before I focused on my next target. Chandelier number two.

With one extra kick I was able to get enough trajectory to let go and grab for the second chandelier, though I fumbled a little, and it took a second to get both hands firmly locked on the curved metal arm. This was the biggest chandelier, so my lower body swings had to be huge. I felt like a trapeze artist and knew the only way I was going to hit chandelier number three was with the stomach muscles of a wrestler. The upper galleries were filling back in with onlookers, and the one I was aiming for was beginning to look too crowded to land.

Except two of the guys on the other side were young-ish and dressed not so nicely as the rest of the crowd in the courtroom. They seemed to be encouraging my progress across the chandeliers, and when I managed to hit chandelier number three, they let out a cheer.

Well, okay then. I might have allies.

Hawk had organized the bailiffs to cover the downstairs exits, and two of them had joined the upstairs gallery throng, one on either side of the room. Which meant there were doors up there, too. I kicked hard and swung my body back in a big arc. My arms were getting tired, and I knew I had one shot to hit the railing on the other side. And then one bailiff to contend with before the others figured out where I was headed. The two young ruffians ahead of me were shouting encouragement and waving me in, and I hoped they were of the catching variety rather than the throwing sort. The third chandelier swung straight with the weight of my body, and I pulled my legs up to jackknife toward the far railing – then let go.

I actually felt graceful as I hung in the air, and time seemed to suspend. Even the crowd held its breath.

But I wasn't going to make it. I'd lost too much momentum between the three chandeliers, and didn't have enough swing to reach the railing. My hands were outstretched, but I could already tell I'd miss it by about a foot.

Crap.

I caught a glimpse below me and saw Hawk grinning like a feral predator, waiting for me to crash to the ground. Something red gleamed in his eyes and I shut my own, waiting for an impact.

That never came.

Strong hands grabbed my arm, and the instinct to clutch them gave me the grip I needed. The two ruffians held whatever parts of me they could reach, and then hauled me up and over the railing to the collective gasp and a little applause from down below.

The lone bailiff on our side of the gallery elbowed forward and tried to grab me, but my foot caught him squarely in the chest and sent him backwards. I stumbled with the force of the kick, and one of my ruffian friends caught me before I could hit the ground.

"Ye all righ' then, mate?"

I grinned at them both. "Never better. Thanks for the help."

"Twern't nothin'. Most fun we've 'ad at court in, well, ever, I s'pose."

The bailiff was struggling to his feet behind my new friends, and Hawk was shouting orders at the ones downstairs in a way that was going to be bad for my health if I didn't bolt. "Do you mind?" I grabbed the ratty looking cap from the head of the smaller guy and tossed him my own, much newer one. Then I threw my head at the bailiff, and the ruffian grinned in a way that reminded me of Ringo.

"Not to worry, mate. Yer off."

I tossed them a wave and ran for the door. Two more bailiffs had nearly reached the top of the stairs, so I vaulted the stair rail and hit the landing about ten feet down. That earned another couple of cheers from the ruffians who watched from the top of the stairs and some growls from the bailiffs I'd just avoided. I shoved the ruffian's cap on my head and hunched down in a feeble attempt at height-reduction. The gallery outside the courtroom was still teeming with people who had escaped the pandemonium I'd caused inside, and I slid down the rest of the bannister and slipped into the crowd.

I spotted Hawk a moment later, scanning the masses for signs of me. He was actually looking too, as if he'd memorized something about me and would find that troublemaker no matter what. I ducked behind a column and decided to try a very risky move.

I yanked the cap off my head and quickly unbraided my hair. Then my topcoat came off and I turned it inside out so the silk lining showed instead of dark blue wool. I ripped off my tie and unbuttoned the top button of my white shirt, then tied the topcoat around my waist in a weak impersonation of a skirt. With my hair down, maybe, just maybe, I'd be mistaken for a girl in the throngs of people that milled about in the gallery.

When I stepped out from behind the column, I felt Hawk's gaze slide over me and I shivered, but I turned and walked toward the opposite hallway where the stairs down to the Descendants' Council room were hidden. I moved with purpose, but without urgency, and I hoped long hair and the flash of silk from the jacket would keep me anonymously female in the crowd.

I shot one last look over my shoulder before stepping into the hallway off the gallery. Hawk was still scanning the crowd, and the expression on his face had lost almost all of its humanity. There was something definitely murderous in his eyes, and I felt myself duck as I slipped out of sight of him.

Hands grabbed me and I almost punched, until Ringo whispered in my ear. "Took ye long enough."

I grinned at him in the dim hall light. "Shut it, Urchin." Then I hugged him. Hard. His hug back was just as hard, but he let me go abruptly.

"Come on, Clocker. Yer ma's waitin' fer us down below."

We made it to the hidden door and down the stairs and didn't speak again until we entered the Descendants' Council room. Ringo looked around with something like awe. "Didn't know such places existed in London. Thought I'd found all the best hidin' spots, I did."

Charlie stepped out from the shadows at the edge of the room, and her voice was quiet when she spoke. "Ringo. Yer safe."

He spun to her, and within two strides was in front of her. I thought he was going to throw his arms around her, or maybe even kiss her, but he visibly restrained himself and instead, picked up her hand and held it in both of his.

"I told ye they couldn't keep me from ye."

A light burned in her eyes, but everything else was tied up in the same restraint Ringo had. Her gaze flicked over to me. "And now ye'll be goin' anyway." It wasn't a question, and Ringo seemed about to answer, but then lost his voice.

"What'd you do to get caught?"

Ringo turned at the sound of my voice. He was so rarely truly angry that the expression on his face surprised me with its bitterness. "I was set up. Made to go down fer a string o' Lizzer's own thievin'. 'E's got a copper in 'is pocket, too. Nabbed me on the way 'ome with our dinner in me 'ands." He looked back at Charlie and his tone softened again. "And no way to get word to 'ye, neither."

"'E'll be after ye again when word gets out yer gone." Charlie spoke softly, but I could feel the protectiveness in her voice.

"I'm not leavin' ye alone, Char." He pronounced her nickname 'Shar,' short for Charlotte, I guessed.

"We can take you both." My mom stepped up next to me. "But, it'll have to be you, Saira. I'm not strong enough."

"Ye'd do that?" Ringo's gaze was on both of us, and Mom nodded.

"If you want to come, you're welcome. We can keep you at Elian Manor for the time being, at least until we figure something else out."

Charlie looked at Ringo, her eyes wide, then at me. "Ye'd take me, too?"

I stepped up and took her hand. "Come on. You won't be able to feel my hand *between*, but I won't let go."

Ringo grinned at me and took his place on her other side. "And if ye think I'm lettin' go of ye, yer addled."

I led them to the carved spiral portal and waited until everyone was holding on. "Home, then?"

Ringo squeezed Charlie's hand and looked over her head at me. "Home is where yer people are, ain't it?"

Tom – June, 1429

The sound of the door jerked me out of the dream. It was the same dream I had every time I closed my eyes, so I rarely did. Close them. Sleep. I was never sure if the screaming was in my head or in my throat, but my eyes didn't have to be closed to see the blood.

The cold morning air blew in behind Léon, the guy Bishop Wilder had found to keep me fed. I didn't know if he was keeping Wilder fed, too. The Vampire bishop had already taken vials of blood from me. Vials and vials of blood. In the two months since he'd grabbed me out of 1554 he'd drawn enough blood to make another person. That kind of blood production required a lot of protein consumption, but even with extra meat and eggs, I was too weak to be much of a threat to him, even without the chains.

Yes, chains.

My cousin Adam would have made an utterly inappropriate joke about bondage if he'd seen me, wearing metal wrist cuffs that could be looped through with the iron chain at my bed. The leg irons had gone on the first time I tried to fight back. The last time I tried, he bled me into unconsciousness.

The stone walls, flickering candle light, and Dr. Frankenstein laboratory look of the tower room Wilder kept me in just added to the melodrama of my situation, as if chains weren't dramatic enough. Léon was about nineteen or twenty, and from a distance we could be mistaken for brothers. At this point I was probably just as skinny as he was, since blood loss will do that to a chap, and my Gypsy blood looked a lot like his Jewishness did. Léon's father was the butcher from whom Wilder bought meat. I supposed kosher meat, in an age with no refrigeration, made sense if he didn't want to kill me with botulism. I was sure his plans for killing me were much messier than that.

I knew where and when I was because of Léon. When – 1429: medieval times. Where – the Hôtel de Sens in the Marais district of Paris. Léon said the Archbishop of Sens was building the castle as a Paris residence. Most of the structure was finished, but it was a shell, and except for a very solid tower room, apparently the main rooms downstairs were bare. I didn't think it was meant to be inhabited yet, though I'd once heard Wilder speak to another man in the corridor outside my tower. I hadn't seen the man, but his voice was of the villainous variety and sent an involuntary shiver up my spine.

Wilder had left the lab about an hour before, and based on the little bit of light I could see through the high window, he was doing his Vampire dead-to-the-world thing. Léon only came during daylight. I didn't know if that was the deal his father had made for his employment, or if he was just smart, but it meant that whenever Léon was around, I could breathe.

He stoked the embers in the fireplace back into flames, and then stuck the two burlap-wrapped packages he'd brought with him into the coals. Finally, he turned to look at me.

"Monsieur failed to kill you again last night?"

"Sorry to disappoint." We were speaking French. The man I'd thought was my father, Phillip Landers, had made sure I could speak his native language from the time I could walk. Léon's medieval French was a little different, but we got by.

Léon smirked. "How much did he take?"

"Another two flasks"

He poured me a glass of water and brought it over. "Here. You should drink."

I accepted the water gratefully. Léon pulled a tin out of his pocket and sat next to me. "Let me see your wrists."

I held them out, but had to support them on the table. I wasn't strong enough to hold them in the air. Léon's finger hovered over the track marks on the inside of my elbow. Wilder wasn't gentle when he bled me, although considering he wasn't using his teeth, I guessed I was still lucky. Léon twisted off the lid of the tin, and the pungent scent of an herbal salve filled my nose.

"A new formula?"

"My grand-mère suggested yarrow." Léon pushed the metal cuffs about an inch up my wrist and scooped out a finger full of salve. "The infection doesn't look so angry." I tried not to flinch from the pressure of his touch on the minced meat that used to be my skin. When the cuffs first went on I thought I could break out of them, and I spent the days working my wrists to find a weakness in the metal. The weakness was in my skin though, and Léon finally found the wounds when they began to stink.

"Thank your grand-mère for me." He smiled a little and moved on to the next wrist. Léon was close enough that I could see the hollows under his eyes, and I didn't think they'd been there a month ago. "You're not sleeping well?"

He shrugged. "The wolves, you know? My father lost an arrow in one last night, while three more made off with half a side of beef."

"I heard them. They seemed to echo through the whole city."

"It is common enough for a small pack to get in through breaches in the city walls during the winter when hunting is scarce, but this summertime cooperation among several packs is unnatural. I am very pleased we have the cattle on the island where the wolves cannot go. Even so, I have spent many nights there in recent months."

He finished with my wrist and got up to clean his hands. His voice was tight, and he didn't look at me when he spoke. "They killed two children last night. A boy and a girl."

I exhaled. "That's over thirty people now."

Léon looked a little sick. "There are bloodstains on the cobblestones that will not wash clean. I see them when I walk, and I cross to avoid them."

I tried and failed to picture what he saw outside. I hadn't been farther than the window in this room since Wilder had brought me here. Léon pulled a chess piece, the black knight, out of his tunic pocket and absently ran it through his fingers.

His voice was quiet. "Did the Monsieur leave here at all last night?"

"You think it was him, not the wolves?"

He didn't meet my eyes. "The threats he made to my father …"

"Wilder's a monster, but he wouldn't leave blood." The room was deathly quiet around us, as if the stone walls absorbed anything that sounded like life. "Why do you carry the knight?"

Léon looked down as if he was surprised to find it in his hand. "My father's chess set has only this one, so rather than play an uneven game he has substituted two black stones for the knights. It is my task to find another knight in the marketplace to match this one."

My eyes felt heavy and I fought to keep them open. "Is there any such thing as a perfect match?"

He looked at the piece he flipped between his fingers. "If one strives for perfection in and of itself, then, no. There is no such thing." Then he met my eyes. "But if one strives only to find the piece that compliments, that stands nobly alone, yet is made better with companionship, then yes, I believe a match is possible."

"Even when one of the pieces is a bloodless, spineless scarecrow?" The words came out more bitterly than I meant to say them.

"Bloodless does not mean spineless, as your chains will attest." His tone was wry, but then quieted. "Yes, even scarecrows find their match."

It was as if the eyes that looked at me saw past the weakness and vulnerability to the person inside--the one who remembered how to make a joke, how to laugh, how to live.

Léon felt like a piece of sanity in something that seemed so insane. I was a prisoner chained to a bed in the tower of an unfinished medieval castle, for God's sake. Not that the divine could have anything to do with the madness that had become my existence. There were no battles raging in Léon, nothing at war, and the peace he brought with him into the room felt better than the balm with which he coated my wrists. I didn't want to sleep and miss any part of that peace. Not when everything else I battled, including my own mind, was descended from War.

"Sleep now. I will stay and keep watch."

I smirked. "The monster sleeps now, too. There's nothing to watch for."

"There are the wolves." Léon sat next to my bed and his eyes found mine. "And the dreams."

It was the same nightmare every time. I had never told Léon what I screamed about, because no one should ever have to picture himself dying in a sea of blood.

"You were humming when you came in. Sing the song to me."

My eyes were closing, no matter how hard I tried to stay awake. Léon reached for my hand and began to sing, as if his touch and his voice could protect me from the madness.

 ## Darkness

I took a deep breath of the cool night air as we came out of the garden spiral at Elian Manor. I didn't need my mom's necklace to bring us back, and there was no way she could have Clocked three people anyway. But I should have been feeling worse than I was, and frankly, I felt fine.

Mom gasped and steadied herself against the wall, and Ringo was trying to hold the puke down. Charlie had been at my side when we'd gone through the portal, and I searched for her face in the slash of moonlight that lit the garden. I blinked when I found it. Her eyes were shining, and she had a smile that defied all nausea-filled-Clocking logic.

"That was Clocking." Charlie's voice was like an exhale, and I blinked again. She had liked it.

"You don't feel sick?"

She tilted her head a little to one side, like a bird. "Hunger or fear makes me feel sick. That feelin' was magic."

Okay, that was interesting. I wondered if maybe she was the reason Clocking all those people had been easier for me than it usually was. She did, after all, have a little Clocker in her.

I hadn't really studied Charlie recently. The first time I met her she'd been disguised as a boy with thin, blond hair and skinny, pale sticks for limbs. She had looked a little like a dandelion then, ready to blow away. But since Ringo had taken her into his flat, she looked less weedy and more like the flower version: still skinny, still blond, but with a little softness around her mouth, eyes, and body. While I was watching Charlie, Archer melted out of the shadows.

I'd been expecting it, because he's good that way, but he surprised Charlie, and I could see her fold into herself like a flower closing its petals.

His eyes locked on mine with an instant of relief, then landed on Ringo. "Since when do you get caught?"

Ringo straightened and grinned at his friend. "Since I grew a conscience and cared that I showed up fer work at the docks." He clasped Archer's shoulder, and they hugged like long-lost brothers. Charlie's wariness relaxed fractionally as she watched them together, and after Archer had kissed my mother's cheek, he turned to her and held out his hand.

"I don't believe we've formally met, yet. Archer Devereux."

They hadn't? Right. Nineteenth century Archer had been sick when Ringo and I first encountered Charlie and her sister, Mary Kelly, the last of Jack the Ripper's victims, and then he'd been turned. Twenty-first-century Archer couldn't Clock back to that time with me because his nineteenth-century self was already there.

Charlie gave him a tentative smile. "I 'eard all about ye, of course. Yer not scary like I thought ye'd be." He struggled to hold back a smile as she offered him her small hand. "Charlotte Kelly. But ye can call me Charlie if ye like."

"Which do you prefer?" Archer's deep voice gave me chills even when he spoke to other people. Yeah, I had it bad.

"Any's fine. I feel like Charlie most of the time. Charlotte only when I'm safe."

Archer smiled. "Charlotte, then. It's very nice to meet you."

That made her smile more confident, and I noticed Ringo watching the exchange with a grin on his face. I loved it when Archer turned on his horse-whisperer charm to calm the skittishness out of people. A useful skill for someone whom most people feared.

"Anyone come tonight?" I asked him.

Archer smirked. "Your Dodo set up camp in the root cellar about an hour ago. The Bear is watching him at the moment."

"Mr. Shaw's 'ere? I want 'im to give Char one of them pox shots." Ringo had been vaccinated against smallpox and influenza the last time he was here, and the way he said Mr. Shaw's name with reverence made me smile.

My mom raised an eyebrow. "Dodo?"

"The guy who chased me across Tower Bridge. He looks like a Rothchild, only bigger." I turned to Archer. "What's the plan?"

"We don't know if he's armed, so cornering him in the root cellar could get one of us shot. Shaw and I thought we'd ambush him when he emerges, presumably to try to grab you."

I nodded. "Do you need me as bait or want me at a post?"

Ringo's eyes narrowed as he studied me. "Yer different."

"Than what? A hedgehog?"

He smirked. "Nah, yer still all prickly like one o' them. Yer different like, I don't know, part of a thing – a team, I 'spose - not runnin' it … or from it."

For about a second I thought about getting annoyed, but frankly, I was feeling too lazy for annoyance. So I settled for acceptance. "There are too many other things to run from."

He wore a half-smile and regarded me thoughtfully, but didn't say anything else. Archer had watched the exchange with amusement, and then got back to the business at hand.

"I don't think we need to dangle you as bait, but I do want you to be the last resort trap. Just in case he gets past us, your sword and dagger skills work well in close quarters."

"If he gets past you guys, he's going to know it's a trap."

"But if he doesn't see you outside, he might still go in after you."

I thought about it for half a second, then nodded.

"Where do ye want me?" Ringo didn't miss a beat, and I adored him for it.

"You're with me. Shaw has a groundsman with him, and Claire, you should probably take Charlotte and Millicent into the keep, just in case this one's of the hostage-taking variety."

"I'll stay with Saira if it's all the same to ye." Charlie's small voice sounded shaky and brave, and Archer regarded her for a moment.

"Do you have any defensive skills?"

"I'm small, I hide easily, and I'm handy with a skillet."

Archer sounded confused. "I'm not sure how much good cooking skills will do you."

Charlie cocked her head with that bird look and stared him straight in the eyes. "How 'bout bludgeonin' skills? Will they do me?"

Ringo was trying not to laugh. And failing. "That one's got an arm on 'er like a blacksmith. 'Specially when a cast iron fryin' pan's in 'er 'and."

I snickered, and Archer just managed to keep from laughing. Just. "Right. Well, then, you might want to stop by the kitchens on your way upstairs."

"Come on," I said to Charlie. "Let's go scrounge some weapons." I turned to Archer before we left. "I don't like the idea of a predator on the loose if you're down for the day, so if he doesn't show before dawn, we need to go after him." Archer opened his mouth to protest, but I didn't let him. "I know Mr. Shaw could probably take him on his own, but unless you are willing to sleep in the keep for the day, you're too vulnerable. And if, as you say, he's not above hostage-taking, all he'd have to do is grab your body, and I'd do anything they said to get you back."

Archer blew out a breath as his eyes searched my face. "The feeling's mutual, my love."

"Good. So, we agree?"

He smiled at me. "Yes, we agree."

The surprise was back on Ringo's face, and it entertained me. I caught the lingering look he gave Charlie as we went inside the manor house, and that entertained me, too. I think the prospect of capturing a Monger had put me in a good mood.

I grabbed an extra carving knife from the kitchens to go along with the daggers I still wore under my clothes, and Charlie picked up cast iron pans like she was weighing for balance and quality. She finally chose a medium-sized one and we slipped upstairs, careful not to wake the cook.

We passed my mother on the stairs and she spoke quietly. "Millicent laughed at me when I suggested we go to the keep. She basically dared anyone to come and take her from her bed."

I grimaced. "She's way more dangerous than any Monger."

My mom smiled, but she was tired and it showed.

"You reset your clock when you went back, didn't you?" It hadn't been that long since she'd last gone to her native time, but even seven months all at once made a difference.

She winced. "It's that obvious?"

"No, you're gorgeous. But it's more than just tired."

My mom wasn't vain like some of the women I used to see in L.A. But those women would also have paid good money for skin like hers – smooth and just barely colored by the summer sun. She reached out and adjusted the collar on the coat I'd hastily put back on, and I kissed her cheek. "Thank you for coming with me, Mom."

"I love you, darling." She sighed and rolled her shoulders. "Ugh, if I didn't think it would shock him, I'd ask Bob for a neck massage."

I raised an eyebrow and grinned. "A neck massage would shock him?"

She smiled. "The request would. Perhaps when he's no longer on guard duty." Then she turned to Charlie. "Welcome to Elian Manor, dear. Once this nonsense is over I'll show you to a room you may call yours as long as you like."

Charlie looked wide-eyed with surprise, but my mother was already down the stairs before she opened her mouth to say anything. I continued up to the family wing of the house, and Charlie ran to keep up with me. Her eyes were wide as she took everything in around her. Millicent liked to keep the hall sconces on dimmers, so the effect was a little like candlelight, and, I had to admit, very pretty.

Charlie didn't speak until we had closed the door to my bedroom. The room had been my mom's when she was growing up in this house, and I liked it for the view over the kitchen garden.

"This is your 'ouse?" Charlie's voice was a breathy gasp.

58

"Crazy, isn't it? Technically, it's my mom's house, but I didn't grow up here. We only moved back this year."

"It is a … proper manor!"

I grinned at the awe on her face. "It took me a week to learn my way around. I can show you, or you can just explore it on your own. My favorites are the wardrobes. There are clothes from probably every era since the 1600s in them, and more in the attics. That's where I found my outfit for tonight."

I was peeling off the jacket and shirt as I spoke. Nineteenth-century men's clothes weren't too bad, as those things went, but they weren't jeans and t-shirts either. Charlie watched me strip down to my camisole and underwear with some embarrassment. It didn't bother me, though. I probably seemed like a freak to her since I was so tall and she was so tiny. I guessed Charlie was about sixteen, but she was about the size of my friend Olivia, who is descended from Picts, the tiny race who had lived on the British Isles before the Romans came. I thought Charlie's diminutive size probably had more to do with not having enough food when she was growing.

"I have a t-shirt you can wear, and if you roll them, my sweats will probably fit you if you want to change."

"Do I have to?" Charlie's voice was small again, and I looked at her sharply.

"Of course not. I just can't stand all the fabric you guys wear. It gets tangled around my legs when I'm trying to run or if I have to fight. I just thought, since you used to dress like a boy anyway …"

She exhaled. "I 'ad to wear trousers so the blokes Mary brought to the room didn't look twice at me. Wearin' a dress now reminds me I'm safe."

A twinge in my chest was some combination of pain and sympathy. "I get that, actually. I usually dress like a boy because I'm too practical, and maybe too lazy, to get all fancy. And when I'm free-running it's actually safer to look sort of anonymously male. But I compensate by wearing cute, girly underwear that only I can see. And I do my toes in crazy colors."

59

I wiggled my bare toes to show off my latest, sparkly turquoise pedicure. Turquoise toenails made me absurdly happy. Charlie giggled.

"It's very silly to 'ave blue toes."

"I know, right? That's why I do it. They were hot pink last week."

I pulled up a pair of black skinny jeans and grabbed a dark gray t-shirt from a drawer. Charlie smirked when she read the words on it – *Dinosaurs didn't read and look what happened to them.*

"Ringo taught me readin'."

I remembered all the books Ringo had stacked on every surface in his flat. "This house is full of books. You're welcome to read anything you find interesting." I was lacing my boots so I didn't see Charlie's expression at first, but her voice was so tentative I had to look up.

"Do ye think yer ma might 'ave work for me? Maybe in the kitchens, or cleanin'? I don't know anythin' about workin' in a big 'ouse like this, but I'm a fast learner."

My surprise must have been visible because the hopeful look on her face shuttered, and she took a step back. "It's alright if there's no place fer me 'ere. I just 'oped, you know?"

"Charlie, my mom wasn't kidding about giving you a bedroom here. A guest bedroom, not one of the maid's quarters. You're welcome whether you work or not, though if you get bored and want to help out, I'm sure no one's going to say no. You don't have to earn your keep. You're my friend. You can stay as long as you want to."

Her eyes brimmed with tears, and I wrapped her up in a hug. "Your life has not been easy in ways I can't even imagine. This life might not be either, but no matter what, you have a place to stay, okay?"

I could feel her nodding against my shoulder, and then I had to wipe my own eyes. Some of the wariness on her face had finally cleared, and I wondered if she had ever truly relaxed, even with Ringo.

I looked out the window to the garden, wondering if the guys were still in view. There was no movement in the walled garden, but directly below me I caught the edge of something. The smallest motion, maybe even Jeeves' cat, but something in my gut prickled.

"I think maybe we should work out some hiding places." I flicked off the lamp next to me, leaving only the one by the bed still lit, then stepped back out of sight of the window. "I'm not sure anyone will ever make it up here, but we should hide now just in case."

The wariness was back in Charlie's face, and she picked up the cast iron frying pan. I pointed behind her. "Wardrobe."

She nodded and silently slipped inside.

I turned off the other lamp and waited a second for my eyesight to adjust. Then I slipped back to the window and stood next to it, peering down at whatever was moving outside.

There it was again. A flicker of motion. Definitely not feline, but what was it?

The movement outside the house was gone, but the prickling remained in my guts. Something wasn't right. Something … was coming.

I put the kitchen knife on the desk next to me and clutched my daggers in each hand. The prickling didn't change, and I could feel a Monger coming on like the flu, steadily getting closer and more icky.

And then the floor creaked. Right outside my door.

My teeth clenched, and I crouched down next to the desk. Not a proper hiding place, but maybe not obvious unless a lamp was turned on. There were no overhead lights in the bedrooms at Elian Manor, an old-fashioned quirk about which I was suddenly very glad.

If I hadn't been watching the door so intently I never would have known it was opening. The movement was glacial and completely silent. Just a centimeter or two at a time. I'd stopped breathing and knew if that door didn't open all the way soon I would pass out from a lack of oxygen.

The door finally stopped moving when the opening was just wide enough for a person to pass through. My daggers were out in front of me, ready to be thrown at the first sign of *enemy*.

There were no other sounds in the house. Nothing moving in the shadows, nothing creaking down the hall. I wasn't sure who was outside my door, but I didn't think any of my friends were stupid enough to sneak into an armed chick's room. And if it was an enemy, how the hell did he get past my friends?

My shoulders were starting to lock up from the tension, and I was afraid to blink. There. Something moved near the door handle. Something not ... solid.

The darkness rippled, if such a thing is possible, and if I'd been a cartoon character I would have rubbed my eyes in disbelief. Nothing solid entered my room, but it got darker anyway. I didn't move a muscle, even as they were screaming at me to run away. Monger-nausea was roiling, and my heartbeat started tripping over itself in an effort to make me move.

The rippling darkness came fully into the room, and a sudden yell cut through the night outside the manor. "He's gone!" It was Mr. Shaw's voice, and it held an edge of panic. It also sounded very far away.

"Upstairs! To Saira!" I totally seconded the urgency in Archer's voice. Yes, please, my mind almost whimpered.

The darkness moved faster now. It hesitated at the bed, then started toward the wardrobe. Crap! I stood up suddenly, possessed by all things heroic and stupid, and yelled, "Here!"

Really, it was an impressive yell. I even startled myself with the sheer volume, and I realized I was yelling to the guys outside to get up here and save my terrified booty before I did something idiotic, like draw attention to myself.

Oh wait, I'd already done that.

The darkness rushed at me and I started slashing.

Note to self — daggers are not swords. They aren't slashing weapons. They're stabbing ones. I was slashing like I'd just walked through a massive spider web and was doing the get-it-off dance.

Darkness is pretty hard to cut though, and the only thing I was succeeding at was freaking out. The darkness hadn't touched me yet – yes, I realized how ridiculous that sounded, but I had the sense that this Monger-darkness had mass somewhere behind all that invisibility.

I could hear heavy feet pounding up the main staircase and knew it would take someone about five seconds to get to my room. Three, if it was Ringo.

And then the darkness grabbed me. And I screamed.

I slashed at the darkness with my free dagger and thought I might have connected with something because the grip convulsed and nearly broke my arm with its force.

Crap. That hurt.

And suddenly I had a flash of malice. I didn't know if I saw it, or just felt it, but it was blinding and seething with nastiness. I almost dropped my dagger.

And then … THUNK.

The grip on my arm let go and I dove away from it.

And then I watched the outline of a man go crashing through my bedroom window.

My bedroom door slammed open the next instant and Archer yelled, "Saira!"

"I'm here."

Like me, Archer didn't need more than a sliver of light to see, and the dimmed hall sconces were more than bright enough to find me. A heartbeat later I was in his arms clutched to his chest, and the pounding of his pulse matched mine.

Charlie stood behind him, just outside the open wardrobe. She had the frying pan raised in her hands and a stunned expression on her face. That explained the THUNK I'd heard, and a smile wobbled onto my lips.

I struggled to the window. Jagged shards of glass littered my desk, and the gaping hole was definitely big enough to have accommodated a fleeing man. I searched the ground with my newly educated eyes. Neither man nor darkness was visible below, and I shuddered as I turned to face Archer and Charlie.

"It's gone."

"It?" Archer's voice was incredulous.

"It was *Other*." Charlie squeaked. Actually squeaked. It would have been cute if what she said hadn't been so freaking scary.

"Other, as in from the Otherworld?" I stared at her and she nodded, wide-eyed. I explained to Archer. "Charlie is an Otherworld seer. Not Seer, like Descendant of Fate, but she can literally see things that aren't from this world. Miss Simpson said she's known of one other person who could see Others. "

"My mother could do it, too."

"What did you see, Charlotte?"

"It was cloaking itself in darkness, but that was just a ... thing it put on, like a skin. But it wasn't a pure Other, because Saira could see it, too."

"It was Monger, too."

Mr. Shaw and Ringo burst into the room. "Rothchild's gone."

Ringo took one look at Charlie and rushed to her side. He unpeeled her grip from the frying pan handle and then wrapped his arms around her shoulders. She leaned back into him, but kept her eyes on the rest of us.

"So Dodo's part Otherworlder," I said. "Isn't that special. But why didn't he go dark when he went after me on the bridge?"

"Maybe he underestimated you before?" Archer's voice had a smirk under it that made me feel good. As if underestimating me was a mistake people only made once.

"Maybe there's an energy expenditure associated with going dark? I like that description, by the way. It explains how he got past all of us outside." Mr. Shaw managed to sound vaguely professorial no matter what he said. Ringo nodded.

"That makes sense. Ye said 'e was a Rothchild. Related to yer old roommate, Saira?"

"Archer thinks he's an older brother, but if he's only half Monger, he's a half brother."

"There are Others that can hide *in* a body, not just hide *as* one." Charlie's voice was getting stronger, and I guessed she was finding confidence in the fact that everyone in the room took her seriously.

"You mean, maybe the Darkness just took Dodo over and decided to ride around in him?"

"Somethin' like that." Charlie gave me the ghost of a smile.

"Fascinating." Mr. Shaw always sounded like Spock when he said that.

"Freaking scary. I'm not feeling too confident about my chances against him if he comes back." I didn't like the involuntary shudders that kept creeping up my spine.

"You should go to the keep with your mother. At least to sleep." Archer's voice was low in my ear.

The thought of sleeping in the warded keep of Elian Manor made me shiver, but with chills, not the creeps. "I don't think I can sleep through the cold of the ward there."

"I wish I could tell you to rest with me, but it'll be dawn soon, and I'm afraid I will become a liability to you if he should find us."

Considering I didn't even know Archer's daytime resting place at Elian Manor, I thought that was unlikely, but Mr. Shaw saved me from answering. "You should both go to the keep. Get some rest, and I'll do some more research on 1429 with your mother. When you wake up tonight we will hopefully have a workable plan to keep you away from the Otherworlder."

I sighed. I really was exhausted. "Charlie and Ringo, go find rooms in the east wing. I don't care where, and no one else will either. Just get some rest, okay?" Ringo nodded, and Charlie picked up her frying pan again. It made me smile.

I looked at Archer. "Go do whatever you need to do to hunt. You're too cold when you haven't eaten, and I'm going to need all the body heat I can steal from you." I was bossy when I was tired - probably other times, too – but Archer nodded quietly. I knew he hunted for deer in the woods surrounding Elian whenever he needed to, so I could keep my squeamishness about his eating habits turned down low. He'd only killed one person that I knew about, and that guy was a Were bent on killing Archer. I tried not to think about it too much, though. I was good at mental hide and seek. If I couldn't see it, it couldn't see me.

I grabbed a pillow and a duvet and dragged myself out of the bedroom. Ringo and Charlie peeled off at the intersection of the east and west wings, and I could tell they were both tripping over the bags under their eyes, too.

Archer escorted me to the keep and kissed me gently before I went inside. I could hear him talking to Mr. Shaw as they walked away.

Mom was asleep on the sofa, so I curled up on the soft Persian rug, pulled my duvet over me, and lay thinking about Dodo. I didn't know if the Monger hierarchy knew their pet soldier wasn't entirely human, but I imagined he was incredibly effective at snatch and grab.

Why let a little thing like humanity get in the way?

HISTORY

The streets teemed with wolves. Their snarls and growls filled the night with a warning of bloodshed, and the scent of beasts was sharp and wild in the air. The stone walls of a castle-like building guarded our backs. We couldn't be surrounded, but we couldn't run either.

One wolf, though maybe not as big as the others, was clearly the leader. It was a tawny, reddish color with a dark tail that made the tail look bobbed, and the others flanked it protectively.

Tawny stared into my eyes and neither of us blinked. It was a test of dominance, and to blink was to die.

I gasped awake with heart-pounding disorientation. No wolves. Not the streets. Not my room. Finally, the hand stroking my hair brought me back to full consciousness. Archer. And a vision.

I turned my face up to his. "Wolves?"

"Apparently."

I closed my eyes, took a deep breath, and sat up. Then immediately dove back under the duvet and snuggled into the warm spot my sleeping body had made next to Archer. "Cold."

Archer chuckled and held me close. Even his scent was warm and faintly spiced with cinnamon or cardamom. We rarely slept next to each other because I worked during daylight hours, so it was a luxury to wake up in his arms.

"Have you had that vision before?"

Archer shook his head. "It's new."

"Actually, it looked old. The streets were cobbled. And the thing behind us, the castle? That thing had turrets."

He smiled grimly. "A lot of turrets are still standing now, but I agree, it didn't feel modern."

I closed my eyes. "Crap. I'm not ready to start Clocking again. The trip back to get Ringo was fine because I kind of know the Victorian rules. And Victorians believe in bathing." I grimaced and Archer laughed, a deep rumble in his chest. "And don't even get me started on street-dumping chamber pots. Seriously? Why even bother. Just dangle your business out the window and let fly. It's the same thing."

Archer's rumble had become full-blown laughter, and it was doing a good job of erasing the bad taste residue from the wolf vision.

I sat up again, pulling the duvet with me to wrap around my shoulders. Archer's bare chest was uncovered, and I automatically reached my hand out to trace the line of a scar. He had slept in pajama bottoms, and I had to swallow a giggle at the idea of a Vampire in pajamas.

Archer grabbed my hand – the one that was absently tracing his scar – and brought it to his lips to kiss. Something in his eyes told me not to let my fingers go walking on his bare chest, so I dragged my gaze away and focused on the portrait of the Immortals that hung on the far wall.

"You ever notice how Miss Simpson looks a little like Aislin's grandmother?"

A person could get whiplash from my subject changes.

Archer followed my gaze. "Technically, she's descended from Fate, right? It's not so strange that they might have similar features."

But now that I'd thought it I couldn't let it go, and I got up to shiver my way across the room to the painting. "Her nose is the same, and the shape of her eyes. Even her lips are the same color. I bet if we could find a picture of Miss Simpson from when she was young, she'd look just like Aislin in this portrait."

"Have you ever asked Doran about this painting? He's the artist, right?"

I made a face somewhere between a scowl and a sour lemon. "Like I ever have a chance to ask him anything." I grabbed Archer's big cashmere sweater and pulled the t-shirt from underneath it. Then I tossed him the t-shirt. "Here, you don't get cold." He shot me a look of mock outrage and I raised an eyebrow. "It's your fault anyway. You created a monster when you gave me my first cashmere sweater. Suck it up."

He smirked. "You just said 'suck' to a Vampire."

"Yeah, that wasn't too smart, was it? Especially since I'm stealing this sweater, too."

He tried to grab me as I passed by, but I dodged out of the way with a shriek. A second later I was in his arms being tickled when the door to the keep slammed open. Mr. Shaw stood there in full scary mode. We sprang apart.

"I heard a scream."

"You heard a shriek. There's a difference." Mr. Shaw didn't scare me, even when he was seconds away from shifting into a Bear. I planted my fists on my hips and glared at him because he did startle me with the door. Then I smiled.

"Thanks for coming to my rescue, though."

"You're welcome." His tone was gruff, and he still wore a scowl, but he wasn't mad.

I slipped on my boots and pulled Archer's sweater over my head. Archer growled at me playfully and I shot him a grin. "See you guys in the library."

Mr. Shaw grumbled. "We'll be a few minutes. I need to talk Devereux into parting with a bit more of his blood."

That stopped me in my tracks. "What have you found?" Mr. Shaw had been experimenting with the kind of blood mixtures we thought Bishop Wilder had been seeking when Archer first met him, back when Jack the Ripper was hunting down part-Clocker girls for him. We wondered if it would give us a clue as to *why* he'd been doing it, and that information might help us stop him. Archer had donated his own Vampire blood, which was like a major biohazard for any Immortal Descendant to handle, and Mr. Shaw was mixing it with his Shifter blood and any other Descendant blood he could get. I'd given to the cause, and I thought the Arman twins had, too. My mom had even volunteered, but she went so pale at the sight of the needle that Mr. Shaw refused to do it.

"I'm getting some fascinating results, but they're unpredictable, so I need to run some more tests. Connor's been helping me in the lab at school, and I have to say, my nephew might just be a better scientist than I am."

I snorted. "Don't tell him that."

Mr. Shaw cracked a smile. "I can't decide if he's brilliantly confident, or just a know-it-all pain-in-the-arse."

I laughed as I swept out of the room. "Both."

I took off at a run once I was out of sight. I didn't usually free-run through Elian Manor because Millicent would have kittens if she caught me sliding down bannisters and vaulting the servants' stairs. But today I didn't really care if Millicent yelled. I had wolves to think about – much more terrifying than she could ever be.

I grabbed a peach from the sideboard on my way through the dining room. It looked like dinner had already happened, and I was very happy to have missed the formal dress requirement of an evening meal at Elian Manor.

Charlie and Ringo were in the library with my mom when I got there. Ringo had on a white dress shirt, open at the collar, and dark slacks. I knew the wardrobes had male clothes too, because it's where I'd found the Victorian menswear I'd worn to go get Ringo. But I hadn't expected Ringo to look so handsome all dressed up. I'd seen him in homespun, and in jeans and a t-shirt, but somehow the dress shirt made him look older than sixteen.

"Wow, you guys must have been at dinner. You look great."

"Miss Sanda brought me this. I was afraid it was too short, but she said it worked with my colorin'." Charlie held out the sides of a light blue, fifties-style dress with a fitted bodice and a circle skirt.

"It's perfect. You were born in the wrong century. You should always wear clothes from the 1950s. In fact, get Sanda to show you where that closet is, and maybe that should be your bedroom."

Charlie shot a quick glance at my mom and then smiled shyly. I looked at my mother, who was searching the computer in the corner. "Mom, who would have been here in the fifties?"

"Millicent."

"Oh, right. Never mind."

Charlie looked up. "Actually, she complimented me on it. 'Er ladyship said the style suited me."

Well, that was unexpected. Ringo was up on the ladder, poking through the top shelf books. He was trying to keep a solemn expression, but I could see his eyes gleaming.

"What'd you guys do today?" I asked him.

Ringo re-shelved the book he was holding and descended the ladder. "Mr. Shaw and I dismantled the Monger's bolt 'ole. T'weren't nothing to identify 'im in there."

"What'd you do with his stuff?"

"Jeeves stashed it. The bedroll looked right useful, and 'e said 'e'd loan it to me if … ye know." Ringo's voice trailed off and my mom looked up.

"If you go camping, or if you go back?"

He looked a little sheepish. I guess my mom inspired that, because I'd never seen Ringo look anything other than completely confident. "Back, I guess."

"Ringo, you heard the conversation Millicent and I had over dinner. You and Charlie both are welcome here. You are my daughter's friends. You've helped her survive unimaginable things several times, and I know she looks at you, Ringo, like a brother. Aside from the fact that I genuinely like you and feel I will learn to like Charlie very much, I am forever in your debt. This house is far bigger than our small family will ever need, and it deserves to be filled with people we love. So, please, find bedrooms in the house you like and make them your own for as long as you want to be here."

I wasn't surprised at my mom's speech, or her generosity, but her words made me tear up and I was so proud to be her kid. I went to her and put my arms around her shoulders. "Thanks, Mom," I whispered. She kissed me on the cheek.

"Mrs. Elian, ye've done us both a great 'onor with yer generousness, and we'd very 'appily accept yer 'ospitality for a time. I'll need to make my own way, so it won't be for long. But ye and Saira feel like family to us. Family we 'aven't ever 'ad, and we are lucky to know ye."

"Good. I'm sick of worrying about you both." I said it in a scolding tone, but couldn't keep a straight face to save my life. And in a very grown up manner, Ringo made a face at me, so I burst out laughing. I think if Charlie had been a modern teenager, she would have rolled her eyes at the pair of us.

"Archer and Mr. Shaw are on their way here, and he's probably already told Mr. Shaw this, so I'll tell you guys. Archer had a vision right before we woke up. Of us, in an old city somewhere, surrounded by wolves."

"Sorry, did ye say wolves in a city?" Ringo asked skeptically.

"I know, right? Doesn't make sense. Except the building we were next to was huge, with turrets like a castle, and the streets were cobblestone."

My mom started typing something into the computer. "What are you searching?"

"Wolves. 1429."

"Really, why that year?"

"Doran said it was a simple, one-ring jump to find Wilder. Maybe your wolves are related."

Charlie was listening to our conversation with bigger and bigger eyes. "There were wolves in Paris."

Ringo and I stared at her. "What?" I tried not to sound incredulous. I really did.

"She's right." My mom was staring at the computer screen. "The wolves of Paris is historical fact. In 1429, after a long, hard winter, the walls around Paris had fallen into disrepair, and the wolves started coming in to hunt people. There were packs of them, and they seemed to be led by one alpha, one the Parisians called Courtaud, or "Bobtail." It was reddish in color and led the packs to kill nearly forty people."

"I saw Courtaud, and it was definitely the alpha. It tried to stare down Archer."

Mr. Shaw and Archer had just entered the library together.

"Wolves don't stare down humans." Mr. Shaw's voice sliced through the shock in the room.

"This one did," Archer verified. He came to stand near me, and his hand rested lightly on my shoulder. It felt good there. Solid. Like he always had my back.

"How did ye know about the wolves of Paris, Char?" Ringo's voice was quiet and I could see why. Charlie's eyes were still saucers on her face. Maybe it was the time jump, or the company she was suddenly keeping – we definitely weren't for the faint-hearted.

"My ma. Our bedtime stories were filled with tales of Others. The wolves were one of those tales." I knew every pair of eyes in the room was locked on Charlie, and yet her chin went higher and her back straighter with every word. Like she was daring us to tell her she was wrong.

My mom whispered from the corner. "Wilder?"

"Ye mean the one who turned 'is lordship and kept ye prisoner?" Mom nodded, but Charlie shook her head. "The Other in the wolf tale took children. 'Undreds of 'em. 'E was caught, tried, and 'ung for 'is crimes. My ma called 'im Bluebeard, on account of a tale someone 'ad written about 'im."

Mom's fingers clattered on the computer keyboard, and a moment later she read from the screen. "The story of Bluebeard is thought to have been based on the medieval French aristocrat Baron Gilles de Rais, who was tried and convicted of the murder of children. He is believed to have killed between seventy and two hundred children over a period of fourteen years, beginning in 1429." She stared and color drained from her face. "De Rais was thought to have ties to the Bishops of Sens, and at one point may have even stayed at their Paris residence as a guest of an interim bishop from England. There is speculation that some of the young victims of the wolves of Paris were actually victims of Gilles de Rais."

"An interim bishop from England? Are you kidding?" My heart began to race.

"We don't know it's Wilder."

"Right. And he doesn't have a habit of hanging out with murderous ogres either." The good news just kept piling on.

"'The Baron de Rais wasn't an ogre, far as my ma knew. They're short and squat and can't do nothing to 'ide the ugliness. 'E was just Other."

All eyes were on Charlie again, and I burst out laughing. It was a defense mechanism against the horror of maybe finding Wilder, but I didn't care. "Ogres actually exist? No way!"

I could tell her expression was warring between indignation and humor. Humor won, and the corners of her mouth turned up in one of those really pretty smiles she usually saved for Ringo.

"So, based on the clues dropped by Doran, the vision Archer has had of wolves, and the mention of an English bishop, it seems Wilder may be hiding in Paris in 1429." Trust Mr. Shaw to bring us back to the business at hand.

"1429 was a whole year long, and Paris is a big city. *When* in 1429, and *where* in Paris are two very big questions on a long list of big questions that we don't know the answers to." Funny, for a second there, I actually sounded rational and careful. As if leaping head-first into bad plans wasn't my specialty.

Ringo suddenly hopped down off the ladder, searched the upper shelves for a few heartbeats, then slid the ladder to another spot in the room and climbed it to pull a book down. It was big and looked old. "Remember this book, Saira?"

I looked at the cover. *Townhouse Architecture of England and France.* "Should I?"

He grinned with perfect Ringo cheekiness. "I'm impressed yer library 'ere 'as it. Ye yelled at me fer minnin' one like it at King's College the time we found Archer there."

I did remember that book. Ringo told me then he needed to know his way around those houses if he was going to steal from them.

"Well, that was my first book, see? And I learned it by heart after ye both taught me to read." He flipped through pages of the book he'd set on the table in front of him, then found what he was looking for. "When ye said turrets and Paris, I could picture it exactly."

He stepped back from the page, and Archer moved closer to look. "The Hôtel de Sens, in the Marais district of Paris. It was the primary residence of the Archbishops of Sens in Paris during the 1400s."

"The Paris residence of the Bishops of Sens. Where de Rais and the English Bishop stayed." My eyes were glued to the pages in front of me.

The drawing that stared back at me was a sepia colored pen and ink, and showed a horse-drawn carriage out front. Which made sense considering Ringo had first seen this book in 1888.

I looked up at Archer. "This is it. The castle from your vision."

Archer was by my side, and then looked up from the drawing to meet my eyes.

"Can you use this?"

"This drawing is detailed enough; I could probably get us just across the street, if I take out the horse, carriage, and people."

Mr. Shaw stared at me. "How are you going to make sure it's 1429?"

My expression was grim, and I knew Archer had already come to the same conclusion because his was, too. "I'll picture the wolves."

SHIFTER BONE

It felt like an explosion had sucked all the oxygen from the room. My mom and Mr. Shaw shouted at the same time, and even Charlie yelled the word, "No!" startling herself. But Ringo was the one who got my attention when he mouthed silent words.

"Take me with you."

"Why?" My eyes were locked on his, and I knew Archer had seen him, too. "Why would you want to go with us?" My gaze flicked to Charlie, and I knew he understood the silent message. Why would you leave Charlie here alone?

"Because my two best friends - actually, my brother and my sister – are going off to face wolves and search for a rabid Vampire. Ye're goin' t' need my skills, and I'm 'bout the only one who can put up with the lot o' ye. So, I'm goin'."

He spoke quietly, and it was in the kind of voice that shut everyone else up.

"I'm going, too," Mr. Shaw growled.

My eyes opened wide at that. "What? Why?"

"Because you need an alpha to control the wolves."

"But you're a Bear." Nothing like stating the obvious as a way to win favor.

Mr. Shaw's scowl was even blacker than before. "A Bear does just fine against wolves."

My mom, of all people, was the voice of reason in the room. "A Bear will do fine against two or three wolves, Bob. But this is two or three packs. If the wolves didn't take you down, the Parisians, with their arrows and swords, would."

I shrugged. "Connor's an alpha Wolf." My friend Connor Edwards was home from school for the summer, but he was one of the most alpha Shifters I knew.

"No!" That came from my mom and Mr. Shaw together.

"He's fourteen." My mom looked stricken.

Ringo spoke under his breath. "'E'd love it." I raised a "right?" eyebrow at him and he smirked, but kept it to himself.

"Don't you know any other alpha Wolves you could call on, Bob?" My mom came over to where he stood. He rested a hand on the small of her back, probably without even realizing he did it.

"None who would do it." His voice was a tired sigh.

"What about the Shifter bone. Could you not use that to become a Wolf?"

Mr. Shaw jerked back suddenly, as if to step away from my mom. "That bone's clan business. What do you know of it?" He had an accusatory tone I didn't like. Apparently, neither did my mom.

Her shoulders tightened defensively, and her expression shuttered closed. "You forget, I was married to the Shifter clan heir." Her voice had an edge to it that sounded angry, but I felt the pain underneath it like a punch to the gut.

Mr. Shaw didn't seem to hear the pain at all and whipped out his own defensiveness. "Right. Your husband. The Shaw heir and son of the last clan chief to have the Shifter bone in his possession. Between the massacre and the loss of the Shifter bone, it's a wonder the Shaw Family even kept its name. Thank you for dinner, Claire. I have work to do."

He left the library with just the barest glance at the rest of us, and when he was out of the room, my mother's ramrod straight posture sagged.

"What's the Shifter bone, Mom?"

She sounded defeated. "It's the Shifter clan artifact, like our Clocker necklace."

"And the Seer's cuff."

She nodded. "The bone is ancient. No one even knows what kind of animal it came from, or even if it's human. But the carvings are intricate and have filled it with Shifter magic. It allows a Shifter who wears it to change into any animal he chooses."

"So a Bear could Shift into a Wolf?"

"Exactly. I hadn't realized they never found it after your grandfather died … and I'm certainly not privy to clan business anymore." She gazed at the door Mr. Shaw had closed behind him, then rubbed her shoulders and glanced at me. "I'm tired. I'll have the servants make up a bed for you in the keep, at least until we can attack this thing with the Mongers head-on." She smiled sadly. "Good night, my loves."

I stood up quickly. "Wait, Mom." I followed her out to the hall, where she waited for me, looking defeated. "Why did he get so mad?"

She touched my face softly. "Bob Shaw has been very patient with me, and I suppose the fact that I know such closely held clan secrets that he didn't tell me himself is a bit too big a reminder of my feelings for your father."

"But you're in love with Mr. Shaw, aren't you?"

The sad smile was back. "Yes, I suppose I am."

"You should maybe tell him that, don't you think?"

She pulled my hand up to her mouth and kissed it. "I wish I could claim credit for your wisdom, but I can't, so I'll take advantage of it and learn from you instead. Good night, sweet girl. And thank you."

Archer looked up as I re-entered the library.

"Is she okay?" he asked.

"I don't know. She's fine, I guess, but he made her feel bad. He might as well have accused her of being married to a murderer who spilled Family secrets to a Clocker."

"We all know your father didn't kill the council."

"Doesn't matter. It's part of the legend now." I got up suddenly. "I need to get out of my head. Who wants to go running with me?"

"Me!" Ringo stepped forward with a grin.

Archer smiled, even though he looked worried. "There's an old barn a half mile away on the next hill. Last one there re-shelves the books."

"You're on!" I caught Charlie's eye. "Do you want to come free-running with us?"

She pulled a slim book off a shelf and shook her head. "I'm off to the bath."

Ringo held his hand out, and she squeezed it quickly before she left the room. He looked baffled when he turned to us. "It's 'er third bath since we got 'ere. She wasn't dirty to begin with."

I grinned at him. "It's a chick thing."

"No chicken I ever saw liked a bath."

Archer laughed and clapped his friend on the back. "Let's go."

It was still early, as night went, and warm enough to run without jackets. Archer had taken us to the third floor to sight the barn, and I'd stopped to wave to Jeeves in his garage flat, a habit since the first time I'd stayed at Elian manor.

And then we were off.

The first part was a straight run across fields filled with sleeping wildflowers and long summer grass. It felt good to sprint. There was just enough bite in the air to stop the sweat, and I stretched my legs as long as they could go. Archer's stride matched mine because we were the same height, but Ringo was faster, so we stayed together effortlessly.

At the first fence I veered toward the woods. It wasn't technically parkour when I took a detour to make the run more interesting, but there were better obstacles in the forest surrounding Elian Manor, and I was in the mood to scramble. I had taken the lead with the direction change, so the first combo was mine. I launched off a tree stump to the top of a boulder. The drop from there was about six feet, so I front-flipped the descent just to be fancy. I could hear Ringo laugh behind me. It was that sound of pure joy that comes with a body doing what you ask it to do.

It's what I loved about free-running.

Then Ringo passed me, and he set the style. He liked flips, and he was a monkey when he climbed, so he pulled himself up onto a low branch to leap to the next tree, then somersaulted down off it. A very flashy move, and I pulled it off with only slightly less grace.

When we hurdled the low fence at the last field, Archer took the lead. This was his hill and he powered straight up it, across the top of ancient stone wall remains, and over split wood fences meant to keep sheep in.

Then the barn came into view and it was on. There was a rock wall and a gully between us and the old wooden structure. Ringo flew up the wall like he had suction cups on his hands and feet, but I paid attention to the split-second timing of his hand and foot placement, so I was right behind him.

At the top of the wall, Ringo did a straight drop down, then vaulted the gully to scramble up the other side. I was about to do the same, but I took a breath to look at the view. It gave Archer the second he needed to catch me, right before I jumped.

Not down. Out.

I pushed off the wall and leapt forward. I aimed for the bank across the gully – for the patch of alfalfa grown there. It had deep roots, and I knew I could grab it to keep myself from falling backwards into the gully. If I had enough arc to hit the other side.

I did. But my feet started backsliding immediately. I grabbed a clump of alfalfa, stopped the skidding feet, and started back up the hill.

I heard Archer whistle appreciatively and follow with his own leap across the gully, but I was already neck and neck with Ringo. I grinned at the surprise in his eyes, and then dug deep for a final burst of speed and shot up a split rail fence, launched off the top, and touched the door of the barn one finger-length ahead of Ringo.

Yes!

We were both doubled over and panting through grins and laughter when Archer hit the door two seconds later. He was barely winded, which was probably more a function of the fact he didn't need air than being in better condition than us. He looked up to the weathervane on top of the barn.

"Shall we?"

I swallowed a gasp and then nodded. "Let's do it."

This wasn't a race, so much as a creative climb with extra points for difficulty. My route took me up the drainpipe to the hayloft window, with a free-climb up to the pitched roof, and all three of us made it to the top within a minute of each other.

There was enough moon to see Elian Manor in the distance, and we sat in companionable silence for a few minutes, letting heart rates go back to normal and soaking in the view.

I finally said out loud what had been creeping around the corner in my brain. "I'm going to go back to see my dad."

Nobody's breath caught; no one stiffened in an obvious way. Archer spoke calmly. "When?"

"When am I going, or *to when* am I going?"

"To when."

I'd given this some thought while we ran. "Probably about a year after he was incarcerated at Bedlam. My mom told me they'd moved him into his permanent room by that time, and I can talk to him through the grate in the cellar."

"Aren't ye changin' things to go back and talk to 'im?"

I shook my head. "I thought about that, but he seemed to recognize my voice when we first talked. He just played it cool because I didn't know him then."

I turned to Archer. "You don't seem surprised."

"I'm not. As soon as you were able to direct your Clocking off the default range, I knew it was only a matter of time before you went back, and learning that Will Shaw's father was the last to have the Shifter bone, well, that was an obvious enticement."

"Not to mention the fact that my dad was the last one to see his father alive."

"I'm surprised your mum didn't realize you'd want to go back."

"Whatever's going on with her and Mr. Shaw had her all twisted up." I looked anxiously at him. "You're okay with me going?"

81

He pulled me in close to him, his fingers absently playing with my braid. "I'm just sorry I can't go with you. I think I would have liked your dad."

"Ye want company? I'll go wi' ye."

Ringo was a year younger than me, so I could probably miss his natural lifetime if I Clocked it just right, but as nice as it would be to have a friend there, this was something I needed to do on my own. I shook my head. "Thanks, but I'm going to do this one alone." I turned to Archer. "I should probably go tonight. That way I'm out of here if Dodo comes back for a command performance."

Archer stood up and dusted off his jeans, then helped me to my feet and gave me a light kiss on the lips. He turned to Ringo. "Last one back sits guard duty."

Bedlam – July, 1872

I'd been Clocking other people with me so often, the trip *between* times by myself was practically nausea free. The only tricky part was making sure to concentrate on 1872. I knew the Bedlam cellar well enough that I could default that part, but other than repeating the year over and over in my mind, I didn't have a foolproof way of making sure I landed in the right time.

The cellar underneath Bethlem Royal Hospital, otherwise known as Bedlam, was pretty much like I remembered it from my journeys there in 1888. Crates were stacked against the walls, and old furniture was stashed in odd places, sort of like an antiques showroom where every surface is covered in discarded items. It was a picker's dream, and it all got smashed to bits when the cellar caved in. Or, would cave in, in about sixteen years.

I covered the beam of my mini Maglite with my palm and used the red glow of my hand to navigate my way to the ceiling grate under Will Shaw's room.

"Will. Will Shaw." My voice was just above a whisper, and after a moment I heard movement above me. "Will, are you there?"

Another moment of silence, and then a man's whisper came through the grate. "I am Will Shaw."

Tension leeched away at the sound of his voice, and tears prickled behind my eyelids. "Hi, Will." My actual voice came out above the whisper. Still low-pitched, but audible. There was a longer hesitation above me.

"Hello."

Tears threatened, and then slightly manic laughter for no other reason than that I'd actually found him again. I suppressed the giggles as well as I could, but the sound still trickled out and I could feel Will Shaw's confusion. But he just listened to me laugh until I finally caught my breath.

"I'm sorry. I must sound crazy."

"No, there's no madness in your laughter." He said it so matter-of-factly I suddenly remembered he lived in an insane asylum. Mad laughter must be part of the soundtrack. "It was quite beautiful, in fact."

Oh. Wow. "Thank you."

I took a breath. He was waiting for my lead, and now I didn't know what to say. So I blurted instead.

"My name is Saira Elian." I wondered if he knew about me yet.

"Sai…" I could hear Will swallow. "Saira Elian. I have a baby daughter with that name."

"Yeah, that's me. Except, well, it's only been a year for you, but I'll be eighteen next week."

"July 25th. I remember."

The day he sent my mom forward to escape the Mongers. The day he lost us.

The next breath was shakier. I felt like I was messing with a man's life by being here, talking to him. "I'm sorry, Will." I was back to whispering again, mostly so I wouldn't cry.

"Saira," his voice was firm. A dad voice. "You have nothing to be sorry for. You are my most precious gift, whether you are here talking to me through a grate, or out in the world living your life. Do not apologize to me. Not ever."

The dad voice was the thing that did it. Let me wrestle control of the tears. It was sort of a "buck up little camper" thing, and it worked. I exhaled and started again.

"Do you have time to talk, Dad?" I didn't mean to say dad, it just sort of slipped out.

There was a smile in his voice, and I could hear him settle in above me. "I have all the time in the world for you."

So I talked.

I started at the beginning, in the tunnels under Venice. I faltered when I described how I'd met him before, and that I'd watched him die to save all of us. I just couldn't edit that part out, and I hoped I hadn't massively changed his future choices with this conversation. Somehow, I didn't think he would do anything differently, though. I got stronger again as I told him about Archer and about Wilder, the prophecy, and Elizabeth Tudor. He laughed sometimes, usually at Ringo's honest logic, but mostly he was silent. Just listening. It felt a little like what I imagined confession might feel like, not being able to see who I was talking to, the darkness making me brave.

When I was done talking I felt wrung out and limp like a wet dishcloth, but strong, too. I had done all those things, and I hadn't cracked under the weight or responsibility of them.

Will's voice broke gruffly above me. "I am so proud of you."

Nothing like a man in tears to turn the floodgates on. And with tears of that magnitude must come laughter, otherwise the snot just takes over. "I'm kinda badass, huh?"

His laughter was laced with tears, too. "If I knew what that meant, I might agree with you. But I'll say this. You, my daughter, are extraordinary."

"Thank you." I struggled to find my voice.

We both struggled, I think, because it was a moment before he spoke again.

"This Shaw, the Bear. He's a good man?"

I hadn't really gone into much detail about Mr. Shaw and my mom. It felt sort of unnecessary and hurtful. "Yeah, he's good. He wants to help us take on Wilder, but we need an alpha Wolf, and no one ever found the Shifter bone after your dad …"

Will grunted. "I'm surprised no one discovered where I hid it."

"*You* hid it?"

"In the council room. Before they took me."

I exhaled sharply. "I've been there. Where did you put it?"

"In the Shifter panel."

"*In* it?"

"There's a deeply carved groove designed to look like a knot in the tree. As children, my brother and I used to hide messages for each other in the knot whenever our father brought us to council meetings. I suppose it is possible Brian never looked there."

"Or he did, but because the Shifters cut all the Shaws out of politics, maybe he wasn't feeling too generous?"

Will took a deep breath, like my words had hurt. "My brother is a good man. Much less selfish than I ever was."

Anger burned at my edges. "You mean selfish because you loved my mom and forced their prejudice out into the open?"

"We all knew there was to be no mixing."

"Why? Why not mix?" It's not easy to whisper a yell, and I struggled with volume. But I wasn't holding back on this. "Why is it okay that anyone gets a say in who someone loves?"

"The love isn't wrong, but they fear what it leads to. All the way back to the original Immortals and the birth of Jera and Goran's son. They didn't just create a mixed child, they created a new Immortal. You can imagine how the idea of sharing power with one more Immortal was received by Duncan."

"You mean, the original Monger? But he's just one guy. How could he have so much influence, especially over the other Immortals?"

There was a pause, like Will was deciding how much to tell me. "When I was a child I was allowed to sit at my father's feet during council meetings as long as I stayed silent. Other Family Heads often forgot I was there, and the things I learned in that room weren't meant for a child's ears."

The image that hit my brain was of JFK Jr. hiding under his dad's desk in the Oval Office. Weird.

"As you know, all the Immortals have an artifact, like the Shifter bone and Clocker necklace. In this time, no one has ever known for sure what the Mongers' artifact was. Is it true for your time as well?

"I've never heard of the Monger artifact, so I guess it is."

He grunted, and then continued speaking. "Well, my father and some of the others speculated it could be a ruby ring they had occasionally seen the head of the Monger Family toying with during council meetings."

The image of the blood-red stone Ringo found in Slick's office flashed in my brain. "I might have seen it."

Will's voice was suddenly sharp with fear. "You've seen the Monger ring?"

"Yeah, I think so, hidden under a Monger's desk. I didn't touch it though. It looked too scary."

"Oh, thank God," he sighed with obvious relief. "Rothchild had it on his hand when your mother and I faced the council. I had a similar reaction to yours, and the moment I saw it, I began planning our escape. I had no facts upon which to base my assumption of its possible power, other than instinct, but if the ring was, in fact, the Family talisman, I expected that it somehow increased their native power – a truly frightening prospect with Mongers." There was a sharp breath above me, like my dad had to steel himself to continue.

"In fact, once Rothchild began speaking, there was nothing we could do or say to sway the council." His voice was intense. "Saira, stay away from that ring and anyone who wears it. There is something dangerous in its power. When Rothchild spoke…" There was an awful edge to his voice. Something self-loathing and toxic. "When Rothchild spoke of the wrongness of my love for Claire, and the dangers of allowing it, even I began to believe him."

My heart was pounding in my chest. Like I was the one reliving that unimaginable day of the council massacre. My dad took a ragged breath and finally continued. "It wasn't until Rothchild laid his hands on Claire – held her with that ring – that I finally lost control. It was as if the effort to regain my own will broke the hold I had over my Family skill, and I became unable to control my Shifts." Another ragged breath. "Please stay away from that ring."

"I will, Dad. I promise." I felt like I needed to calm him down. Like something in the air was shimmering in the room above me, and he was close to Shifting. Will Shaw's animal was a Mountain Lion. I'd seen it once, as he battled Bishop Wilder, and he was magnificent and deadly and everything I ever imagined a lion would be.

His voice was muffled when he finally spoke again, like his head was in his hands. "Did you inherit the ability to Shift from me?"

It's something I'd wondered when I'd first discovered my dad was a Shifter. "I got my height from you, and I run and climb and probably fall like a cat. But I've never Shifted."

"Well, as I don't know any other half-Shifters, I can't tell you if your animal will ever fully manifest. Shifter children are trained from the time they are small to understand their skills. Obviously, there's been no one to equip you." He sounded sad again, and tired. We'd been talking a long time.

"Dad?"

"Yes, love."

"I'm going to go try to find the Shifter bone now. I'm stalled in my quest to stop Wilder unless we can deal with the wolves."

He sighed. "As I've missed a lifetime of opportunities to dispense to my daughter nuggets of wisdom, I feel I should send you away with some bit of advice my life has taught me." He hesitated a moment, like he was sifting through the Rolodex, deciding which card to pull. His voice broke a little when he spoke again.

"I would never change having loved your mother. In fact, I should never have hidden it, because it's only when things remain in the shadows that they have the power to be used against one. The lesson I learned far too late is one I hope you'll embrace - live your life as if everyone will discover what you do and who you are. If no one holds your secrets, there's nothing to compel you to make choices that are not your own."

I smiled, even though he couldn't see it. Maybe he could hear it. "Kind of like living out loud, instead of in whispers. I like that."

"Living out loud." There was warmth in his voice. "You have an excellent way with words, Saira."

"So, besides coming out as a mixed-blood, do you have any other suggestions?"

His tone was thoughtful. "You told me you've accepted that you're part of the Seer's prophecy. Fulfilling it gives you and every other mixed-blood Descendant that chance to leave the shadows."

"No pressure."

He chuckled. "Thank you for coming here, and for sharing your adventures with me. Your laughter and the sound of your voice will echo in my dreams for a long time to come, I think."

"I'll come back when I can." I stood up and brushed the dust off my jeans.

"I look forward to it."

"Good night, Dad."

The council room was quiet and deserted, but the air had a closed, heavy feeling that was different than how it seemed when I'd been there with Mom in 1889. I remembered it had only been a year since the council massacre, and I tried not to look for bloodstains.

The Shifter tree panel was right next to the spiral, and now that I knew the knot was deep enough to hide something in, I couldn't imagine how anyone could miss it. I have a thing about reaching into places I can't see, but this was shallow, and my fingers found the cool, soft edges of the carved bone almost immediately.

I held the Shifter bone up to see the aged and timeworn relic. It was carved into an intricate twisted symbol, similar to something from Maori lore, and a leather cord was looped through one end. I put it over my head to keep it safe, and immediately a shiver went down my spine. I couldn't tell if it was the magic of the bone or the ghosts of the dead council disturbed by my presence that raised goosebumps, but unlike the stupid chick who always *goes into* the creepy house where the guy in the hockey mask waits with a chainsaw, I wasn't sticking around to find out.

I tucked the Shifter bone under my sweater and Clocked back home.

 **SHIFTED**

The sounds of fighting filled the pre-dawn air.

The garden was empty, which meant Archer was part of that fight, and I hit the ground – literally fell to the ground after Clocking – and then picked myself up and ran.

I climbed the garden wall to try an overhead perspective first. No sense running right into the fray until I knew what the fight looked like.

It looked weird.

Archer and Ringo were fighting with … air.

One would get punched, and the other would immediately strike the spot the punch had come from. Sometimes they connected, sometimes they didn't.

Mostly, they were just getting bloody.

Archer was taking the brunt of it. I assumed it was Dodo raining blows on him, because the idea of another creature like the one riding Dodo after us was too terrifying to contemplate. Dodo must have decided Ringo was just an annoyance, because he was only sporting a bloody nose and would probably have a black eye. Archer, on the other hand, was getting beaten to a pulp by a creature who didn't seem to care about infectious Vampire blood. Which was concerning, because Dodo was a Monger, susceptible to Vampiric infection, and the world did *not* need another double-deadly Monger.

I could see the ripples in the night air when Dodo stepped back from his last, horrifying punch to Archer's temple. While

Archer was trying to keep his feet, and Ringo was swinging wildly in the wrong direction, Dodo unsheathed something shiny.

I only saw it for a second, but I knew the thing in that creature's hand could cut and stab and kill.

I didn't think.

I just …

Shifted.

One moment I was me on top of the garden wall. The next moment the air around me shimmered, but from inside my cells. I say shimmered not because there was light attached, but because it was all movement. Shifting molecules, exquisitely painful and glorious, like deeply scratching the biggest itch of the most insidious case of chicken pox – with a wire brush.

And in the space between an inhaled breath that screamed "What the …?" and the exhale that finished that sentence in a particularly impressive expletive, I'd Shifted.

Into a Cougar.

I might have said Mountain Lion if I'd been looking at me, but I was inside the gorgeous beast and inside felt like Cougar. No bad jokes about aging desperate housewives suited the amazing creature I had become.

I was a Cougar.

A very pissed off Cougar.

I leapt off the wall with a grace I'd never imagined I could feel, and strength – sheer feline strength – coursed through me.

The fighters don't see me. They clearly aren't looking because I am magnificent, and they should run away in terror from my deadly strength.

My Cat was bossy, and I let her be. She wanted to be above the fighters, to choose her quarry with dangerous accuracy. I let her take me into a tree above them where we perched, watching the rippling night attack.

With his blade.

No! I saw blood well from a gash in Archer's arm where he'd somehow blocked the knife from gouging his ribs.

My mate. That was my mate that had been blooded by the blade of the rippled night.

91

My Cat wanted to kill the creature that held the knife. She sighted him, and then leapt from the tree. She aimed for his back, intending to take him down.

The creature must have heard us because it twisted away.

I can see it clearly now, behind the face of the Monger. The creature has lost its hold on the night, and the Monger it rides is terrified of me.

There was yelling and scrambling, and the night was flooded with the scent of fear. *It is an elixir, that fear, like the best chocolate or the sweetest ripe strawberry.* It made my Cat preen and her gaze find focus on the prey before her.

The creature who rides the Monger will die.

It was enough! Enough to force him back, to make the Monger visible; she didn't need to kill him!

Silly girl, she said.

My God! I was Sybil, arguing with my Cat.

But she was stronger than me. She was calling the shots, and they involved stalking toward the Monger with deadly grace. His face was a mask of fear. The yelling intensified behind her, and she could smell gunpowder. Someone had brought a gun to the party, which meant she had to do this fast. She couldn't play with him and fill the air with delicious fear.

I tried to hold her back but she shoved me deep inside.

And she lunged.

A shotgun blasted.

She twisted the Monger around to take the shots.

And she tore out his throat.

"Saira!"

I struggled up from blackness. From the depths of unconsciousness. I tried to open my eyes.

Failed.

"She's comin' 'round."

Tried again.

"Saira?" Archer's voice. His hand smoothed the hair back from my face.

I opened my eyes. The sky was beginning to color with the coming dawn, and Archer hovered over me. "You shouldn't be out."

He choked back something that sounded like a teary laugh. "Neither should you."

I tried to sit up and the world spun. Archer held me to his chest until I could keep myself steady. To his right, Ringo sat in the dirt, dried blood smeared across his face, one eye swelling shut.

I shoved Archer away. "The Monger! Where is he?"

I caught the grim look Ringo shot Archer over my shoulder, and then I knew.

I killed him.

I stumbled up and away from them to puke on Millicent's roses. Oh, God. I killed him.

"Jeeves has gone to take care of things." Archer was at my side, holding my hair, stroking my back with a gentle hand.

I choked back sobs. "Take care of things? What does that even mean? Does that mean go to the police or, or ... bury the body?"

"I didn't know you could Shift." Archer's voice was low and hurt.

"I can't." I was crying for real now. "I'm not a Shifter. I can't."

He pulled me back into his chest as sobs wracked my body.

I whispered into his shirt. "I don't want to."

The sun was about to break into the sky, and I dragged Archer inside the manor with me. Ringo trailed behind, watching me silently. I got us to the keep and closed the door to the windowless room just as Archer's energy failed him. He had just enough momentum left to strip his filthy, bloody clothes off and climb into the bedroll my mom had made on the floor before unconsciousness took him away.

I crumpled to the floor near his head and leaned against the wall.

Ringo lowered himself down with uncharacteristic stiffness and winced as he probed his eye socket for breaks.

"So, how was yer night?"

My bark of laughter got hung up on a leftover sob. "Well, it started in Bedlam, moved to Old Bailey, and ended in a man's death. How was yours?"

He shrugged. "I've had better."

"What happened after I left?"

"Nothin' for a long while. Then the tom tug kicked a rock, and we were on 'im like stink. 'Course, 'e wasn't no slouch in the beatin' business."

I looked over at Archer's face. The blood had dried in smears, but the bruises were already starting to age into lovely greens and yellows. He would probably be completely healed when he got up tonight. Ringo's face was less battered, but would take a lot longer to heal.

"Do you need some ice for that?" I indicated his eye, and Ringo shrugged.

"It's already closed. I'll be okay."

We sat in silence for a moment. He didn't push, but I knew we weren't done talking.

"I talked to my dad for a long time tonight. About everything."

"'E knows 'e's goin' to die, then?"

"He didn't seem too worried about that. He just said how proud he was of me and to trust myself. Oh, and he gave me a piece of fatherly advice, too." I smiled. It had been weird to feel like someone's daughter, but I kind of liked it. "He said to live out loud, with no secrets that anyone can use against me."

"Good advice, that."

"Sort of tough to do in a culture that would give me to the Mongers if I outed myself."

"That's what yer doin', isn't it? Changin' the culture?"

"Am I? Last I heard, I was fulfilling an old Seer prophecy."

"Remind me of it, again." Ringo closed his eyes. He really was beat to hell.

I took a breath and thought I'd have to dig in the memory banks, but the words just sort of flowed out of me.

"Fated for one, born to another
The child must seek to claim the Mother
The Stream will split and branches will fight
Death will divide, and lovers unite
The child of opposites will be the one
To heal the Dream that War's undone."

"Right. That's the one." He opened his eyes and looked at me. "So, what's it mean?"

"Hell if I know."

He gave me a half-grin. "Then let's pick it apart."

"Okay, the twins figured out that *Fated for one, born to another* was me, because I was technically supposed to be born in 1871, but Mom Clocked us forward so I was born into a different time. And the child seeking to claim the mother – me again, when I went back to 1888 to get Mom."

"Right. Those are the identifyin' bits. Now what's the meat of it?"

"That's the part I don't know. *The Stream will split and branches will fight.* Maybe that means the time stream will split? Oh, God. I hope not. What a colossal nightmare that would be. *Death will divide, and lovers unite.* That sounds ominous. I'm not sure I want to know."

"Those are just things that'll happen. Ye know that. The real 'eart o' this prophecy is in the last two lines. *The child of opposites will be the one, to heal the Dream that War's undone.* War, that's Duncan, right? What's the dream 'e undid? That's the question ye should be askin' after. What'd War do that needs fixin'?"

"Could be the Mongers, too. They're the Descendants of War."

"Nah, look at the language. *The child must seek to claim the Mother* is something that 'adn't 'appened when the prophecy was made. But *the Dream that War's undone*, that's past. That's an old wrong to be righted. The Mongers are likely just the effects."

I stared at Ringo like he was a fascinating new species of something cool and colorful. "You're pretty brilliant for a kid off the streets, you know?"

His half-grin was back. "Took ye long enough to figure that out."

"Okay, genius. Why did I suddenly Shift tonight when I've never shown the slightest sign of Shifting before in my life?"

He looked at me in silence, then finally said, "Ye didn't just go back to have a chat with yer da, did ye?"

"No. He told me that he hid the Shifter bone in the council room after the massacre. It's a little freaky to realize we were standing right next to it in Old Bailey."

Ringo looked at me oddly. "And did ye pick up the Shifter bone before ye came back 'ere?"

"Of course." I pulled the Shifter bone pendant out from under my shirt, which must have stayed on around my Cat's neck. My fingers stalled, and I stared at Ringo. "This? You think this let me Shift?"

"It's meant to give a Shifter control enough to Shift into any beast. Why not give an 'alf-Shifter control enough to Shift into 'er own."

I ripped the leather cord over my head and dropped the Shifter bone on the thick Persian carpet between us. My fingers were shaking, and I suddenly felt like I couldn't get enough air in my lungs. "You take it. Get it to Mr. Shaw. I don't ever want to touch the thing again."

"Ye saved Archer's life, Saira."

"I *killed* a man!" I could feel hysteria starting to build in my chest, strangling the air out of my lungs. I'd managed to shove the memories of having Shifted into the background of my consciousness, but it was still there, like the turd on the rug you don't want to admit seeing because then you have to clean it up.

Ringo waved a hand airily. "Nah, ye just tore 'is throat out. Jeeves killed 'im first with the shotgun. 'Twas lucky 'e didn't 'it ye, too."

I shuddered and curled my arms tightly around my knees. I wanted to vomit again as I remembered the taste of blood in my mouth. And … liking it.

I must have looked green because Ringo nodded his head toward Archer's sleeping form. "Curl up wi' yer man. Ye need sleep, and from the looks o' ye, comfort, too." He picked up the leather cord and tucked the Shifter bone into his pocket. "I'll slip out fer a bit o' shut eye, too."

"Thank you, Ringo. For everything."

He winked the eye that was still open as he got up. "Ye talked to yer da, Saira. Dream 'bout that."

 TAKEN

Ringo was saying my name through the fog of sleep, and it took a bit to realize he was trying to wake me up. It must have been near dusk because all of Ringo's noise managed to pull Archer out of his Vampire sleep, too.

"Wake yerselves, you two. We'll have to track down Mr. Shaw at yer school, Saira. No one 'ere's seen 'im since last night."

"You're mean."

"Yeah, well, yer breath stinks."

That got me up. He was probably right, since I'd basically passed out fully dressed this morning. I didn't need Archer to get a whiff of my shoddy oral hygiene.

"I'm going to shower, and I'm starving. I'll meet you guys in the dining room in ten."

Archer peered at me through barely cracked eyelids. He still had crusty blood on his face, but the bruises had totally healed.

I reached out to stroke his cheek. "You should probably wash up, too. People might get a little weirded out seeing blood on your face."

Archer winced and rubbed his face as I slipped out of the keep.

Just under ten minutes later I had washed hair and fresh breath, and in a nod to the fact that Millicent prefers formal dress at dinner, I was wearing a silky, black, long-sleeved t-shirt with my black jeans. It was the best I would do since we were probably going out right after we ate.

Ringo was already there, wearing jeans and a dress shirt.

"Yer ma left these for me in my room," he answered my questioning look.

"Nice boots, too."

He grinned and showed them off. "She's a generous lady, yer ma. 'Lot like 'er daughter."

Archer walked in looking like a movie star, with still-wet hair, black slacks, and a sapphire blue dress shirt. "Wow! You clean up pretty."

He grinned at my frankly admiring gaze and kissed me on the cheek. "Says the most beautiful woman in any room." His voice was low and rumbled through me like a heartbeat.

Millicent swept into the dining room dressed like a queen. The woman had some seriously stunning jewels, and I guess dinner was as good a time as any to wear them. It beat keeping them locked up in a safe full time.

Tonight's ensemble included a heavy gold chain that hung down over her formidable chest, with a single emerald drop pendant. It was simple and beautiful and looked like something a diver might have scooped up off the bottom of the ocean from the wreck of a Spanish galleon.

I kissed her cheek, and I could tell it surprised her. "How are you feeling?"

"Obviously I must look awful, or you wouldn't ask."

"Actually, you look beautiful, and that necklace is stunning. I asked because you had a headache the other night, and I haven't seen you since then."

The suspicion in her eyes softened slightly. "I'm well, thank you." She fingered the emerald and looked closely at me. "But you're not, are you? What happened?"

I sighed. "Can we call Jeeves to join us for dinner tonight?"

Millicent's eyes widened as she searched mine, but finally she nodded to a maid I hadn't seen standing in the corner. "Please call Jeeves in, Mary. Ask him to dress for dinner."

Poor guy. I'd just set him up for the microscope. But my guilt needed wiping, and looking at it in bright light was the only way I knew how to clean it up.

My mom and Charlie came in together. Charlie was in another awesome 50's style dress, and I watched Ringo track her from the moment she entered the room. She and Mom were laughing at something, and my chest tightened at the sight. It wasn't jealousy at their ease with each other; it was a sad kind of happiness. They could give each other something they both craved, but it was the craving – for family, maybe – that made me sad.

Mom gave me a hug, and Charlie stood next to Ringo with a shy smile. Jeeves came barreling into the room in a way that anyone else would have seen as a quiet, dignified entrance. I saw barreling, because I knew just how dignified he usually was.

"My lady, I'm very sorry if I've held you up in any way."

"Join us, Jeeves."

He didn't look at me at all. He just nodded and held the chair out for Millicent to take her place at the head of the table. My mom was at the other end, and the rest of us were arrayed around the sides. The moment Millicent sat was the cue for everyone else, and almost instantly there was a maid at my elbow offering me soup.

Archer and Ringo were on either side of Millicent, and Jeeves sat closest to my mom. I waited, because I knew from painful experience that Millicent started dinner conversations. Anyone else who tried to got a verbal slapdown of the talking-to-a-five-year-old variety.

"I believe there is something Saira wishes to discuss," she finally announced.

I took my cue immediately. "A couple of things, but they're related. First, I found the Shifter bone."

My mom's sharp intake of breath was the only sound in the room. Everyone had stopped eating, and Millicent and Mom were staring at me. "Where was it?" Mom whispered.

"It was hidden in the council room."

"The council room was built in 1907 with the redesign of Old Bailey. If I'm not mistaken, the Shifter bone was rumored to have gone missing in 1871." Millicent's tone clearly said she didn't believe me.

"The *new* council room was built in 1907. The bone was in the *old* council room, where my dad hid it for his brother."

Mom's eyes widened. "But Brian never found it. And we were just there, too." Her eyes bored into mine. "It was in the knot of the Shifter tree, right?"

"You knew about Will's hiding spot?"

A sad smile tilted her mouth. "He told me all of his hiding spots, and I told him mine."

Millicent's sharp voice cut through the room, and I wanted to snarl at her to let Mom have her happy memory. "How, exactly, did you know to look there for the Shifter bone, and why were you seeking it?"

"*Why* is a big story. *How* is a small one. I went back to talk to my dad."

Mom seemed resigned. Millicent looked horrified. Charlie suddenly perked up.

Oh, no.

"Charlie," My voice was gentle. "I can't take you to any time you already were. We can't be in the same place twice – time just, sort of, kicks us out and won't let us land. Otherwise I'd love to take you to see your mom."

The light dimmed in her eyes, and she looked like a little origami bird that had just been rained on.

"I'm so sorry. The most I can do is take you to see her before you were born. But even that's a risk to the time stream."

"No, I'm fine. It was just a thought."

My mom slid next to her and put an arm around her thin shoulders, and Ringo just stopped himself from doing the same.

"So, you wax poetic about risking the time stream and yet you endangered it yourself to see that beast." There was venom in Millicent's voice, and my eyes narrowed dangerously at her.

"The second part of my news is that I Shifted last night and killed a man."

As satisfying as the surprise on Millicent's face was, I hated the gasp of horror that came from my mom. Her eyes were wide and her face had drained of its color. I didn't think it was possible for

101

someone to feel worse about what I'd done than I did. But apparently, it was.

"Oh Saira. No!" Her whisper was barely a breath, but it held a scream-full of pain.

"No, Saira." Jeeves spoke clearly, and then he took a deep, shaky breath. "It wasn't the Lion who killed the intruder. It was my shot that hit him in the heart."

"Right before I tore his throat open." My tone was grim, and my mom choked back a sob. I turned to her. "I was wearing the Shifter bone to keep it safe. I didn't plan to Shift. It just … happened."

"A Lion." Mom was still strangling on her voice, and I fought back tears.

"Just like Will. Yeah."

There was so much I needed to say to my mom, but I couldn't find the place to start. So I turned to Jeeves instead. "What do we need to do about the Monger?"

"'E's dead, right? What's t' do about 'im?" Ringo's tone suggested I was an idiot for asking the question. I glared at him.

"We tell someone."

"Who? Who are ye goin' t' tell that won't 'aul ye right away?"

"People don't just kill other people, Ringo. It's not like we can just bury him and forget the whole thing happened."

He glared back at me. "And why not? If the Mongers go askin' 'bout 'im and 'is whereabouts, they would 'ave to admit 'e was 'ere. Who else would know t'ask?"

"He's right, Saira. Whoever sent Rothchild here is the only one who could ever ask us about him. And to do that, they'd be admitting they sent him." Archer spoke in the low tones he reserved for skittish animals, but I still felt the hysteria rising.

"But he's someone's family. He's Raven's and Patrick's brother. He can't just disappear like he doesn't matter to people. It's not right!"

Archer's tone got hard and fierce, and I flinched from the anger in it. "No! What's not right is that the Mongers are kidnapping people and using an Otherworlder to do it. It's not right that Rothchild intended to take you and would have killed me. And it's not right that neither you nor I can walk freely because one Family of Immortal Descendants believes they have the right to remove us from existence. None of that is right, and frankly, I'm glad Rothchild's dead. The Mongers I see are bad enough. An invisible one is something I never want to encounter again."

Millicent was glaring at us, and she finally spoke up. "How is it possible for anything to be invisible?" Scorn and disbelief. Two of my favorite tones of voice.

Charlie spoke before I could answer. "It's possible, ma'am. I saw 'im for an Otherworlder, the thing ridin' the Monger's back. It drew on the Monger for the power t' turn 'im clear. 'E was still there, 'e just 'ad no visible substance."

Millicent sat back in silence – a rare occurrence – and regarded Charlie thoughtfully.

"I'm with 'is lordship on this. That one was a nasty piece of work." Ringo shuddered quietly.

Millicent looked at Jeeves. "Did you see this … creature?"

Jeeves lifted his chin, and I knew it was costing him something to speak plainly to the force of nature that was Lady Millicent Elian. "I saw Lord Devereux and young Ringo being beaten by thin air. Whatever was hitting them was strong enough to inflict injury, but the fact that they couldn't see it was the biggest liability. I went to get the shotgun, and when I returned, a Lion was about to take down a man. I wasn't quite sure if I was shooting at the Lion or the man, but it was the man whom I hit. When he died, the air moved behind him as if something else went with him. That's what I saw, ma'am."

"And what has become of the body of this man?"

"It's been buried, ma'am."

"And what became of the Lion?"

Jeeves' gaze didn't waver for an instant. "It – she became Saira. She was unconscious and unclothed, and I felt my duty was better served removing the body, ma'am."

Unclothed? "Wait. I was naked?"

Millicent almost snorted. "Well, what did you imagine happened to a Shifter's clothes?"

I looked at Archer. "I just assumed I was bloody and you changed me into sweats." I was suddenly mortified at the idea of having been unconscious and naked. I knew I had been completely safe in the company of two very Victorian men, but that didn't change the fact that they'd seen me bare-bootied. Oh, God. My cheeks flamed, and I just barely resisted hiding my face.

Archer's voice was quiet and gentle. "I was far more concerned that you were unconscious."

"And I went for yer clothes, so I didn't see nothin'." Ringo's blush was almost as red as mine, and I shot him a grateful smile.

"Reason number three never to Shift again," I mumbled.

"What are one and two?" Charlie looked at me with frank curiosity.

I peeled back my fingers. "One: I killed someone."

"You did not kill him. I did." Jeeves was adamant on the point, and his tone didn't allow for argument. I wasn't really up for a semantics battle anyway.

"And two: I couldn't control the Lion. She was the boss, and *no one* gets to be the boss of me. Just ask Millicent." I shot her a weary smile, and shock-of-shocks, she grimaced back.

I looked down the table at my mom, who had been stricken silent by the news that I had Shifted. All the strength I'd seen when we'd Clocked together had vanished, and she seemed so fragile again. Maybe it was worry, or maybe fear. Whatever it was, I didn't feel like my mom was strong enough for me to lean on while I figured this thing out. It hurt, but I knew Archer was stronger and could be my rock when I needed one.

He saw me watching my mom and shot me a quick smile. I felt something lift off my chest, just enough so I could take a breath. I gave a tiny jerk of my head toward the door, and he nodded. Ringo had seen the exchange and was already setting down his napkin.

"Please excuse us; we need to find Mr. Shaw to figure out our next move." I stood, and finally, Jeeves met my eyes. "I'm really sorry you had to deal with my mess, Jeeves. But thank you."

"Nichts zu danken." He said it with a small smile.

My high school German deciphered his statement as "not to thank," which sounded like "there's nothing to thank me for" to my ears. I responded in the same language. "Vielen Dank." Many thanks.

Archer had pulled my chair out for me, and we were almost at the door when my mom finally spoke. "Try the lab at school. It's where he goes to think."

"Thanks. We will." Interesting that Mr. Shaw had anything to think about. It made me wonder if there was more to the disagreement between them than I had heard.

We retrieved Archer's Aston Martin from behind the stables, and after Ringo had picked his eyeballs up from the ground, dusted them off, and popped them back in his head, he slid into the back seat like it was made of pure silver and he was the fanciest thing since sliced bread to be riding in it.

I laughed at the rapturous joy on his face as we pulled down the long driveway. "You're going to have to teach him to drive this, you know that, right?"

Archer grinned into the rear-view mirror. "A driver's license may be tricky, but we'll work something out."

It wasn't a long drive between Elian Manor and St. Brigid's School, and I was a very different girl than the one who had arrived in the back of a Rolls Royce, wearing flip flops and a blanket, not even a year ago. Now the towers looked less like fangs and more like a safe haven from invisible Mongers and political nightmares, and I had friends by my side to face whatever the future held for us.

The school was closed for the summer, but no one had fixed the broken solarium window, so I didn't even need Ringo's breaking and entering skills. The light was on under Mr. Shaw's office door, and I knocked. No answer.

"Mr. Shaw?" Silence. I tried the handle and it turned, but stepping into my teacher's office when he wasn't in felt wrong, so I opened the door really slowly. "Are you in here?" I said louder.

Papers littered the floor. That wasn't good. I shoved against something solid and pushed the door all the way open. Mr. Shaw's office looked like the set of a disaster movie, or maybe a zombie apocalypse minus the brain tissue. His beautiful, battered desk was on its back, the file cabinet was open with the contents all over the room, and the bookshelves were empty.

Empty. "No!" There, on the floor among the scattered books and papers in a twisted pile of brass and broken glass, was Will Shaw's 1850s microscope. It was a thing Mr. Shaw prized long before I ever knew him, and the ramifications of its destruction were huge.

Archer had pushed in past me and was doing an efficient scan of the room. "He Shifted." My head jerked up, and I saw the disintegrated remains of Mr. Shaw's clothes behind the desk. I looked closer at the overturned chair and saw claw marks. Bear claw marks.

"And he fought them, too."

My eye was caught by the small kit up high on a shelf that hadn't been swept clear like most of the others. I remembered it contained the experimental compound he'd used a couple of months before on Connor's Were bite to draw out the contaminant.

"We need to check the lab."

The science labs were in a different wing under the unused dorm rooms, presumably in case someone accidentally blew something up. Mr. Shaw had been using a smaller lab for his private research work, and when we got there, the door was locked.

"Whatever happened to him, they didn't come here." The relief in my voice was at odds with the fear and adrenalin pounding in my veins.

The lab door suddenly opened from the inside, and Connor Edwards, my science geek Shifter friend, appeared in front of us. I bit back a shriek. His eyes were huge, and he seemed to be in shock.

"Mongers took him."

COUNCIL

We retreated up to the Clocker Tower to talk. It seemed like the safest place because I could get us out of there through the portal in the painting if I needed to.

Connor told us he'd been working with his uncle in the lab, which was how he'd spent a lot of his summer. His mother had been happy he was with her brother, and since she was basically raising three kids alone, one less in the house made things easier on her.

"Where's your dad?"

"He died after Sophia was born."

I stared at Connor. "I'm so sorry. How come I didn't know that?"

He shrugged. "I don't really talk about it. But yeah, that's why Uncle Bob is always around. He tries to do a lot of the dad stuff with me and my brother."

"I didn't have a da either." Ringo piped in from his seat on the edge of the desk.

Archer grimaced. "I think we're all a little deficient in the father department."

It was true. Connor and I had been raised by our mothers, Ringo had raised himself, and Archer had grown up under the thumb of a total jerk. I spoke quietly. "Mr. Shaw's been as close to a dad as I've ever known, and we need him back. Tell us what happened tonight, Connor."

He took a deep breath. The wide-eyed shakiness had diminished but wasn't completely gone yet. "I showed up this afternoon, and Uncle Bob was in the middle of a complicated sequence of gene splicing that he'd been at all night." Connor looked at Archer. "You have some very cool blood, you know that?"

"Thanks so much. I'll be sure and tell Wilder that when I see him next."

The irony was lost on Connor, and I could see his confidence returning with the excitement in his eyes. "No, seriously. Your blood's like the Borg. It doesn't have to kill anything because it assimilates everything it comes into contact with."

"You have Star Trek blood. How cool are you?" I wasn't sure he knew the reference, but then again, Archer had probably seen the entire series from the beginning. It was the kind of cultural reference he usually surprised me with.

"Figure out how to assimilate normal cell death and the ability to go out in the sun, and then I'm cool." Archer kissed me lightly on the nose, which I knew was a move designed to distract me from the harsh realities he had to deal with every day.

"See, that's the thing!" Connor's voice had risen in his excitement. "Uncle Bob thinks there might be something he could introduce into your bloodstream that could do exactly that – kick-start the cell death again. Sort of like the reverse of what cancer does to normal cells."

Archer and I stared at Connor. I think my mouth might have even fallen open. "He thinks he can cure Vampirism?"

"I'm not sure if cure is the right word, because he hasn't found anything yet that will clear the porphyria out. But there might be a way to override its effects. Kind of like planting a computer virus in the Borg hive mind."

"So, Mr. Shaw was working on that?" I wasn't sure how I felt about that. Excited? Terrified? So I retreated into calm and collected.

"Yeah, and when he gets in that zone he's impossible to talk to. So I just picked up with the Descendant combinations we've been working with. By the way, Saira, your blood is totally anomalous."

"What's anomalous mean?" Ringo had stayed mostly silent, but he followed the conversation with interest.

Connor grinned. "She's a freak."

"And you're not, *Wolf*?" I would have punched him, too, but I was too lazy to get up.

"Actually, no. I'm uncomplicated Shifter. There's nothing interesting about my blood at all. You're the only true mixed-blood we have samples from since Tom's ..."

"Not here." I finished the sentence for him when he faltered. I didn't want to hear "dead," which was the other way to end it.

"Right. Well, even when we mix different Descendants into the Vampire blood, we can't get the same kind of ratios of the Descendant genes yours has."

"Well, yeah, because there's no Vampire blood in mine."

Connor looked up, like he was questioning how anyone could be so dim. "Obviously we added your blood to his for the control."

"What did that do?"

"They mixed, but it wasn't the same. It seems that mixing the Descendant genes in utero kicks out a different genetic component that we haven't identified yet, and we can't recreate it in the lab."

"Awesome. I am a freak." That actually didn't bother me. I liked knowing I couldn't have been created in a test tube.

"Not a surprise, but good t' 'ave it confirmed, eh?"

I picked up a pencil and threw it at Ringo, who ducked away laughing.

Connor grinned at our banter and then continued, his smile fading away as he spoke. "Uncle Bob finally looked up around six and only just realized I was there. He said his sister would cheerfully murder him if he sent me back to her hungry, so I should keep working and he'd go find us something to eat. About half an hour later he still hadn't come back, so I went in search. I swung by his office on my way to the kitchen in case he got distracted by an e-mail or something. There were Mongers in the office with him."

"Did they see you?"

Connor shook his head. "I Shifted so I could jump in if I needed to, but Uncle Bob saw me in the hall through the open door and he shook his head, basically telling me not to come in."

"Who was in the office with him?" Archer asked quietly.

"The Monger Head, the bloke who hates Saira, and three other really big guys who looked like Russian mobster types."

"So, Markham Rothchild and … Seth Walters?" I weighed in. The list of people who hated me might be longer than I thought.

"Yeah, the Aryan-looking one who's mad all the time. Him."

"Why were they here?"

Connor's breath shook, but he kept his voice strong. "To question my uncle about what we're doing in the lab. Somehow they knew, or guessed, we're mixing blood. I'm thinking it was the Rothbitch who told them since I've seen her at school a couple of times this summer. They said mixed-bloods are illegal, so mixing blood is too. It's like we're operating a meth lab as far as they're concerned."

Archer's voice rumbled. "It would take more than five Mongers to take down his Bear, and we know he Shifted."

"Yeah, well, Rothchild brought up that he knew I'd been working with my uncle in the labs, and unless Uncle Bob went quietly with them, my house would be their next stop."

Archer sighed. "So of course he went with them."

"He was going to, but one of the goons saw me lurking in the hall and pulled out some kind of dart gun thing. He aimed, and Uncle Bob Shifted. I was already bounding away so I didn't see what happened next, but I assume the other guys jumped him until the goon could turn his dart gun on the Bear and shoot him. Whatever tranquilizer they used was super-powered. I've never seen anyone take Uncle Bob out when he was in Bear form." Connor's voice caught in his throat. "He Shifted back to human form once the tranquilizer kicked in, so they were basically dragging a naked man down the hall. I tried to go after them, but the goon with the dart gun turned it on me, and only just missed. If they'd knocked me out, I'd have gone human too, and they probably would have taken me with them. I figured someone needed to know what happened to Uncle Bob, so I let them take him away."

He sounded on the verge of tears, but he shook off my attempt to comfort him.

"Ye didn't *let* them do anythin'. They were takin' 'im. Ye just made sure there was a witness." Trust Ringo to say exactly the right thing.

"Did they say where, exactly, they were taking him? Maybe I can Clock in and get him."

Connor shook his head. "If they said it, I didn't hear it."

I looked at Archer. "My mom can take this to the council. She'll have the Armans and the Shifter clans behind her for sure. I don't know what the Mongers are doing, or how they think they can get away with it, but they messed up this time. They left a witness."

He nodded. "Right. Back to the manor, then?"

I turned to Connor. "Does your mom know what happened? Do we need to call her?"

"I told her I'd be staying here with Uncle Bob, so I'd see her in the morning. I didn't want to worry her before I figured out what to do."

An interesting choice, and not one most fourteen-year-olds would make. "Well, then come with us to Elian Manor and we'll figure out what to do next, okay?"

Connor nodded. "Thanks."

Ringo put his arm around Connor's shoulder. "I'm sorry 'bout the circumstances, but it's good to see ye."

Connor gave a short bark of laughter. "Is it weird that I didn't even notice you shouldn't be here?"

Ringo grinned. "Nah. The strange bit is that I feel righ' at 'ome."

I smiled at them both. "Home is where your people are."

Ringo winked back at me. "That's what I said."

My mom and Millicent had gone to their separate corners of the house with headaches, and Sanda thought they, and Charlie,

111

were likely all fast asleep by now. We decided that nothing official could be done in the middle of the night, so we settled around the big farm table in the kitchen to talk.

I heated up a plate of leftover chicken and potatoes for Connor, and then sat down on the long bench next to Archer.

"I love big country kitchens. If this were my house, we'd have every meal at this table." The Elian Manor cook, Rosie, wasn't big on Family company while she worked, so I never got to hang out in there except after dark. I was pretty sure the only two rooms I needed in my house were a kitchen with a huge table and a library full of books.

"It'll be yer house, no?" Ringo grabbed a peach and took a big bite. I noticed he always went for the fruit first and realized it would have been nearly impossible to get when he was growing up on Victorian streets.

"Probably not. If my mom stops Clocking she could theoretically live forever, and between Mongers and Wilder, my life expectancy is looking pretty grim."

"Well, that's a cheery thought." Archer pulled me to him as he straddled the bench, and I nestled my back against his chest.

"Do you think your mum would let me take some blood from her?" Connor spoke between bites of food.

"You'd probably have to blindfold her to do it, but yeah, she volunteered."

He gave me an odd look at the blindfold comment, but shrugged it off. "Good. Because I want to see if I can combine it with Mr. Shaw's and get something similar to yours."

I watched Connor eat with his fingers and thought about the Wolf he became. "Do you ever eat when you're in Wolf form?"

He looked up and shrugged. "Sometimes. But it's pretty gross. The Wolf's not a dainty eater, and the smell of blood when I'm in human form makes me nauseous."

"Do you think of the Wolf as separate from you?"

This time he didn't just shrug the answer, he regarded me for a long moment before speaking. "The Wolf is separate, but he's me, too. He wants different things than I do occasionally, and sometimes I even feel what he wants when I'm in human form. But we learn from the time we're really young how to control our animal so it's desires don't override ours." His eyes didn't leave mine. "Why?"

"I Shifted last night."

Connor's eyes widened, and he put down his food. "Into what?"

I realized we hadn't really had deep conversations about my dad, so I filled him in on the basics.

"Wait, you found the Shifter bone? That's kind of an epically big deal, Saira."

"We needed it so Mr. Shaw could become an alpha Wolf and help us deal with the wolves of Paris."

He gave me a look as laden with "duh" as something non-verbal could be. "Because you don't know any actual alpha Wolves?"

"Hey, I suggested you, but my mom and Mr. Shaw had a conniption because you're fourteen."

He snorted. "Alpha is alpha. My uncle knows that better than anyone. He had to take down an older Bear from another clan when he was thirteen."

That surprised me. "Why?"

"The guy was starting to lose control over his Bear."

Whatever appetite I'd been working up was gone in a heartbeat. "Oh."

Archer could hear all the unsaid things in my voice. He spoke gently. "It's not the same thing, Saira."

Connor gave him an odd look, then turned to me. "What's not the same? What did you do?"

Ringo jumped in before I could bare my guilty conscience. "Archer an' me were attacked, and the thing was killin' us. She Shifted an' 'er Lion saved us both." He shot me a "so there" look that dared me to contradict him.

Connor's eyebrows rose. "Well, that explains the Shift. Strong emotions can bring the animal up. What'd you do to the guy?"

"'E's gone." Ringo's proclamation pretty much shut the conversation down, and I picked at a loose thread in my jeans so I didn't have to meet anyone's eyes.

Archer could feel my tension, and he ran his fingers up and down my arm. His touch soothed something tight in me, and I finally looked up.

"God, we have so much to do."

Ringo cocked his head. "What's on the list?"

"Mr. Shaw, the wolves, and Bishop Wilder. And that's not even counting all the missing people the Mongers have probably taken."

Ringo shrugged. "Seems easy 'nough. We do 'em in that order. Mr. Shaw, the wolves, Bishop Wilder. If we run across any o' the missin' on the way, we take 'em, too."

"What's this about missing people?" Connor had just swallowed a giant mouthful of chicken and barely got the words out.

We filled him in on the sequence of events that had brought us to Elian Manor for the weekend. He looked startled when I mentioned the visit to the Armans' house.

"I know Daisy Rowen. Alex's cousin is in her twenties and really nice. She's also not ugly, if you know what I mean." His tone of voice was admiring, and I grinned at fourteen-year-old way of saying she was very pretty. "I didn't know she was a mixed-blood." Connor tilted his head in a way that reminded me of his Wolf.

"Apparently she is." I said.

Connor looked thoughtful for a long time. "How many other mixed-bloods are hiding in plain sight?"

I shrugged. "A better question might be, how did the Mongers know about them, and why now? Why risk the wrath of the council if it gets out that the Mongers are surreptitiously kidnapping Descendants by the dozens?"

Archer's voice rumbled in his chest, and I felt it through my back. "There was nothing low profile about taking Shaw. Whatever their plan, they seem to be very confident of success."

A piece of a conversation suddenly flashed through my brain. "You remember that red-stone ring you found in Walters' office when we got the genealogy?"

Ringo looked up from the peach pit he was spinning on the table. "Yeah. Ye though it was evil."

"It might very well be." I turned to Archer and Connor. "My dad thought it might be the Monger Family artifact. He thinks it somehow broke his control over his Lion."

Connor looked a little sick.

I nodded. "He said the Monger head of 1871 – the guy was a Rothchild, too, I think - he was wearing it the day of the council massacre."

Archer looked grim. "Whatever their ring does could be the game-changer they're counting on."

"My dad told me to run if I ever saw it on any Monger's hand."

"Is it just a Shifter thing, or does it affect everyone, I wonder?" Archer was playing with my fingers on the tabletop.

"As if breaking Shifters isn't bad enough?" Connor's voice sounded strangled.

"I should 'ave nicked it when I 'ad the chance." Ringo's tone was grim.

I shook my head. "No way. That thing felt like something that should be tossed into the volcanic fires of Mordor."

Connor scoffed. "C'mon. The One Ring?"

I shuddered. "You didn't see it. I swear the ruby winked at me."

Archer laughed and kissed my hair. "You should all sleep if you're going to deal with the Descendants' Council tomorrow."

"What are you going to do?"

"I think I might take a drive into London and give myself a tour of Old Bailey."

"You don't think they'd be holding him near the council room?"

He shrugged. "It's a place to start."

We all stood up from the kitchen table, and Connor cleared his dishes while the rest of us put away food. I looked around at the other two guys. "So, first thing tomorrow we go to Mom with the news about Mr. Shaw, and then we do whatever it takes to get him out. We should also start poking around for anything that'll help us in 1429."

Connor nodded. "I'm going to have to tell my mum about Uncle Bob tomorrow, too."

"Not looking forward to that conversation, are you?"

Connor winced. "Not really."

Ringo nodded at him. "C'mon, I'll find a room for ye to sleep in." Ringo met my eyes past Connor's head, and I mouthed "thank you" to him before they left the kitchen.

Archer came up behind me and wrapped his arms around my waist. He nuzzled my hair. "You always smell like vanilla, you know that?"

I turned around and put my arms around his neck. "And you smell like a warm spice." I kissed him, and I could feel his grin on my lips.

"A warm spice, huh?"

"Mmm hmm. Cardamom or nutmeg."

He kissed me again, the kind of kiss that made the butterflies dance in my chest. Their wings tickled my insides and made my heart pound in time to their beat. His hands threaded through my hair as he pulled me to him with a soft groan, and suddenly every nerve ending was on fire in a way that felt like hunger. I gasped and pulled away. "What was that?"

His eyes searched mine. "What happened?"

A whisper of something deep inside me unfurled, and I thought I felt the stirrings of the animal under the slamming of my heart. My breath caught in my throat, and I whispered. "I just felt the Lion."

Archer's eyes were locked on mine. Slowly, he put both hands on the sides of my face, and then pulled me to him to kiss my lips. I clutched his shirt, suddenly terrified of the pounding heart that his touch inspired. "I love you," he said to my lips. "I love you and the Lion inside you."

The sob got tangled in butterfly wings in my chest. Archer let me pull back from him, but he brushed the hair off my face and held my gaze. "There's nothing to be afraid of."

I choked out a laugh. "Says the Vampire."

He smiled. "Exactly. You're not scared of me, and I'm much more terrifying than you could ever be." He pulled me in to hold me tightly to his chest. It felt good and safe and right in his arms, and I thought I could stay there forever.

"Go to sleep. I'll find you in the library tonight, okay?"

I nodded. "Be safe, please?"

"You, too." A kiss, and then he slipped out of the kitchen door and into the night.

I found my way up to my room using my night vision and whatever dim wall sconces had been left on. My ability to see in the dark had taken on a much more feline cast, and for the first time in my life, I was afraid of my own skills.

After breakfast, we traveled to London in Millicent's Silver Cloud Rolls Royce. My mom had been grim-faced and nearly silent since we'd told her about Mr. Shaw being taken away by the Mongers. I rode in the back seat between her and Millicent, who insisted on going along for an official Head of Family handover with Mom. Connor rode in the front seat with Jeeves in case we needed to produce a witness, but my mom wouldn't let Ringo come. People who knew of my trips to the past might wonder about his origins, and there was some question of ethics when it came to displacing people from their native times.

The Armans had called a special council meeting after our visit on Friday, and it was set to start at noon. Connor had held off on calling his mom, hoping he would have good news to tell her after the council met. I thought his logic was a little flawed, especially if she tried to contact her brother before Connor could explain, but it was clear the kid was trying to protect her, not lie to her. I didn't think Connor Edwards had had much of a childhood after his father died.

When Jeeves finally pulled into a driveway behind Old Bailey, my mom turned to me. "You and Connor should wait in the car. If we need you, we'll send someone to get you."

"Mom—"I began to protest, but she cut me off. "No, I'm not bending on this, Saira. I'm going to have enough trouble convincing the council Markham is behind the kidnappings. I can't have anyone questioning my fitness to head the Clocker Families by pointing to your parentage."

That stung. It almost sounded like she regretted having a mixed-blood kid. She must have seen it on my face though, because she pulled me in for a rough hug. "Don't for a minute think I'm not proud of you. But I'll break if they take another person I love from me, do you understand?"

And then I got it. She'd already lost my dad to Descendant politics. And now Mr. Shaw was being held by Mongers for a variation on the same thing. "Find out where they've got him, if nothing else. We'll go bust him out if we have to." I said it with a wry smile on my face, and it was enough to crack the mask of fear that covered hers.

Jeeves had already helped Millicent to the curb and was coming around to Mom's side of the car. "I love you." She seemed to be memorizing my face.

I smiled a real smile. "I love you, too, Mom."

When she'd closed the car door behind her and Jeeves was walking them both to a side entrance, Connor hung an arm over the back of the seat and rested his chin on it. "So, when are we going in?"

"If Jeeves comes right back out, we'll wait to tell him what we're doing, just so he doesn't go in after us. If he stays inside with Millicent, we'll give them thirty seconds to get settled before we follow."

Connor grinned. "That's what I thought."

A couple more cars pulled up outside the building entrance. I recognized the chauffeur-driven Mercedes Maybach the Armans arrived in, but their driver didn't stay. Once they were inside, he pulled down the street and sat parked by the curb. A big Cadillac SUV arrived, and a guy I didn't recognize climbed out of the driver's side.

"That's Ian MacDonald. He's the head of the Shifter clans. And those are his sons, Jamie and Geordie. Geordie's a pompous jerk, but Jamie's not so bad, and he's next in line for head." I watched the three men closely. Ian MacDonald was a big man, and at this point I just assumed size ran in their genes. He also moved with the kind of power that comes with great weight. He wasn't heavy-looking in his human form, but before I could ask, Connor answered. "He's a Buffalo, and both his sons, too."

"That doesn't seem very useful in England."

"Well, they're more like shaggy Highland bulls, but we don't say that out loud."

The door had barely closed behind them when another SUV pulled up. This one looked more like a tank, and I had the sense that the guys who peeled themselves out of the front and back of it were like a tactical force. There was a lot of scanning the street and talking into throat mics before the man I recognized as Markham Rothchild stepped out of the back.

My guts twisted into knots, and I wasn't sure if it was Monger-induced nausea or hatred that did it.

To be fair, I didn't actually know the head of the Monger Family, so hating him was extreme. Rational thought didn't come into it though. His Family's policies had hurt me and people I loved.

"Mongers." Connor's eyes narrowed as he watched the precision movements of the team surrounding Rothchild.

"What gave them away?"

"Are you kidding? Who else comes to a council meeting with bodyguards?"

"I don't see Seth Walters. I'd expect him here as chief bully."

"Maybe he's already inside. There's no way he'd miss this."

"Right." The Mongers had all disappeared inside the building, and the only people still outside were pedestrians walking by on Old Bailey Street at the far end of the alley. "You ready?"

"Let's do it."

We slid out of the Rolls and tried to look casual as we strolled up to the door everyone else had gone in. "You've been here before, right?"

"Not this building. I've been to the old one, in the 1800s."

"That's helpful."

I grinned at him. "What's the worst that could happen?"

"I'm not even going to answer that." Connor pulled open the door and we stepped inside a cool, dark hallway. My eyes adjusted to the gloom immediately, as did Connor's Wolf eyes. There was a staircase directly in front of us, but the hall we were in wrapped around behind it.

"Let's see if there's a cupboard under these stairs."

"Shouldn't we be looking for a fireplace to flash out of?"

I scowled at him. "You obviously watched the movies instead of reading the books. The floo networks into the Ministry of Magic were for flash. The regular employee entrance was through a toilet."

Connor laughed. "The image of Markham Rothchild entering the Descendants' Council from a toilet makes him far less scary."

"Better than picturing him in his underwear." I shuddered for effect, but the light banter was doing a lot to calm my nerves. There was a door under the back staircase, which fit with my memory of the original building. We could hear faint voices below us as we tiptoed down the stairs.

"...more than forty people missing."

"I don't know why you assume my Family had anything to do with it."

"Oh, come on, Markham. Every Family but yours has lost people." That was Mr. Arman's voice. We were at the bottom of the stairs now and able to hear more clearly. The door was open just a crack, but it would be a disaster if we were seen.

"Yes, Ms. Elian? You have something to add?" The male voice was gruff, and I thought it might belong to Ian MacDonald.

"Please call me Claire."

"Only if you call me Mac."

I could hear the smile in my mom's voice. "Thank you, Mac. Yes, I do have something to add. Last night at St. Brigid's School, Mongers abducted Bob Shaw."

I couldn't help myself; I had to look into the room to see how people were taking the news. Only part of the big council table was visible, but I could see several of the onlookers sitting off to the side. The MacDonald sons were there along with about eight or nine other people I didn't know. And Seth Walters, lounged in his chair with the kind of arrogance I'd come to expect from him. His arm was draped across the back of an empty chair beside him, and his fingers were alternately tapping and twisting.

Wait. Twisting? A brief flash of gold and red on his finger.

"Crap!" I whispered as silently as a yell could be. "He has the Monger ring."

Behind me, Connor inhaled. "Who, Markham?"

I shook my head. "Walters." So far he hadn't said anything, but if he opened his mouth … I couldn't even finish that thought.

There had been murmured discussions in the council room at my mom's news, and Mac sounded angry when he finally called things back to order. "What possible reason could you people have for arresting one of the most respected teachers at that school?"

Markham's voice was slimy and dismissive. "No one's been arrested." Then he ignored Mac and addressed my mom. "I'm curious where you heard such an outrageous story, Claire."

"You may call me Ms. Elian, and my source was there and witnessed your people take him. Do you really think I would expose that person to your bullying tactics, Mr. Rothchild?"

Connor had come up right behind me to look past my shoulder, and I could feel the fear coming off him. I knew my mom wouldn't cave, but he didn't.

"This is unacceptable, Markham. We've never appointed the Mongers the police of Descendants, and it must stop." I recognized Mrs. Arman's cultured tones even though I couldn't see her face.

"What is unacceptable is the idea that you people, with your flagrant disregard of ancient Descendant laws, could possibly police yourselves." Markham Rothchild's voice had lost the pretense of civility.

"Where are you holding Shaw, Rothchild?" Mac was growling now.

"We're not."

"Release him immediately."

Rothchild smiled in a slimy, "make me" kind of way, and it sent a shiver up my spine. "It entertains me you think I'd ever take an order from you."

Oh. My. God. The guy was a kindergarten bully. I could see Mac start to shimmer around the edges a little, and I thought he was about to Shift. And the only thing that could come of that was Markham Rothchild knocked on his butt by a Highland bull.

I saw the younger Macs tense in their seats, but then Seth Walters got lazily to his feet.

"If I may speak to the council."

I clapped my hands over my ears and backed away from the door in horror. "Go!" I whisper-screamed to Connor. I was already running up the stairs. "Go, go, go!"

We must have made a huge racket as we bolted, but the only thing I cared about was getting far, far away from that voice.

I led Connor past the staircase toward the front of Old Bailey where the regular courts were in session. If anyone was going to follow us, I hoped they wouldn't go into the public part of the building. We slowed to a fast walk to get out past the guards, but once we hit the street we were running again.

Connor had done enough free-running classes with me that he could keep up as I pulled us away from the major thoroughfares.

We hopped a wall and darted through a small churchyard, across the top of the far wall, and down to an alley that led us to Paternoster Square. From there, we dodged and wove our way past

St. Paul's Cathedral and down the steps to St. Paul's tube station. I shot a quick look around before we descended from street level, but it looked like we hadn't been followed.

Connor handed me his Oyster card for the underground while he quickly bought a ticket. I hate leaping over turnstiles because it feels like stealing, so I was happy he was prepared. We didn't actually exchange words until we were safely on a train with the doors shut behind us.

"We should change at Bank and head down to Tower Bridge."

Connor just nodded, still trying to catch his breath.

"We can get back to Elian Manor from Bishop Cleary's."

"Okay."

His voice sounded odd, and I looked at him sharply. "You okay?"

He shrugged. "A little freaked out."

"Yeah."

He was silent as we switched trains and didn't speak again until we were headed toward the Tower Bridge station. "The Monger power. It's a real thing, huh?"

I searched his gaze. Connor was scared. "I guess we'll find out when my mom and Millicent get home."

"You think Walters could have compelled her to give up her source."

"Crap. I guess it's theoretically possible, if the ring actually has that kind of power."

He nodded again, but didn't meet my eyes.

"I think we need to go back tonight." I willed him to look me in the eyes, and finally, he did.

"By 'back' you mean in time?"

"Yeah."

A longer moment of silence.

"Yeah."

Tom – July, 1429

I thought I really might be going mad.

I had felt my ability to reason softening with the lack of sleep, lack of blood, and lack of anything resembling comfort. I started to mark the passage of time in measures of pain and loneliness. Fear became too hard to hold onto. I just didn't have the energy anymore.

There was a goose quill shoved in my arm and tied to it with a strip of linen. There'd been a lot of cursing when Wilder first realized hypodermic needles wouldn't be invented for four hundred years. If his immortal soul wasn't already damned, it would have been after that tirade. But necessity is the mother of invention, and he didn't want to risk contaminating my blood before he was ready to kill me. Therefore, a goose quill, sharpened to a point like one of those straws that poke through juice bags – my unfortunate arm in place of the bag - the other end cut at the tip and dripping into a glass bottle. It was thick and crude glass, and Wilder had paid Léon's father a lot of money to find a glasshouse to make the long, thin bottles to his specifications. I learned that from Léon when he'd asked me once what Wilder had commissioned the bottles for. I showed him the cabinet where Wilder stored the stoppered blood vials. Léon didn't speak the rest of that visit, and we never discussed it again, but he took extra care tending the wounds left by the goose quills after that. I tucked those moments of kindness in around the pain, like a blanket to soothe and comfort the writhing soul inside.

The glass bottle was nearly full, and I could sense Wilder moving around the room. I usually closed my eyes when he was near. I didn't want to know when he was finally going to kill me, and anticipating my death had gone the way of fear. It took too much energy.

"The wolves are restless again tonight, Tom. Shall I take you out to the roof so you can watch them feast on children?"

"Take me to the street and let me feed them. Though at this point I'm more like beef jerky than meat. It'll save you the bother of having to get rid of my body."

I felt his eyes on me. I shouldn't have been able to, but my awareness of him was like sandpaper on whatever was left on my nerves – unfathomable and painful. "You're feisty tonight."

I turned my head away from the direction of his voice and spoke to the wall. "I've stopped caring."

He removed the bottle, and I winced as he jostled the end of the quill. I hated to show that I could still feel pain, but unlike a normal hypodermic needle that only hurt going in, the pain with the goose quills grew with every beat of my heart and every pump of my blood. Stabbing the veins with the quill could only be done once per location because each wound continued to bleed internally long after the quill was removed, and the bruises were so blue they looked black. Even if I'd wanted to sleep, the pain wouldn't let me. I'd been running a low fever for days, and I hoped my blood was contaminated with some horrible infection that would kill him, too.

Hope was too strong a word. I'd lost the taste for hope a lifetime ago.

Wilder had been silent as he corked the full bottle and replaced it with an empty one that he secured to my arm with another strip of linen. He wore leather gloves whenever he touched me so as not to accidentally mingle our blood. I remembered Saira saying he had a doctor do all the blood draws on her mum, but here in the Hôtel de Sens, it was just Wilder and me.

And sometimes, after Wilder had gone to rest, Léon.

I closed my eyes and let pictures of my friend play in my head like a film. He was quick to tease me about the most gruesome parts of my care, which usually erased the embarrassment of it. Every day he pretended surprise at finding me still alive; I thought it covered his worry I wouldn't be. His touch was always gentle on my wounds, even when his comments were designed to sting me out of my self-pity. Léon somehow knew how to reach the parts of me that were retreating from the horror and the pain, but he was only with me during the days, and night times without him had become unbearable.

"I think I don't like this side of you, Tom. I believe I prefer it when you feel things." Wilder's voice intruded on the sliver of peace I'd found, and I added it to the list of things I hated him for.

I broke my own rule about looking at him, and I turned to face Wilder. His usual arrogance was in place, but it was frayed around the edges, like something was wearing on him. I wished it was me that was getting to him, but I knew I was nothing more than a carcass to be bled. There was something though. I decided to poke at it.

"What would you like me to feel, Wilder?" I saw his mouth tighten. He hated when anyone used a name other than his title, so of course, I never called him Bishop. "Would you like me to be afraid? People fear the unknown, but I know I'm going to die. In fact, I'm already dying because you've drained so much blood from me. There's nothing left for me to fear, Wilder."

The candlelight glinted off his teeth, and I thought he might practice the effect in the mirror. "There is always pain."

I shrugged. "You're right. There's always pain. Every moment of every day I'm in pain. Increasing the pain would only be different, not better, not worse, and difference is about the only thing I have left to look forward to. So bring it, bad guy. Do your best."

He narrowed his eyes, considering me, and I met his gaze. I was so tired. Tired in the way people who've been in a coma must feel when they finally wake up, except I was doing the opposite. I could feel parts of myself slipping away. The only thing left behind was beef jerky and pain. I closed my eyes and felt the madness creep into the empty playing field. Well, madness was better than nothing at all.

Wilder stood up and snorted in disgust. He ripped the quill out of my arm and yanked the linen strip tight to stop the bleeding. This time I managed to fight the grunt of pain because the madness took it, bit into it, and swallowed it whole.

I think I might even have smiled.

Preparation

Connor and I brought Archer's sword collection back to Elian Manor with us. Bishop Cleary had loaned us a bag to carry the loose knives and daggers in, and we packed the weapons into two cases, so each of us carried one. I'd given him a rundown of our weekend, then hugged him goodbye tightly. His grip was just as strong as mine was, and his voice sounded gruff. "Come back home when you can."

Home. My room in Bishop Cleary's flat had been as much a home to me as any other place I'd lived, and more than most. Because Bishop Cleary was definitely one of my people.

I'd called Elian Manor, and Jeeves came to pick us up. He was waiting in the less obvious Range Rover outside Guy's Chapel.

"Your mother will be pleased you're safe." Jeeves loaded our cases and bag into the back of the SUV, and his voice was only a little accusing.

"Yeah, sorry about that. Were Millicent and Mom mad?"

"Actually, they seemed unconcerned. It was therefore not until we'd returned to the manor that I realized they didn't know where you were."

That was the freakiest thing he could have said, and the look Connor and I exchanged in the back seat was one that usually had an inventive expletive attached to it.

"Didn't that strike you as weird?"

Jeeves caught my eyes in the rearview mirror. "It's not my place to have opinions."

"Maybe Millicent doesn't want to hear your opinions, but you definitely have them."

His eyes flicked to me again before he focused on the road. "The Ladies Elian seemed ... confused when they left the council meeting, and they were utterly silent on the ride back to the manor."

"So, you don't know anything that happened at the meeting?"

"For all I know they could have been discussing the weather." There was an edge of anger in his voice that surprised me.

"What's going on, Jeeves?"

He took a deep breath, like it cost him something to answer. "I like Mr. Shaw, and I find I don't sit still very well when there is something to be done."

I watched him in the rear view mirror. "Do you want to meet us in the library at sunset? We need to get out of Dodge for a while, but we need a plan to find Mr. Shaw, too."

"I'd be honored to help in whatever way I can, Miss Elian."

I looked over at Connor. He was staring out the window as we left the city behind. "Hey, Jeeves?"

"Yes, Miss Elian."

"Can we make a quick detour to ..." I poked Connor. "Where do you live?"

I'd startled him, but he answered quietly. "Bridgeview House, Foxglove Lane in Brentwood."

Jeeves nodded his head. "I know the house. Yes, of course I can take you there."

"We'll be fast." I poked Connor again and he poked me back, on principle, probably. "We don't want to be there if Mongers come."

He grimaced. "Right. That." His eyes found mine briefly. "Thanks."

Connor's house looked like it had been the first one on the street, before there were even streets. It had the look of an old farmhouse, but Foxglove Lane had built up around it, and most of the other houses were from the 1930s or '40s.

"Cool house."

129

"Yeah, thanks. It was my grandmother's, and she passed it down to my mum. I think it was built in the 1820s or something like that. The original Shaws all lived in it, but Uncle Bob didn't want it. He said it was time for the house to have a new Family name living there."

The original Shaws all lived in the house? I suddenly had a thought that had never occurred to me before. "We're related, you know that?"

He stared at me. "Huh? Oh, right. Yeah."

"Your Family came down through Brian Shaw, right?"

"Yeah, I guess."

"So we're first cousins, a thousand times removed or something like that."

He shook his head. "It's so weird that you're Brian Shaw's niece. He's legendary in my Family."

We climbed out of the Range Rover, and I was immediately surrounded by a pack of growling, barking dogs. Connor gave a quick, sharp whistle, and the dogs instantly fell silent, practically freezing in place. He met me on my side of the car and gave another short whistle. The dogs came to life again and swirled around him in happy greeting. One of them, a big, dark red mix of something resembling a boxer, jumped into Connor's arms and wrapped her front legs over his shoulders in a hug. He held her weight and rubbed his face against hers. "Hi, sweet girl. Did you miss me?" When he put her down she stayed right next to his legs, even in the middle of the pack of very excited dogs.

Connor turned to me with a big grin on his face. "Saira, this is Natasha." He indicated the red dog next to him. "And that's Boris, Rocky, Bullwinkle, Bugs, Speedy, Porky, and Elmer." He pointed to each dog in turn, and despite the common theme, every dog fit its name perfectly. I burst out laughing, and his grin got even bigger. "I know, right?"

We turned to walk into the house and I poked him again, just for good measure. "Quite the alpha, huh?"

"Of course."

The house smelled like baking bread, and we followed the scent into the kitchen. The dogs had settled into a swirling mass, with some leading the way and others following. A little Jack Russell terrier, the one named Rocky, had attached herself to me, and when I bent down to scratch her, she leapt into my arms to cuddle. So, when I entered the kitchen I had a dog cradled in my arm, and I was scratching her belly. Which meant I had no free hands to defend myself.

"Ahhh!" A huge, raptor-clawed hawk dropped out of the air. I hunched over the dog in my arms to protect her from the hawk, which sent it fluttering up, its wings tangling in my hair. On the outside I might have looked fairly calm because my main concern was that the hawk didn't get the dog. On the inside I was a shrieking, screaming, hiding-under-the-table mess.

"Logan! Get off her!"

The hawk settled its wings as it landed on my shoulder. I knew it could feel my heart pounding in my chest, and I sincerely hoped hawks weren't attracted to the scent of fear like – well, like lions were.

"The hawk is named after your brother?" I tried for a calm voice that came out sounding broken. Rocky had settled back in the crook of my arm and was looking up at the hawk with furious eyes.

"The Hawk *is* my brother."

Okay, I wasn't expecting that. I was also definitely unprepared for the size and weight of the beast whose deadly talons were gripping my shoulder with surprising gentleness.

I turned to look at the predator bird sitting so calmly on my shoulder. He looked back at me with little dancing eyes. So I spoke to him. "A pretty dramatic entrance, there, Raptor. Perching on your brother's friends is kind of weird, don't you think?"

The grip on my shoulder tightened fractionally as he launched himself off my shoulder and out of the kitchen. Rocky nudged my hand to keep rubbing her belly as if a giant bird of prey hadn't just been hovering over her, and Connor set the kettle on the Aga cooker to boil.

And I thought my family was odd.

"Was that really your little brother?"

Connor winced. "Yeah. Sorry about that. He thinks it's funny to freak out the new people.

I tried to contain the grin, but failed. "He's right. It took everything I had in me not to run out the door screeching."

"That's what most girls do."

I glared at him. "Most girls would kick your butt for saying that."

He grinned. "You did pretty well, all things considered. Rocky appreciated the protection, even though she's used to it."

"She looked pissed."

"Probably because you stopped scratching her stomach."

"To save her life." It was hard to sound indignant when laughter threatened.

A blond kid, about eleven years old with dancing eyes, and hair that stuck up in about five different directions, walked barefoot into the kitchen. He scooped up one of the dogs, maybe Elmer, and nuzzled it affectionately.

"Hey, Logan," I said. "Way to freak out the company." Logan looked like the Calvin and Hobbes version of his brother, and when he grinned at the casual tone in my voice he was the spitting image of the six-year-old troublemaker.

"You're not nearly as satisfying as some of mum's friends. Those ladies could give banshees a run for their money."

"I thought the animal you Shifted into was hereditary."

Logan looked quickly at Connor, who gave him a nod. "It is."

My eyes traveled between the two of them. "And you can Shift into raptor form because ...?"

"Because they're cool."

"Clearly."

He grinned at the sarcastic tone. "I can Shift into any animal I want to."

I stared at him. "Is that normal?"

He shrugged. "Normal is boring."

Connor handed me a mug he'd just filled with boiling water. "No, it's not normal. We don't know anyone else who can do it, and we don't really advertise his skills."

"Except to shrieking ladies."

"Nah, they just think we've got strange pets."

I studied Logan over the rim of my mug. "Your uncle knows, of course."

"Are you kidding? He's been sticking me with needles for testing since I was six."

Connor perched on a barstool at the counter. "That's when it manifested. Before that, he was just a Wolf cub like me."

"Has Mr. Shaw found anything different in your blood?"

"Nope. I look exactly the same under a microscope as anyone else in our Family."

I blew on my tea and considered this. "You know, the Shifter bone does the same thing for whoever wears it."

Connor told his brother. "Saira found the Shifter bone, by the way, but no one knows about it yet."

"Cool. What are you going to do with it?" Logan looked at me, as if I had any say over the Shifter artifact.

"Give it to your uncle." I stared at Connor. "Except…"

"Who's the regal-looking chap in the fancy car?" Mrs. Edwards swept into the kitchen with a big basketful of garden vegetables in her arms and a smaller basket of eggs perched precariously on top. "Hi. You must be Saira." She sat the baskets down on the counter, blew a piece of blond hair out of her eyes, and shook my hand. "I'm Elizabeth Edwards."

"It's really nice to meet you, Mrs. Edwards. The fancy car guy was our ride here." I struggled to suppress a smile. Jeeves might like being called regal.

She smiled as she busied herself unloading the baskets. "Call me Liz." She looked at Connor. "Hello love, how was work with Bob last night?"

Connor didn't answer right away, and his mom looked at him with sharp eyes that missed nothing. Liz Edwards was tall, like her brother, Mr. Shaw, and she had long blond hair tied back in a messy bun. She was tan with laugh lines around her eyes, and she looked quick to smile. But she wasn't smiling now.

"What happened?"

"Mongers came to St. Brigid's and took him in for questioning."

I shot a quick look at Logan to see how he reacted to that news and was met by the golden eyes of a Cheetah, sitting calmly on his chair. I guess I would have played animal charades if I could have, too, but it was hard to gauge the emotional reactions of an African predator.

Liz scowled. "About what, and where were you?"

"In the lab. I saw them, but they didn't see me. They said it was because he was mixing blood."

"Why did he go with them?"

Connor opened his mouth to speak but no sound came out, so I continued. "They knew about Connor helping him, and they threatened to come after him if Mr. Shaw didn't go with them."

"Right." It was more of an exhale than an actual word, and the leaning she was doing against the counter suddenly became more of a holding-herself-up-to-not-freak-out-her-kids move. "Well, then we need to get you out of here."

Wow. Liz Edwards was strong. I could see what it cost her to say the words, and yet her tone was totally practical and no nonsense.

"Actually, Mum, Saira needs my help."

She looked at him a long moment, then turned her gaze to me. "When?"

"Now?" I was trying not to be intimidated by her directness.

"No, *to when* will you be taking him?"

She was good. And there was no question that I wouldn't tell her anything she asked. "1429."

Connor's mother blinked. Just once. That was all. I wanted to be her when I grew up.

"I want to go to the middle ages! Take me, too." Logan was suddenly a totally unconcerned naked boy, who apparently couldn't bite his tongue any longer.

134

I made a point of looking straight in his eyes. "Sorry, Bud. Your uncle would cheerfully have me shot if I took both your mom's protectors away. As of now, there haven't been any threats against the rest of you, but you never know with Mongers."

I could see the conflicted pride my words inspired, and Liz shot me a quick, grateful look.

"What about my brother. What can I do there?" Liz had directed her question to me.

Something shimmered in the corner of my vision, and when I looked, a young brown Bear was sitting in Logan's seat.

"We're working on that, Mum," Connor answered. "The Elians' driver, Jeeves, might get in touch with you if he needs help getting Uncle Bob out."

She was trying to hold back a grin, and I could suddenly see both her boys in her face. "Really? His name is Jeeves?"

"Yeah, really."

Logan had Shifted into a Bush Baby and was looking at me through huge brown eyes. I suddenly wanted to hold him and tickle his belly just to watch those eyes get even bigger. He must have sensed his cuteness factor was getting to me because he chittered at me, then ran up my arm and pulled my hair before retreating to his seat again.

So I stuck out my tongue. And so did he.

Liz hadn't seen my exchange with her youngest son because she had reached around the counter to pull Connor into her arms. She inhaled his scent like she was memorizing her boy. I loved that he hung in there on her hug and then kissed her cheek when she finally let go.

She looked at me over Connor's head. "You will take care of each other?"

"Ringo and Archer are going, too, so we'll be covered." Connor was leaning down to scratch Natasha behind her ears. "Kiss Sophia for me?"

"Of course. She's at the neighbors' playing with their new puppies."

"Because we need more dogs?" Connor teased his mom, and she tousled his hair.

Connor held his arm out for Logan, still in Bush Baby form, to scamper up. Logan rode on his brother's shoulder, facing forward, with one hand resting on Connor's ear as we walked to the front door. "Take care of them, okay?" Connor's voice was pitched low for his brother's ears.

The Bush Baby nodded.

"Hey, Logan?" The Bush Baby dropped to the ground behind Connor. A second later, Logan's head popped up from over his brother's shoulder. I appreciated finishing the thought to the human child, rather than another creature. "Don't let the Mongers get wind of your skills, okay?"

He made a face. "The only wind they get is the kind I cut."

I laughed. "Nice. Seriously, though. They may decide you're a fascinating specimen to add to their collection."

"And I may just decide to become a fascinating specimen of a venomous spider. I dare anyone to try to collect me."

He suddenly Shifted back into his Hawk and flew up to settle on a branch of a big tree overlooking the front of the house. It was as if he was taking up a sentry post. I gave him a quick wave before Connor and I went away with big hugs from Liz.

Connor looked back and waved from the Range Rover as we drove away, escorted down the road by the pack of barking dogs. His eyes were a little shiny when he turned to face forward.

Elian Manor seemed too big, too quiet, and too tame after my visit to Bridgeview House. Clearly we needed dogs and lots of them, but having people staying there with us was a good start. Cat strolled past us as we climbed out of the car. He was carrying a dead mouse in his mouth, and I complimented him.

"Nice one."

He gave me a look, then flicked his tail at me and pranced away as if to say, "Don't you wish you could do it."

I wanted a dog.

136

"Would you teach me how to train a dog to do the hug thing Natasha does with you?"

Connor laughed as we walked up the steps to the kitchen door. "I didn't train her to do that. That's how I carried her around when she was a puppy."

"Does any of your dog pack dynamic have to do with you being an alpha?"

"Yeah, but they'll respect anyone who's an alpha, not just a Shifter. You just have to act like the boss and they'll treat you like one. You should have no problem with that." He gave me an impish grin, and I batted him playfully.

"Och, there ye are. Come wi' me, both o' ye." Sanda appeared in the hall as we headed toward the staircase, her Hobbit-sized shape somehow the biggest presence in any room.

We followed her up the stairs to the third floor. "Sanda, have you seen my mother?"

"Aye, but she's restin' now. It'll take a few hours 'fore she's fit for company, and even then, not completely."

"Do you know something about the Monger ring?" Sanda was descended from the ancient Pict people, and I trusted her to know about things I barely understood. Even secret Family things.

"What I know for sure and what I suspect are two different things."

"What do you suspect, then?"

She caught my eyes for a second before opening the door. "Ye know that thing ye can do with a watch and a suggestion?"

"You mean hypnosis?"

"Near as the People 'ave figured, a Monger wearin' that ring can do somethin' like that, only stronger. Those that wonder about it 'ave an 'abit of disappearin' though, so it's best not to wonder out loud."

She opened the door to a room I'd never entered. It was big, with windows that overlooked the driveway, and might have been a playroom for the children of the house in years long past. Now, there were sewing tables set up and bolts of linen fabric leaning against walls. Charlie was working with a needle and thread on a chair by the window, and Ringo emerged from behind a screen wearing a shirt and fitted pants of a dark blue linen. His eyes lit up at the sight of us.

"There ye are. I was wonderin' if I needed to come find ye."

Charlie finished tying a knot and then shook out the thing she'd been working on. She gave me a quick smile, and then spoke to Ringo. "'Ere, try this on for fit over the top of the shirt."

It was a tunic of dark green wool, and Ringo shrugged it on and belted it. It hit just above his knees, and with the belt tightened, it looked a little like a 1950s shirtwaist dress. Charlie consulted a big, very old-looking book on the cutting table, and then looked at Ringo. "I think it'll do. What about you, Saira?"

She turned the book toward me, and I saw it was a reproduction of a painting dated 1422 and set in Burgundy, France. There were elaborately dressed noble men and women in the foreground wearing complicated headgear and looking constipated, and in the background were the tradespeople dressed very similarly to what Ringo wore now. I included Sanda in my astonishment. "You guys just made these?"

Sanda had a mouthful of pins, so her normal gravel voice was back to unintelligible as she tried to speak. So she gestured to Charlie to translate.

"Sanda knew it was just a matter of time before ye went back to find 'imself, so she recruited us to 'elp with the cuttin' and the stitchin'." Charlie beamed at Sanda. "I never 'ad much chance to learn tailorin' before, but Sanda's a fine teacher, and now I 'ave another skill to take wi' me wherever I go."

I looked back at Ringo as he refitted the belt and searched the tunic for pockets. "You're amazing. Thank you."

"We 'ave them cut for all four of ye. Ringo said ye'd be better in men's clothes than ladies', but I made yours from a piece of red wool instead of the dark colors the lads got. The hose and shirts are done for all o' ye, and we've an extra set we can fit to Connor, but the shoulders in the tunics needed to be measured before we could stitch 'em."

Sanda was behind me the next moment with a measuring tape stretched across my shoulders. She grunted, then did the same to Connor, then noted the numbers on a piece of paper.

I spoke in an undertone. "I haven't talked to my mom yet, but is the hypnosis a permanent thing or will she eventually get back to normal?"

"Yer da, he was able to fight it right away, but the fightin' cost 'im. Others take some time to find their way back to the truth. Personally, I think it's more to do with 'ow badly the person wants the truth, and 'ow easy the lie is to live with."

"Is she still herself?"

Sanda measured the piece of tunic she was working on, a lovely dark red wool that I assumed was for me. "Mostly. The little fierceness she 'ad is softened. Ye forget. She was exposed to the ring once before. We don't know if the effects build up."

"Oh crap." I whispered. My mom had been in the council room when Will Shaw fought off the power of the ring. There was sympathy in Sanda's eyes.

"Did anyone see Millicent after the council meeting?" I couldn't imagine anything getting past her indomitable will.

"I saw her." Charlie spoke quietly.

"How'd she seem to you?"

"She didn't say much. Just made a 'alf-'earted attempt to tell the new girl, Laura, off for leavin' the lye in the pantry, but I could tell she didn't really mean it."

"Is that normal, Sanda?"

Sanda didn't look up from her sewing when she spoke. "I've worked for 'er ladyship since before she was *the* Lady Elian. I've never once seen her 'old her tongue 'bout somethin' that wasn't right. And leavin' lye in a pantry can get someone killed."

"Does it off-gas or something?"

Sanda shook her head. "Looks like sugar."

"Oh."

I looked around the work room to distract myself from anything to do with the Monger ring. My gaze landed on Ringo. "I don't suppose you were able to scrounge any trade goods, were you?"

He flung his head toward some cloth bags tossed in the corner. "Wikipedia told me what they 'ad for tools, and we guessed at the rest."

Connor seemed a little shell-shocked at all the activity in the room. "You've done this before, obviously."

I smiled. "Never with so much help, but yeah. The big, old manor houses are great for supply shopping."

"I guess I never really thought about what goes into time travel."

Charlie was turning pages of the big book with gentle fingers, and I realized it was probably really old. "Where'd you find the book?"

"A top shelf in the library. Part of a collection there just 'ad dates on the spines." Ringo was trying to make a strap to tie a knife to his leg, and I thought it was probably a good idea to figure out the weapons thing under my clothes, too. Connor must have had the same thought because he headed toward the door. "I'll go get Archer's weapons."

"Cool. Thanks." I moved closer to Charlie's table. The printing in the book was actually careful handwriting, and every couple of pages was another painting showing people doing various things, but always in a specific landscape and identified by year and location.

"Hang on. Go back a page?"

There was a painting of a military camp. Men in armor and round helmets aiming arrows across a moat at a walled city. It was dated 1429 and titled *Siege of Orléans*.

"Orléans, in France? I don't remember reading about a siege there in the research we were doing with Mom and Mr. Shaw."

Ringo shrugged. "There wasn't one. I spent the day with yer books – and for the record, I think the Elian Manor library is far better than the one at yer school. From everythin' I read about 1429, the Burgundians were workin' with the English against the French, and they 'eld Paris and southern France. 'Enry VI of

140

England was King of France at the time, and there were some minor skirmishes with the 'Ouse o' Valois, but nothin' to write 'ome 'bout."

I was trying to pick my way through the formally written text. It was in French, which I had a very rudimentary knowledge of. One semester of high school French before switching to German did not a fluent reader make, so I was mostly just letting words jump out and embrace me. "This says something about King Charles VII being crowned in Reims in 1429. There's a ton of other stuff here, but I don't really read French."

Ringo looked at me in surprise. "Well, it's wrong. The books I've been readin' say very clearly the English continued to 'old France after winning the battle of Agincourt – the major English victory in 1415. 'Enry V of England was named 'eir by the old Mad King Charles, the French ruler. Henry died a few years later and left France to 'is little son, 'Enry VI. I'll go get 'em and show ye."

"Bring my mom's laptop up too, will you? I want to search for some of these names."

I continued turning pages when Charlie went back to her stitching. I didn't know what I was looking for, especially since I couldn't really read it. I just loved the feeling and the smell of the old book.

A piece of folded paper slipped out from between the pages. The paper was old and had some faded handwriting inside it.

"Blois. Convoy to Orléans. Jeanne d'Arc et Gilles de Rais. 29 April, 1429." I read the note out loud, but to me it still sounded like something written in code. Sanda shrugged and continued with her sewing, but Charlie looked up sharply.

"What?" I asked her.

"Baron Gilles De Rais. Bluebeard."

Ugh. I dropped the note like it was contaminated. "The child killer." I shuddered. "Why would his name be on a note in my family's house?"

I really didn't like the implications of that, whatever they were. An unsettled feeling was making me restless, and I went to the window. The sky had clouded over dramatically, and it looked like it was going to rain. I didn't know what time it was; the way the light looked, it could have been evening already.

I could hear the guys talking as they came down the hall, and Archer's voice in the mix gave me a little thrill. It was crazy how much I missed him during the day, which I only noticed the moment I knew I'd get to see him. He was carrying one of the weapons cases in one hand and my mom's laptop in the other. His eyes found mine the minute he entered the room. Archer smiled in a way I felt to my toes, and I knew my return grin was probably huge and idiotic. Oh well, sometimes being in love felt a little like an inside joke I couldn't stop laughing at.

He joined me at the window when he'd emptied his arms. I, of course, was very happy to refill them. He kissed me softly and spoke in low tones as we ignored everyone else in the room and looked out the window.

"Connor told me about the council meeting. Are you okay?"

"Worried about Mom, but yeah. I'm fine."

"Have you seen her yet?"

I shook my head 'no', then looked into his eyes. "How about you? Did you find anything in London?"

"Not related to Shaw, or wherever the Mongers might be keeping him, but I tried to trace some of the other people they've taken. Maybe they're holding all their captives together."

"Find anything?"

"A street sweeper thought she saw some men escorting a young woman, similar to the description of Alex's cousin Daisy, through a closed gate and onto the grounds of the British Museum."

I stared at him. "Why would they hold prisoners there? It's not like no one's going to notice forty people just hanging around a major tourist attraction."

"The place is locked up after hours, and I crawled around the grounds for a bit before the guard traffic started getting nosy. Except for the pub, the area outside the walls shuts down at night. I couldn't find anyone else who'd seen anything."

"So I guess we need to search the grounds during the day, or find someone who knows the museum really well."

He kissed me gently. "We have to get Connor out of here."

"You could hide him while I look for Mr. Shaw."

"Or he could help us get into Paris."

The thing with Wilder had been painful for so long I'd stopped feeling it, but the Mongers taking Mr. Shaw felt personal. Archer's grip around my waist tightened. "Believe me, I know. There's nothing I want to do more than tear every Monger limb from limb until they let him go. But we're not the only people who can look for him here. And you *are* the only one who can get to Wilder."

I felt hollow inside. Take my friends into danger, or leave a friend captive? Such a delightful choice. But I knew it wasn't a choice, not really. I held Archer's gaze. "I need to talk to Mom first."

"Shall we go now?"

I hadn't realized I wanted him to go with me until he said that. It loosened some of the tight fist that had wrapped itself around my heart when we ran from the council. "Yeah. Hang on just a second though, I want to check something."

I booted up Mom's laptop and was mildly impressed the wireless signal reached the third floor. I looked around at my friends while I was waiting for the internet to load. "By the way, who here, besides Archer, speaks French?"

Connor's hand went up. "School since I was eight and camp in Provence every summer."

Charlie nodded shyly. "I 'ave a few words. The washerwoman I worked with used to practice 'em on me. She went to Workin' Women's College at night to be a ladies' maid."

Ringo grinned. "I don't speak a bit o' it."

"And I have one semester of high school French, which is just enough to order in a restaurant but useless for anything else."

"Well, then you're just going to have to stick with me." Archer kissed my head and then focused on the computer screen. "What are you looking for?"

143

I indicated the book and the note now open on the page. "The note mentions a date in 1429 and the name of that serial child killer that Charlie was telling us about. Might be a coincidence, but I come from time travelers. I don't really believe in coincidences."

He picked it up and held it so I could. Google the names. "Nothing on Jeanne d'Arc. The date is when the Siege of Orléans ended." I skimmed through the Wikipedia entry about the siege quickly. "English troops arrived in support of the Burgundians who surrounded the city. No aid or supplies could get through the blockade, so the city opened its gates and the French were defeated."

Ringo came over holding two modern history books open to specific pages. "That's what these say, too." He pointed to the reproduction of a painting in one. "This one even shows the same archers outside the Orléans city walls."

I carefully turned the pages of the old book back to the same painting so Ringo could compare them. "Same one."

Archer read the formal handwriting of the old book with interest. "But that's *not* what it says here." His finger skimmed over the page as he easily translated the words I had struggled with. "This book claims that the Siege of Orléans ended in victory for the French when Jeanne d'Arc, in English it would be Joan of Arc, arrived with relief for the city." He sucked in a breath. "This says she was only seventeen years old at the time."

Archer skimmed further down with a speed that would have impressed me if I hadn't already known he'd spent a big chunk of his last century learning everything he could get his hands on, including languages. "This calls her the Maid of Orléans, who had been foretold by an old prophecy as one who would help crown the King of France. She claimed to have been sent visions by God telling her that she was to help rid France of the English."

That got my attention in a way nothing else about her had. "She had visions? Do you think this Joan of Arc could have been a Seer?" We had done so much historical research into famous Descendants looking for possible targets for Wilder's blood-skills hunt that I wasn't surprised by anything anymore.

144

Archer looked up. "It's entirely possible. Who lets a seventeen-year-old girl lead men into battle?"

I grinned at him. "Oh, I don't know. Old Vampires, maybe?"

He grunted and smirked at me. "According to this book, Joan of Arc turned the long-standing Anglo-French war into a religious war for French freedom. After her arrival in Orléans, the French soldiers began fighting the battles differently, and they started to win."

"How old did you say she was?" Connor weighed in from across the room.

"Seventeen."

"Are you sure she wasn't Monger?"

"It might explain the battle tactics, but how did she get them to let a girl lead them?"

Archer continued skimming the book. "Within nine weeks of Joan of Arc's arrival at Orléans, the siege was lifted. She then went on with Charles VII and his army to Reims, where he was crowned King on July 17, 1429."

Ringo shook his head. "I'm tellin' ye, every modern 'istory book I've read about the 'Undred Years' War – and I've read a lot – says Charles VII never became King of France."

Archer looked up at me significantly. "And this very old book says he did – in 1429."

The silence in the room was deafening as everything fell into place.

"Oh crap," I breathed. "Someone split time."

Every pair of eyes in the room was locked on mine as the full weight of the realization set in. Archer flipped to the front of the big book. There were Roman numerals etched into the bottom of the title page. "This was published in 1522."

Ringo flipped to the front of each of his books. "This one was 1934, and this one was 1899."

I did a rapid-sort through the information we had. A book from the Clocker Family library, published in 1522, had a different history than the modern history books and even the internet.

I let out a breath. "So, sometime between 1522 and 1899 someone went back and changed history? That's a huge window."

"Includes Wilder," Ringo grimaced.

"And every other Clocker who lived during those three hundred and seventy-seven years." I started pulling up Google maps of France, and Paris in particular. They weren't from medieval times, but they were something.

Ringo shook his head. "Who else besides Wilder had an interest in messin' about with 'istory?"

Archer leaned forward and pulled the laptop toward him. "That's the place to start. Who would have benefited from a different king on the French throne at that time?"

"Only every English noble with ties to France." I was suddenly exhausted, and I knew it was just resistance to doing the research work that lay in front of us.

Archer smirked. "That includes my family, then."

"Yeah, but they weren't Clockers."

"Guys, we can debate this all night, or we can go do what we know we need to do and figure it out as we go." Who knew Connor would be such a man of action?"

"Do we even need to change it back? I mean, it's been this way since sometime after 1522 and before 1899." My arguments were losing steam.

"Ye know the chances are it's Wilder doin' the changin' anyway." Ringo and Connor together were a force of nature.

"So, we should just jump in head-first and figure out what happened when we get there? How do we know time wasn't split way further back than 1429?"

Archer's fingers moved rapidly over the keyboard; then he got up to check the old book. "Here. The battle of Agincourt on St. Crispin's Day, 1415. This is the same as the history I've always known, so at least we know the split didn't happen before 1415."

Ringo shrugged. "It's Wilder doin' it. Who else would it be?"

I gave him a tired smile. "I guess I'm with you on that. The idea it could be anyone else gives me chills." I turned to Archer.

"Jeeves has agreed to help find Mr. Shaw, and he's probably waiting down in the library for us. You want to go fill him in while I talk to my mom?"

"Are you sure you're okay?"

I nodded and turned to the whole group. "Can you guys get everything together that we'll need to Clock out? We'll probably need Jeeves and some of his guys to watch our backs when we go, just in case the Mongers are out, and we should pack some food, too."

Charlie was up and already heading toward the door. "I can pack the food. Everyone 'as a shoulder bag and can carry some."

I shot her a grateful smile, and then swept it around the room. "Thanks, you guys. For everything."

Archer pulled me in for a hug and spoke into my ear. "Nichts zu danken."

The house was quiet despite the fact that it was just after dark, and the east wing where my mom slept danced with shadows from the wall sconces. I knocked softly on her bedroom door.

"Come in."

Her room was lit only by the lamp next to her bed, and she looked up at me from where she lay. It looked like she'd been staring at the ceiling.

"Are you okay, Mom?"

A vague smile touched her mouth, but not her eyes. "Just a headache. I'll be fine in the morning."

"What happened in the council meeting this morning?"

She frowned, and it seemed like she was struggling. "Markham was … he was quite rude. And Bob … Bob has been taken in for questioning." The words trickled out of her, and a flash of hope hit me.

"Why, Mom? Why did they take Mr. Shaw?"

She closed her eyes as if she was trying to find the answer, trying to squeeze it out of her brain. Finally, she opened them again with a sigh. "I can't do it, Saira. I can't hope that someday he'll be free to choose me. I loved a man like that once, and it nearly killed me to lose him. I can't do it again."

Wait, what?

Oh, that's right. My mother's lovely, generous, beautiful brain had been tampered with by a Monger bent on kidnapping her daughter and everyone else who mixed blood. And just like that, my insta-rage at her weakness evaporated. She'd been corrupted. My mother in her right mind would never, never have left Mr. Shaw out to dry. All I could do was hope the damage was reversible. And I had to see how deep it ran. "What are they going to do about the witness?"

"What witness, honey?"

"Someone saw the Mongers take Mr. Shaw. That's how we know it happened."

My mom's eyes seemed to clear for a second, and she gripped my arm tightly. "Saira, no one can know about Connor's part in it. I would never allow them to harm a child."

That, at least, I believed.

I leaned over and kissed her cheek. "I love you, Mom. Try to get some rest."

"Thank you, honey. I love you, too."

Her eyes were closing dreamily, and I stood up to go. I turned out the nightstand light when I left her room. A small part of me wondered if she'd even remember I'd been there.

CLOCKING OUT

I detoured to the library before heading back up to the third floor. Archer and Jeeves were still there, talking solemnly.

Archer looked worried when he saw me. I must have looked bad. "How did it go?"

"Not great. They somehow convinced her Mr. Shaw wasn't worth fighting for, so she's not even going to try to find him."

Archer sighed and turned to Jeeves. "So, Claire's out. Millicent, too, probably."

"Liz Edwards, Mr. Shaw's sister – she's definitely in. The Mongers may go there to find Connor, but hopefully they'll leave her alone."

"I'll keep an eye on the Edwards family as well."

"Thank you, Jeeves."

The night sky was full dark now, and we both knew we had to go. Archer clapped Jeeves on the shoulder with one arm. "We'll be out to the garden in a few minutes."

"We'll be waiting."

Ringo and Connor were already dressed and anxious to go when we got upstairs. Sanda had just finished a hem on Archer's tunic. I quickly shoved the extra underwear, socks, and camisoles I'd grabbed from my room into my satchel. I was *not* getting stuck without clean undergarments on this trip. Ringo showed us how to get into our medieval costumes while Sanda made quick adjustments for fit. The linen of the long shirt was actually quite soft, the pants were more like thick tights, and the wool tunic was big and long enough to allow us to improvise some weapons holsters. I ended up strapping my two daggers to the outsides of my thighs, in a sort of Lara Croft way, except without the miraculous boy shorts that would be up my booty in two seconds.

Despite all the fabric, the tunics were cut and belted in a way that didn't look like a dress. There hadn't been time to make the fur-lined, soft-leather boots the people in the paintings wore, so we just wore our own low boots and hoped no one would get close enough to notice our shoes.

But despite all the wardrobe perfection Sanda and Charlie had pulled off, I still had one big problem. The dumb hats the people in the book wore would do nothing to hide my long hair, and according to medieval fashion, men's hair was never longer than shoulder-length. So, while Archer was improvising sword belts for the other guys, I pulled my hair back tightly, gathered it into a low ponytail, and picked up a big pair of cutting shears.

"No!"

Sanda was the one who yelled at me. Too late. I'd already made the cut. When I shook my hair out, it just brushed the tops of my shoulders. I consulted the painting in the book again to make sure I could get away with shoulder-length hair, then met Sanda's eyes.

"I had to do it."

She looked stricken. "'Twas such lovely 'air ye 'ad, Saira."

My expression softened. I'd never really thought of Sanda as being overly emotional. Or emotional at all, really. She seemed far too practical for something so unpredictable. "It'll grow back."

Archer smiled and took the shears from me. "Let me straighten the edges." He trimmed some jagged pieces, working efficiently and quickly, and then ran his fingers through what was left. "You look beautiful."

I shook my head with a smile. "I don't want to look beautiful. I want to look male."

Ringo snorted across the room. "Not a chance."

"Hey, I fooled you, once."

"Just 'cause ye were tall and fast."

I smirked at him. "Well, I didn't get slow or short since then."

He raised an eyebrow. "Yer still too pretty, but at least ye don't 'ave to 'ide the 'air anymore."

"Exactly."

Archer and Ringo sheathed broadswords at the sides of their belts while Connor and I grabbed shorter ones that could swing around to the back. We had satchels slung across our chests and had wrapped the hooded cloaks, which were a staple to survival, around our shoulders. I suddenly felt like I needed a bow and arrows to complete the Robin Hood look.

Sanda had gotten over my haircut and was beaming at the four of us like a proud parent.

"Where's Charlie? Didn't she make it back from the kitchen yet?"

No one had seen her, and Ringo looked suddenly worried.

"Come on. We'll get her on our way out to the garden." I bent over to kiss Sanda on the cheek as I headed toward the door. "Thank you, Sanda."

Her eyes were gleaming, and she put both her hands to my cheeks to look at me. "My gran used to tell of getting kit and costume together for the Elian family before they'd travel. My ma showed me the storerooms and all the supplies t' do so. Kittin' ye out like this 'as brought me close t' my family again. I'm so proud of ye for what yer doin'." She gave me a firm kiss on the forehead, and then did the same for Archer, Ringo, and finally, Connor.

"All four o' ye come back to me. I'll need yer word on it now."

I grinned. "I'll be back."

"And me," piped Connor.

"Ye couldn't keep me away, Mistress Sanda." Always the gentleman, Ringo.

Archer kissed both her cheeks and held her hands as he looked into her eyes. "You have my word that I'll return and bring this lot with me, if I have to chain them to me to do it."

Sanda grinned. "Yer a good 'un, Archer Devereux. My gran always said it, an' I'll say it as well. You be safe."

The eerie quiet of the house stilled our exuberance as we crept down to the kitchen. The lights were off, and Connor was about to reach for them, but Archer stopped him. I could feel Ringo's nerves tighten as he whispered into the room.

"Char. Ye 'ere?"

The big schoolhouse clock on the wall echoed my own heartbeat, but it was the only sound in the room.

Ringo looked at us, still whispering. "I'm goin' up to 'er room. Somethin's not right."

He turned and started toward the door. "Ringo, wait." I stopped him.

A flash of movement outside the kitchen. Someone was out there. Maybe just Cat, or maybe Jeeves and the gardener, but warning bells were starting to ring in my head. I looked at Archer in the dim light the glowed from the oven. He must have read my mind because he nodded.

"Saira and Ringo, go out the front door. I'll take Connor with me, and we'll meet in the garden."

It was the smartest way to split us up, and we moved with quiet efficiency through the house. The heavy front door was locked, and I hated to leave my mom and Millicent vulnerable by unlocking it, but no one had ever seen fit to give me a key, so it was my only option.

Ringo and I bolted for the garages once we were outside. Jeeves' place was dark, too, and I hoped it was him I'd just seen moving outside the kitchen window.

But where was Charlie?

I knew Archer and Connor would get to the garden first, and when I heard the clang of metal, we both ran.

The scene in the yard was totally surreal. Jeeves and the gardener were being held at the end of Jeeves' rifle by some guy in a ski mask. My gut instantly told me Monger, but honestly, that could have described any or all of the four guys attacking my friends. If the balaclava ski masks and black clothes they wore didn't give away their bad-guy status, the fact that they were all armed with something definitely did. Archer was sword-fighting –

yes, sword-fighting – a guy holding a big metal pole. The Monger was outclassed in the weapons department, and I knew Archer could take him, but that left a third guy holding Charlie, and a fourth guy waving a gun between her and Connor.

Connor's short sword was out, but the gun would win, and he knew it. I was so glad he'd frozen in place, because I was afraid if he moved, he'd get shot.

The screech when I stopped was practically audible, but I had my sword out an instant later and went to help Archer. Two instants later the big metal pole was thrown to the ground, and the Monger took off on foot. That left three swords and two guns. And Ringo.

He had used the momentary distraction of my arrival to leap up to the garden wall and creep along the top in a fair imitation of my Lion. The shotgun guy had his back to the wall, and Jeeves and the gardener had the good sense not to give away the presence of the medieval Spiderman behind him. Ringo caught my eye to warn me, and then dropped down on top of Shotgun Guy with a yell that sounded primitive and scary. He knocked the gun away and in a flash, Jeeves had it pointed back at the Monger.

Ringo's yell was the distraction Archer and I needed to lunge at the other gun. Archer knocked it away with his sword, and I flipped a dagger at the guy holding Charlie. It hit his shoulder and bounced off, but it startled him enough that he dropped her.

And if Charlie was good at anything at all, it was reflexes. That girl had lightning fast ones and was inside the garden walls before Ringo was even back on his feet.

Jeeves motioned the other two Mongers over with his rifle, and they joined the third, who was being tied up with a piece of twine by the gardener. Archer retrieved the pistol from the ground and handed it to the gardener, who held it like it was a viper ready to strike. Then he turned to Jeeves.

"Shall we call someone, or can you take this from here?"

"I have it, sir. Thank you for your assistance." I appreciated that Jeeves didn't call Archer by his name around the Mongers. It was a small thing, but gave them that much less ammunition against Mom and Millicent.

Archer looked at the rest of us. "Right, then. Shall we?"

Jeeves was already herding the Mongers toward the garages, so they hopefully wouldn't see us slip into the walled garden and think we were up to something. Because the medieval clothes and swords weren't dead giveaways.

Charlie waited for us by the Clocker spiral. She looked so out of place in her pretty gray dress among all the homespun wool and linen clothes we wore. It didn't help that her eyes were like saucers and her breath still came in gasps.

She flung herself at Ringo when she saw him, and he held her tightly and unselfconsciously. The circumstances could have been better, but I was really happy to see them finally get past all the decorum that kept them at arm's length from each other.

When Charlie finally stopped gasping, she turned to face me.

"I'm comin' with ye."

There was total silence in the garden. Even the crickets seemed to hold their breath. I half expected Ringo to launch himself in opposition, saying it's too dangerous and she wasn't prepared – everything I was thinking. But he just looked at me. And so did Connor. Archer studied Charlie for a long moment before he turned to me.

"Charlotte can help."

"With the *Other*, the Bluebeard one. And with Clocking." Charlie's tone was proud and strong. I was impressed, and she wasn't wrong. The times I'd Clocked more than two people, I had suffered. Even when my mom was the primary source of our Clocking, I'd still felt all the same symptoms that being *between* brought on, only muted. But Charlie seemed to be like a fuel source for me *between*. Like she amplified my Clocking ability and overrode the nausea and weakness. I had no idea how we'd protect her in 1429, but no matter what, we couldn't protect her here when we were gone.

"Okay," I exhaled. "Let's roll."

THE WOLVES OF PARIS – JULY, 1429

We were taking a huge risk Clocking into the middle of Paris with five people. There was no part of stealth mode to this plan. The drawing of the view of the Hôtel de Sens from across the cobblestone street was the only reference I had to guide me to our destination. And because I was Clocking to an unfamiliar location and focusing on a specific year – 1429 – I had to let the season go to default. Too many variables at once were dangerous, especially with five people in tow. So, it would be July, 1429 when we landed in the square in front of the Hôtel de Sens. That much, at least, I could control.

It was easier to focus when Charlie was linked in because keeping it together wasn't such a pressing need. She did that. She kept it together, almost like she closed a circuit on the energy it took to Clock. And when we landed, it was like I'd been on a long car ride or a short boat ride – only mildly queasy, and more importantly, able to draw my sword right away.

Archer, Ringo, and Connor needed a minute.

My eyes searched the dark corner of the street where we'd fallen. I had a sword in my hand, which felt ridiculous but seemed necessary somehow, and three of my people were in various stages of vomitousness. All things considered, a memorable way to start my first visit to Paris.

The street was deserted though. Rue de Figuier, presumably named for the giant fig tree at my back, started at the Hôtel de Sens and wandered north, away from the Seine River. I'd studied a modern map, but a Google street view could hardly prepare me for the reality of the scene in front of me.

In French, the word 'hôtel' is more about being a grand townhouse than a place for travelers to stay. And just like in Archer's vision, this one looked truly medieval, with turrets and towers and all the decorative pointy bits that defined its age. There were lit torches in brackets attached to the stone walls, but otherwise, the few buildings scattered around the Hôtel de Sens were dark.

"Is everyone okay?" I whispered. Because it was bad enough we'd just appeared out of nowhere, but to be speaking modern English, too? I could see burning at the stake in our future if we weren't very careful.

Charlie nodded, and shivered. Her thin sweater was no match for the night, much less the times, so I sheathed the sword and wrapped my hooded cloak around her shoulders.

The guys were done heaving and hurling and had pulled themselves together. We instinctively fanned out so we could see all sides of us and still protect our backs. I nodded at the building behind Archer.

"It looks right, doesn't it?"

He glanced over his shoulder at the Hôtel de Sens. "Yes. Which means there are wolves. Leave us your clothes, Connor. We can't afford to lose them when you Shift."

I had the feeling they'd been having private logistics conversations, but I wanted in. "Wait. What are you going to do once you're a Wolf?"

Connor was stripping off his belt and boots and handing stuff to Archer. "Find the alpha and challenge him."

I was a little appalled. "So, a fight straight away?"

"It's how we do it. Any reconnaissance is done up-wind. As soon as the pack scents another wolf, it's on."

"Does the rest of the pack get in on the fight? Do we have to jump in with swords and knives to keep you alive?"

"Nah. Dominance fights are one-on-one. The pack wants the strongest wolf to lead them, and the only one who really cares if the weaker one dies is its mate."

"You people are brutal."

Connor shrugged. He was down to his shirt and pants, and he motioned to me and Charlie. "Turn around. I don't want to shock you with my manliness."

I stifled a laugh and did as he said. Considering he and his manliness were fourteen, I was more in danger of hurting his ego than being shocked.

He continued whispering, but with a chatter in his teeth. "It may seem brutal, but it's fair. We don't hold grudges, and we don't kill unless it's necessary to eat or live. If I can get away with not killing this alpha, I'll have a pretty good shot at sleeping later, too."

Before I could ponder what he meant, I could feel the air change behind me. I gave him a second before I turned back around to find his Wolf grinning at me with his teeth bared.

Connor's Wolf was gorgeous, and I just barely resisted running my fingers through his fur. He wasn't a pet, and that would have felt way too intimate, but the silver of his coat looked so elegant and wild at the same time, it was hard to keep my hands to myself. He really was pretty spectacular.

"I wish I could do that." There was awe in Ringo's voice, and I realized he'd never seen Connor's Wolf before. The Wolf turned his grin to Ringo then nudged Archer's hand, shot a look at me, and took off down the Rue de Figuier.

Archer finished packing Connor's clothes into his satchel and slung it over his shoulder with his own bag. "We need to get food for everyone and something for Charlie to wear."

Charlie scoffed. "O' course, there's a big pile o' food on the kitchen table at Elian Manor, just waitin' to be packed in yer bags."

"What happened back there, by the way?" I turned to Charlie.

"They nabbed me, plain and simple."

"They couldn't have known who you are?"

"No, but they might just have been looking for leverage." Archer's whispered voice carried across to us. "It's almost better for your mother and Millicent that Walters did his thing with the ring. He won't expect them to be culpable in anything."

"Oh gee, here, let me brainwash you so I can leave you alone." Ironic whispers are hard to pull off, and I could hear my voice rising.

Ringo shot me a look. "Shut it, Saira. Yer angry and ye have a right to be, but that's not our job right now. Gettin' Wilder is."

I took a breath and nodded. "Sorry. I was just starting to get her back, and I'm mad that she's gone again."

Archer reached for my hand. "I know." As much as I wanted him to tell me everything would be okay, I was glad he didn't. Because none of us knew if it would, and the not knowing sucked.

"Well, until the wolves come, we may as well do a little reconnaissance of our own." He turned to Ringo. "I'll take Charlie with me while you and Saira look for upper floor access?"

I loved that he was basically asking Ringo's permission to be the one to protect his girl. Ringo nodded, and then swung himself up into the big fig tree. "'Ere. 'And me up yer bags and I'll stash 'em." When we were stripped of everything but clothes and weapons he dropped back down and nodded at me. "Ye ready?"

"Let's do it." We darted across the street and hugged the walls of the hôtel. If Wilder was actually here, he'd be awake, and I doubted a couple of knives and swords would have much effect if he surprised us.

I spotted a promising tree overhanging a section of roof that would do nicely. The only tricky part was the spiderwalk that would have to be done between the hôtel wall and the smooth trunk to get up into the tree branches. The medieval tunic wasn't as bad as Elizabethan skirts had been for climbing, but Ringo-the-monkey still beat me to the top of the tree.

The view was pretty incredible.

We could see the river Seine from there, and the small islands in the middle of it. They looked full of grassy farmland, which was so hard to imagine from the pictures of modern Paris I knew. The buildings in the rest of the Marais district seemed to be mostly one or two stories tall, though another big townhouse and a church were also visible.

Ringo wasn't looking at the view though. "The room below is empty and the window looks easy. Shall we?"

Honestly, I wasn't ready. I didn't feel armed enough, or strong enough, or even brave enough to take on Bishop Wilder in all his time-traveling, future-seeing Vampireness. I wanted Archer at my back, or by my side. And Ringo, and Connor in his Wolf form. And maybe even Charlie if she had a frying pan handy.

I was chickening out.

And Ringo knew it.

"I'll go in, Saira. I'll scout t' make sure 'e's 'ere. Ye can wait on the roof and give me a signal if ye see danger."

I shot him a you're-out-of-your-mind look and shoved my nerves down to somewhere in my knee region, hoping the fear wasn't big enough to actually paralyze those knees. I started moving toward the roof and was almost to the no-return point when the howling began.

Wolves. And our friends were down there.

Ringo was already backing up to the tree trunk, and within a few moments we'd jumped down to the outside of the wall and were running back to the street. I heard the sounds of snarling and growling and hoped it didn't mean something, or someone, was being ripped to shreds.

The sight of Archer and Charlie, backs to the wall of the Hôtel de Sens, surrounded by wolves, was so familiar it rocked me for a minute. Except in Archer's vision it was me next to him, not Charlie.

"We need to get Charlie out of there." My whisper was low, but Ringo could still hear it over the gasping of my breath.

Archer had his broadsword, but Charlie had only a rock.

"Right."

"Let's split the wolves up. I'll stay here and get their attention, while you go to the other side of the pack and grab Charlie when they come after me." I pulled my short sword out of the scabbard at my belt, and then unhitched a dagger from my thigh.

He looked at me a second, looked at them, and then nodded. "I'm off."

In less than a breath he was free-running across the street. He barrel-vaulted an abandoned cart and slid under another one parked nearby. I started running at the wolves, yelling at them to come and get me. I sounded like a twelve-year-old with a common sense deficiency taunting bullies.

Archer used the distraction to lunge at the wolves who'd been sneaking up on his Charlie side, which cleared a path for her to get to Ringo. That girl had some serious reflexes, and the minute the coast was clear, she bolted.

Ringo grabbed her and they ran back to the fig tree. Archer had edged closer to me until we were side-by-side with our backs to the wall. It was exactly his vision, and in that moment I saw Courtaud, the red-gold alpha, closing in on Archer from the side.

"On your left!"

Courtaud lunged at Archer, who dodged the gnashing teeth with inhuman speed. Two mangy-looking wolves near me used his distraction to attack from the other side, but I slashed down with my short sword and connected with one of them. His yip alerted Archer, who swung his sword to the right just in time. The Mangies slunk back again to rejoin the pack.

There were about fifteen wolves around us, and while Archer parried with Courtaud and the bigger wolves, I was left to fight off the other half. From the corner of my eye I saw Ringo hoist Charlie up into the fig tree and draw his sword to run at the pack near me. My sword was too short to keep their teeth away, and every time I missed I could feel another wolf get ready to lunge.

With Ringo diverting attention, I was able to wound another one of the smaller gray wolves, who pulled itself out of the pack to skulk away. I had to swing for a black one when it went for Archer's right side, but my hits weren't doing anything more than nicking the beasts. Their thick fur and quick reflexes kept them safe from most of the damage I tried to inflict.

Ringo caught a ratty tan one in the leg, and it yelped before running away. A dirt-colored one took its place, with a reddish one right behind. I saw Courtaud draw back, and for a second I thought he was going to retreat, but he was just coiling to spring at Archer while he fought off the big black beast.

"Archer!"

Everything shifted into slow motion in my brain. Courtaud leaped with bared teeth. Archer's eyes followed my voice. The big black lunged and tore at Archer's leg. Ringo stumbled on a blood slick. Charlie screamed.

"No!"

And then it hit. A huge silver beast flew through the air and took Courtaud down. The midair collision was horrific and sounded like fists pounding flesh. The landing was worse.

The big black's teeth were wrapped around Archer's boot, and he buried his sword between its shoulders. It fell limp to the ground, stained yellow fangs embedded in his boot leather.

Ringo was on the ground. The dirt wolf tore into his thigh, and I screamed and tried to hurl my sword, but it wouldn't leave my hand. It was too close.

And what if I missed?

Charlie threw her rock at the dirt wolf, which bounced off its skull. The beast stumbled back from Ringo, its maw covered in Ringo's blood. I ran at it and plunged my sword into its side, then twisted with all my strength to keep the beast from landing on my friend.

Charlie flew down out of the tree and fell by Ringo's side. Her hands pressed down on the wound in his thigh. I felt the red wolf behind me and yanked my sword from the dead wolf to spin on the red. My sudden move clipped him in the jaw, and he yelped backward and slunk away, his eyes never leaving mine.

When I turned back to Charlie, she was talking to Ringo under her breath, calling him names that sounded like insults, demanding he stay with her or she'd leave him. The kind of nonsense a person says when they're scared. When the one they love could die.

Blood ran through her fingers from the wound in his thigh. It wasn't spurting, but the artery was leaking, and she pressed down hard so she could fumble with my cloak around her neck, rip it off, and press it into the gash.

It was all still slow motion to me. Even the slamming of my heart had slowed to something that echoed through the night. The cobblestones were slick with blood, and the vicious sounds of a wolf battle dragged my eyes back to the street.

Connor's Wolf was circling Courtaud, his jaws snapping aggressively. The other wolves had slunk back from the fight and were frozen, watching their leader and the silver Wolf. Courtaud lunged for Connor's throat. Connor was faster and twisted away, and then used his bigger size to crash into Courtaud. The red-gold wolf snarled and lashed out with his teeth, and again, Connor was faster.

Archer stood ready, his sword out, the big black kicked away so his feet were clear. He had Connor's back, and he watched the fight intently. The other wolves were still staying back, so I knelt by Ringo's side.

He was pale and in pain, and his eyes were locked on Charlie's, but he was breathing. Charlie pulled up the cloak to check the wound. The blood had slowed to a trickle, but I could see through the torn fabric of his pants that the gash was deep and jagged. I looked at his eyes again. They'd moved to mine as he watched my face.

"That bad, eh?"

I could barely hear his voice over the sounds of wolves fighting.

Charlie's voice had risen in volume but was still the calm, talking-to-herself tone when she spoke. "Ye'll live if ye don't fester."

He choked back a bitter laugh. "'Ave ye got the green medicine wi' ye, Saira?"

Of course I did. I got up to get my pack, still stuck in the tree, and the snarl of a gray wolf nearby made me snap. I whipped my other dagger off my thigh and flung it at the creature. The blade embedded into the wolf's chest, and as it stumbled away I got a flash of its surprise and pain, and underneath that was a glimpse of what seemed like a whole lifetime of hunger and fear.

My eyes filled with tears, which pissed me off even more because now I couldn't see. I would not feel sorry for it - the damn thing had my dagger in it. The snarls and growls of the fight grew louder behind me, and I turned to see Courtaud hurl himself at Connor's silver Wolf again. Connor took the blow and went down, but he brought Courtaud with him, his jaws locked around the alpha's neck.

Courtaud froze, and Connor flipped around so he was standing over the red-gold wolf. His teeth hadn't let go, but they weren't tearing the flesh. The two wolves stared into each other's eyes for a lifetime that lasted about five seconds before Courtaud's body relaxed, and he stretched his head back to offer his submission.

It was over.

I quickly scanned the other wolves. They hadn't moved from their retreat, and some had crouched down, ears back, in a position I recognized as submissive.

Connor's Wolf held Courtaud down for another breath, and I used that breath to retrieve our packs. I could feel the worry emanating from Archer across the street.

I dropped to Ringo's side and fished the tin of green medicine from my pack. I opened it and held it out to Charlie. "Scoop some with your fingers and press it into the wound. I'll get something to bind it with."

The bandages weren't in my pack, they were in Archer's, and I hurled Connor's clothes across to where his Wolf still pinned Courtaud to the cobblestones while I rooted for them.

Ringo kept his grunts of pain nearly soundless as Charlie slathered the gash with the antibiotic salve Mr. Shaw had taught me to make, and again when I wrapped a long strip of linen around it to stop the small trickle of blood that still escaped the torn flesh.

I felt the air shimmer while I was working, and when I'd tied off the edges of the bandage, I wasn't surprised to see that Connor had Shifted back to his human form. He pulled on his clothes as if being naked in the streets of Paris while standing over a wolf was just part of the job, though Archer still held his sword in a position I knew was ready to defend if necessary.

And then Connor said something in French that made Archer stare, and made the wolf at his feet flinch.

"What? What did he say?" I was back to whispering, mostly from shock.

"I think 'e told it to Shift." Charlie's voice was quiet, but her eyes had moved to the scene in the street.

Courtaud hesitated, still staring up at Connor. I couldn't find malice in the eyes anymore, just intensity. And then the air shimmered, and the Wolf at Connor's feet became human.

And female.

The girl was naked, of course, but it was that she was a girl that stunned us all. Charlie gasped quietly, Connor took a step back, and Archer's sword touched the ground. I did the most irrational thing of all. I stood up and yelled at her.

"What the hell were you thinking? Your wolves have been *killing* children! Who are you, and how could you lead them to do that?"

The girl stood up, and Connor tossed her his cloak. I was barely conscious of her nudity as I advanced on her, and she seemed equally unfazed by it as she swung the cloak around her bare shoulders.

Her eyes never left mine as she spoke to Connor in French. Connor translated automatically. "She wonders at the fierce woman who dares to scream at her in the language of her oppressors." He turned to me. "You're yelling in English. They've been at war with the English for decades. Shut it, Saira."

I glared at the girl but I recognized the idiocy of yelling, much less yelling in English, outside the place we thought Wilder lived. So I did shut it. And instead shot daggers with my eyes.

Naked Girl shot back, and we had our own silent pissing contest with death glares. Archer finally broke the stand-off when he sheathed his sword and stepped forward, speaking in French.

Naked Girl answered Archer's question in rapid-fire, fairly guttural-sounding French, and then she made a strange, growling noise deep in her throat that sent the remaining wolves scattering. Within a minute we humans were the only things left in the street.

Charlie had helped Ringo up to a seated position, and he winced as he shifted his leg around in front of him. Naked Girl shot him a look with a sneer attached and said something in a tone that made him flip her off the English way with the back of his hand thrust up in an up-yours gesture. I was the only one who heard Charlie's whispered voice. "Bitch."

"Who is she?" I asked.

Archer was speaking to her again, and she glared at him silently. But when Connor used a tone of voice on her that was like 'I'm the boss of you, so do it,' she grudgingly gestured toward the river.

"'Is lordship wants to know where she keeps 'er clothes, or maybe where 'er camp is. I couldn't tell exactly." Charlie's voice was thin and scared.

Archer and Connor came to sling their bags over their shoulders, and Archer helped Ringo to his feet. "How bad?" He spoke to Ringo.

"'Urts like 'ell."

Archer met my eyes behind him, and I grimaced to let him know that was an understatement. He slung Ringo's arm over his shoulder and got his arm around Ringo's wiry torso.

Connor picked up Ringo's pack, then looked at him and spoke quietly. "I'm sorry I didn't get here sooner. Their trail led all over the district, and I had to dodge a pissed-off shopkeeper with a handful of rocks."

Ringo gave him a wan smile. "No worries. Yer a bloody good brawler in Wolf form."

We started to follow Naked Girl who was trudging down the street in her red-riding-hood cloak and nothing else. The scene felt totally surreal to me, and my brain was having trouble processing the fact that we'd just had a fight with a pack of wolves, Ringo was hurt, Connor was alpha, and Courtaud was a Naked Girl Shifter. I fell into step beside Archer.

"This isn't good, is it." I wasn't asking a question.

Archer sounded grim. "Not good at all."

THE SEINE

I took a little detour to track the gray wolf with my dagger in its chest and get my weapon back. Ripping the dagger out of dead wolf-corpse was grimly unsatisfying, and I was in a macabre mood when I rejoined my friends.

Naked Girl led us to the Seine River and then alongside it until the river curved south. There was a city wall intersecting the river at the curve that looked either badly built or beaten down by weather. Big cracks ran along the mortar lines of the stones, and chunks of rock were missing in places. One of those gaps was clearly big enough for a wolf to get through, and almost big enough for a man.

She stopped and spoke to Connor in her guttural French. He listened, and then translated for me.

"Her camp is outside the wall. The wolves are there, but she said Ringo can't go because they're hungry and they'll smell blood."

"Who is she?"

They spoke again, and Connor translated. "Her name is Jehanne."

"Why did she let the wolves kill kids?"

Connor translated my words, and Jehanne shot me a look of pure venom but didn't say anything. Connor used his badass alpha voice on her again, and she grudgingly answered his question.

"She uses the wolves to attack English army camps outside Paris, but there aren't enough kills of soldiers to keep the wolves fed, so she lets them come into the city to take what they need. She says the Burgundians control Paris and they're in league with

167

England, so she doesn't feel bad about it. God charged her to kick the English out of France, apparently."

"Well, isn't that special."

Jehanne was speaking again, and this time Archer answered. They went back and forth a few times before he translated for me. His mouth was grim. "She only wants Connor to go back to her camp with her, since he's her alpha now."

I interrupted him. "No way is he going there alone to be challenged by some other pack wolf."

"That's what I told her. She suggested I could go, too, but that leaves you and Charlie carrying Ringo."

"I don't need carryin'." Despite the blood loss and pain, Ringo was like a kid, jumping in whenever his name was mentioned.

"Shut up. You do, too." And, apparently, I was also six years old.

Archer spoke before Ringo could argue. "You need food and rest. We all do. And if it's possible to clean that wound properly, we need to do it. I've seen too many men lose legs to infection."

That got him. Part of Ringo's identity was wrapped up in his ability to run. I understood it, because it was in mine, too. And while I knew the advancements in prosthetic technology made limb-loss deal-able for twenty-first century athletes, Ringo's only experience with amputation would be the painful sailor's peg-leg that made men old before their time.

Ringo exhaled. "Right. Where are we goin' t' do that?"

Archer seemed to be studying the river, and I shook my head. "If the Seine is anything like the

Thames, that water is foul."

"It can be boiled."

"If we had a fire."

Archer's eyes narrowed as he stared into the dark night. "There are islands in the middle of the river. They didn't get built up until the 1600s, so perhaps we can make a camp of sorts there. Charlie can tend Ringo, and the wolves can't cross the water."

"Neither can we." I was tired and coming down off an adrenaline high, and it made me whiny. "Sorry. That's not helping, is it?"

Archer smiled at me and some of the tightness in me unfurled. I leaned into him, and he wrapped an arm around my waist.

"Guys, she's going to leave." Connor called to us. "I'm going with her." He hacked at a chunk of wall with his sword, and when it came down, the opening was big enough for a person to go through.

"I'm coming with you." I was looking at Archer when I answered Connor. Archer closed his eyes for a moment, inhaled, and then met my eyes.

"That works. I'll find a boat, take Ringo and Charlie across, and then come back here for the two of you. An hour before dawn and not later, though, okay?"

I nodded and kissed him. "I love you." It was a whisper meant for his ears only, but the hint of a smile tugged at the corner of Ringo's mouth before he could stifle it.

My eyes landed on him. "You, too, wolf-bait." He grimaced, but the smile stayed put. I fished the tin of green medicine out of my pack and handed it to Charlie. "Here. Use it up if you need to. I can make more." Then I gave her a quick hug, which startled her, but she didn't flinch away. "Thank you for being here," I whispered into her ear. She nodded mutely and looked over at Ringo as if the idea of not being here to take care of him was too terrifying to contemplate.

I held Archer's gaze. "An hour before dawn. We'll be here."

"Watch yourself with her." His eyes flicked to where Jehanne stood impatiently. She was pretending not to pay attention to us, but I knew she was absorbing everything. "She's Shifter, but she's something else, too. I'm not sure what, but the colors I get off her are all over the place."

Archer could read people's intentions as colors. Kind of like an aura, only more about whether they were telling the truth than about who they were. "Was she lying about the whole mission from God thing?"

He shook his head. "It's the one thing she believes with total certainty. Everything else is layered with omission and lies."

"Awesome. So we have that to wade through. It's a good thing you and Connor have British educations and can speak French. I'm completely lost about anything other than body language."

"Then watch that and let Connor listen to the words. Her body language will probably tell more truths than her voice does."

I gave Archer another quick kiss and then went to Connor's side. "Right. Let's do this."

Just before I slipped through the wall, I looked back to see Archer easing Ringo down to the dirt and Charlie crouching down beside him. A sharp fear that I wouldn't see them again suddenly pulsed through me, and I firmly shoved it away. It was the only down side to loving people – the terror that they would one day be gone.

The landscape outside the walls of Paris was almost wild. We were in a thick forest and didn't have far to go to get to Jehanne's camp. It was nearly impossible to stumble into, and we wouldn't have found it without her to guide us.

Connor told me in a quiet voice that he would have to Shift when we got to camp, just to make certain his dominance over the actual wolves was solid. Also, to make sure they didn't eat me. Which was nice of him.

I studied Jehanne as we walked. She was still barefoot and naked under the cloak and seemed unaffected by the nighttime chill. Her hair was sort of the reddish color of her Wolf coat, with streaks of blond running through the tangles. It looked like it had been cut with a knife at about jaw length and was stick straight. She was young, maybe even younger than me, but strong, and she moved like she was coiled wire, hard, tight, and ready to spring at any moment. The hardness wasn't just in her body though. Her expressions were hard, too, and it made her look older than she probably was. She actually reminded me of her Wolf, coiled and fierce, and I had the impression there wasn't much that had been soft or safe in her life.

It made me feel a little sorry for her. She must have sensed it, or maybe she had a little of Archer's skill, because she turned sharply, looked me in the eyes, and spit at my feet before continuing into the camp. Charming.

A lean-to shelter was rigged against a tree. It seemed more den-like than for human habitation, and I wondered if she spent much time in her human form.

"Is she the only Shifter in the pack?"

Connor translated the question to Jehanne, and she nodded as she pulled on pants similar to ours and slipped a ragged linen shirt over her head. She put Connor's cloak back over her clothes, and he didn't say anything about needing it back.

"Is not caring who sees you naked a Shifter thing?"

Connor shrugged. "Sort of. We're so used to getting naked when we Shift it just sort of loses its charge, you know?"

There were scars around Jehanne's wrists and ankles. They looked kind of fresh, and some of the skin was pink and raw.

"What happened?" I pitched my question louder for her ears, and indicated her wrists. She spit again when she answered, but this time the phlegm wasn't directed at me. Necessarily.

Connor translated. "When she and her people lost at Orléans, the English put her in irons. It was a week before they left her untended long enough for her to Shift. Her Wolf paws were small enough to slip through the manacles, and she escaped."

My eyes narrowed. "Orléans? Why was she there?"

I could feel wolf eyes staring at us through the trees, and Jehanne's gaze was distinctly wolfish when she answered Connor's question. Even though it was in French, her answer was directed at me.

"As I said before, I was sent by God's angel to rid France of the English."

Connor translated rapidly between us, but our conversation was with each other.

"How did God's angel speak to you?" I thought I did a decent job of keeping my tone even and curious, instead of revealing the weird, panicky feeling that was starting to prickle my lungs.

She hesitated before answering. "In dreams. He comes to me in dreams."

Prickly-lung-panic turned to full on hollow-stomach-churn.

"What's the English translation for her name?"

Connor shot me a strange look. "Jehanne? I don't know, probably Jeanne or Joan, why?"

Certainty hit me like a fist, and my voice came out in a strangled whisper. "She's Joan of Arc. From the true time stream."

"The chick who got the French king crowned?"

I turned to Connor. "Does she look like she got anyone crowned?" I had a sudden thought. "Ask her the date."

He did, and it seemed like she had to calculate before she answered.

"Near the end of July, she's not sure."

"The king was supposed to have been crowned on July 17th, 1429. Ask her what happened in Orléans. How did she get captured?"

He translated rapidly, and Jehanne's voice turned venomous again when she answered.

"They anticipated our arrival at the city, and they captured us before we were able to deliver the aid we brought to the people of Orléans. It was as if they could see the future and know the exact location of our camp." The bitterness in her voice was palpable.

"They could have had a Seer with them." I didn't really believe it, but I wanted other possibilities besides someone messing with the time stream.

Connor shook his head. "That wouldn't make two different histories."

"You're right. I just don't want to admit that some Clocker screwed up. Because then I'd feel like I have to fix it."

"You said it yourself, though. Why do you have to do anything? What's been done has been in our history for hundreds of years. What does it matter if Charles doesn't get to be king this year?"

I tossed my head at Jehanne. "It matters to her."

172

"How do we know that? Maybe she goes on to live a boring, peaceful life now that she's not messing around in French politics."

I snorted. "Right. She's terrorizing Paris with a pack of wolves. How is that going to end?"

Speaking of wolves …

"Um, you may want to do your alpha thing now. We're pretty much surrounded." While we'd been talking, the wild pack had been creeping closer, and I could see more eyes watching us from the woods beyond the camp's perimeter.

"Here, hold this. And either turn around or learn to deal because I might be doing this a lot."

Connor quickly stripped out of his clothes, and I just held out my arms to be a hanger. If I'd had a brother, I'd probably be used to a guy's naked body, but I also refused to be embarrassed or squeamish. Thankfully, he was a fast stripper and Shifted almost immediately.

I found myself watching the transformation with fascination. There was something so beautiful about the shimmery air around his body as it blurred and changed. Watching Connor Shift gave me an entirely different perspective on a human body, and I found myself appreciating the Shifting process with my artist brain. The animal form he wore was so striking that for about a second I wasn't so terrified of the Shifter side of myself.

And then he growled, and all the warm fuzzies evaporated into thin air. Connor's Wolf was lethal. He was dominant, and alpha, and about to throw down with any wolf who dared to challenge him.

Two of the wolves, a big dark one and a scrappy-looking reddish one, were edging closer while the others kept their places surrounding the camp. I couldn't back up very far to give Connor room because it would put me in range of two or three other beasts, and the idea of all those teeth at my back sent goose bumps up and down my spine.

Not that the teeth in front of me weren't doing the same thing. But the wild wolves had frozen in place. And then I realized why. Connor's big silver Wolf stood, more massive than I'd ever seen him, hackles up and teeth bared, like he owned the clearing. Like every inch of it belonged to him. Even I felt the dominance of his stance, as if I had to ask permission to be there. I knew what alpha meant, but I guess I'd never really seen what it looked like. He wasn't terrifying, I think because he wasn't trying to be. Connor was just the boss, and even Jehanne, who had been leaning against a tree in a seemingly casual pose, had lowered her head and wouldn't meet his eyes.

He snapped his teeth at two or three of the wild wolves for good measure, and they flattened themselves to the ground. None of them would meet his eyes, and when he turned them to me, I fought the instinct to do the same. I squared my shoulders and looked straight back at him.

I wasn't sure why I'd done it, and if I'd been a Wolf I don't think I could have. But I don't think my Lion would let me look away, and I was glad. I understand that wolf pack hierarchies exist to keep the peace, but I had spent a fair amount of time on city streets when I was growing up, and there are times that confidence is the only thing that will keep a person safe. Especially a free-running tagger girl whose playground was storm drains and deserted alleys.

Then Connor's Wolf walked to my side and stood there in silence, glaring at the wild wolves, and especially, at Jehanne. She scowled when she looked away, and I could tell his proximity to me chapped her. The goose bumps on my spine went away, and I realized what he'd just done. The new alpha Wolf of this wild pack had just established my own dominance to make me safe among these wolves. I didn't really know much about lupine politics, but I hoped it would hold even when he wasn't with me.

"We need to get back to the river." I spoke under my breath, but Connor's Wolf ears had no trouble hearing me. He took one last fierce look around the clearing at the pack, growled menacingly in his chest, and then Shifted back to his human form.

I tossed him the trousers first and looked away to find Jehanne watching me with open hostility. "What's your problem?" It didn't matter that she didn't speak English, she knew from my tone what I'd just said.

She spit on the ground and said something in French that made Connor scoff as he translated.

"She said they burn women like you."

"I'm the witch? She's the one who has visions and changes into a Wolf every five minutes."

Connor stifled a laugh and Jehanne spoke again.

His mouth tightened into a grim line at her words, but he didn't automatically translate for me. She just watched me with glittering eyes.

"What? What did she say?"

He finally answered. "Any woman who mates with a devil and consorts with a Wolf deserves to burn."

"So, Archer's the devil, obviously." I couldn't help the snort of derision. "But how am I consorting with you?"

He sighed deeply. "I had to effectively name you 'mate' so my alpha standing in the pack would extend to you. If I just named you dominant, than any wolf could challenge you for your position, and probably would."

I stared at my fourteen-year-old, tall, skinny, blond friend and couldn't help the laugh that barked out. He winced, and I realized I wasn't being very nice.

"I'm sorry, that was mean. I appreciate what you did, and I hope it doesn't mess you up in some way."

He looked confused. "Mess me up, how?"

I grinned at him. "I don't know. Jehanne's been looking at you like she wants to lick you."

The look of disgust on his face was priceless. "You are *so* not funny. C'mon, let's get out of here." He spoke quickly to Jehanne and she tried to talk back, but he snapped at her sharply. She finally cowed and then nodded sullenly to whatever he'd just commanded.

He did some human version of his Wolf's growl as a parting shot, and then we left the clearing. Connor led the way, and I could feel at least two or three wild wolves traveling with us.

"What'd you say to her before we left?" I kept my voice low, although the wild wolves obviously couldn't understand me.

"I forbade them from going through the walls into Paris."

"How can you enforce that? If they're hungry, they'll go for the easy meat."

He shot me a look over his shoulder. "They're not hungry, Saira. It's summertime and there's plenty of meat in these woods. She *took* them into Paris."

A sudden rage surged through me – the kind that made me more quiet and fierce. "She can't possibly believe her God told her to murder children! I mean, it's bad enough to believe an ethnocentric God is going to throw his weight behind one king over another. That girl is completely nuts."

"No argument here." Connor's voice was quiet, too. "You're kind of scary when you get righteous."

I grunted, still annoyed. "Yeah, well, you're a scary alpha Wolf. What's your point?"

He chuckled and led the way back to the crumbling city wall.

Archer was just landing a primitive wooden skiff when we arrived at the river. The small splashes from his paddles were the only man-made sounds I could hear in the pre-dawn night. The little flush of heat that filled my chest at the sight of him felt like an internal happy dance, and I know the size of the smile on my face was completely inappropriate to the excursion we'd just been on.

"You found a boat!" My whisper was too excited, and I had to tone it down before I sounded moronic.

"You made it back safely." There was happiness in his voice that made me think I wasn't the only goofball in the group. He helped me in and then kissed me lingeringly on the lips. The happy dance music had turned into a rocker's acoustic ballad and a slow dance took over. Connor cleared his throat dramatically behind us.

"Move along, move along." He flashed a wolfish grin at me when I turned to growl at him. Archer just laughed and pulled Connor into the boat before shoving off with a paddle.

"Is Ringo okay?"

The smile faded from Archer's face and my heart constricted. "I don't know. His flesh was torn and I stitched it up as best I could, but if an infection threatens, you'll have to take him back for treatment."

I stared at Archer. "Back where? Mr. Shaw's locked up, and Ringo doesn't have anything even close to ID or the kind of papers he'd need in a hospital. And that's if we're even safe at Elian Manor, which I'm not convinced of."

Connor looked stunned. "I just assumed any one of us could go back any time if something went wrong. But you're right. None of us is really safe at home right now."

Archer looked thoughtful. "I suppose, in the worst case scenario, you could take him to the Missus. But you'd have to go back to before he was born."

"I guess she wouldn't freak out too badly about me just showing up before I've ever met her, since it's basically what I did with you and Mom when the cellar collapsed. But I can do a lot of the plant medicine now, so I'll only take him if he starts to infect."

The river was so dark and quiet that being on a boat in the middle of it felt like I imagined the world did to Archer when he slept. I had tried to wake him from his daytime slumber before, and it truly seemed like he just wasn't there. Like he had departed his body and his soul had gone wandering. I knew there were people who didn't believe Vampires had a soul, which was ridiculous. The thing that made them Vampires was cell-death suspension, so to say they were soulless would be to say the soul was cellular. It was one of the few things in life I took on faith – the idea of a soul being something sort of infinite. As if souls could, and did, go on even after the body died.

I snickered at the philosophical conversation I was having with myself, and I could feel Archer's eyes on me.

"Just debating the existence of the soul."

His soft laughter whispered on the air. "Some of the deepest conversations I've ever had happened just before dawn."

I leaned my head against him and settled in, feeling his muscles ripple with very pull of the oars. "Like what?"

He chuckled. "You want a story?"

"Yes, please." The motion of the boat on the river and the nearness of Archer were making me sleepy.

"Who, besides us, is crazy enough to stay up this late?" Connor was tired, too. His voice was heavy and fading fast.

"Well, during the war there was Ravi. We had the night shift, and since even the enemy had to sleep sometimes, there was very little code breaking to do from two to five a.m."

"Code breaking? You mean you were at Bletchley Park?" I forgot Connor hadn't been with us when Archer discussed his experiences during World War II.

"It was one of my favorite jobs. And Ravi – even then he was deeply interested in history. We had long discussions about how civilizations became technological first-world cultures or stayed backward third-world cultures, always on the brink of starvation."

"That's easy," Connor said. "It had to do with geography. If food and shelter were easy to get, people had time to develop art and innovation. If they lived in a desert, or in extreme temperatures that made food scarce, life was all about trying to survive." His confidence made me smile, and I was content to just lie back and listen.

"You're very wise, Master Edwards, for one so young," Archer responded. "But now take that a step further and it gets more complicated. What if you apply the same principle to individual people? Compare those for whom money, food, and shelter are easy to those who have to struggle for every meal and work endless jobs just to keep shelter over their heads. Do the innovators come from hardship, or from ease?"

"I think some of the more interesting people I know came from some pretty harsh childhood experiences."

"What makes them interesting?"

I loved this conversation Archer and Connor were having. To my tired brain it was like being lulled to sleep by classical music – lyrical, complex, fascinating, and ultimately, soothing.

"An interesting person learns how to deal with the hard stuff constructively. They tend not to fold under pressure or stress, and they can usually laugh at the small stuff. They also value the intangible things more, like family and friendships and loyalty because they can't be bought, they have to be earned."

"What about the privileged people you know. Are any of them interesting?"

"Yeah, the ones who aren't defined by what they have. Adam and Ava are totally interesting, even though they take monthly trips to Paris and live in a huge townhouse."

I thought I could feel Archer's smile. "It seems to me, Connor, that it's the people who haven't allowed their circumstances to define them - the ones who choose their own paths, regardless of what's come before – who interest you."

Connor thought about that for a long moment. "I had to think about who my friends are, and yeah, you're definitely right. Ringo obviously came from nothing, but he soaks up information like a sponge. You came from money, and you're the best educated guy I know, but you got attacked by a Vampire. And Saira pretty much raised herself with no dad, no place to call home, and no clue as to who her family really was."

"What about you, Connor? What makes you so interesting?"

Connor laughed a little, but I wasn't sure how much humor there was underneath the surface. "Let's see – dad's dead; mum's family is considered inferior and damaged because of something a distant ancestor didn't actually do; I had to start being the man of the family before I was ten, so I'm far too responsible to be considered "fun" by most kids at school; I'm smart and therefore either a know-it-all or a giant geek to most people; and my best friends are criminals and outlaws. So, take your pick."

"I'm not an outlaw," I mumbled.

"You're totally an outlaw, and when it's the Mongers you're running from, it's cool to be an outlaw."

"Oh. Okay."

"We're here." Archer's whispered tone shifted from conversational, and suddenly both guys became all business, beaching and tying up the boat with quick efficiency. The sky was starting to color with something other than black, and I knew the sun was probably about twenty minutes away from full rise. In the dim darkness I was able to make out a little of the landscape. It looked pastoral, like literally, a pasture. We were walking through wild grass across fairly even terrain.

I whispered to Archer, "Does anyone live here?"

"As far as I can tell, no. They've brought cattle over here to graze, so people do come, but I didn't see any signs of permanent habitation."

There were a couple of small trees giving some variation to the landscape, but no buildings. "Where will you sleep?"

Archer had said the sun on his skin felt like radiation burns might – he could survive it, but it wouldn't be pleasant. "There's a lean-to for storing hay, and a cloak draped over me should make up for any deficiencies in its shade. Maybe you can make sure I'm still in deep shadows when you wake up so I don't spend the next few days walking around like a Chernobyl victim?"

He said it so casually, but I had the feeling it cost him a lot to need my help. "Of course." But then I remembered and wrinkled my nose. "We'll have to be under your cloak though, mine is covered in Ringo's blood."

"Charlie rinsed it and it's hanging up to dry."

We were approaching a big tree, and under its heavy branches was a sort of shepherd's lean-to hut. There were bales of hay near the open side, and behind them was a space that seemed fairly well-protected. Charlie looked like she had just sat up and was blinking herself awake when we entered the lean-to. Ringo was still asleep on a padding of loose hay next to her.

"How is he?" Archer whispered to Charlie as he bent down to check Ringo's head for fever.

"'E's not stirrin'. I keep checkin' 'e's breathin' though, and 'is temperature seems good."

Archer shifted over so I could crouch next to them. Ringo's skin was cool to the touch and his breathing was deep; he was just really deeply asleep. I didn't think ex-thieves ever slept so well. "His leg is still bound?"

"The cloth wrappin' ye had in yer bag was clean, and it's well packed with yer salve after 'is lordship stitched it closed."

Archer winced. "It's Archer. I haven't been a lord in a very long time."

Charlie's chin tipped a little higher, and she said proudly, "Well, yer 'is lordship to my lad, so ye are to me, too."

I smiled at her in the darkness. My lad. I liked it. I reached across Ringo to squeeze her hand quickly. "C'mon guys, let's get some sleep in while we can. We'll need some daylight to scout the Hôtel de Sens in case Bishop Wilder really is there."

Charlie nodded and settled back down next to Ringo. She put one hand on his arm, but otherwise slept as close to him as was physically possible without actually touching. Connor curled up, half-seated, against a bale of hay and was asleep in maybe thirty seconds, tops. Archer spread part of his cloak on the hay for us to lie on and wrapped the rest of it over us like a blanket. He pulled me in close to him, my back to his front, and draped his arm across my hip possessively. His other arm cushioned my head, and I settled back into him. When the others' breathing had deepened, he whispered into my ear.

"It's just you and Connor later today in the Marais."

He was right, and it was the first time I'd actually thought it through. Ringo was out, Charlie had to stay with him, and Archer would be down until sunset. And if Wilder was at the Hôtel de Sens, sunset was when he would rise, too.

"Yeah." I knew how much he hated to go down during the day because it meant he couldn't be with me.

"He might not want to admit it, but he'll need you to watch his back. He's responsible, but he doesn't have the experience surviving that you have."

That surprised me. I hadn't expected Archer to be more worried about Connor than about me, and I liked it.

"He can always turn Wolf if he has to run."

"They have some firearms in this time. If they see a lone wolf in Paris now, they'll kill it on sight."

181

I tried to put myself in the Parisian's shoes. If I saw a wolf running through the streets, especially after all the children who'd been taken, I'd probably kill it too.

Which reminded me that I hadn't told Archer what Connor and I had learned in the woods. "By the way, Jehanne is Joan of Arc." I heard his breath catch. "She was captured by the English outside of Orléans and only escaped from irons when she was finally able to Shift into her Wolf."

His silence lasted a long time.

"So, time has split."

"We've known that since we saw the old book."

"True but we weren't so close to the split before."

"It's not really what we came here for." I tried to believe that, really I did. But even as I said it out loud, I knew I was lying.

Archer chuckled. "So you'd step over a fallen child to chase the purse-snatcher?"

"You know I wouldn't."

He kissed my hair. "I know you wouldn't."

"I don't like her."

"It's hard to like someone who would lead wolves into Paris to kill people."

"Connor told her she couldn't bring them back into the city. She didn't like it, and some of her wolves started coming at me. He had to go dominant Wolf on them to get them to back off."

Archer's hand stopped its absent-minded stroking of my hip. "So they believe you're his mate."

I turned to face him, surprised. "Wait, how do you know that's what he had to do?"

He frowned. "Our estate was surrounded by woods. As a boy, if I wanted to wander I had to know the rules of the wildlife in whose territory I ran. Pack hierarchy is very well-known to farmers and their sons."

I was silent for a moment, absorbing the idea that it could possibly bother him. "She basically accused me of witchcraft for being with both of you."

"And how did young Connor deal with all of this?"

"Like an embarrassed fourteen-year-old with too much responsibility." I faced him and wrapped my arm around his waist. "Does this bother you?"

Archer exhaled, closed his eyes, then finally smiled tiredly. "The caveman in me doesn't care for his claim, and the caretaker in me is concerned that he's so used to being responsible he's in danger of losing the joy and freedom of being young."

I couldn't help the quiet scoff that slipped out. "When's the last time you got to feel joy and freedom?"

I felt his smile. "Every time I hold you in my arms."

LéON

A hand gripped me tightly, and I woke up with a gasp. Charlie hovered above my face with a finger to her lips and a terrified expression in her eyes. I sat up, carefully disentangling Archer's dead-weight arms from around me, and emerged out from under the heavy cloak I tugged over him more completely. A tiny part of my brain vaguely wondered what it would be like to spend a night wrapped in arms that moved, with breathing that changed, and even restless movement that woke me up.

Charlie's whisper was so quiet I had to lip-read to understand her. "There's someone out there."

Awesome. Nothing like starting the day out with a hit of adrenaline. The sun was sort of out behind puffy clouds, and high in the sky. It was probably around noon, and there was no way Archer could wake now. I looked over at Connor – he was sleeping the zombie-sleep of a growing teenaged boy – and Ringo … I'd deal with Ringo later.

I crept out of the lean-to and squinted into the daylight. The tree we were under was one of a couple big, old linden trees dotting the fields, and near the closest one was a youngish-looking guy, maybe about nineteen or twenty, talking to a cow.

Yep. Talking to it.

He had a big brush in his hand and was grooming the thing like it was a horse, brushing down its sides, smoothing his hand over her flanks – she was definitely female given the size of her udders – and murmuring to her as he worked.

A couple other cows stood nearby munching on grass, only vaguely interested in the guy and what he was up to. He seemed fairly tall for the times; maybe not as tall as me, but close, with a hard, lean build that moved easily. His dark hair was messy but looked clean, and even across the field his chiseled features were all edges and planes, kind of like an awkward-looking runway model.

The guy did a final sweep of the brush down the cow's side, and then sat himself on a rock at udder height. I realized the cow was positioned perfectly for this natural stool, and when the guy reached behind him for an earthenware jug I hadn't noticed before, I knew.

"He just seduced the cow into giving up her milk."

I'd actually seen farmers milking cows – there were several farms around Elian Manor, and one of the wives made cheese that Millicent used to send me to pick up for her – but I'd never seen anyone sweet-talk a cow before he milked her. A California slogan about happy cows came to mind, and I shook my head at myself. California wouldn't exist as a state for another four hundred years.

"I never 'ad milk fresh from a cow before. Is it good?" Charlie asked.

"Yeah, it is. Creamier than you'd expect, and warm from the cow's body, which is weird. But it's good."

I looked at the wistful expression on Charlie's face, and I knew she was hungry. We all were, and somehow I needed to be the provider for my small band of teenaged guys and a wisp of a girl who had spent most of her young life with not enough to eat.

"Where are the bags? I need to find something to trade for milk." I whispered so I didn't draw attention to us, but also so I didn't wake the guys. I thought Charlie and I might be able to handle this okay by ourselves, and I was sick of the language barrier putting me in a secondary position in conversations.

She handed me Ringo's bag, and I rifled through it. I had no idea what anything was worth in this time, and I didn't want to make myself a target for thieving if I looked like I had too much, so I tucked a pencil and some rolled-up paper in one pocket of my tunic, and a pair of old spectacles wrapped in an embroidered linen handkerchief in the other. I also had my daggers strapped to my thighs just in case.

I felt all kinds of badass with daggers.

Charlie was still just wearing her fifties-style dress, which wasn't as big a problem as her bare legs were, so I took out the longest pair of socks I had and gave them to her to put on. Because she was so small, they reached to her knees and looked like tights under the dress. Fortunately it was a simple gray dress and not something with bright flowers printed on it, so she looked only a little different than the rest of us in our tunics and tight pants.

When we were both ready, I shot her a quick, bright smile before slipping out of the lean-to. The Abercrombie-model guy had his back to us as he milked the cow, so I directed our trajectory to approach him from the side. Mostly so we didn't give away that we'd slept in the lean-to, but also because I didn't want to startle him … or the cow.

The closer we got to Abercrombie, the more interesting-looking he got. He had olive-toned skin and a sharp, aquiline nose. His cheekbones were high, and his eyes were rimmed with long, dark lashes. We got close enough that I could hear him humming to the cow before he finally looked up to see us.

A slight widening of his eyes was his only reaction, and I was impressed at his self-control.

"Bonjour." That was about the limit of my French, but I said it with a passable accent.

He smiled warily and returned the greeting.

Now I had no choice but to speak in English, and I used my hands to pantomime what I wanted. "We'd like to trade for some milk." My hands went into my pockets and he flinched, so I brought the contents of both pockets out slowly. I gestured to the milk jug he had almost filled, then pantomimed a trade. He got it.

Abercrombie beckoned me closer so he could study the articles in my hands. He gingerly picked up the spectacles and put them on his nose. His eyes widened in surprise as he looked around at the magnified view. Then he touched the fine linen of the handkerchief and seemed to marvel at the thinness of the paper.

Then he put them all back in my hands, and I could feel Charlie's disappointment behind me. He wasn't interested.

Abercrombie said something in French, and Charlie stumbled through a translation.

"I think 'e needs the milk for a sick friend." There was longing in her voice, and he must have heard it, too. He pulled a cup from inside his pack and handed it to Charlie. She was afraid to take it, so then he gestured that I should hold it.

It took two hands to hold the heavy jug of milk, and he carefully poured the creamy drink right to the top of the cup and then spoke to Charlie again.

"He said I should drink this."

"He's right; you should."

I gave Abercrombie a grateful smile over her head and then watched her take a tentative sip of the creamy milk. Charlie gave a tiny gasp, and she took a bigger sip. When she finally pulled the cup away from her mouth, she had a cream mustache and a delighted smile. "Oh. That's good."

I gave Abercrombie a nod, and said the only other French word I knew. "Merci."

He smiled and then turned back to the cow, patted her leg soothingly, and continued his humming and milking.

Charlie finished the milk in another gulp and then carefully placed the empty cup on his pack before backing away.

Watching him work, I became fascinated with the sharp edges of the guy's face. So I took a couple steps backward, out of range of the cow's legs, and sat on the ground. Charlie looked nervous when I pulled out the pencil and the roll of paper, but she settled herself just behind me so she could see what I was doing, but out of the guy's direct line of sight.

He looked over at me for a surprised moment, and then turned his attention back to his milking. My fingers itched to capture some of those lines in his face on paper, and I thought I might end up with a cubist-type drawing that no one would believe came from an actual face.

I craved the challenge.

The pencil had no eraser, because that little piece of rubber hadn't been invented yet, and was thick enough that I could rub the lead with my fingertip to shade for skin tone. Charlie moved in closer behind me, and I remembered that she was an artist, too — her fantastic drawings of Others had decorated the flat she shared with Ringo in 1889.

The shapes in his face were almost all straight, and I was right, my drawing definitely had a cubist feel. Until I got to the eyes. They were the one soft place to land, and with the heavy lashes framing them they almost looked feminine. Like 1920s-silent-movie-starlet feminine, with fake, stick-on lashes top and bottom.

He only looked over at us once more, to see what I was doing, I guess. And when I was finally done with my sketch, and Charlie let out a little gasp, Abercrombie finally patted the cow's leg, stood up, stretched casually, and came over to see what I'd drawn.

This time I got more than widened eyes from him.

"Oh!" he said, or at least the French-accented version of the sound.

I held it out to him, and he took it gingerly, like he was afraid to get it dirty. His remarkable-looking eyes roved over the whole image, and one hand went up to his nose, a cheek, his jaw, as if he didn't believe it was really him. My heart suddenly twisted in my chest at the memory of Ringo doing the same thing when I'd sketched him the first time.

I motioned as I said the words. "It's for you."

He stared at me, said something with a no in it, and tried to hand it back.

I waved it away. "Thank you for the milk."

He looked stricken and strode back to his pack to get the cup. He handed it back to Charlie, thrust the drawing back in my hands, then refilled the cup carefully from the fresh jug. He said something longer in French this time that made Charlie stare.

"What did he say?"

"I think 'e knows about the lads." Charlie shot a look back toward the shelter.

"Okay, wow. He knew and didn't freak out?"

Charlie snorted. "They're all dead to the world. Not much to be concerned 'bout."

I nodded to her. "The guys could definitely use the protein, but they should stay in there. I don't think this guy is dangerous to us, but I don't want to back him into a corner either."

She nodded, gave Abercrombie a quick smile, and hurried away to the lean-to.

I handed the drawing back to him. "Really, it's for you."

He tried to shake his head no, but his eyes kept darting to the image on the paper. He wouldn't accept it from my hands, so I went to his pack and tucked it inside.

A small tin fell out as I was laying the pack on the ground. I picked it up to replace it and the pungent odors of herbs hit me. I gestured to the tin. "May I?"

He nodded warily, and I opened it. A scent very similar to my green medicine permeated the greasy salve inside. I sniffed it, trying to figure out what made it slightly different than what I made, while Abercrombie watched me carefully. I made him jump when I suddenly called across to the lean-to. "Charlie, can you bring my green medicine with you?"

After a few seconds, she emerged from the lean-to and held up the tin. She was halfway across the small field when Connor eased himself out of the shelter and crouched next to a bale of hay. He was watchful and tense and didn't smile when I waved to him. He really did take responsibility seriously. It was hard to reconcile with the soccer-playing, skateboarding fourteen-year-olds I knew in Los Angeles. I appreciated that he listened to Charlie, though, and didn't venture out of range of the lean-to.

"Is something wrong?" The girl was a little breathless, and after she'd given me the green medicine, Abercrombie refilled her cup to the brim again.

"I think he has a medicine like mine." I handed him my tin, and he opened it curiously.

"I'll be right back," Charlie said, as she darted back toward the lean-to.

The guy tentatively touched the salve I'd made, rubbed his fingers together, and smelled it, then gestured for me to do the same. His salve was very similar to mine – I could smell the willow bark, burdock root, and chamomile straight away. There was lavender, rosemary and eucalyptus, too.

"What's different?" I asked him. The meaning of my question must have been clear enough because he held his hand out for his salve and then smelled them both side-by-side. Then his eyes lit up, and he handed them both to me. He patted the cow on the rump as he went past her to the big linden tree, and then said something that was probably "come here" in French.

He took a small knife out of his pocket and scraped something off the tree bark, then held the knife out to me to examine. I could see Connor tense in the distance, but I ignored him and held out my hand.

"It's tree moss."

"Tree … moss." His attempt at English was awkward and halting, but I appreciated it.

I tapped the tree. "Tree," then the stuff in my hand, "moss. Tree moss."

"Tree moss." This attempt was better. He pointed at the stuff in my hand and said "Usnea."

I knew that word from botany class. "Usnea."

He smiled, and then proceeded to tell me something long and involved that I caught almost nothing of. But Connor was coming over, and I could see Abercrombie tense up.

"Hang on, Connor. The guy has been generous with his milk. He won't trade us the whole jug because he has a sick friend who needs it, but he gave us those cups for nothing. Lose the scowl because I need your help translating."

To his credit, Connor relaxed his face and stopped where he was about ten feet away from us. Then he spoke to Abercrombie behind me.

"What'd you say?" I asked.

"Thanks for the milk."

Right. "Could you ask him what usnea is used for?"

190

"What's that?"

"Just ask him. It's an ingredient in his version of green medicine that's different than mine."

A whole back and forth conversation went on, but I was starting to identify the sounds of individual words that I'd have to ask about later. Connor approached us as they talked, and it didn't seem to bother Abercrombie that he did.

"He said it has antibiotic properties."

"He did not. They didn't know about the germ theory of disease until the mid-1500s."

Connor grinned at me. "You dare lecture me on germ theory? I kicked your butt in that class and you know it. This guy …" He turned to Abercrombie and had a quick conversation. "Léon said his father is a butcher, and his grandmother figured out that the salves she makes keep infections out of the cuts his dad gets when he's butchering animals. The basic idea is solid even if his grandmother can't explain why it works."

I looked at the two salves in my hand, then up at Léon. The name fit him – it was strong and sharp. "Can I borrow a little of this for a wolf bite on my friend's leg?" If it worked with meat pathogens, it might work with carnivore ones, too.

Connor translated automatically, and Léon's eyebrows rose in surprise. He answered Connor, and then nodded to me.

"He's surprised that anyone survived a wolf attack. They've been killing so many in Paris." Connor's voice got tight with anger, and I knew how he felt. "But as long as you leave him some for his friend, you can have what you need."

"Merci." I gave him a quick smile and ran back to the lean-to with the tin of Léon's salve in my hand. Ringo was sitting up against the back wall with Charlie. His color was okay, but he looked really tired, and considering how deeply he'd slept on the hard ground, his body must be fighting pretty hard.

"Good morning. How are you feeling?"

"Like somethin' a cat dragged in, gutted, then left parts around fer ye t' step in." Ringo's tone wasn't bitter or cheerful – both of which I could have expected. It sounded flat, and that worried me.

191

"Thanks for that visual. I'll be carrying it around in my head all day." I grimaced theatrically and it got a smile from him, but not more. "I need to unwrap the bandages and check your wound. Can you deal, or do you want Charlie to do it?"

"Saira, don't step lightly 'round me. If ye start 'oldin' back, I'm goin' t' know somethin's wrong, and I'd rather 'ear it straight than wonder."

That sounded more like Ringo, and I smiled at him. "Good, then shift over and give me room to work."

He snorted, but did what he was told, and within a couple of minutes I had the linen bandages unknotted and open. "Archer and I talked about where I could take you if this festered. Not home, because Mr. Shaw is the only doctor I'd trust, and I can't just walk into a pharmacy to get antibiotics without a prescription."

I examined the puckering edges of the wound. The stitching Archer had done was good, under the circumstances, but Ringo's skin was very pale, and the flesh around the stitches was slightly pink.

"The Missus would know just by looking at this how you're doing."

Ringo nodded. "I don't want to go anywhere, but if ye had to move me, I'd go to 'er."

I didn't smell anything, but it hadn't been long enough for a proper infection to set in, and I needed to know whether to cut the stitches open to clean and re-pack the wound. I looked up at Ringo.

"Okay, this might be weird, but I need Connor's Wolf to smell this and make sure there's nothing putrid starting in there."

Ringo winced. "Ye paint a pretty fancy picture yerself. But whatever ye think needs doin' so I don't lose the leg, I ask that ye do it."

I looked at Charlie. "Could you run over to Connor and ask him to bring his Wolf here?"

She gave me a quick smile and took off across the field.

I turned back to Ringo. "You're not going to lose this leg, but I can't have you taking forever to heal either." I glanced at Archer's motionless body. "I need to work with you on the day shift."

He grimaced. "Connor's young, and Charlie's just a slip of a girl." He watched her cross the field. "I think I'm in love with 'er."

"I know."

"Ye do? 'Ow?"

I smiled. "Really? Your eyes track her through a room. You find every excuse in the book to be next to her. And when you actually do let yourself accidentally touch her, it's with so much wonder and awe, it feels … worshipful."

Ringo laughed quietly. "Ye've just described the way 'is lordship is with ye. I suppose it must be love, then."

Did modern guys look at their girlfriends the same way? I thought I should probably watch Adam more carefully when he was with Alex, because if he didn't look at her like she was on a pedestal, someone was going to have to teach him to.

The near-silent padding of feet was the only warning I had that Connor was coming, and I made room for the huge silver Wolf to come into the shelter next to me. Ringo looked up at him with fearless appreciation. "God, yer a stunnin' beast, Connor. What I wouldn't give to do what ye can do."

Connor's Wolf huffed in something that sounded like appreciation, and he bent his head down to the unwrapped wound on Ringo's leg. A look of concentration hit the Wolf's eyes as he smelled first the flesh, and then the bandage. He gave Ringo a slight nudge before ambling back out from under the lean-to.

"Does it 'urt, to Shift?" There was whispered awe in Ringo's voice.

"I'm not really sure I can describe it well because I was freaking out a little when it happened to me." I took a deep breath and tried to form it into words. "I felt like my body became a thousand fragments of light that opened up and then rearranged themselves into the Lion. It felt amazing and powerful and freaking scary all at once. And then when it was done, I felt like I had settled into a part of myself I'd never connected with before, and it was like … coming home after being away a really long time."

"My favorite part is the senses." Connor was pulling his tunic over his head as he re-entered the shelter. "Everything is brighter and stronger, scents have texture, and flavors are almost colorful. I feel like I can hear a whisper a hundred miles away, and darkness just makes it more fun."

"You're kind of a poet, young Edwards." I grinned at him.

His smile dimmed a little as he turned back to Ringo. "It's not infected, yet. But it's not perfectly healthy tissue either."

I nodded and opened Léon's tin. "Okay, I just needed to know if I had to cut the stitching open to clean it again, or if I could just slather this stuff on and hope it draws whatever's in there out."

"I vote no cutting. I can help keep a nose on it tonight and tomorrow, and if it does turn into an infection, I can tell before he gets feverish."

"You're kind of handy to have around, Wolf."

He grinned. "Remember that next time you need to Clock somewhere."

"Make it through this one unscathed and I'll consider it"

He left the lean-to with a chuckle as I coated Ringo's wound with Léon's medicine. I filled Ringo in on what we knew about the butcher's son as I re-wrapped his leg with fresh linens. I saved the old linen to boil, just in case we ever lit a fire or found a pot. I'd gotten pretty conservative with things since I started Clocking places where I didn't have money.

I finished the knot on his bandage and rubbed the residual salve into my hands. "I need to return this, and then Connor and I have to get to Paris."

"Do ye know the way back to the Marais?"

I nodded. "I think so. I spent a lot of time studying the modern map of Paris, so I have a fair idea of distance at least."

"Bring me back a croissant, would ye?"

I laughed and slung a bag of stuff to trade over my shoulder as I left the lean-to. "I'll do my best."

De Rais

The day had actually warmed up enough to be uncomfortable, and I wished I could take off the tunic that allowed me to stay vaguely male-looking. Jehanne had recognized me as female, which I'm sure was because she was one too, but I didn't think Léon had. His eyes had rested easily on mine and Connor's, but he wouldn't do more than steal quick glances at Charlie. They hadn't been looks of desire, more like embarrassment at having to address her at all.

Connor and I did some trading at a food market stall a few blocks away from where we stashed the boat, then took the bread and cheese right back to the island. Léon was gone by then too, and I assumed he'd gone to bring the milk to his sick friend.

So, it was late afternoon by the time Connor and I could head back to the Hôtel de Sens.

The city bustled with people, but it was so totally different from the way I'd always imagined Paris to be that I might have blown the fantasy of that city for good. The stench was bad. Maybe even worse than London had been in Tudor times. Granted, I hadn't spent a lot of time wandering around greater London then, and maybe the area just outside the Marais was the Parisian equivalent to Whitechapel, but the city was like a cobblestoned version of hell.

I hadn't noticed it the night before, probably because everyone was inside, hiding from the threat of wolves. But in the light of day, with pockmarked, filthy, toothless people hunched in crooked doorways, and children wearing nothing more than a long shirt and a layer of dirt lying listlessly beside them, this place was a nightmare.

"And I thought Bedlam was bad." I said it under my breath, but Connor's ears were sharp, even in human form.

"The rag hanging on that wall just moved." His voice was low too, and I realized it could be very bad for us if we were heard speaking English.

I followed his gaze to a bundle of dirty rags, and then gasped. "That's not a rag, that's a baby!" My whisper carried further than I meant it to. Connor shushed me sharply, but I was still incredulous.

"Why would anyone hang a baby on the wall?"

It wasn't dead, it had definitely moved, but the poor thing was swaddled so tightly it was in a stupor. It didn't look older than about a year, and the person I assumed must be the mother was sitting in the doorway peeling potatoes.

"What do you think would happen if I went over there and pulled the kid down?" It was hard to keep whispering. Connor looked as appalled as I felt, and I remembered his little sister had been a baby when he took over as man of his family.

"I'd applaud, and everyone else would jump you." He was looking around at the suspicious glares that were starting to come our way.

"We could take them." I was suddenly feeling very sure of the sword at my belt and the daggers under my tunic.

"So, we'd murder the parents to punish them for hanging their kid up like a side of beef?"

"Ugh. I hate it when you're right."

"Yeah, I'm not too happy about it myself," Connor grumbled.

"I'd feel better about it if I didn't imagine the hook she has inside the house, too."

We had reluctantly turned away and were headed back toward the square outside the Hôtel de Sens when people began to yell. Somewhere, a street or two away, a panic was growing, but it was in French, and even Connor was struggling to understand the words, which he translated and editorialized for me.

"Le loup. The wolf. Crap!"

Neither of us really stopped to think, we just ran.

Two streets away we found the crowd in the square. Women were hurrying away with screaming children under their arms, while men arrived carrying knives and meat cleavers. Suddenly, Jehanne was in front of Connor, with words tumbling out in a panic. He turned to me with a wild look on his face.

"She says three of the pack have gone rogue and are out of control. We have to Shift and drive them out of the city."

The people's panic was contagious, and I could feel it settle into my chest where it raised my voice and constricted my breath. "You can't Shift. They'll kill you, too!"

"Saira, we'll get to a less populated area, but we have to do this. We have to make these wolves an example, or I'll lose control of the pack and they'll keep killing."

Jehanne said something in rapid-fire French, and Connor yanked off his bag, unfastened his sword belt, and ripped the tunic off over his head. He dumped all three in my hands. "I have to go."

"Wait—"

Before I could finish the thought, he and Jehanne were off and running, weaving their way through the crowd to get out of the square.

"Crap!"

A big guy in a blue velvet tunic stood a few yards away from where Jehanne had been, and he looked over at my exclamation. I shifted my eyes and ducked my head away to disguise the fact that the English word had come from me, and I suddenly felt conspicuous with all of Connor's gear in my hands. I needed to find someplace to stash it so I could go after them. I hated the idea that he would be running around Paris in his Wolf suit during broad daylight.

I ducked down a side alley to get out of the main square, and I felt someone follow me. Whoever it was didn't make a sound, but that was even more nerve-wracking because it meant he or she was trying to be stealthy. I lengthened my stride to get out of the confines of the alley as fast as possible, and had just made it to the street at the other end when I felt a hand on my shoulder.

How did he get so close? Why didn't I hear him approach?

"You are the one Jehanne calls Saira?" The voice was deep, and thick with a French accent. But it spoke in English. The panic that had gripped my chest loosened the tiniest bit with the knowledge the voice knew Jehanne, and I turned slowly to face the English speaker.

It was Blue Velvet, from the square. He was tall and probably topped me by about five inches. His beard and hair were so black they were almost blue with the reflected color of his tunic, and he looked rich enough to pay someone to keep him clean and well-groomed. Not your average ruffian, and I relaxed a fraction more.

"Who are you?"

"I am Gilles de Montmorency-Laval, Baron de Rais. Jehanne told me to look out for Saira. You are her?"

I nodded and was about to ask how he knew Jehanne.

Except he punched me.

In the solar plexus, so hard the breath flew out of me at hurricane speed, and I dropped to the cobblestone street like a brick. I couldn't breathe. Could not put air in my lungs to save my life.

My mouth was open, and I heard my futile gasps for breath from a distance, as if I wasn't in my body anymore. It hurt way too much to be inside my skin, so I wasn't surprised I'd taken a powder.

Still no breath.

Nope.

Nothing.

My brain was starting to starve for oxygen. My eyes were open, but the only thing in my swimming vision were a pair of leather and cork boots. I watched with detachment as the right foot drew back and then launched at my ribs. Really?

I dimly noticed the sound of ribs cracking before pain exploded like white-hot fire over the airless meat my lungs had become.

I couldn't understand why I was still conscious. I couldn't even breathe enough to cry out. I lay on the filthy stones with my mouth open trying to suck air like a beached guppy. My arms were clutched around my middle, but some small, rational part of my brain knew he'd break one if he kicked me again. Didn't matter. I couldn't unlock them anyway.

Distantly, so distantly I thought I might be dreaming, I heard someone call my name.

The leather and cork boots paused, as if Blue Velvet were debating another kick for good measure. But there was another shout, closer now, that I swore was Connor yelling for me.

I didn't want him to find me if Blue Velvet stuck around. The bastard was big and strong and would wipe the floor with Connor. Mercifully, the boots strolled away from my gasping body and seemed to saunter down the alley to the street.

"Saira!"

Finally, a slip of air made its way through flattened lungs and released as something vaguely squeaky.

"Saira." Less panicked, and closer. In the alley and running toward me. Thank God for Wolf ears.

Connor dropped to his knees beside me and gathered my head into his arms. He tried to pick me up, but the squeak turned sharp when a fierce pain whipped through my ribcage.

"Ribs." I managed a whisper, and he froze.

"Who did this? What happened to you?" Connor was crying, and my heart hurt more than even my lungs at the pain and fear in his voice. "I'm so sorry I left you. I'm so sorry." His tears dripped down his nose and hit my forehead.

"Stop." I had a little more voice in the whisper. A little more air in my lungs. "Stop crying. Not your fault." Connor's terror was subsiding with every word I spoke, so I tried a couple more. "Jehanne sent him." That did it. Fear turned to anger.

"She led me away on a hunt for wolves that were long gone, just to make sure you were alone. I'm such an idiot!"

More air seeped in, enough for a smile attempt. "You're not an idiot. Just did a dumb thing."

"Same thing." Now he sounded bitter.

"Different." I struggled to sit up, and he helped me find a way around the shooting pain of the cracked rib. At least I hoped it was just cracked. But breathing was easier when I sat, and I finally filled my lungs to something resembling normal capacity.

"It's not okay to call yourself an idiot." I wheezed a little when I took the next breath, but at least it was enough to talk. "What if Logan heard you, or Sophia. You're their big brother. They idolize you, and if you say you're an idiot, what does that make them for loving you?"

I watched the self-recrimination seep into something thoughtful.

"We all do dumb things, Connor. We're only idiots if we don't learn from them."

His bark of laughter held no humor in it. "Never leave your wingman, right?"

I smiled at him and pushed back a piece of hair that had flopped over his eye. "Something like that. Your penance is that you have to help me up, and then carry everything back to the island."

I held my arms up for him to pull me, and then whimpered when he did. My ribs hurt, and my gut felt like I'd been hit with a log.

It took a few steps before I could stand fully upright, and I still wheezed a little when I inhaled too fast. I gave him the rundown of events that led to the sucker punch. He hadn't seen Blue Velvet, either before he went racing away with Jehanne or when he found me in the alley. Connor said she led him through a maze of winding streets, and he never actually Shifted before she just disappeared.

"That chick needs to be paid a visit by a big bad Wolf." Connor was still angry.

"Probably. But we're down to three able bodies at the moment. We can't afford any more battle wounds if we're going after Wilder." I stumbled on an uneven cobblestone. "Ow. Crap. Don't ever get kicked in the ribs, okay?"

I felt like we were moving backwards in our quest to find the Vampire. And I really didn't like having a two-front war on our hands – Jehanne and her Blue Velvet henchman on one side, and Wilder, current whereabouts unconfirmed, on the other. Hopefully the wolves were still under Connor's domination.

"Are you going to need to put in an appearance with the wolves tonight?"

"Probably." He didn't sound concerned. More like resigned.

"You want back-up?"

He looked at me, holding myself gingerly as I stepped carefully to avoid potholes, and grimaced. "Maybe I can get Archer to come along and watch my back. It's not the wolves I'm worried about though, it's the guy with Jehanne. Anyone who hits a woman can be counted on to fight dirty."

Connor had to row us across the Seine River to the island, and I was pretty useless at helping to dock and tie up the boat, too. He slung both satchels, weighted down with a wheel of cheese and a bunch of grapes we had traded red silk embroidery thread for, over his shoulders, and we trudged across the field toward the lean-to. The sun was setting, and I hoped Archer would be awake soon. I didn't feel like being strong for a little while, and he would let me wallow, at least until I'd had enough.

When we arrived at the lean-to, it was empty. But there was a note stuck to one of the hay bales. Charlie had found us a hut, and we should join them on the far end of the island.

I was trying very hard not to cry. I was ready to let someone else take care of me, and even walking the hundred yards across the field was more than I felt capable of.

Archer was outside with an arm-load of wood when he saw us. He must have noticed how I was moving, because he dropped the wood a second later and was sprinting across the field. Before he could gather me into his arms, I held up a hand.

"Cracked rib. Maybe broken."

His eyes searched mine, maybe looking for hurts I wasn't disclosing. "How?"

"Kicked."

He took a step back.

"And punched." Connor's voice was back to morose. "My fault."

Archer stared at him. "You punched her?"

The horror on Connor's face would have been funny if he hadn't been so serious about it. "Clearly not."

"Then it's not your fault." Archer's tone didn't allow for argument, not even from me as he swung me up into his arms and carried me to the thatched-roof hut.

The inside of the hut held two cots slightly wider than twin beds that were strung with rope and cushioned with a thick layer of rushes. They were off the ground, so the insects didn't seem to have made their homes in the dried plant bundles, and I thought that with cloaks to protect against the pokey bits, they might actually be comfortable.

There was another pile of rushes on the ground, and a crude table with a bench pulled up to it. There were even some clay vessels and cups stacked neatly on a shelf.

"What is this place? It looks like someone's home."

"Léon said we could use it." Charlie looked proud of herself.

"Léon?"

"He and his father and uncle come out here for a month each year. They butcher and salt the beef Léon's father sells in his butcher shop. There's a special way they have to do it, which is why it takes so long." Charlie was practically breathless at relaying all that information.

"They're Jewish." Archer had set me down on one of the cots and was gently lifting my tunic over my head.

I looked at him oddly. "How do you know?"

He shook his head. "There's a mezuzah on the doorway." As if that explained everything to the vaguely Christian-by-default chick with no formal religious training. Then he inhaled sharply as he raised the hem of my linen shirt up to reveal my rib cage. His expression froze into a hard mask.

"Who did this to you?"

"He was with Jehanne. She lured Connor away with a made-up wolf emergency, and the next thing I knew, this huge, bearded guy in blue velvet was asking me if I was called Saira."

Archer's teeth and fists were clenched, and it was with effort that he unclenched a hand enough to gently prod for injury. "Did you get his name?"

"Well, he spoke in heavily accented English, which was what got my attention in the first place. But he said his name in full French, so I only caught the beginning and end. Gilles-something-something-Ray."

Charlie gasped. "Baron Gilles de Rais?"

I stared at her. Oh crap. Under all the fancy names he spouted were those, and I suddenly recognized them. "He said it so fast, I didn't realize…"

"That was Bluebeard."

Tom – July, 1429

I drank his blood.

Why do such a self-destructive thing? I asked myself a hundred times before I did it. Because I didn't want to die was the answer every time.

And I was dying.

I barely had enough energy to raise my head without help anymore, and sitting up was nearly impossible. I needed fluid and protein to make blood, so Léon brought me fresh milk when he could. When he came today, he said he met a girl who made a drawing of him. Something broke in me. I couldn't look at him after that, not even when he tried to show me the portrait. If I looked at him I'd tell him everything, and none of those words would ever change what I was, or that I was dying.

My blood filled flasks and tubes along the counters and shelves of Wilder's laboratory. He was drinking it steadily now, and I could feel the Monger in him being refueled with aggression and the urge to destroy.

He wasted my blood, too, and sent flasks flying across the room when he didn't get the Seer's visions he expected. I didn't tell him his rage was proof it was working.

He was gaining my Monger rage. It seemed unleashed in him, as if all the control I'd kept wrapped around it had broken with the pain, and it was angry and vengeful. I had somehow become the focus of my own rage.

The power he wanted was from my Seer blood – my mother's blood. But since Wilder had begun consuming it, he hadn't had a single vision of the future. Not one. I knew this because he had screamed those words at me in a fit of rage, right before he threw his wine glass at my head.

I was unconscious for two hours.

No visions from drinking a Seer's blood. What did it mean? Who the hell cared? Before Wilder grabbed me in that cellar under the Tower of London, I had visions all the time. They had become fugue-Sight, one after the other, always flashes, and full of Mongers. I hadn't had a vision since that night, and I didn't miss them. Sure, it would have been great to See someone coming to rescue me. But that wasn't in my future. I had no future.

But last night Wilder did something stupid.

The vein in my arm was near collapse when he finally drew the goose quill out. The flask was barely half full, and he was furious. He smashed it to the ground, shouting insults at me as if they had any power, as if anything mattered anymore except whether there would be another breath.

The flask shattered, and a piece of flying glass cut the inside of his forearm. I noticed the blood welling there before he did, and I tracked its progress as it rolled down his arm and dripped into a flask of milk Léon had brought from his island. One drop. Two. Three. Barely enough to stain the liquid pink. The fourth drop hit the table, and that's the one he saw.

It sobered him instantly, and he wiped it with his shirt, then went to the far side of the room to tend his wound.

Just then, sounds of banging came from below. It sounded like someone was pounding on the door, and Wilder snarled, "It's not a night for visitors."

What visitors could *you* possibly have? I didn't have the strength to say it, and even the voice in my head was weak. Wilder grabbed one of the flasks of day-old blood from the counter, uncorked it, and slugged it straight from the bottle. He used to pour it in a wine glass and pretend to be civilized. That ended weeks ago as his frustration grew at his lack of Sight.

I hated him with every cell and molecule in my body. That hatred was winning the war with apathy when it came to my survival.

The pounding on the door downstairs persisted, and Wilder finally stalked out of the secret tower room muttering about unwelcome and unwanted guests. My eyes found the flask of milk on the table next to my bed. I hadn't moved without help in days. I didn't know if I still could.

I pulled strength from my bones, from the memory I had of muscles that used to run and climb and jump with Saira and Adam and the Wolf kid. I was good then because I worked at it. I practiced harder than they did. I ran in secret, and at night. The Vampire knew I was training, but he never told Saira he saw me struggle over walls she could fly over, stumble into branches she ducked with ease. I didn't know why he kept my secret, but I was grateful. It took a few months, but eventually I could keep up. I couldn't be left behind when we ran.

It didn't matter in the end, though. No one would ever come for me here, so I was left behind anyway.

Underneath the disappointment I tucked a piece of that strength away, and it's what I drew up into my body to reach for the flask of milk.

It was all excruciating now. And yet I still didn't want to die. My arm came into view, and I almost dropped it again just so I didn't have to see the wounds that didn't close anymore. The wounds were horrific, swollen with pus that burst from the edges of half-formed scabs and dripped down my arms like snake venom. I was revolting to look at, and my conviction faltered. What was left to save? But a spark of will forced my arm farther, out beyond the edge of the bed, toward the table where the flask sat.

The flask into which the Vampire's blood had dripped.

The trembling started as my fingers reached out. I worried about the flask, about being able to hold it. My hand didn't want to close, but I forced my fingers into claws, and they wrapped loosely around the neck of the flask. The shaking was worse, and I was afraid I would tremble the milk right to the floor. I needed this to work. I needed to find the strength to pick up the flask.

Slowly, excruciatingly, I drew the flask across the table toward me. There was no strength left – nothing but will and fear put motion in my arm. And when it was at the edge, I had to close my fingers around the smooth glass and lift. It wasn't a grip, it was a flinch that held as I drew the flask to my mouth.

I was shaking again, and when I got the flask to my chest I almost dropped it. But I held on, and somehow managed to tilt my head up to put it to my mouth. A splash of milk slid down my throat and I forced myself to drink as much as I could swallow. Three drops of the Vampire's blood had tinged the milk pink, and I prayed it was enough.

That's a lie. I didn't pray. I didn't believe a God could love me and leave me here to die like this. I willed it to be enough, and my will was the only thing I had faith in any more.

I drank the monster's blood.

Jehanne

"The guy's a monster." Even breathing hurt my ribs. "But he's a well-known one. We can't just skewer de Rais in a dark alley somewhere or we'll be messing with the time stream."

Ringo laughed at me. "Skewer 'im in a dark alley? Aren't ye a bold one now?"

"If she doesn't, I will." Archer had finished his poking and prodding and was surveying the damage to my mid-section. "I don't think they're broken, but there's definitely bruising of the muscle tissue."

"Last time I broke my ribs, I got a cough that wouldn't end. 'Urt like the devil, it did. Time before that was alright, though. No cough." Ringo was stretching out his leg to test the muscles. He winced slightly, but lifted it higher than I expected.

"So, your point, besides the fact you either fight or fall way too much, is I'll be fine?"

He moved his foot gingerly. "Yeah, ye'll live. Can't say the same for the baron though."

I looked sharply at him. "We can't go after de Rais."

Connor spoke up. "The guy killed hundreds of kids."

I was going to launch into an argument about temporal ethics, and my head was already exploding. I lay back on the cot and surrendered. "Archer, please tell them why the baron can't die yet."

"Sure, he can."

I closed my eyes. "Not you, too."

"I know why you think we can't dispose of him; because what if, among those two hundred or more kids he killed, there had been another Mozart, or another Einstein?"

Connor drawled, "Or another Hitler?"

"Shut up. You're not helping," I snarled at Connor.

Archer continued. "The future could be altered dramatically if someone extraordinary is among the kids who live because de Rais was skewered in a dark alley before he could get to them."

I was nodding to agree with Archer, and was about to say something, but he cut me off.

"Except this isn't the right history."

I stared at him, even as Ringo and Connor nodded. How did they get it and I didn't?

Archer smiled grimly at me. "Joan of Arc did not lead the armies to victory in Orléans. We're on the new time line, not the original. We're exempt from anomalies on this one since it isn't supposed to exist anyway."

"You're going to hunt down de Rais because nothing we do matters on this time line?"

"We know we need to fix the split. So, yes. This time line is a throwaway."

"Why? Why do *we* need to fix it? Why isn't there some time-cop Clocker squad from another century that fixes time-splits?" I was being whiny because I hurt, and all I wanted to do was curl up and nurse my wounds. I already knew this answer, I just didn't want to look at it right now.

"We found it, so it's our responsibility."

Connor nodded. "In our house, whoever finds the dog puke cleans it up, because if Mum spots it and knows you were just there, your life is basically forfeit."

I couldn't help the laugh, but I wasn't feeling humorous. "Well, then by that logic, what the hell are we doing here? Why even bother trying to find Wilder on this time line because killing him now wouldn't matter to the right future anyway?"

All the air got sucked out of the room and into four sets of lungs that gasped in unison.

"Bollocks." Ringo quietly swore. I liked the American version of that particular curse word better, but it would do.

I looked around at my friends. Their expressions said they already knew what I was going to say next, and none of them liked it.

"I guess we're going to Orléans."

The time streams had split because of something that happened at Orléans, so we had to go there if we wanted to prevent the split from happening and get back on the time stream with the correct history. The problem was, none of us had ever been to Orléans, and the only image I'd ever seen was in the old book at Elian Manor. The medieval painting of soldiers laying siege outside the city walls was a two-dimensional view right in the middle of a battle scene. Not something to trust Clocking to, and certainly not the place I wanted to land. After a quick discussion, we decided the safest way to get ourselves to Orléans was to travel there over land, pick a location where we could Clock safely, and then go back to the specific date from there.

Safe was entirely relative, of course, considering what could happen to travelers in these times, but I'd rather take my chances with highwaymen and thieves than getting lost *between*.

Archer took off in the boat to find out the best way to travel and promised to return with food for everyone. I knew he was probably hungry himself, but we had a tacit agreement not to discuss his dietary requirements.

The rest of us talked through whatever we knew of the battle of Orléans, Joan of Arc, and Gilles de Rais until we were going around in circles. When there was nothing new left to hammer out, my friends began to settle in for the night. We all knew that whatever rest we could get now might be the last consistent sleep we got for a while.

I'd been asleep for maybe three hours when I heard a scuffing noise outside the hut. I sat up without groaning, which was something, but I felt every clench of muscle in my mid-section like a fresh punch. Ringo's eyes found mine in the dark.

"It's Archer," I whispered to him. I don't know why I knew that, except I was developing a sense for him, sort of predator mixed with mate, that let me feel his presence.

"'E's not alone."

"No." I could hear the extra footsteps, too. Ringo sat up, but I knew getting up would be out of the question. "I'll go see."

I stifled the squeak of pain that threatened with standing, but once I was up, breathing seemed easier. And my legs worked fine, so I moved only a little gingerly to the door.

There was a loose wood slat to one side with just enough space to see through. Archer was there, with his back to me, doing something to whoever was with him. His shoulders jerked, and he reached behind his neck to massage the muscles there. Which meant he was tense, and that didn't bode well for the person in front of him.

He must have had the same sixth sense as I did, because he turned quickly to me and whispered, "Come."

I opened the door and slid outside into the cool night. There was just enough moonlight to see clearly, and I was surprised to find Jehanne standing in front of Archer.

She looked pissed.

Her hands were tied in front of her – tightly with linen, so even if she Shifted, her Wolf's paws couldn't slip out like they'd done with the English irons – and there was a blindfold pushed up on her forehead. Archer must have just uncovered her eyes.

She saw me and spat at my feet. "Putain."

Even I knew what that meant. I was working up to a nasty comeback when Archer reached out to touch her on the arm. She suddenly leapt backward with a look of white-faced terror, and she attempted to cross herself with her bound hands.

"What did you just do?"

"Reminded her she's not the biggest badass of all." He used one of my favorite words to describe himself, and it made me fall a little harder in love. I struggled to hold back a smile.

"How?" I asked very sweetly.

"I touched her."

I knew that's what he'd done. And I also knew Jehanne had just seen something in Archer's eyes that said he'd kill her without a second thought. I had seen it before, directed at my least favorite Monger on the planet, Seth Walters, and that look was definitely on the list of things I didn't want to meet in a dark alley.

Speaking of dark alleys, Archer had a very healthy-looking glow to his skin that was not just from moonlight. "You found the Baron, didn't you?"

"Yes."

Right. And that was all he had to say on the matter.

The door opened behind me, and Connor shuffled out to lean against the door frame. His expression darkened when he saw Jehanne, and he spoke to her in French.

"He's telling her that no God would condone her personal vendetta against you, and that by threatening you she harms herself."

I looked at Connor in wonder as he stared at Jehanne in the darkness.

"Pretty deep for a kid."

"I haven't been one of those for a long time." He hadn't taken his eyes off her, and finally she flinched away from his gaze and looked at the ground.

"Right. Now that the pissing contest is won, we need information." Archer smiled briefly at Connor and then launched into French.

Connor looked impressed at what Archer was saying. "He's asking what went wrong at Orléans. What did she expect to work that failed, as if the English had known what was coming?"

Evidently, Jehanne was as surprised by the direct questions as I was. She seemed to think about her answer, and for the first time, spoke without the guarded anger I'd seen since we'd first met. Connor translated her answer for me as she gave it.

"It was my dream to see our Frenchmen scale those walls and knock the filthy English off the battlements."

Archer said something in return, and again, Connor was impressed.

"He's asking about the visions God sent. What happened that was different than what she had seen in those dreams?"

Her answer came with much more certainty. "The bridge. God showed me how to fill a boat with fire and set it alight under the bridge where the English soldiers crossed to Orléans. I saw thousands fall into the water and drown in their armor, and I knew it was how we could defeat them. But somehow they found the fireboat and moved it out into open water, and we were lost."

"What day did you set the fireboat?" I understood Archer's question even before Connor translated.

"Saturday, the seventh of May. I was shot with an arrow to the shoulder that day."

Archer continued questioning her about her visions, but it seemed that God stopped talking to her after that day, which had begun with scaling the Tourelle, a tower in the defensive wall around the city, and had ended with the failed fireboat explosion under the bridge.

May the seventh. That was the day history changed.

Of course, landing on a specific day in the middle of war was going to be like hitting a spinning target with a pea-shooter during a hurricane, but at least we had a date.

Archer finished his questions and then turned to both of us. "Anything I missed?"

"Were there any Clockers among the soldiers she fought at Orléans?"

He translated my question without using the word "Clocker," and she looked at me oddly.

"What is a traveler in time?"

Uh, okay. I tried a different tack. "What other Immortal Descendants have you known?"

When he translated that, she looked startled, and then suspicious.

"God is the only immortal I know, and his son, Jesus, the only descendant."

I restrained the eye roll and took a breath. "What about other Shifters? Which parent did she get that skill from?"

Her eyes narrowed when Archer translated. "If you mean the Wolf, that is a gift from God. Neither of my parents has been deemed worthy of an honor such as He has bestowed upon me, nor have they heard His Word."

Connor spoke English in an undertone. "So, basically, she's a Shifter, maybe with Seer mixed in, with no idea who she really is."

"Looks like it." I would have been surprised if my own experience hadn't been exactly that. A mixed-blood Clocker/Shifter with no idea what I could do or who I was until just last year.

"You'd think you might ask a couple questions if you suddenly went Wolf, though, right?"

"Not if it's a gift from God and you've been having visions all your life." Archer was still watching her closely, and it seemed to make her nervous. Good.

I turned to him. "When are we leaving?"

"Just before dawn. I've booked passage for us on a riverboat going south to Montargis. From there we'll go on horseback the rest of the way."

Jehanne had been listening avidly, despite the conversation being in English, and she spoke to Archer. Connor was appalled at her words, and only filled me in when I elbowed him.

"She wants to go with us."

"What? Why?"

"She thinks she lost her access to God when she lost the battle of Orléans." He was scowling as Jehanne spoke. Personally, I didn't think God worked that way, but that was the least of my arguments against her joining us.

When Jehanne was done, Archer turned to me. "I don't want her with us any more than you do."

"It's that obvious, is it?" My tone was loaded with irony.

"I don't trust her, and I can think of a dozen reasons why it's a bad idea."

"Are you kidding? The girl is a complete nutter!" Trust Connor to get to the heart of the matter.

"Quite possibly, and yet she is the only person in our current acquaintance who knows exactly what happened three months ago and, maybe more importantly, what didn't happen."

Archer made a strong point, but the screaming in my head that it was a bad idea just wouldn't shut up. "What's in it for her?"

"She honestly believes she was destined for something, and that she fell from God's grace when she failed."

"Losing the battle of Orléans isn't what made her fall from grace, if you ask me – or any of the kids those wolves have killed." I wasn't giving in on this. Whatever else Jehanne had done, leading a pack of wolves into Paris to feed on Parisians was murder.

Archer looked at me a long moment, then turned and spoke to her in French. Her expression tightened, and then she answered me directly, with Archer translating as she spoke.

"I am responsible for their deaths, it is true. But I gave them a quick end instead of the torture Baron de Rais had planned for each of those children. He had marked every one of them, and I merely directed the wolves to take them before he could."

I took a deep breath. Nothing about what she said made what she'd done okay with me. But Archer murmured something that wasn't her words. "She is telling the truth as she believes it, Saira. The color around her is bright blue."

I met his eyes. "I hate this."

"I know. But I think it's a chance we shouldn't pass up."

"I don't like her."

"Neither does any of us. But I do feel sorry for her. She has Immortal Descendant gifts she knows nothing about, an unfulfilled destiny, and nothing but anger and disappointment left to drive her. It's almost more dangerous to leave her here to cause mayhem than to take her with us."

I looked grimly at Connor, who stared back with a semi-scowl on his face, then at Jehanne. The intensity of her gaze was unsettling, and it startled me when she spoke again.

"She apologizes for her insults. She did not recognize you as our leader when she first met you, and realizes now it was a mistake." Archer's voice had the slightest edge of smirk to it.

"Kiss ass," I whispered under my breath. And then finally, I did indulge in the eye roll I'd been keeping at bay. "What's the worst that could happen?"

Connor stayed outside to sit with Jehanne, mostly to keep watch on her, but also to make sure she recognized his Wolf as dominant over hers. If anything, he was less excited about her coming with us to Orléans than I was. Her ploy to get me beat up by de Rais still chapped him and he had laid into her about it, but he wasn't forgiving himself easily.

Archer filled us in on the travel plans while I attempted some stretches, and Charlie snuggled, half-awake, against Ringo's shoulder to listen in.

"The river boat is owned by a man named Maximillian, who is probably in his late thirties and has been a captain on the river since he was a small boy. His wife, Sophie, travels with him, and they make their living from hauling whatever cargo or passengers they can between Paris and Montargis."

"Is Montargis a big city? I've never heard of it before."

"It's the end of the line for the Loing River, which is as far as you can get into the Loire Valley from Paris on the water."

"Why the river? Why not just get horses or a coach from here?"

Archer included Ringo in his answer. "Because you two have injuries that need to heal, and they won't if you're on a horse or a bumpy road. It takes six days to get to the Loire Valley by boat …"

"Six days?" I don't know why I was so surprised. France was a much bigger country than England, and train schedules had no part in medieval travel.

Archer smiled at my horror. "Six days in which to heal your bodies, grill Jehanne for every bit of information we can get, and maybe learn a little French."

I scowled at him and he laughed. "And here you thought school was out for the summer."

"Oh, I definitely need to learn French – I just hate the idea of being stuck on a boat for six days with that chick."

"I'll be the first one to toss 'er overboard if she so much as blinks funny." Ringo wasn't kidding, and I loved him for it.

I leaned against Archer and felt a kind of peace sweep through me at his touch. "So, what really scared Jehanne when she called me a slut? You didn't show her fangs or anything like that, did you?"

He chuckled. "Nothing quite so stereotypical."

"Then what?"

Ringo spoke up. "'Ye touched 'er, right? Ye passed along a vision."

Archer raised an appreciative eyebrow at Ringo. "Very good. I consulted with Ms. Simpson about Elizabeth Tudor's ability to pass along her visions, and she graciously worked with me to improve my own skill."

"You had a vision?"

He shook his head. "I replayed one."

"Which one?"

Archer regarded me for a long moment, and I knew he didn't want to tell me. "One I woke up with this evening –" A longer silence, which I didn't break, then finally, "of myself and de Rais."

I touched Archer's cheek, and he almost flinched away from me. But then he didn't, and his skin felt warm under my fingertips. "Did you kill him, or just drink?"

"It doesn't really matter. She saw what she needed to see."

"Well, it was effective. Thank you."

He sighed and pulled me in close to him. "Fangs would've been good, too."

I stared up at him. "You don't really have them, do you?"

"You mean the retractable, razor-sharp canines that they botch in True Blood and Twilight?"

I giggled. "Come on, show me."

He grinned at me with his perfectly normal, slightly crooked teeth. "Not a chance."

THE RIVER

Dawn was just beginning to color the sky when we arrived at the boat docks. Crude wooden piers stretched out like gnarled fingers into the Seine, and shallow-bottomed boats of different sizes were tied up alongside them.

Archer walked with Ringo to help support his weight on his injured side, and I was moving a little slower than usual because breathing still hurt, but we made it to the docks in time to get everyone settled.

Max reminded me of an art teacher I once had in Oregon. All over the place, with the kind of energy for everything that made me tired just looking at him. But he wasn't just fast-twitch busy; there was an inherent happiness under it all, like life was just so great he couldn't wait to taste and smell and touch everything. I also soon discovered Max had a Frenchman's passion for food. Archer had arranged for crates of food to be delivered to the docks – he traded some of the bits of broken gold jewelry my mom had given him – and before we could load any of them onto the boat, Max opened each one like it was Christmas, exclaimed over all the contents, and then decided what should go where according to its need to stay fresh.

Max's wife, Sophie, was the complete opposite of him. The enthusiasm and passion in Max was serenity and ease in his wife. She was about 5'7" tall, with thick, dark hair and the kind of curves that looked deceptively soft, but which I knew were full of muscle. She handled the packing of the boat with calm efficiency, and her smiles at Max's exclamations of joy over the fresh bread and big wheel of cheese were affectionate and private.

When Archer introduced us all, Max shook everyone's hand effusively, like the human version of a big puppy jumping all over us, but Sophie studied us. She used the distraction of his big personality to mask what she was doing, but I noticed, and so did Charlie. She saw the order in which we were presented, and heard things in Archer's voice as he said each name that added to the impressions she was already forming. And then later, as we loaded things in, Sophie sought me out to ask about meals, and placement of personal bags, and most importantly, to show me the shade they'd rigged for Archer and me to sleep under during the day. Charlie was usually on hand to translate, or we made do with hand gestures and pantomime, but I thought it was pretty fascinating that Sophie chose me – one of the non-French speakers among us – to be the voice of the group.

We were underway before full dawn. Max navigated the shallows with a long pole, and Connor and Ringo sat on either side ready with oars. Ringo insisted on taking a first shift at the oar, saying that if he didn't get some exercise he was going to wither away into a useless lump.

Archer's tarp was rigged between two benches, and there was a bedroll spread out on the floor of the boat for us. He had explained that he had an allergy to the sun, so he and I would take the night rowing shifts. Sophie thought it was a very efficient way to travel, and she said she would rig this kind of shelter on every trip to allow for night rowers to sleep.

So we were under the tarp, snuggled in our own cave in the middle of the boat.

"I like them." I didn't want to say Max and Sophie's names to draw their attention to my whispers, but Archer knew who I meant.

"I thought you would. She reminds me a little of my brother's wife, always quietly supporting him in a way such that few people noticed how strong and capable she was."

I smiled sleepily. "Not like me, all up in everyone's face?"

Archer stroked my hair. "There's no one like you."

219

I scoffed. "That bad, huh?"

"You make things happen that seem impossible. When you set your mind to something, you create the opportunities for it, and then you go after them. I've never met anyone more powerful or determined than you. It would be quite intimidating, if I didn't know where you were ticklish."

He grabbed for me with tickling fingers, and I barely muffled a shriek before he pulled me close to his chest. I poked him one last time for good measure, and he tightened his arm around me as he kissed my hair. I could feel him start to slip into his daytime sleep, and I lay awake a few minutes longer listening to the dip of the oars in the water and the sounds of the city waking up along the banks of the river. I fell asleep with a smile on my lips.

It was well past noon when I woke up. Archer was still asleep beside me, so I tuned my hearing in to figure out who was doing what outside our little shelter. There were murmured voices in French coming from the front of the boat, which I assumed were Sophie and Max. I tuned them out because I couldn't understand enough French yet to make the effort to listen in worth my while.

The rhythmic slap of oar into the river was soothing, and it punctuated a quiet conversation in English between Charlie and Ringo. Their voices were low enough that I doubted anyone else could hear them, but between their location on the boat and my hearing, I couldn't help but listen.

Charlie spoke with certainty. "I've seen 'is kind before. They like the water, and they've a fair bit o' joy in 'em all the time. But in tough spots they run for it, and ye can't count on 'em in a fight. 'Is kind'll always save their own skin first."

"Do ye think she's one, too?" Ringo must have been asking about Sophie, which meant Charlie had been talking about Max.

"No. She's 'uman all the way." Ah, so it wasn't Max's character they were discussing. It was an Otherness. That was interesting. I trusted Charlie's Other-sight, and wondered what, if anything, Max's Otherness meant for us as we traveled down the Seine with him.

Charlie spoke again in an even softer voice. "And ye? 'Ow are ye really feelin'?"

"The leg 'urts, but it's better."

"That's not what I'm askin'."

"Ye mean what do I think about this that we're doin'?"

"Yeah, that, and 'bout the people we're with."

Ringo was silent a moment, and the murmur of French voices from the bow had paused, too.

"Wilder feels dead to me already. Like 'e isn't worth pursuin' anymore. I know that's what we came 'ere for in the first place, but somethin' tells me 'e's already done."

"'Ow do ye figure that?" Charlie seemed skeptical, and I was glad she asked the question, because I probably would have popped my head out and asked the same thing.

Ringo scoffed. "Cause this is the wrong time line, and I've always 'ad a sense for things 'avin' to do with my survival. The thing with Wilder at this moment just feels ... beside the point."

"What about the rest of it?"

"I trust Saira and Archer. This feels like what we're meant to be doin'. But what about ye? What are ye thinkin' about this whole adventure yer on?"

She inhaled sharply. "I shouldn't be 'ere, Ringo. I'm not ... enough for any of it."

"'Ey. It's not right what yer sayin'."

Charlie's voice sounded teary. "Ye 'ad to rescue me from the Mongers, and again from the wolves. I'm not strong or fast, and I can't run like ye and Saira do. Give me a fryin' pan and I might be able to knock ye on the 'ead, but without it, I'm just not ... enough."

In my head I was yelling at her, telling her that was a load of crap. But I knew my anger was misplaced, because it hadn't been that long ago that I questioned whether I was enough to fulfill a prophecy, and because I still struggled with my own doubts about being capable enough to do what needed to be done.

I snuggled closer to Archer's body. Even when he was sleeping, he could still comfort me.

Ringo didn't yell, and he didn't try to talk her into believing all the ways she was strong. His tone was matter-of-fact and very straightforward. "Well, I chose ye, didn't I? If ye don't believe yer enough, yer callin' into question my judgment. And that calls to question my judgment about 'Is lordship and Saira and Connor, too. And I'm not changin' my mind 'bout them, just like I'm not changin' it about ye. So, I guess the only thing left for ye to do is change yer own."

I would have applauded if I could have without giving my eavesdropping away. And in fact, I was starting to feel a little slimy for it, so I decided to interrupt them with some waking up noises. I yawned and stretched, and murmured a little as I rolled over and crawled out of the little shelter.

I blinked blearily in the sunlight and squinted around the boat at everyone.

Charlie looked a little white-faced, like she'd just been yelled at, Sophie waved at me from the front of the boat, and Connor stared out at the water grimly as he rowed. Jehanne sat across from him, looking pissed, and Ringo hit me with a smirk that said he knew I'd been listening.

So I owned it. "He's right, you know."

Charlie's head snapped around to me. She definitely hadn't considered that I could have overheard him. "You insult him by believing you're anything less than amazing. Because he chose you, and he has pretty great taste in people." I smiled at her to take the sting out of my words, but her face flamed anyway.

"Most days I don't feel so very far from Whitechapel."

I quirked a smile at her. "Really? Have you looked around lately?" I did actually look around, for the first time since emerging from the sleeping cave. The banks of the river were green and lush, full of big trees and flowering bushes. We were just approaching a small village with little huts dotting the fields. As we rounded a bend, a massive tower stood tall on a hill in the distance, and I was slapped with the realization, again, that we were in medieval France, where wars were fought with bows and arrows, and castle fortifications included boiling oil.

"Quite a view, isn't it?" Charlie finally had her own quirky smile back on her face.

I nodded my head toward Max, setting up a crude fishing line off the side of the boat. "Really?"

After a startled second, she caught my meaning and nodded. "Not trouble, but don't count on 'im to 'ave yer back."

"'Ow much did ye actually 'ear of our talkin'?" Ringo looked at me suspiciously.

"Sorry. I woke up right when you were discussing him."

He looked at me thoughtfully as he pulled the oar.

"I'm going back to Paris when this is done." I said. Maybe I was warning him, maybe just hoping he'd still be in.

He nodded. "And I'll go with ye, of course."

"Thank you."

There was a whole bunch of stuff we weren't saying, but it was kind of speculative naval-gazing stuff about what we'd find when we got back to Paris, what would change, and whether any of it would have mattered at all? So instead, I asked Charlie to start teaching me French.

Ringo laughed at everything that request covered up, and tossed out badly pronounced body parts he'd heard down at the quay in London. Charlie pretended shock, but she came in with her own off-color words picked up at the food markets she used to steal from as a little girl. French bakers were apparently even more descriptive than sailors. By the time we went ashore to have our evening meal and use the field facilities – basically, go for a squat – I had a fairly interesting vocabulary to try out on Archer.

Dinner was kind of amazing. Max had caught several fish he said were pike, and had gutted and cleaned them with Jehanne's help in about fifteen minutes. Sophie had me go with her to forage some thyme and wild onions, and we stuffed the fresh herbs inside and then coated the outside with some olive oil before roasting them on sticks in the fire. With the fresh bread and cheese and some apples Charlie found in an abandoned orchard, it was a total feast.

Archer had gone hunting while the rest of us ate, and the hunger in Jehanne's eyes when he brought back a gutted and dressed wild rabbit was a tad unsettling. Connor was keeping a sharp eye on her, and I saw him tense at her reaction to the fresh meat.

When the rabbit was stuffed with the leftover onions and was roasting on its own stick to have for breakfast, Max settled in with a pipe and told us tales about the river we'd traveled that day. There were fish in it, he said, as long as a man, and strange-looking, armored fish that were so rare he'd only known of two people besides himself who had ever seen one. I knew that any fish that had gone extinct before the 1500s was considered prehistoric, and I wondered if that's what he was talking about.

I settled in against Archer and ignored the sharp-edged looks Jehanne sent me across the fire. When silence stretched for a couple of minutes after Max was finished talking, Charlie cleared her voice and began to sing a quiet ballad in English about a nine-year-old boy imprisoned for stealing handkerchiefs. Her voice was as haunting as the lyrics, and afterwards, the quiet settled in like a sigh.

Finally, Archer stood and offered his hand to me. "My lady, I believe it's our turn to row."

When the boat was back on the water and everyone but Sophie was tucked into various corners of the hull to sleep, Archer and I took our place at the oars.

We sat close enough to each other on either side of the boat that we could speak in low tones and hopefully not keep everyone else awake. Sophie was at the tiller behind us, and a lantern hung from the bow.

It only took a few minutes before we were rowing in an easy, synchronized rhythm, and it felt, somehow, like a metaphor for how we worked together. Just a couple minutes to find each other's pace before we ran side by side. It's how we ran home from the Tower, on the days Archer caught me, and how he taught me to sword and knife fight, too. The oars dipped quietly in and out of the water, and I counted the days since the last time things had felt normal. Because, of course, midnight free-running and weapons training was normal.

I gasped suddenly, and Archer's attention snapped to me. "What's wrong?"

I made a sound somewhere between a snort and a chuckle. "Nothing. Except I think today's my birthday."

"It's at midnight tonight." Archer's voice was calm with certainty.

"It is?" I mentally ran down the nights – that was easier than counting days – and realized he was right. "Right. So, I'm seventeen for another, what, twenty minutes?"

I could feel his smile in the darkness. "Something like that."

"You remembered." It actually touched me more than I thought it could that he remembered my birthday in all the chaos and madness.

"My love, I've been celebrating your birthday for more than a hundred years."

Wow. Okay. "How?"

"How do I celebrate?"

"Yeah. I'm trying not to be overwhelmed or weirded out by how intense that sounds." I had come to terms with the idea that Archer had loved me since 1888, but it actually hurt to think of him waiting around for a century until I was even born.

He chuckled. "I suppose it does sound a little obsessive, even for me. But I don't think I'm as bad as I seem on paper."

"Yeah, that whole too-good-to-be-true thing can be kind of a bummer," I teased. The momentary freak-out was over, and now I just had a case of the warm fuzzies. I was also intensely curious. "Seriously, though. How did you spend every July 25th?"

"Talking to you."

"So, that must've gone over well with the people you hung out with."

He laughed. "Remember when we first met, I told you I didn't have cronies because Immortal Descendants weren't sane topics of conversation for my peers?"

My voice got a little smaller. "I'm guessing the nocturnal habits of the undead weren't really conducive to making friends either?"

"Ravi really was one of the few people in my life I've ever considered a friend. After you, of course, and now Ringo."

"And Mr. Shaw and Connor and Charlie and Ava and maybe even Adam …" Suspiciously absent from that list was Tom, who would have considered Archer to be a friend if he had lived.

"Well, they're all your fault. I had done a fair job of convincing myself I didn't need friends until you showed up in my life that night in Whitechapel."

"Clearly you were delusional. And apparently still are. What do you mean, you talked to me on my birthdays?"

He laughed. "Just that. I started talking around midnight – just telling you things I'd seen and done throughout the year. The best place I'd gone running, the most interesting person I'd met or seen, someone's cooking I'd smelled that you would love, or a photograph I wish I'd taken. Sometimes I'd share conversations I'd overheard, or a piece of music." He chuckled again. "The year I heard *Dust in the Wind*, I learned it so I could sing it to you on your birthday."

"Would you sing it now?"

I knew the lyrics to the old Kansas song, but until Archer's quiet a cappella voice sang the haunting melody about the inevitability of death, I had never really paid attention to the words. His voice was much deeper than the one in my head, and on the second verse, my voice unconsciously joined his. Then he dropped to a deeper harmony for the chorus, and by the time the last notes died away across the space between us, I knew I never wanted to spend another birthday away from him.

"Thank you," I whispered.

"That was much better than I did the first time. I didn't know you knew any seventies music."

"Anything in a minor key."

"Hmm. Me, too."

We were quiet for a few oar pulls while a not-unpleasant burn set into my shoulders from the repetitive motion. Crickets were singing from both shores as we passed on the right side of a small river island, and a fox's eyes glowed at us from its edge.

"What would you tell me tonight?"

Archer made a sound in his throat that was something between a hum and a rumble, the kind of sound that sent chills across my skin when it came from behind me, in my ear.

"Well, last year's birthday conversation was full of anticipation. I tried to imagine what you were doing that night in Venice. Had you been out tagging, or had your mum done something special to celebrate turning seventeen?"

I smiled. "We made a cake together and then took a walk to the art wall at the beach. Then I did a little free-running at the playground, since it was after dark and I wouldn't scare the kids, and one of my favorite street artists did a sketch of me flying off the monkey bars and gave it to my mom. It actually was a great birthday."

"Thank you for that visual image. It sounds wonderful."

"Yeah, it was one of the better ones. I think my mom was starting to finally understand my art, and we were dealing okay with all the things we weren't saying to each other."

"What a difference a year makes?"

"No kidding." I could never have pictured this life for myself a year ago.

"You'd be proud of me. I didn't actually start stalking you outside Elian Manor until September."

I laughed. "That's some pretty major restraint, buddy."

"You have no idea. I do think Jeeves might have seen me in the woods once or twice, and I had to start buttering up the gardener's dogs with beef bones."

He was silent for a long moment, and then he choked on his voice a little. "And when I saw you running down the road, in the boots, jeans, and hoodie that had been burned into my brain that night in Whitechapel, I very nearly crashed the Aston Martin. I could barely believe it was you after so many decades of wondering and dreaming about seeing you again. And even after I dropped you at the Upminster station, knowing I wouldn't see you until the following night, I prowled the area around Whitechapel, just in case something changed and you came back before dawn."

My heart constricted in my chest. My experiences of those early days of Archer were a whole galaxy apart from his. I remembered getting a big case of overwhelm in the woods outside Elian Manor when he told me how he felt, and now I can't imagine how he held himself back. I took a couple of deep, slow breaths to regulate the pounding of my heart.

He continued speaking quietly. "So, on this birthday, I would tell you about the night we met again. How dumbstruck I was that my memories of your energy and your smile and your wild beauty were transparent ghosts in comparison to the living, breathing, stunning girl who jumped into my car. You took my breath away. You made my heart remember to beat. The scent of you filled blanks in my memory I hadn't known were there. And then I spent those first weeks utterly terrified to lose you. I'm not even certain how I was able to function as a rational being some nights. I would have killed Bob Shaw if you hadn't gotten between us the night he was training you to kill ... me, I suppose."

"Not you. Never you." My voice broke on its whisper.

"And in the end, when it was completely out of my hands, I finally surrendered to the reality of what it meant to love you. And it truly was surrender or break into a thousand pieces every day." He took a deep breath. "Fear for your safety paralyzed me, but you, my beautiful woman, are always moving. So I had to break free of the fear in order to run with you, and since that day, and every day I choose not to fear, I have known more freedom and happiness than I ever imagined was possible."

I took a shaky breath, and tears prickled at the backs of my eyes. I could hear a smile in Archer's voice when he continued speaking.

"I thought finding you again would be about you – about learning your likes and dislikes, reading your moods, uncovering your passions. What I didn't expect is that it's been about me, too. I thought I knew myself well – after more than a century of life, I expected to. But I didn't realize that being myself *with* you was not

228

just simply loving you. I had to grow and change and adjust myself to stand next to you. I've become stronger to be strong for you. I've become more tolerant and less afraid, even as I let myself *feel* everything, rather than risk missing anything I could feel with you. And the things I feel …" He scoffed at himself, and his voice went husky. "I thought blood lust was a challenge to control."

I couldn't breathe. Definitely couldn't speak and risk breaking the spell he'd woven, or cooling the heat that had lodged inside me at his words. We were rowing a medieval river boat full of people on our way to war, and all I wanted was to have Archer wrap around me, to let my hands explore his skin, to taste him and feel his desire for me. Because that's what the heat was. Total desire. I had no real idea what to do with it, no experience to fall back on. Usually, our circumstances were a big enough barrier that desire couldn't dig in and take hold. But not even that was working right now. And I wanted to feel it. I craved the heat that had built inside me with the caress of his words.

His whispered voice was ragged. "Happy Birthday, Saira."

I almost moaned.

"Thank you," I whispered back.

I took a breath and let the flush of heat begin to escape. One last mental image of his hands on my body, and then I shook it free.

"You just changed color." His low voice was almost back to normal.

"What?"

"Something lightened in you. The color surrounding you is a lovely rich rose."

Okay. That was impressive. "Really?"

"What did you let go?"

It was midnight. On my birthday. I was eighteen. Talking to a man who just bared his soul to me.

"I want you."

He inhaled.

"But I can't do anything about, it so I let it go."

There was a long silence, but I didn't let it worm into my confidence. I'd been totally honest, and it felt good to actually say exactly what I'd been thinking.

Archer broke the silence. "So, at some point we'll need to discuss marriage and morality and our future, but I think if that conversation happened right now, I might have to throw us both overboard and swim for shore." His tone sounded casual and conversational, and I laughed.

"Thank you. A marriage and morality conversation might just do me in."

He joined me in laughter, and I felt the heat inside become warmth that wrapped around us both and held us in an easy embrace.

HEALING

Our days passed quietly on the river. My ribs had healed to the point that a green bruise was the only remnant of de Rais' attack, and the nights of rowing had strengthened my upper body beyond what even sword-fight training had done.

Ringo began using the bow of the boat for balance training after Connor's Wolf nose declared the bite wound on his thigh free from infection, and we all went for a free-run just before dawn and just after dusk, whenever we set in to land for meals.

Jehanne spent most of her time helping Max with the boat, and he didn't care that she rarely spoke, because he talked enough for both of them. That allowed Sophie the chance to rest so she could navigate the river at night while Archer and I manned the oars. Archer had relieved Connor of his responsibility over Jehanne, and Connor was much happier not being tethered to the morose and judgmental girl.

The mornings I spent asleep in Archer's arms were as torturous as they were soothing. I was exhausted by the time we handed over the oars, but the heat his words had stoked in me always ignited the minute his body was pressed against mine. But sleep was the only thing that ever happened under the shade cloth, and I woke up every afternoon with a hunger that had nothing to do with food.

Ringo and Charlie had settled back into the easy relationship I assumed they'd had in 1889 when they shared his flat. There was a shorthand between them, and it was growing between Ringo and Connor, too. The conversations I woke to reminded me of the ones Archer, Ringo, and I used to have about books and college courses, except these were mostly about science and technology – subjects Connor knew an insane amount about, and Ringo was fascinated by.

A whole afternoon was spent arguing the merits of the Hadron Collider, while another day, Charlie, Ringo, and Connor went back and forth with the best life hacks they knew. Charlie knew that eating ten almonds is a painkiller and that eggs can be preserved a very long time by burying them completely in salt. Ringo said if a tooth gets knocked out, put it in coconut water before shoving it back into place so it adheres better, and you can make a water filter with a pail full of rocks, pebbles, coarse sand, and fine sand. Connor was full of life hacks, of course, but most of his were technology based. Drying out a wet electronic in a bag of rice sounded useful, and pancakes made by pouring batter over frying bacon was just decadent.

I had brought a book with me, which was bulky even in paperback, but I figured it would raise fewer eyebrows than my e-reader would have. I started reading out loud to Charlie to interrupt a very involved discussion the boys were having about Skyrim vs. Call of Duty and the merits of fantasy role play video games vs. first person shooters. I had never seen either of them shut up so completely as when I started to read.

"It was night again. The Waystone Inn lay in silence, and it was a silence of three parts."

Ringo got a faraway smile on his face, and Connor listened like he didn't want to miss a word of the story. Two hours later, my voice was hoarse and I needed water like a desert wanderer, and still the cries of "one more chapter" went up among my friends.

Before we stopped for dinner, Connor, Charlie, and Sophie would undertake my French lessons. Sophie and Charlie were there to keep the boys from turning me into a sailor, and in turn, we were teaching Sophie some words in English. Evenings on the beach were always the equivalent of a pot-luck dinner between whatever fish Max and Jehanne caught, whatever meat the other guys hunted, and the plant food and herbs the girls found. It was interesting to me how we divided ourselves along gender lines, but it didn't feel like we were put into a place. More like we just organized ourselves according to our skills.

My favorite times on the river though were after dinner when someone would sing, and then on the boat after everyone else had settled to sleep. The conversations Archer and I had covered every topic imaginable, even politics and religion. I didn't know, for example, that Archer had strongly opposed the parts of the Treaty of Versailles that made Germany pay more than $30 billion in war reparations. He said the allies backed Germany into an economic corner that allowed someone like Adolf Hitler to come to power. He had also revised his opinion on some aspects of religion since the last time we'd talked about it – in 1888. The rise of religion in US politics was disturbing, he said. And the number of people who stood behind religion to wave their flags of hatred and intolerance disgusted him.

The best conversations were the personal ones, though. Stories of what we'd done, what we'd felt, who we'd seen and known. Sometimes one of the others would either wake up or admit they hadn't been sleeping and join in our late-night talks. Archer, Ringo, Charlie, Connor, and I became a family on the river Seine. We teased each other, tried to make each other laugh, told stories, and shared secrets. And mostly, we healed.

Along the river there were some fascinating sights to see, too. In Melun there was a bridge with a flour mill spanning across the water. Max insisted on putting every fishing line he had into the river under the bridge because the eels were fat from the grains that fell in from the mill. I'd never eaten eel before, but he caught six huge ones, and it was so much food the other guys didn't need to go hunting that night.

We also passed castles on the islands in Melun and Nemours. There were several churches, of course, and evidence that the war had come this far upriver. It looked like a fire had taken out most of the village of Nemours in the not-too-distant past. Some of the buildings had been replaced and looked new; others were ramshackle shelters whose owners made no attempt to create a home.

"The English burned many villages along the Loing River when the people of Montargis drove them out," Max told us one evening as we passed another village trying to rebuild. "The siege failed two years ago, but the people still struggle to recover."

Jehanne's words carried over the dip of oars in the water. "What happened in Montargis?"

Max smiled as if it had been his own actions that saved the day. "The people broke through the walls of two holding ponds and sent a cascade of water down to the English. Many were drowned."

Her smile at the idea of drowning Englishmen was creepy, and I shuddered. She must have caught the motion because she turned to me and spat harshly, "You believe they should have been allowed to live? To continue starving French children in their homes and killing Frenchmen in the name of their pretender king?"

Connor was translating automatically, but I actually understood about half of what she said on my own. Her tone of voice would have conveyed the rest, even without the translation. This girl had either ignored me or been completely rude since we'd met, and it took every ounce of self-control I had to keep my voice reasonable and calm, because I knew my words wouldn't be.

"No, Jehanne. It was the look of happiness in your eyes at the idea of drowning people that bothered me. It doesn't matter to me whether they're English or French or German, even. Drowning seems like a horrible way to die."

She smiled with all her teeth showing, and some small part of my mind saw they were beginning to rot. It made the smile that much more menacing. "Exactly. That was why the explosion of the bridge at Orléans would have been a master stroke."

I felt sick. That fireboat that didn't blow up might be exactly what we needed to change to set history back on the right course. The image of men in armor falling into the river and sinking like rocks filled my head, and I had to turn away from Jehanne's ugly grin.

"Don't let her get to you, Saira." Connor's voice was low.

"She's gotten to you, too, hasn't she?"

He nodded, miserably. "My Wolf wants to rip her Wolf's throat out. In a pack, she would challenge me every day until she killed me, so I would have to kill her first or risk losing the pack, or my life. It's the kind of thing that can tear a pack apart in the wild."

"I'm so sorry we saddled you with her before." I really was sorry. He'd been carrying the burden of his own family so long he just shouldered extra responsibility without complaint.

He shrugged. "It's fine. I mean, why else am I here, right?"

I stared at him. "No. It's not fine. And you're here for a lot of reasons, but having to babysit a delusional psychopath isn't one of them."

He snickered at that. "She's not actually a psychopath that I can tell. I mean, the Wolf can usually sniff out that brand of insanity, believe it or not. But delusional? Definitely. Although honestly, I can't imagine what it would be like to get Seer visions and have no idea what they are."

He was right about that, and a tiny part of the wall I'd put up against her splintered. Just a little, though. It was hard not to patch the cracks every time she glared at me.

We noticed that Max was steering us down a tributary off the main river, and both Ringo and Connor raised an eyebrow at me questioningly. I shook my head with an "I have no idea" look.

Connor spoke to Max. "Why are we turning?"

"There is a town ahead that makes things of wool. I have a load of dyes to trade before we continue on our way."

"That wasn't the agreement that Archer made with you. The agreement was that you would take us straight to Montargis – no stops except to eat and restock food." Connor sounded like a young man not to cross, and I thought Archer would be proud of him.

"Château-Landon is ten minutes ahead. I'll make my trade, and we'll be on our way." Max wasn't budging on this, and I saw Jehanne shoot him a satisfied smirk. Huh. Interesting.

Sophie was at the front of the boat picking debris out of a fishing net. I sat next to her and pulled one end of the net up to help. Our conversation was halting at first since I was using most of the appropriate French I knew, and she understood a few words of English to fill in the gaps. But it was a relief to be able to speak to her directly.

"Why does Jehanne want to go to Château-Landon?" I spoke in low tones, and Sophie shot a quick, hard look at where Jehanne and Max sat together near the tiller.

"She has convinced my husband to trade the dye there instead of Montargis because it is a place of many churches."

It took me a minute to understand the many churches part, but as we rounded a bend in the tributary, it suddenly made perfect sense.

High above the river was an edifice that looked like a church and a castle all rolled into one. I must have gasped out loud, because Sophie answered the unspoken question. "The Saint-Séverin Royal Abbey. It is the center of the complex of chapels and monasteries. Many pilgrims come to Château-Landon to pray to God."

Of course. Jehanne needed to get her God back. I looked at the hard lines around Sophie's mouth. I had the feeling she didn't care for the amount of time Jehanne spent with her husband. I felt bad about that, but not too bad. Time Jehanne spent with Max was time she didn't spend with us.

The sun was just setting as we pulled the boat to the shore just below the Saint-Séverin Abbey. It was perched on a hill that rose probably a hundred feet above us, but even from this distance I could see fire damage on one of the towers. The abbey was built directly into the rock, and it was supported by huge buttresses that gave it a very manly, tough-guy look. A strange way to describe a church, but there was nothing feminine or graceful about the lines of the place at all.

Ringo was in a foul mood about Max having ignored Connor, and when Archer emerged from under the shade cloth, looking barely rumpled as usual, he pulled him aside to speak quietly. The rest of us disembarked, and Jehanne immediately strode off toward the village.

Connor wasn't pleased with her sudden departure and was about to go after her, but I stopped him. "She's going to pray. It's why we're here."

I looked over to find Archer staring at Max for a long moment. I wondered what he saw, but then Ringo said something again, and Archer turned his attention back to their conversation. Charlie was already walking with Sophie toward the woods when Ringo jumped off the boat and ran after her.

Archer caught up and handed us each our bags.

"What's this?" We almost never took our stuff off the boat, and except for the daggers I always wore, I usually had empty hands when we were onshore.

Archer shrugged. "We should restock our personal food supplies while we're here." He watched Charlie and Ringo head into the woods. "And they both need trousers, so perhaps we can make a trade ourselves."

Something in his eyes told me there was a much bigger message under his words, but Max was close by securing the lines of the boat to thick wooden posts stuck into the shore. Archer's gaze traveled up to the fire-damaged stone walls of the abbey before he looked at me again. "I think you should let us do the talking, Saira. Something tells me the English are not appreciated in Château-Landon."

I grumbled teasingly. "And yet I'm the only non-English one in the bunch."

He kissed me quickly on the lips. "That's not what your passport says, my love."

I had a thought as the three of us started toward the town. "Do you even have a passport?"

"Of course."

"Of course, how? I mean, it's a little tough to walk into the post office with a hundred-fifty year old birth certificate and not get arrested."

He raised one eyebrow in that look that had a whole conversation attached. "I know a guy."

I looked at Connor with a "do you believe it?" look. He smirked back with a shrug. "He knows a guy."

I filled Archer in on the possible motive behind Max's change of plans. He nodded thoughtfully. "Maybe we should visit the abbey after the markets close?"

Connor shot him a sly glance. "Sure you won't burn up stepping on consecrated ground?"

I burst out laughing, and Archer cuffed him upside the head. He narrowed his eyes at Connor with a smile. "You and your scientific facts are more likely to have trouble with creationists than I am."

I was careful to keep my mouth shut as we entered the thinning market crowd, but it was hard. I wanted to talk to the guys about everything we saw. Some of the people were dressed in the dirty, timeworn version of our tunics and trousers, but many had clothes made of richly-colored wool with intricate embroidery around collars and sleeves. Even the children who ran past our legs, dodging in and out of the lamplight shadows, had wool caps dyed indigo blue and deep wine red.

Most of the stalls had bolts of wool fabric, but here and there were seamstress and tailor stalls with the medieval version of ready-to-wear clothes. Most everything was man-sized, and surprisingly, there was a big variety of people in the market. Several big farmers strode by with sacks of grain on their backs or children perched on shoulders. The women were smaller, more like Charlie-sized, but I was definitely surprised to see so many tall men.

We passed a stall where a wrinkled woman with pure white hair sat embroidering a child's tunic. The clothes at her table seemed designed for women and children, and a soft green tunic caught my eye. It had tiny daisies embroidered around the collar and would look perfect on Charlie.

I was about to call out to Archer to come back and realized there was no way to hide my Englishness, even if I spoke in my limited French. So I turned to the wizened old woman and started pantomiming. I held up the tunic, and then mimicked pulling on trousers. She understood what I meant, then reached under the table and pulled out a stack of trousers in the same soft wool.

I quickly realized she wasn't speaking either, and we carried on our whole conversation in silence, with smiles on our faces. I rifled through my bag for something to trade for the daisy tunic and a pair of blue trousers that seemed like they'd fit my small friend. The old woman watched me with interest and amusement in her eyes, and then I found the perfect thing.

I carefully placed a small packet of steel needles and three skeins of silk embroidery thread on the daisy tunic. The old woman's expression sharpened immediately, and she reached out a tentative hand for the needles. I thought for sure she'd go straight for the thread, but then I saw what she'd been working with. It was made of bone and was twice as thick as the biggest of the needles I'd offered. She looked into my eyes, and the amusement had turned to awe. Her hand shook as she picked up the needles and thread, and I hoped I hadn't just created a huge frustration for her when she tried to thread the tiny eyes.

She pushed the tunic and trousers across the stall to me, then looked around quickly and grabbed a small linen handkerchief. There was an interesting pattern of geometric shapes embroidered around the edge, and it looked kind of Middle Eastern or Moorish. She added that to the stack and then pressed her hands to her lips in the universal sign for thank you. I touched my chest and then gave her a big smile before tucking the clothes into my bag and the handkerchief in my pocket.

When I turned away from the stall, I was surprised to see Archer and Connor standing off to one side watching me with giant grins on their faces. I was ridiculously proud of my negotiation and practically bounded over to them. Archer laughed at my excitement as I showed him my purchases. I had stayed silent, and before we left, I turned back to throw a wave to the old woman. She didn't see me though. She was engrossed in trying to thread her new needles by the light of the candle in her stall.

It was almost full dark by the time we left the market, and I was bursting to talk. But Archer didn't stop until we'd climbed up several twisting streets toward the abbey. He finally turned off the cobbled street onto a path cut into the side of the hill. There were no houses within earshot when he pulled a bottle of ale from his bag and passed it to me.

I took a sip, winced at the sharp taste, and whispered, "Can I talk now?"

"Quietly." He passed the ale to Connor and then grinned at me. "That was some masterful negotiating. The clothes are for Charlie, I take it?"

I nodded happily. "The old woman was so excited about the needles, I almost felt bad I didn't have more." I pulled the tunic out of my bag and showed the guys the embroidered daisies. "She does amazing work, doesn't she?"

Archer fingered the wool cloth. "These are quite fine quality. Much nicer than the trousers we found to replace Ringo's torn ones."

"Do they know where we went?"

"I told Ringo to meet us at the abbey if we weren't back at the riverbank in time for dinner."

"So, you knew we were going up there even before we left the boat?"

Archer grinned mischievously. "I've wanted to see the Saint-Séverin Abbey since I was at King's College."

That got a punch from me. "And you couldn't have told us that before Ringo got all up in Max's face about stopping?"

"I was still down, wasn't I? Besides, your deduction of Jehanne's motive was very good. I didn't want to steal your thunder."

He was teasing me, but I couldn't help the eye roll. It just sort of escaped of its own will. I tried to catch it and turn it into a "mon dieu" look to the heavens, but it might as well have been wrapped in rice and seaweed.

"We got some meat pies to snack on if we miss dinner, but we should probably get up there before they close the abbey doors, or something." Connor was reaching into his bag and pulled out two meat pastries. I hadn't had anything baked since the bread ran out the first day on the river, and I barely resisted the moan that threatened with the first bite.

"They won't close them," Archer told us. "The abbey was built in the twelfth century as a rest stop for soldiers coming back from the Crusades. They keep the doors open in honor of that history."

We continued our whispered conversation as we climbed the hill to the base of the Saint-Séverin Abbey. The view would have been spectacular if it had been full of electric lights, but the front steps of the abbey were ablaze with candles. It really did look like a welcome place for travelers, and I decided to soften my harsh stand on organized religion for this place.

The giant doors were like something that belonged to a castle to keep marauders out, yet one of them stood open enough for a person to step through. I thought the doors must be so heavy that keeping one open was probably a good idea.

It was also a good defensive move, I saw, as we entered one by one. A very large priest stood just inside the doors, watching us with a smile. Archer had gone first, so the priest was speaking to him in French. Connor didn't dare translate for me in such close quarters, so I picked out as much as I could. It seemed the priest was telling us we had to leave our swords at the front door, and Archer motioned for both of us to unbuckle ours like he was already doing. It wasn't a bad policy, considering the open-door nature of the church, but seemed surprisingly liberal, considering the abbey had been burned recently, presumably by English troops.

One other sword had been left by the door, and we arranged ours a little to the side of it. I didn't feel bad about my dagger non-disclosure. These were tough times, and although I wasn't planning to use them in church, I felt better with them close at hand.

The main room was cavernous and fairly plainly built. It mostly looked like it had been carved from the rocky hillside, but there were painted frescoes on the walls in vibrant, beautiful colors that looked like they might have been freshly applied over some of the burn damage.

One of them made me gasp. It was a stunning image of a huge, black tree, stylized so it was all trunk and branches, with very thin leaves all over. Under the tree were five robed and hooded people – two women and three men. A bearded man was in the middle, reaching toward the crows that seemed to be darting among the branches. I walked over to the fresco and stood as close as I dared. It wasn't close enough to see details in the faces, but the people's hoods covered all the eyes except the bearded man's. And his seemed to look out of the wall and into mine.

I stepped back, and the illusion was gone. Then forward, and he looked at me again.

There was a chuckle behind me, and the large priest said something in French. I almost opened my mouth to respond, but quickly remembered I was supposed to be mute and signaled that I couldn't speak.

A glimmer of something like humor or understanding danced in his eyes, and he pantomimed the robed guy looking out from the painting as he told the story in French. He was an eloquent enough storyteller with his hands that I understood the basic ideas, and his black curly hair made him look like a slightly wild Italian, so I dubbed him Dante in my head. I nodded and smiled, then stepped in to really look at the details. Archer came over and engaged Dante in a conversation about the painting. I loved that about him. I clearly wanted to know more, so he was trying to ask the questions I would ask.

I heard the word "immortel" and looked up sharply. Dante was watching for Archer's reaction as he described some aspect of the fresco, but Archer gave him nothing but a pleasantly interested smile. I wished I knew what else he was saying, but Dante's French was too fast for me, so I turned back to the painting and studied it with a new perspective.

The tree reminded me of the Shifter symbol in the Immortal Descendants' council room in London, but then again, it was a tree, and Shifters hadn't cornered the market on trees. I searched the faces of the five figures, but except for Bearded Guy's eyes, everyone else's face was in shadows. The crows that Bearded Guy was reaching for reminded me of death. Maybe it was just the association with Edgar Allen Poe's *The Raven* poem, but they were called a murder of crows for a reason.

I took a step closer to the fresco back into range of Bearded Guy's gaze, which was totally disconcerting and reminded me of Jera, my Immortal ancestor, staring at me from the painting in Elian Manor. And that thought made me look for two things – Doran's signature and a spiral.

The style wasn't right for Doran and the painting was at least a hundred years older than anything I'd seen from him before, but Bearded Guy's eyes were exactly what he would have painted, so I didn't discount it. I eventually spotted the spiral, woven into the bark of the Shifter tree.

I wasn't positive, but if I had to guess, Bearded Guy was Goran, the Immortal Nature, the tree was his symbol, and for whatever reason, there was a time portal painted into this abbey.

Dante had fallen silent, and when I turned toward them I realized he must have seen me find the spiral. He spoke in French and was talking to me, not Archer. I tried to indicate speech loss again, but he ignored my pantomime and continued speaking.

When Archer translated, I realized Dante knew we weren't who we seemed.

"He knows you're a Clocker and wants you to go with him."

I stared at Archer. "That sounds like a very bad plan." I kept my voice low, and Dante didn't seem fazed by the English coming out of my mouth.

Archer spoke to him in French, and Dante answered, though his eyes were still locked on mine.

"I told him I go where you go, and he said only Descendants may enter the … havre. Could be harbor, could be haven. I can't really tell."

"You're a Descendant."

Archer spoke again, and Dante's eyes swiveled to Archer in surprise.

"What did you say?"

Archer's eyes were locked on Dante's, but he answered me. "I told him that like him, I am a Descendant of Death."

"Like him?" I squeaked.

Just then a door at the back of the nave opened and Jehanne emerged, followed by an even bigger guy than Dante-the-dead. Crap. Was Dante really a Vampire? I didn't have the brain space to process this thought because the look on Jehanne's face was murderous, and she was very definitely being escorted to the door.

She didn't look at any of us before being all but thrown out of the church. And once she was out, the bigger guy picked up the sword he must have left there and stood like he was on guard duty. I couldn't tell if he was keeping her out or keeping us in, and it made me very, very nervous.

Because being faced with another Vampire wasn't nerve-wracking enough.

Except when I turned my eyes back to Dante, he had the biggest, shiniest grin on his face I've ever seen. Seriously?

Connor had obviously seen Jehanne's unceremonious ejection from the abbey and was edging his way back to us. I suddenly wanted him at my back very badly because things at my front had gotten weird.

Dante was speaking rapidly to Archer, and then he reached out a hand to shake. The guy looked really excited to meet Archer, and after my experience with Wilder – the only other Vampire I'd ever known – it was mildly disconcerting.

Archer's mouth quirked up in a half smile as he responded to whatever Dante had said. Connor's voice in my ear was like a balm to my disintegrating sense of reality, especially because he sounded as surprised as I felt.

"Archer's telling him about having studied theology at King's College in London, and he also told him that the only other Descendant of Death he's ever met tried to kill him, so please forgive his rudeness earlier." I think I might have scoffed under my breath, because Connor's tone was amused. "Apparently this guy has someone you guys need to meet."

"You need to come, too. The place is for Immortal Descendants only."

"Are you sure it's not a trap designed to capture and kill us?"

I looked to see if Connor was kidding. He wasn't. "Between the three of us, we can take this guy, Vampire or not."

Connor was staring at Dante. "I never thought I'd meet one Sucker in my lifetime, much less two. And not trying to rip our throats out. That's something. How'd he even know what we are?"

I nodded at the fresco. "There's a spiral in that. He saw me find it and wanted to know who we really are."

Connor's eyes widened. "Curiouser and curiouser."

"Said Alice to her feet," I mumbled as I watched the two Vampires laugh at something one had said.

"You're a ridiculously literate nerd, you know that?"

"Pot, meet kettle." I threw an elbow back and caught him in the stomach, then stepped forward to get Archer's attention.

"I think we should probably find out what Dante's talking about with the havre business. I don't like that Ringo and Charlie aren't here yet."

Archer's expression sobered immediately, and Dante turned to me with an equally serious look on his face. He held out his hand to shake mine, except when I did the same, he actually kissed the back of it in a courtly gesture.

"Mademoiselle, I am called Sebastien, but please call me Bas." His English was heavily accented, but I could understand it much better than French.

"I'm Saira. Why do we need to go to the … havre with you?"

"The Saint-Séverin Abbey is known as a safe haven for travelers from the Crusades. What is less well-known is that we are also a haven for those descended from Immortals."

"But that guy just ejected Jehanne, and she's a Descendant, too."

Bas didn't look concerned. "Not every Descendant is granted haven."

Archer returned to French, probably because he didn't want Bas to miss any part of what he was saying. Connor translated for me. "He said we're not here for safe haven, we are just traveling through the area and wanted to see the abbey."

Bas responded in English. "Our bishop has requested that all Descendants allow him the courtesy of greeting them in person."

At the word "bishop" I felt my stomach clench in fear. Archer saw it on my face and responded to Bas in English.

"What Family does your bishop belong to?"

Bas grinned. "Besides being one of God's children, Bishop Klene is of Nature's Family."

I caught Archer's smile and realized I hadn't been the only one who was worried. I nodded to Bas. "We would be happy to greet your bishop before we continue on our way."

His grin widened. "Wonderful. Right this way, please."

Bas led the way toward the nave door that Jehanne had come through, then turned to us. "One moment, please." He looked at Connor questioningly, but I answered before he could ask.

"Nature."

His expression brightened, and he smiled. "I'll announce you, and then you may enter."

Bas closed the door behind him, and Connor looked concerned. "Whatever the bishop said to Jehanne was not good. It's probably not a great idea to say we're associated with her."

"Yeah, sorry about that." I had spoken without thinking, and I regretted making that connection.

"I must say, I'm quite intrigued at the idea of a Vampire priest." There was a light in Archer's eyes I hadn't seen before, and I tried, and failed, to decipher it.

"He was sure excited to meet you."

Archer's quiet voice was thoughtful. "The feeling's mutual."

The door opened again, and Bas swept his arm magnanimously. "Please come in. Bishop Klene is happy to meet you."

"Ladies first." Connor nudged me forward, and I stepped into the tall-ceilinged room. It was filled with ornate furniture and hangings, like the plain abbey behind me had barfed all its grandeur into this room, and I looked around in wonder at all the gold glittering in the light of several candelabras placed around the space.

A man walked forward into a pool of candlelight with his arms outstretched in greeting. He was older with snow-white hair and a heavily lined face, but his body still retained a wiry grace that made me guess he Shifted into something strong and fast.

The smile on his face seemed genuine, and he spoke in accented English as well. "Welcome, welcome. It is my pleasure to welcome Descendants to Saint-Séverin Abbey."

He held my hand between his two warm and calloused palms, then greeted Connor, and finally Archer. "I am Bishop Klene."

My eyes were drawn to the richness of the room beyond the light of the candles, and I absently wondered how they had saved all this gold from the English soldiers who had burned the abbey. Movement at the far end of the room caught my attention, and I realized someone else was in the room with us.

The person stood and walked toward us from the shadows, the rustle of silk skirts giving away the fact that it was a woman.

"We have the honor of another guest at the abbey …" Bishop Klene was saying as the woman stepped into the light.

I gasped.

Crap.

"Ah, but perhaps you already know Lady Valerie Grayson?"

LADY GRAYSON

Lady Valerie Grayson, of the sixteenth century Graysons, had a wary look on her elegant face when she held her hand out to me.

"Saira, it's a pleasure to see you again."

Despite her wariness, something in her voice convinced me she really had wanted to see me. "Lady Grayson. You remember Archer?"

Her eyes flicked to him, and I realized they hadn't actually been introduced when Lady Grayson met me in Elizabeth Tudor's rooms at the Tower of London. He bowed graciously.

"Archer Devereux at your service, madam." The manners of nobility looked a little strange on a guy dressed like a tradesman, but Lady Grayson didn't seem fazed by his wardrobe.

"You are Lord Devereux." It was a statement. She'd been expecting him. "I believe I know your mother's family, though we do not travel in the same circles."

Of course they didn't. First of all, Lady Grayson belonged in 1554 — or at least that was her native time. Second, she was Mistress of the Robes to Queen Mary Tudor, Elizabeth's older sister. And third, Archer's mother was related to the Boleyn Seers, as in Anne Boleyn, which put her at direct political odds with Lady Grayson.

"I have never met that branch of my family, Lady Grayson. May I present Connor Edwards." He smoothly turned the spotlight away from himself, and Connor stepped forward. He mimicked Archer's bow awkwardly.

Lady Grayson's eyes traveled over Connor then dismissed him. I bristled at her rudeness until I realized why she'd done it. "This isn't the same young man I saw with you before."

"That's correct." Archer was good. He didn't give anything away. Lady Grayson didn't like his reticence though, and her eyes narrowed.

"This is unexpected." Her words were almost murmured, but I heard them clearly.

"Which part? Because it seems like you were expecting us, and this meeting was definitely not on my schedule." I didn't try to be rude, I really didn't. But I didn't like being blindsided by this woman.

Lady Grayson turned to Bishop Klene. "May I have a moment to speak to Saira privately?" I wasn't actually sure I wanted a private moment with her, but the bishop bowed gracefully and backed away.

"Of course, madam. Gentlemen, if you'll join me in the nave?" He led the way to the door, and Archer shot me a look loaded full of "just say the word and I'll stay." But as prickly as I got about imperious assumptions, I really wanted to know what Valerie Grayson had to say.

So Archer and Connor departed with the two priests, and I was left alone with Lady Grayson. I had a chance to study her and realized she had dressed for the time period, simplified for travel instead of court. It wasn't dramatically different than what she'd worn in 1554, but there was more fabric – a pretty dark gold brocade – and it was higher waisted and less ornate. I was forcefully reminded that she was my mother's age and noble enough to be part of the queen's court, while I was eighteen and dressed like a tradesman.

I dug around in my head to find my confidence and pull it back up. I thought the only chance I had to be treated as an equal by this woman was if I behaved as one, so I squared my shoulders as she turned to face me.

But then she smiled, and it was such a tired, sad smile that all my armor melted. "I am truly sorry to have surprised you as I've

249

done, Saira. If I thought there was another way …" She held her hand out to me. "Come, let us sit for a moment while I run through all my pretty, rehearsed words to find the ones you will hear."

Her hand was cool in mine, and her skin felt like silk. I thought of all the callouses I'd grown from rowing and wondered what sort of life a woman in her forties could have had that gave her such soft hands. She led me to chairs placed close to the big open hearth, and when we sat, she stared into the fire a long moment before she finally looked at me.

"Henry has caused a rift in the time stream."

Of all the things she could have said, that was not what I expected. To cover my surprise, I studied her face. She met my eyes with something that looked like resignation and determination. Her face was nearly unlined, except for creases around her eyes. Laugh lines, I hoped. Her hair was hidden by a veiled headdress, but the hint of a blonde widow's peak showed underneath. I'd seen her son, and I guessed her husband must have been the source of his relatively exotic coloring.

Her son. "Henry's mission." I remembered the term because it sounded so covert, and the theme song from *Mission Impossible* had played in my head when he said it.

If Lady Grayson was surprised she didn't show it. "Do the Descendants of Jera still have such missions in your native time?"

I shook my head. What I didn't say was that as far as I knew, the number of Jera's Descendants that still existed in my time could fit in the palm of her hand.

"What did my son tell you of his?"

"Only that he was going to 1429, and that his birthdate was the subject of some prophecy."

She inhaled. "My husband is the headmaster of St. Brigid's, and he also has ties to the Descendants' Council, on which he aspires to sit. Henry was not the only Clocker child to be born in time to be sent here for this mission, but my husband's ambitions put my son in position to be the one."

"The one? You make it sound like the messiah, or Neo, or something." Oh good. Whip out a *Matrix* reference. I scoffed at myself in my head, but Lady Grayson didn't bat an eyelash.

"In our history, the English are defeated at Orléans in May, 1429. Charles VII goes on to Reims to be crowned King of France on July 17th, and although this war continued until 1453, the tide was inexorably turned at Orléans."

"By Joan of Arc," I breathed.

"Yes. Somehow, inexplicably, one young, uneducated girl from the French countryside managed to convince the heir to the throne that she was charged by God to give him his kingdom and expel the English from France."

"You know she's a Descendant, right?"

Lady Grayson's voice was smooth. "I thought it was a possibility."

"She's been leading wolves against the city of Paris since her defeat and capture at Orléans."

A sigh accompanied her words. "Yet another twist my son must atone for."

"What, exactly, did Henry do?"

"I am not entirely sure, because, you see, he did not return."

I stared at her. He told me he was going to 1429 at the end of April, and more than three months had passed since then.

"I'm really sorry." And I really was. This whole time travel business was stupidly dangerous, and that's not even taking into account that the guy's purpose was to change a war. "What was he supposed to do?"

She sighed and rubbed her temple. Yeah, I imagined this whole conversation was high on the headache-worthy list for her. "Perhaps we should invite the gentlemen back in for that part of the conversation. It is quite involved, and I fear I am not up to telling it twice."

"Why did you want to speak to me alone, then?"

Lady Grayson looked me in the eyes. "Frankly, my dear, I am tired of arguing with men. My husband and the rest of the Descendants' Council believe Henry has succeeded admirably in his

251

mission as the outcome has allowed their families to retain titles and lands in France. But even if my son was home safely, I feel the wrongness of their plan to change our history. I can already see the effects this change has caused, and I fear for the future in which my grandchildren and their grandchildren will live. You may or may not know the joys and heartaches of becoming a mother, but I sense in you the instinct for family that I, myself, cherish."

She took my hand in hers and held it. "The men have caused the mess which the women must now clean up."

"I'm part of a team, Lady Grayson. Most of whom are men."

She smiled in a way that softened her striking features into something pretty. "You are the center of your team, and they are your family. You are the tie that binds them to each other, as the strongest women always are."

If I was the center of anything, I shared that center with Archer, maybe back to back, supporting each other, and our friends were like spokes in a wheel that couldn't turn without them. We had chosen each other, my friends and I, and we *were* a family.

"The girl who was here earlier – before we came in? That was Joan of Arc."

Lady Grayson looked startled. "I know she was very rude, and Bishop Klene sent her away rather than suffer her libelous accusations against me."

"Against you? What does she know about you?"

"That I am English."

I scoffed. "Well, join the club. She hates me, too."

"She is with your party?"

I couldn't help the face I made, and Lady Grayson's mouth quirked up in a wry smile. "Not by my choice. But she was causing trouble in Paris, and Archer thought she would be useful as we made our way to Orléans."

"So, the vision my Seer had was correct. You truly are intending to go there?" She had gotten up and was leading me toward the door.

"Your Seer? That's how you knew we'd be here?"

"Yes, though my Seer couldn't tell me the nature of your plan."

"Probably because there isn't much of one. Get to Orléans, figure out where we can safely Clock, and go back to the day before things changed to stop the split."

"To stop Henry." Lady Grayson's hand was on the door latch, but her voice had dropped into a range that sounded flat and dead.

"Yeah, I guess so."

She inhaled sharply, and then seemed to make up her mind. She opened the door and stepped into the candlelit nave. "Gentlemen, I thank you for your patience. Would you care to join us now?"

I looked past her shoulder and saw Archer and Connor turn toward us in an instant. Beyond them, Bishop Klene and Bas had started for the front of the abbey, as if someone had just come in.

And then I heard the unmistakable sound of swords being drawn from their scabbards.

I grabbed Lady Grayson's dress and pulled her back into the room as Archer and Connor turned toward the sound of swords. I still hadn't seen who'd entered the church, but a prickling in my gut warned me there could be Mongers among us.

Lady Grayson looked like she was about to protest, but I shot her a stern look and closed the door down to a crack. Through the gap I could just make out the figures of about six or seven men spread out just inside the door of the abbey. I couldn't understand the little French I could hear, but from the way they stood, they didn't seem to have come to pray.

I turned back to Lady Grayson and whispered, "Is there another way out of this room?"

She nodded and pointed toward the fireplace. "It leads to a tunnel that will take us outside." Clearly we weren't pulling a Harry Potter and using the floo network, so I just shrugged and trusted that she knew what she was talking about.

I could see through the crack in the door that Connor was backing up slowly so he could speak to me without giving us away. Archer still stood a little behind Bas, as if he was his wingman, and

I wondered if they could have been friends if we weren't constantly running to or away from something.

"They were told there were Englishmen hiding here. They want to search the abbey." Connor's voice was a fairly low whisper, but I caught the words.

Well, crap. There's no way I could pull off the mute girl business with a bunch of armed men looking for trouble. "There's a way out of here, but all four of us are going. I'm not leaving you and Archer to fight for us."

"If it comes to a fight, we can take them while you run. We'll meet you back at the boat." Connor stepped forward after delivering his order, and I wanted to shoot a blow dart at him. Since when did he get confident enough to give me orders?

He was probably right though. If he Shifted, and if Bas was any good as a fighter, the three of them could take six guys fairly easily.

I turned back to Lady Grayson. "Do you know how to open the passage?"

She nodded tensely and moved to the massive fireplace on the opposite wall. For the first time I noticed animal heads carved in stone under the mantel – bears, lions, wolves – all manner of predators. I watched in awe as she found a space behind the lion's mane and pulled a tiny lever. The wood panel of the wall next to the fireplace popped open to reveal a door large enough for me to walk through with only a slight duck, and I couldn't help the excitement that welled in me. I loved secret passages – especially ones that led underground.

I grabbed a longish stick from a bin next to the fire and lit the end in the flames. Lady Grayson went through the door first, and I closed it down to a crack behind me so the guys could find it if they came this way. Then, with my makeshift torch, I led the way down the stone steps.

"Have you been here before?" My voice was low, but the narrow stone passage made it carry.

"No. Bishop Klene showed it to me just after the rude Jehanne left. He apparently did not trust her response to me, and now I'm quite glad of it."

That was interesting. It hadn't occurred to me that Jehanne could have sent the French after us, but it totally made sense. Even though we could really use her help at Orléans, not having to put up with the death glares every day wouldn't suck.

The passage got smaller and smaller the further we descended. The stairs were roughly hewn into the solid rock, and parts of the walls were actually dirt. It made me feel a little like an ancient Greek hero descending into Hades.

"I intend to go with you to Orléans if you will allow me." Lady Grayson's voice was quiet, but firm. She didn't strike me as a delicate flower, but she also didn't seem especially imperious.

"We've been traveling by boat on the river, and once we get to Montargis our plan was to buy horses for the overland trip to Orléans. If that's fine with you, and unless any of my friends has something to say otherwise, it's okay with me if you travel with us."

"Thank you." Her tone was surprisingly humble for someone used to the privileges of nobility, and I had to admit, so far I'd been impressed with Lady Valerie Grayson.

The tunnel ended abruptly at another wooden door. This was latched from the inside, with a heavy plank resting across it that looked like it hadn't been lifted out of its cradle in a long time. The fire at the end of the stick I carried was starting to sputter, so I handed it to Lady Grayson and went to work on the plank. It took some wiggling, and a splinter under my fingernail, but I finally got the plank free and lifted away from the latch. I cracked the door open just enough to see the night sky. The sky was everywhere – above, in front of, and all around us, and when I stepped outside I realized we were in the cliff, about halfway down the hillside from the abbey.

A narrow track had been carved into the sandstone, but it was overgrown with scrub brush in places and looked like it had only a nodding acquaintance with safety. Above us were sheer cliffs, and the sandstone seemed like it had been carved by rivulets of water on all sides.

I gave Lady Grayson a wan smile. "Put out the fire and use the stick for extra support." My voice was still a whisper because I had no idea how far it would carry. I caught a glimpse of cork-soled boots under her skirts, and was very glad ridiculous footwear wasn't part of her repertoire.

She ground the fire into the dirt and nodded to me. I took a breath, and then led the way down the path. Twice, I had to grab onto exposed roots to keep my balance around loose sandstone, but Lady Grayson followed my lead with every move. It took us about fifteen minutes to navigate the path down to a larger track that looked like more than mountain goats used it, and I hadn't realized how hard it was until we rested. My legs shook and sweat trickled down between my shoulder blades. Lady Grayson's hand shook on her walking stick, and she casually tucked it into her lap so it wouldn't show.

I smiled. I knew that move.

"Why do you smile?" Her whispered voice was strained. The climb had been tough on her.

"Because you did a great job. That was a hard climb, and those skirts didn't make it easier." I made a face. I hated climbing and running in big skirts.

Lady Grayson returned the smile with a sigh as she tucked stray wisps of hair back under her veiled hat. "I should like a costume like you wear – something practical for walking. It never occurred to me to dress as a man when I planned my travel."

I laughed. "It never occurs to me to dress like a girl."

She reached into a pocket of her voluminous skirt and pulled out two small, paper-wrapped pieces. She offered them to me. "Would you like a sweet? I put a bit of pynade into my pockets in the event I encountered children, but I feel rather like a child who has just learned to walk at the moment."

I took one of the pieces and unwrapped it. Inside was something like a honey and nut bark, and it tasted amazing. Pine nuts, honey, and some spices that reminded me of Turkish food. "Thank you, it's wonderful."

She grinned and bit into her own piece. "When I was a child, my father brought me a bag of pynade from a journey he'd taken to Anatolia. I sat by his side eating the sweet, and listened to his stories of bazaars full of exotic and wonderful scents, velvet and silk in every color of the rainbow, and fantastical architecture that looked more like sculptures in ice than anything made of clay or brick."

It hadn't occurred to me that I could use my Clocking skill to go on exotic vacations, and suddenly I wanted to be home in London with Archer searching the Lonely Planet website for vacation inspiration. Or even just stopping a spinning globe with a finger, like I used to do when I was a kid. I wanted to go someplace where I could speak English like a tourist, dress and eat like a local, and wander around holding Archer's hand.

Archer. I needed to get back to him. I listened to the night, but we were too far away from the village to hear anything definitive. A glance at the abbey above us gave me my bearings, and I stood and held my hand out to help Lady Grayson to her feet. She clutched my hand for a brief moment, and then took a shuddering breath. "I can continue."

It took us another fifteen minutes to find a small cart track that appeared to head toward the river. I didn't want to travel on the main road through town if I could avoid it. We didn't speak as we walked, and I sensed Lady Grayson was much more tired than she let on. But I wasn't stopping until I found Archer again, and she didn't complain. When she stumbled on a root, I grabbed her hand instinctively. She clutched mine and didn't let go. We were still holding hands when we finally saw the river.

"The abbey was surrounded by loud Frenchies with swords." Ringo materialized next to me, and I very nearly slugged him. Lady Grayson actually did. It was accidental, but both of them looked so shocked, I burst into a fit of stressed-out giggles.

Her voice was breathy, and she glared at Ringo. "There you are."

Ringo did a double-take. Then his eyes widened, and he dropped into a low bow. "Ma'am. I'm very sorry for scarin' ye."

"You remember me?" She sounded surprised.

"O' course. Yer Lady Grayson, mother of 'Enry, wife to the St. Brigid's 'eadmaster."

I bit back a smile and spotted Charlie behind a tree nearby. I held out my hand to her and she crept forward, her eyes locked on Lady Grayson, who, for her part, was studying Ringo with growing interest.

"And you are?"

"Brother to Saira and 'is lordship. They call me Ringo."

I loved that answer, and I shot him a look that let him know how much. Meanwhile, Charlie had reached my other hand and was staring at Lady Grayson through wisps of hair. The older woman turned to her next, and with one look she went from amusement at Ringo to surprise at seeing Charlie.

"Oh." It was a gasp and a whisper, and Charlie took an instinctive step backward. Lady Grayson's hand shot out, and she reached for Charlie's other hand. For a brief moment I felt like we were playing ring around the roses, but then Lady Grayson dropped my hand and offered both of hers to Charlie.

"You look so like my dearest sister." She choked on her words and had to struggle to get them out. "Mary died last year, and I have missed her as if a piece of my heart was cut away." Lady Grayson wiped a tear away and looked at me. "You must think me mad to have reacted so."

I threw a quick glance at Charlie, but her eyes were locked on Lady Grayson. "My name is Charlotte Kelly, milady." Her voice was so quiet it was almost a whisper, but Lady Grayson swiveled back to Charlie.

"Kelly? You're Irish, then?"

"My father was. My mother was called Mary Reid."

Lady Grayson gasped. "Reid was the name of the man my sister married. Her son, Johnathan, carries his father's name."

I stared at them both. There was a vague resemblance between them, but the coincidence was too massive. "Come on, really?"

Charlie looked at me quickly. "Do ye know what I see when I look at milady, Saira?" I'd never seen so much intensity in her eyes. It was a little intimidating. "I see my mum." Charlie turned her gaze back to Lady Grayson, whose eyes were beginning to fill with tears. "Mum was not nearly so fine, and she'd been sick my whole life, but her eyes were just the same color green, and the same shape. And 'er 'air came to the same widow's peak above 'er brow."

Charlie had just enough Clocker in her that she showed up on the Immortal Descendants genealogy Archer had compiled in 1888, so I supposed it was possible that Lady Grayson was her million times great aunt. But it didn't matter what I thought, because those two were looking at each other like they were family.

I shot a glance at Ringo, but he was watching Charlie with a tender smile on his face. Charlie's mother had died when she was really young, and her older sister hadn't done much to raise her. So if Lady Grayson was willing to step in and be some sort of surrogate mom, that looked fine with Ringo.

"Did Archer and Connor come back?"

Ringo tore his gaze from Charlie and narrowed his eyes at me. "They're not with ye?"

I shook my head. "We left them in a standoff at the abbey. Four against six."

"Who are the others on their team?"

I couldn't help the half grin that accompanied the words. "A Vampire priest and a Shifter bishop."

But Ringo didn't give me the great surprised look I was hoping for. He just shrugged with a smirk. "Good odds, then."

So I shoved him, and he looked mischievous but said nothing.

"Where are Max and Sophie?"

"Gone."

"Wait, what? They left?"

Ringo shrugged. "Charlie and I went huntin' for rabbits, and when we got back to the river, Jehanne was leadin' a band o' armed Frenchies to town, and Max was just castin' off. We showed ourselves just as the Frenchies went out o' sight, and Sophie tossed us a bag o' food, but yeah, they're gone."

Charlie finally shifted her gaze from Lady Grayson's face. "I told ye what Max was like. Nice enough, until there's trouble."

I exhaled, suddenly wiped out. "Right. So we're heading inland to Orléans, then. Without Jehanne."

Ringo made a face. "I'm just as 'appy to be rid o' the chit. All that intensity's exhaustin', ye know?"

"Archer was hoping to pick her brain when we got there, though."

Ringo shuddered. "I'd just as soon stay out o' that 'otbed of insanity, if it please ye."

"You and me, both." I looked around at the clearing and considered our options. I was startled at how exhausted Lady Grayson looked. "Lady Grayson, have you eaten yet?"

She had just taken a seat on a nearby log and shook her head. "I only arrived at the abbey a few hours before you did."

"Through the spiral in the fresco?"

If she was surprised I knew about it, she didn't show it. "I came last month when it was clear Henry was missing. The Seer I traveled with foretold your arrival at the abbey, so I decided to return for you."

Her words were delivered so matter-of-factly that I was already opening my mouth to speak before she'd finished. "The Seer you traveled with?"

Now it was her turn to stare. "You don't travel with a second and a Seer each time you Clock? I assumed that's what this young man was to you." She indicated Ringo, who had the best poker face in the world and yet looked surprised.

"Archer's a Seer, and I don't know what a second is. But no one ever gave me a Clocker handbook and said, 'Here, these are the guys you have to travel with.' There is no Clocker handbook. I'm making this crap up as I go along." I couldn't help the exasperation that crept into my voice.

Lady Grayson looked horrified, probably at the idea that anyone would fly without a net like I'd been doing. "A second is a conduit, a Clocker with a special ability to help carry you across time. Granted, true conduits are somewhat uncommon among

Clockers, yet I'm sure you must have them. They are particularly useful when one Clocks with a Seer in tow because they share the burden."

I looked at Charlie, who seemed just as startled by that information as I was. "That's you."

Lady Grayson's head whipped around to Charlie. "It is quite a rare thing. Are others in your family the same?"

Charlie shook her head. "I didn't even know I had any skills until I met Saira."

"She can't Clock on her own, but when she came with me from 1889, everything was so easy."

Again Lady Grayson was staring – at me this time. "And before that you carried the burden alone?"

I shrugged. "I didn't know any differently."

She looked at Charlie and me for a few heartbeats, and then turned to Ringo. "And what can you do?"

"Watch their backs." Ringo responded before I could open my mouth. Lady Grayson nodded as if that was the obvious and perfect answer.

I reached for my satchel and pulled out some rabbit jerky, which I set on a stump along with a wedge of cheese and a knife. Charlie added some plums from her own satchel, and Ringo pulled a tomato from some unknown part of his wardrobe and began slicing it on the stump.

"So what, exactly, did your Seer See when you came before?"

Lady Grayson reached for a piece of jerky with delicate fingers. Her teeth were surprisingly good for the times, and it was oddly satisfying to see her chew off a bite. Maybe because jerky always struck me as common food, and she was so elegant.

"He Saw you alight from the boat here, under the abbey. I only recognized you two," she indicated Ringo and me, "and Lord Devereux, so I assumed the others were native to this time."

I shook my head. "Connor's a Shifter from my time, and you already know Charlie."

"It is a large party you Clock with, Saira. I must say, I am surprised you do not leave more ripples in your wake."

261

"Believe me, I'd be much happier not Clocking anywhere." The cheese and tomato combination I'd just eaten was like a perfect appetizer bite, and I thought about adding a piece of the rabbit jerky just for variety.

"Forgive me if I doubt your words. I sense a bit of my Henry in you – the prospects for adventure are a welcome product of your heritage. Those of us who prefer home and hearth tend not to make great use of our skills."

I immediately thought of Millicent and my mom. Home was more of a place with them, and considering the home they had, it wasn't a bad thing. "I guess that's why I travel with my people. I'm home wherever they are."

"That, I fear, is not one of Henry's strengths. He is searching for the thing to which he belongs, and this journey was that for him. He thought that by fulfilling his father's dream he would find his place among the powerful and influential of the Families. But he is still young and, though he believes otherwise, has much to learn before he becomes a man of power and influence."

Ringo snorted, and I remembered that he hadn't been terribly impressed during his brief meeting with Henry in the Clocker Tower.

"Did your Seer See anything about your son?" Charlie's quiet voice was like something a person had to reach for. It never quite traveled all the way to the listener's ears, and usually had something apologetic weighing it down.

Lady Grayson looked grim. "No. The only vision he had while in this time was of your arrival here."

The clash of metal rang in the distance, and Ringo and I instantly jumped to our feet.

"Pack away the food and then hide," Ringo directed Charlie. She nodded, and I turned to Lady Grayson.

"If there's fighting, we'll try to keep it away from here. Hide in the woods, or if you have to run, go back to the abbey. We'll find you."

Ringo was already sprinting, and I had to dig deep to catch up. I'd left my sword in the abbey, but my daggers were still with me, and I hoped we'd have the element of surprise on our side.

The skirmish was near the market square in town and was three against seven if you counted the Wolf as a fighter, and I did. Connor had Shifted and was the stealth attacker for Archer and Bas as they fought off six armed Frenchmen and Jehanne. She was in human form and seemed to be the one calling the shots.

The amazing thing was, she was good at it.

She shouted an order at two of her swordsmen and they responded immediately. No questioning look, no rolled eyes at the chick who was giving the orders, just insta-obey. She did it twice more, and each time her fighters ended up in a better position against Archer and Bas than when they started.

Ringo and I had stopped at the edge of the market square, and he was getting ready to draw his own sword when I motioned that we should climb. His eyes had been locked on the battle in front of us, but now as they scanned the buildings, he could see the advantage. In less than a minute we were on a rooftop, and suddenly Jehanne's whole battle plan came into focus.

Archer and Bas were more or less back to back as they fought against the Frenchmen. Connor's Wolf was keeping two of the guys busy on the sidelines, but Jehanne and the other four were attempting to draw the Vampires toward an area where the marketplace dipped down into something like a sewer. It seemed like she wanted them on low ground, and the way she was moving her guys, it's where they were headed.

Ringo used hand signals to tell me where he planned to drop down and join the fighting, and then he was gone. I scanned the battle and realized if I could take out at least one of the guys on Connor's Wolf, he could take out the other one and then join Archer, Bas, and Ringo in the main fight.

No one was looking up, because no one ever does, and I was able to slink across the rooftops to get the clearest shot on the guys fighting the Wolf. I slipped both daggers from their sheaths, took a breath, and narrowed my focus to the center of a chest. That fighter was young and strong, but he was broader than the other guy, and I thought I might have a better chance of hitting my target.

The Wolf lunged like he knew I was above him and was trying to get my target lined up for me. He had to dance out of the way of the other guy's spear, but the big guy was open and looked ready to attack again.

So I let fly.

The dagger left my hand in a perfectly straight line, but its target stepped forward at exactly the same moment. The point was positioned so it would have embedded in the guy's shoulder, but because he moved, it hit his arm instead.

And gave my position away.

A flash of the man's righteous anger filled my vision for a second, and I shook my head. The Wolf used the momentary distraction to take my target down, and when he hit the cobblestones his helmet flew off. The sound his body made on impact made me think he hit his head, and the fact that he didn't get back up confirmed it. The second guy who started after me was shielded from my other dagger by the pitched roof. Connor joined in the main fight, and I saw him take down another of the guys on Archer and Bas.

I used the distractions to jump to another roof, then to a shed, and was on the ground behind Jehanne before my pursuer could change direction.

I still had one dagger left, and Jehanne was focused on directing her remaining fighters like they were her own personal chess pieces. It would be so easy to bury the point between her shoulder blades, but even the fact that I had that thought sent a foreboding chill curling around my guts.

I was not a killer.

"Hey!" I yelled at her, and she spun in surprise to face me.

She said something in French that didn't sound like 'it's nice to see you; would you like some tea,' right before she lunged at me with her sword.

Well, crap. I didn't know what I was expecting, but it wasn't that. Apparently, she didn't have the same aversion to killing that I did because she wasn't kidding around with that sword thrust.

I dove to the side to get out of range of Jehanne's sword and practically fell over Connor's clothes. I could have kissed him for leaving his stuff lying around because his sword was part of the pile.

Connor's sword was weighted differently than mine. For the first minute or two with it, I could only block Jehanne's attempts to skewer me.

The sounds of the fight around me changed slightly, and I thought the tide might have turned against Jehanne's fighters. It didn't mean much for me unless I could keep the sharp edge of her battered sword away from my intestines, which is what I was using both dagger and sword to do at that moment.

The ringing of metal from swords clashing is a distinctive sound that's been lost to history. It should stay lost, as far as I was concerned. It was loud and sharp and carried all the promise of extreme pain.

I thought Jehanne might be close to Shifting, because the look on her face, as she tried again and again to bury her sword in my body, could only be described as feral. I got Connor's sword up just in time to avoid a slash to the neck and was trying to use the dagger in my other hand as a weapon rather than as a puny little shield, when Jehanne suddenly flew at me. Except not with her sword. With her body. Connor's Wolf had barreled into her from behind. He took her out at the knees, and her impact with the ground knocked the wind out of her.

I stared at him standing over her with a fierce growl that said, 'Move and I'll rip your throat out.' Then I looked around to find Archer and Bas disarming a couple of French fighters while Ringo gathered weapons from the ones who had fallen.

Jehanne was struggling to sit up while Connor's Wolf hovered over her menacingly. I had enough presence of mind to kick her sword away, but I was still in a fog of disbelief that I didn't have any fresh holes in my body.

"That girl tried to kill me." I was breathing hard, and my voice was more of a stunned whisper than actual tone, but she heard me and glared like she'd like another shot at it.

Archer came up next to me and peeled the sword out of my grip, finger by finger. I didn't seem capable of it because the muscles were locked into place. He said, "Thank you," in a quiet voice, and I stared at him.

"For what?" I took in the blood on his cheek and arm, and saw Bas behind him clutching his side. They looked like they'd been fighting for weeks.

"We were losing until you came."

"You were way outnumbered. And as much as I hate to admit it, she —" I tossed my head toward Jehanne, who shot a couple eye-daggers at me. "—is a really good battle tactician."

He looked grim and flinched away as I tried to look at the wound on his cheek. "Blood." He warned me. "Don't touch it. Bas and I will see to our wounds."

My heart sank to somewhere around my knee region. Archer would never let me dress or deal with his wounds, and even though I knew it had nothing to do with trust and everything to do with porphyria infection avoidance, it still stung.

"She was driving us to low ground and would have succeeded if you and Ringo hadn't come."

Jehanne spat on the ground next to my feet, and I just barely resisted the urge to kick her. Instead I turned back to Archer. "What are we going to do with her?"

"All my suggestions 'ave sharp sticks and swords in 'em." Ringo's expression was mild, but the glare he shot her had barbs attached.

Bas limped up next to Archer and spoke to him quietly in French. He was looking at Jehanne as he spoke, and Archer translated for me. "Bas said he and Bishop Klene will keep her safe and away from people while we travel to Orléans."

I looked at Bas as he continued speaking to Archer. They weren't very far apart in age – well, apparent age, since I had no idea how long Bas had been a Vampire – and had developed a short-hand with each other that men in combat seemed to. They had probably only spent an hour fighting side by side, but I could already see the beginnings of friendship.

Archer said something back to him and then turned to me. Ringo had taken Connor's place guarding Jehanne, and Connor was just coming around a corner belting his scabbard over his tunic. "Bas suggests we leave tonight. These are local farmers who rose up against the English when they burned the town two years ago, and if she has used our Englishness to rile them, their brothers, sons and fathers will come after us next."

Archer handed Connor the sword he'd taken from my hand and turned back to Bas. They spoke briefly, and Connor translated for me. "They're working out details. The upshot is we're out of here as soon as the blood's gone." Connor nodded toward Archer, who was wiping at the drips from his nose.

"By the way, we're on foot. Max and Sophie bolted at the first sign o' trouble." Ringo's scorn was louder than his voice had been.

Archer winced. "I knew that was coming. Do you have Charlie stashed somewhere?"

"She and 'er ladyship should be at the river waitin' for us."

Archer smiled at me with an expression that was closer to a grimace. "To Orléans, then?"

Why did that sound less appealing than the tea-cup ride with the stomach flu?

CLOCKER TALES

Archer came with us back to the river to get Charlie and Lady Grayson, while Bas took Jehanne up to the Saint-Séverin Abbey. We ate quickly and discussed our travel plans while Archer dunked in the river to scrub off the blood. I actually wouldn't have minded a bath, but between Ringo's disapproval, Lady Grayson's propriety, and Archer's insistence that I stay as far away from his blood as possible, I had to satisfy myself with a face-splash at the edge of the water.

Archer and Bas had agreed to meet at the abbey, which was dark when we returned – a clear sign that visitors were not welcome. Bas ushered us quickly inside and latched the heavy wooden doors behind us. The Shifter tree fresco was in shadows, but my eyes were drawn to the spiral like a moth to a flame. While Bas and Archer spoke in French, I turned to Lady Grayson.

"Do you have the mental coordinates to take us to Orléans?"

She flinched as if I'd just jumped out from behind a door. "Mental coordinates? I don't understand."

Right. Vocabulary. I tried again. "Do you have an image of Orléans you can hold in your mind in order to take us there."

Lady Grayson stared at me. "But one must be in a place in order to travel to that place. We must travel to Orléans and find a spiral in order to Clock to another time from there."

Now it was my turn to look startled. "You can't location jump?"

"You can?"

Ho boy.

268

I tuned into something Archer was telling Ringo. "There's a tributary, the Fusain, that will take us to just outside Choisy-aux-Loges. The castle there has a particularly famous dungeon, which it's best to avoid, but the horse market is apparently excellent, and from there it should only take another two days to Orléans."

"So, we're back on a boat?" I couldn't help the distaste in my voice, and Bas smiled at me before answering in heavily accented English.

"I have a small boat I will give you. It will work for Archer, and I will make a journey to retrieve it another time."

Or maybe, in another time, he wouldn't have to. I mustered a gracious smile and thanked him for his generosity while my brain spun on the conundrums of the time stream split. Would any of these people even remember what is on the other time stream? Jehanne wouldn't be here, that's for sure.

"Where do you have Jehanne?"

Bas's pleasant smile grew tight as he answered in French. Archer translated for me. "She sleeps in a room near the bishop's quarters, but she has Shifted and is now too dangerous to approach. The bishop will have to make her submit in order to have any affect with her."

Connor's expression was grim. "Should I go see what I can do?"

"No. We have bigger things to deal with than a grumpy Wolf. She's not our problem right now, and it was her choices that put her here. Let her deal with the consequences."

He nodded and looked relieved, but I could tell he still felt responsible.

Bas handed out satchels filled with food and supplies for the rest of our journey. Connor was as fascinated by this good-natured, generous Vampire as I was, because of all of us, he was probably the one most deeply steeped in the Vampires-are-bad propaganda that pervaded our time. To be fair, Lady Grayson also kept her distance, but she didn't seem distrustful of him or Archer.

Then again, I wondered if she knew what they were.

Archer and Bas said goodbye with an embrace and a promise to meet again. As we were leaving, Bas touched my hand lightly.

"Your man is good and loyal. If there is ever a time he needs help, come find me."

I looked in his warm, brown eyes and smiled. "What were you before …?"

"Before I was turned? I was a beautiful Eagle."

"Can you still Shift?"

The light in his eyes dimmed a little, and he shook his head. "I have sight, and I have speed, but the Eagle comes from life, and what I am now is from death."

Impulsively, I kissed his cheek. "Be well, Bas."

His smile was back and aimed at me. "And you, Saira."

Bas was a Moor from Spain, Archer told me. He moved to France a hundred years ago when he wanted to study Christianity.

"Moors were Muslim, right?"

"Bas is on a quest to understand the world's relationships to God. He began his journey with his own faith and spent a hundred years studying the evolution and complexities of Islam. He then moved into Sephardic Judaism in North Africa for about fifty years, and then finished that century in Germany with the Ashkenazi Jews. Catholicism in France was next, and since he wants to learn English, he'll continue his Catholic immersion in England. I warned him about the Tudors, and suggested he slip over to Amsterdam for his Protestant conversion in the 1500s until things settle down under Elizabeth."

I stared at Archer. "He's over three hundred years old?"

He grinned. "I tell you he's faith-hopping, and you're fascinated by his age?"

"I'm fascinated by everything about the guy. I want to go back and sit down with him for the next two years, listening to his stories and asking him questions." I couldn't keep the awe out of my voice.

"It's a good thing I like Bas so much, then, or I'd be jealous."

I smirked. "I don't want his body. I want his brain."

"And that's supposed to make me feel better?" He was teasing me, and it felt like a million years since we'd played.

Archer and I were the only two still awake in the boat, which was a good deal bigger than Bas had let on. The Fusain River was narrower than the Loing, but that just pushed the water through faster. Our party was the same size as it had been when we left Paris, without Max and Sophie of course, but swapping Lady Grayson for Jehanne had improved things a hundred percent. Charlie was glued to her side, and Lady Grayson was lovely and warm and generous with her. I could see her interactions with Ringo take on a different tone, too. He was less man-at-one's-back now and more mate-for-my-girl, and so far, it seemed that she liked what she saw.

"Have you met any other Vampires besides Bas?" I asked Archer. We had fixed a lantern to the front of the boat, and the dim light made the water under it sparkle.

"I assume Wilder doesn't count?"

I scoffed. "As if anyone could count less."

Archer shook his head. "It seems the prejudice against my kind hasn't yet become so pervasive and deep in this time. Bas seemed unsurprised to meet me, and Bishop Klene related to him as just another Descendant."

"When St. Brigid's was founded in 1554 there were only four tower wings for the four Families. So it seems like the prejudice had already taken hold by then." I realized I was intolerant of intolerance, because even saying the words annoyed me.

Lady Grayson's soft voice came out of the darkness. "It has. But Death was not forgotten in the building of St. Brigid's. A room was built for him under the school, not to be occupied, of course, but as a nod to his existence. I saw the original construction plans, so I may be one of the few who knows of it."

Funny that Archer was living in Death's room, though neither of us mentioned it to Lady Grayson. Archer spoke quietly. "Do you know other Vampires, then?"

"I do not believe so, but then again, I did not realize you were one until I overheard you speaking about it. I apologize for inserting myself into your conversation, but I find I am fascinated."

"No need for apology, Lady Grayson. Please, join us. There is a bottle of the abbey's red wine in my satchel if you'd care for some?"

Lady Grayson sat up and moved toward our positions in the boat. "I would be quite delighted, Lord Devereux. Thank you."

"Please call me Archer. I have the sense we may end this journey knowing more about each other than most family members do."

"Then I will, on the condition that you both call me Valerie."

That was going to be a tough one for me. She was Lady Grayson to the bone, from the way she held herself, to the way she spoke. It felt disrespectful to be casual with her, but she asked, so now it would be disrespectful not to.

I dug around in Archer's bag to find the corked bottle and a glass, which I handed to Valerie as she sat next to me.

"Will you not join me?"

"I don't really have a taste for wine. Where I grew up it isn't legal to drink until age twenty-one."

Valerie might have been more horrified at that than finding out Archer was a Vampire. "Twenty-one? That's practically half one's life spent without the benefits and delights of wine. Preposterous." She poured herself a glass from the bottle and took a sip.

"Ah, there is nothing in the world like French wine. Archer, are you able to join me in a glass?"

He grimaced. "It is one of my greatest regrets about my condition, sadly. My father had an excellent wine cellar with extraordinary wines from this region in particular, but they're wasted on me now."

Valerie let loose a sigh worthy of an Oscar as she sipped her wine gracefully. "I think I should not become a Vampire then. Though I must admit there is a certain appeal to the idea of permanently stopping the clock. Only I should have done so about twenty years ago when I still had beautiful skin."

Oh. My. God. Become a Vampire to stop the aging process? I caught Archer's eye and gave him my best 'is she for real?' look. He winked and then poured charm all over her.

"You would stop the clock at ten years old?"

Valerie laughed. "Don't be ridiculous, Archer. I am well over forty and you know it."

"Looking at you, I know no such thing."

She sighed again and turned to me. "Manners and charm like his cannot be taught. I like your young man very much, my dear. Now stop with the flattery and let us discuss Vampires."

"Has there ever been a Vampire on the Descendants' council?" Archer spun the questions back around to Valerie, and she seemed intrigued enough to explore the topic with us.

"Everything I have ever known or read about the Families indicates that Death removed himself from the other Immortals after Jera and Goran's child went missing."

"Wait a minute. Went missing? I thought Death killed the child." I hadn't given the origin stories a lot of attention, but I'd also only just heard them this past year, so this one in particular was pretty fresh in my mind.

"There has never been any indication the child was killed, although I suppose missing can be construed as dead when there is no evidence of continued life."

"You sound like a scientist. Connor's wishing he was awake for this conversation," I smirked.

"I am awake." His sleepy voice came from somewhere near the bow of the boat where he had been wrapped up in his cloak.

"Well, come and join the party then." At this point I wouldn't be surprised if Charlie and Ringo were pretending sleep too. But the glimpse I caught of them in the moonlight showed them nestled close, her hand resting on his arm. Even if he was awake, I doubted Ringo would move from that position. Kind of like when a kitten falls asleep in your lap and you'd rather pee in a cup than wake it.

Connor yawned deeply and then shot a quick glance at Valerie and covered his mouth. "Excuse me, ma'am."

"It has been a very long day for all of us. The fact that you are also tired makes me feel much better about my own state of exhaustion."

He scooted me over on my bench and sat down. "I heard what you said about the original Immortals. I was taught that Death either killed the child or had it killed after War stirred the pot about another Immortal being created."

"Well, Duncan was certainly a 'pot-stirrer,' as you say, but the legend I was taught was that soon after the child was born, it disappeared. Whether Death had anything to do with its disappearance remained a mystery, as he also seemed to retire from the public life of the Immortals after that."

"The Immortals had a public life?" I knew I sounded incredulous, but seriously?

"Apparently, they were quite active participants in their Families for a time."

I scoffed. "In an Immortal life span, 'a time' could be anything from a couple hundred years to a few thousand."

"As you say. I believe the same holds true for Death's issue, which, some may argue, is a more valid reason for waging war against them than a baseless argument with Aeron himself."

Connor spoke thoughtfully. "In other words, hunt the Suckers because they're essentially immortal and might decide to take over."

"I wouldn't put it past the Mongers, for sure." I turned to Archer, who had been silent during the whole exchange. "What do you think?"

He looked at Valerie. "How do the Descendants feel about inter-Family marriages and the mixed-blood offspring of those unions during your time?"

She looked at him strangely. "Descendants and the ungifted? It dilutes our skills, but it has never been of great concern."

"Descendant Families with each other." His voice was quiet.

Valerie waved her hand dismissively. "That is not possible. Children from such a union would die, the Immortals made sure of it after Jera and Goran ..." She suddenly turned to stare at me. "You said Jehanne is a Shifter. I assumed she was a Seer. Is she, as you say, mixed?"

"We think so. I am, too."

The stare got bigger. "But you're an Elian."

"And a Shaw."

"How ..."

"Pretty much the usual way, I'm sure."

She sat back, speechless.

Archer tried to explain. "Fundamentally, Death's Descendants are also mixed. The ... sickness that changes our bodies doesn't actually alter our Family skill, it merely incorporates it, or in the case of Bas, subjugates it."

Connor was nodding as Archer spoke, but I could see the confusion on Valerie's face as if she'd said it out loud.

I made my voice gentle, like I was coaxing a dog to trust me. "Archer wasn't born a Descendant of Death. He was infected through a transfer of blood. That infection stopped the aging process in his body, but didn't change the fact that he was born a Seer and still has the visions of one. So, in a sense, he's mixed too – Sucker blood mixed with Seer blood."

"Apparently, something seems to have happened between the Renaissance and the Victorian age which changed the ignorance about mixed-bloods into a hatred of them." Archer sounded like he was thinking out loud, because there's no way Lady Grayson would know about the Victorians.

"Why do you say that?" Valerie still sounded like she'd been whapped upside the head by a two-by-four.

Archer seemed to be lost in thought, so I answered. "At best, the known mixed-bloods are forcibly sterilized so we can't have kids. At worst, we're killed. We've been discovering that a lot more mixed-bloods may exist than anyone knows about, probably because the threats against them are so dire."

"Dear God! Such barbarism! How can the council allow it?"

"In my time, the Mongers have become the enforcers of the Immortal Descendant world."

"In mine, they are merely – what did you call them? Pot-stirrers."

"Which begs the question, why? Why do Mongers become so threatened by mixed-bloods that they start a campaign to hunt them?"

Valerie looked me straight in the eyes. "Are you dangerous?"

I smiled. "Yes. Are you?" I thought about her position of influence in Queen Mary's court, and the courage it took to come here to find her son.

She watched me for a long moment, and I thought maybe she considered those things, too. "Yes, I believe I am."

As we glided down the river, there were many philosophical debates about Immortal Descendant politics, but as fascinating as they were, none of them seemed to get us any closer to answers that made a difference to our purpose. We learned, for example, that in Valerie's time, and for at least a century prior, Clockers went on a mission at nineteen. It was the first time they were allowed to Clock anywhere on their own, though they always had a support Clocker – the conduit – and a Seer with them. Valerie said the support Clocker with Henry was an older woman who had been the conduit for many missions, but Valerie's husband and the council had substituted a different Seer at the last minute for the one originally scheduled. She had heard a rumor he was a sailor or someone who worked on ships, but she had no other information.

Valerie explained that the Clocker missions had been established because the first time any Clocker traveled, it was always a precise one-ring jump to exactly the date, time, and location from which they'd departed – but a hundred and twenty-five years in the past. After the first jump, Clocking became less precise, unless one had the Clocker necklace. Without the necklace, Clocking could sometimes be off by a month or two, but Valerie had heard of adult Clockers who had gone as far afield as several years … or had never returned at all. It had, therefore, been a huge risk for her to come back to the abbey to find us, which was why she hadn't discussed the trip with her husband before she left. Sort of the 'ask forgiveness rather than permission' thing I did, and one of the reasons I was beginning to like Valerie Grayson so much. She said the unpredictability of Clocking was the main reason Clockers rarely left their native times, and why so much importance was placed on a Clocker's first mission.

I was, unsurprisingly, a complete anomaly. My first experience, Clocking back to 1888, seemed to fit the pattern. But since I'd learned to jump off the default range, I could direct my location based on a detailed image, and at least get myself to the right year. Or, if I knew the location well, I could be even more specific with the date. I seemed to have the ability to focus on at least two of the three variables every time I clocked.

Clockers in Tudor times, according to Valerie, were limited by location as well as uncertain timings. They had to physically start from the place they wanted to land, which meant that just after I met him, Henry had traveled across the English Channel and then over land to Orléans. There was an old spiral carved into the city wall, which was fine to leave from in 1554, but he and his two companions had to travel armed because they were Clocking into a war zone. I didn't like not knowing anything about the Seer with Henry – because I had the feeling he was more like a bodyguard than a traveling partner.

It was because of the precise one-ring jump limitation that the council had begun anticipating the birth of different Clockers, and why Henry's birth had been the subject of a Seer's vision. Valerie's anger at her husband was barely hidden as she described his ambition within the council and his push to make sure Henry was chosen for the Orléans mission. The council had identified the battle at Orléans as the turning point in British/French relations. They felt the problems the Tudor court was having with France in the mid-1500s would never have occurred if France was still under England's control. Therefore, history must be changed.

Right. Because that's a good idea.

The magnitude of the idiocy was baffling. Like cheating in chess when checkmate is inevitable. A do-over of a move that set a whole new game in motion, but did the old game just disappear, or did it keep on playing? Was there only ever one stream of time? What if a Clocker aimed for a particular year and ended up on another time stream?

Those were questions that had apparently never occurred to the councils in Tudor England. They seemed to be operating under the "history is what we say it is" philosophy. The more we talked, the more horrified Valerie became at the Clockers of her time.

I told her not to worry. Our Family had managed to nearly extinguish itself by my time; so clearly, natural selection was hard at work.

She didn't understand why I thought that was funny.

Charlie spent her time in quiet conversation with Valerie. She picked her brain about every aspect of society – the Families, how to throw a party, what to read, the intricacies of the class system. I slept through most of it, but I could see the effect on Charlie's confidence. Valerie was a mentor to her, and their relationship was quickly developing into something pretty deep.

Ringo didn't seem threatened or bothered by the amount of time Charlie and Valerie spent together. He and Connor spent their rowing hours in active debates about science, politics, world peace, video games – everything was open for discussion. Connor might have been younger than Ringo in age and experience, but his vast storehouse of knowledge put them on a level playing field.

When the river ended, Archer and Valerie negotiated transportation while the rest of us stayed hidden in the woods. They came back with three sturdy farm horses, and who rode with whom was decided by weight distribution and riding ability. At first it seemed Connor was uncomfortable on the back of Valerie's horse, but it made sense that he go with her. By the end of the night's riding they were chatting like old friends.

Everyone adjusted to Archer's schedule, since it was virtually impossible for him to go unconscious on the back of a horse, and by the end of the second night we had made it to the Loire River.

We set up a makeshift camp at the edge of the woods where Archer could be covered by cloaks under the shelter of the trees while he slept. Ringo and Connor went into town to sell the horses and buy passage for us on one of the boats heading to Orléans. We were only about four hours away by boat, so tonight we would arrive.

Charlie dropped off to sleep almost as soon as she wrapped up in her cloak. Valerie looked over at her with a tender gaze. "She has no family left."

"She has us. And Ringo is her family."

Valerie's eyes found mine. "That young man is extraordinary. He came from nothing and yet knows exactly who he is and what he wants from the world. He will live every moment of his life to the fullest, and he will do it with confidence, grace, and quite a bit of cheek." She smiled. I thought Ringo fit that description exactly, and probably wouldn't even be surprised at it.

"He will also protect and care for Charlie every step of the way. I see his honor and loyalty, and I see the affection between them. They could be together for the rest of their lives and grow into the comfortable closeness that soul mates share." She looked back to Charlie, and this time there was concern in her gaze.

"But she doesn't know who she truly is. She doesn't even know the breadth of what she doesn't know. I fear that if she attaches herself to him now, she will grow up in the shadow of this wonderful, confident young man and will stumble, half a step behind, wherever he goes."

I opened my mouth to deny what she said. Ringo loved Charlie. He didn't admit it yet – his honor and sense of propriety probably didn't let him. But he clearly loved her, and I knew she worshipped him.

"He'd never leave her on her own."

"Of course not. She would have to leave him."

I stared at Valerie. "You're not trying to break them up, are you? Because I warn you now, I won't let you hurt my friends."

Valerie smiled gently. It wasn't the look of someone hatching an evil plan, it was more the look of a woman who had a lot of life under her belt and wanted to spare someone else the heartaches she'd known. "One cannot 'break up' those who are meant to be together. I do, however, intend to offer Charlotte an opportunity to come to court with me. To learn the confidence and poise a young woman must have to know who she is."

"She can't go to court with you. Mary's only going to be queen for another two years." I blurted it out before I could guard my tongue. So far we had avoided talking about the history we all knew would happen but hadn't yet for Valerie.

Her eyes narrowed. "So soon?" Then she sighed. "I knew it would come. The queen is not well, and I have already made my plans to retire to the country before the first frost hits. It will give me three months at court with Charlotte, and then she shall learn how to manage an estate."

I was already shaking my head. "But she'll be outside her native time. She won't age while she's with you, and Ringo will just keep getting older."

"And is she aging here? Or in your time? I think not. And for that matter, who is to say that Ringo will age out of his native time?"

That was true, too. He wasn't a Descendant, but that didn't mean he wasn't subject to the same temporal laws Clockers were, even partial ones like Charlie.

I huffed in exasperation, not sure why I was fighting this so hard. "Charlie's not a full Clocker. She can't get herself back to him when she's done learning ... whatever she would learn with you."

"No, but you could bring him to her and let them decide together what path their futures hold."

"Unless something happens to me, and then we've messed up two more lives."

Valerie's smile was sympathetic. "You have made yourself into a strong, capable, confident young woman, Saira. You have skills I can only dream of and are fearless enough to use them. If Charlotte had even one-tenth of your courage, I would not be having this conversation. But courage rides on the coattails of confidence, and that is not something that can be forced into a person's experience of themselves. Some people are born with it, others never find it. But I do believe confidence can be learned in a nurturing, safe environment. The world you and Archer and Ringo currently inhabit is not safe, and there is no time for nurturing. The best Charlotte can do with you is hold on for the ride."

I couldn't say anything to counter that because it was true. Until Wilder was taken out of the equation and whatever was going on with the Mongers in my time was stopped, we were committed to a course of action that I'd accepted from Fate. Funny how I'd stopped fighting the idea of Aislin's prophecy when I decided to take the theoretical job of "the child." But whoever came with me had to be there by choice, not by default. And I wasn't sure Charlie had really chosen this.

I finally sighed in resignation. "I assume the only reason you brought it up with me is because it'll be my job to eventually reunite them if she went with you."

"That is part of it. But I also recognize your place at the center of this gathering of lovely people. They look to you for friendship, and they trust you. If you were set against the idea of Charlotte coming home with me, she likely would not do it for fear of disappointing you."

"I doubt I have that much influence on any of my friends, and I'm not supporting your plan, but I won't protest if it's something they both want."

She nodded. "Thank you, Saira."

"Why do you want her with you?"

She leveled her gaze on me. "Because Charlotte looks at me with the trust and admiration that I have not seen in my own son's eyes for many years. Perhaps familiarity actually does breed contempt, or perhaps I made mistakes with Henry that I have learned from and will not repeat. In any case, I was only blessed with one child of my body, and he no longer needs me. I have much more room in my heart and my life than I have people to care for, and I want to give what I can to Charlotte."

When I took my fierce protective instinct for Ringo out of the equation, I could see that Charlie was lucky to have someone like Valerie in her life. Charlie's mother had died when she was young, and her sister had never been maternal. I had seen how she gravitated to my own mom, and I thought that maybe Valerie could fulfill a role that really did go into helping to shape how a girl put herself together.

I reached my hand out to Valerie, and she squeezed it. "You're very different than I first thought you were."

She smiled. "You mean imperious and entitled?"

I laughed and didn't answer. She had been imperious, but she wasn't now. Despite her social standing and her place at court, Valerie Grayson was lovely and warm. I hoped we could find Henry, and then I hoped, probably absurdly, that he would have a change of heart and become a good and generous son to his mother.

TOM – AUGUST, 1429

He was coming.

I could hear his heartbeat through the door. The sound of it beat a rhythm that tattooed my skin and pumped blood through my body.

Blood.

It was the eye of the needle through which my focus was threaded. Blood drove the breath from my lungs; it carried the promises of life and death in every cell. I didn't just need it, I had become pure need. Every part of me yearned, desired, wanted, and craved the life-giving substance. It had become air to a drowning man, and I knew that without blood the need would ravage me.

The latch on the door began to lift.

The need pushed me up. Atrophied muscles filled with blood that had somehow replicated inside the wreck that was left of my body. My heart pounded the blood through my veins so hard I thought it would push right out of my chest.

The door opened.

My heart stuttered.

I stood.

The muscles shook, but held. The pounding of my own heart couldn't mask the sound of his when he saw me. I scared him.

His heartbeat raced.

I licked my lips.

"You … live?"

I didn't move. I couldn't. Yet.

"But how?"

283

I smiled.

It must have been a grim-looking thing, that smile, because he took a step backward. Hit the edge of the door. Stumbled.

The need filled the oceans, the world, and the universe. I. Was. Need.

I moved then. Faster than I'd ever moved before. Faster than unused muscles and weakened bones should have allowed. The need was strength and speed and desire.

He screamed then. It chilled me. That scream broke through the tiniest atom of the need. Made me hesitate, but then ...

The need laughed and lunged and tore and drank and drank and drank.

The need became light and warmth and joy. It became the reason for life, the sustenance and purpose, and as I fulfilled it, I felt my body become mine again. But stronger, better, and more real than I'd ever been before.

A profound peace settled around me like a mantle of calm and rightness.

I looked down to thank him for the life he had given me.

But Léon could only stare at me through his dead eyes.

He couldn't even scream anymore.

So I did for him.

THE WALL

The boat captain let us off before the river bent toward Orléans, but on the same side as the city. He had been paid the entire cost of all three horses to wait until sunset to depart, and had barked orders at the kid with the lantern the whole time. The Loire River was three times as wide as the Loing had been, so I didn't know what he was so worried about, but it was clear he was happy to be rid of us.

We had all slept that day, so midnight felt like noon, but the woods around us blocked the moonlight and made stealthy travel a little challenging.

"If one of you will take my stuff, I'll Shift and go ahead to see what we're walking into." Connor's low voice was just above a whisper, but the sound of the cicadas almost overrode it.

"Give them to me." Archer moved forward to take Connor's bag. There was enough light that my night vision was working properly, so I turned my back while Connor stripped off his clothes.

"Should I turn around?" Charlie whispered to me.

"Only if you can see him."

"I can't even see you, and you're right in front of me."

I laughed quietly. "Nudity is normal to Shifters. He doesn't care one way or the other."

I could practically feel the shimmery air around Connor as he Shifted, and suddenly Valerie exclaimed.

"Oh! He's beautiful."

285

I turned back in time to see the Wolf nudge Valerie's hand, and then take off running into the trees. The woods by the river weren't so thick that Archer and I couldn't lead the others forward, but it was slow going without lights.

Archer spoke quietly to me. "We'll have to take everyone back with us, so wherever you draw the spiral needs to be sheltered, out of the main flow of traffic, and ideally with some sort of safe place to stash Charlie and Valerie."

"As soon as we find a safe place to Clock, we have two objectives, right?" I looked to Archer for confirmation, and then continued. "Find Jehanne to keep an eye on her so things play out like her visions predict." I was ticking my fingers. "And find Henry and get him to abandon his plan, so history can continue in the direction it's supposed to go."

"If it's about the bridge blowing up, we'll need to factor that into our priorities."

I exhaled sharply. "Right. Hopefully we don't have to deal with that – it'll just happen because it's meant to." The idea of taking an active part in any of the killing that would happen in Orléans was way more than I wanted to contemplate. "Ringo and I know what Henry looks like. Once we land in the past, we should search for him while you and Connor try to find Jehanne."

He exhaled softly. "That makes sense. I hate the idea of separating, but it's the best use of our resources." He bent to pick something, and then held it out to me. "Here. For your tea."

I crushed the tops of the chamomile between my fingers and inhaled the slightly sweet scent of pineapple. The chances of actually taking the time to boil water and make tea were slim, but I loved that he thought about it.

"Elizabeth said something to me once … She said I loved like I thought I had a choice in the matter." I tucked the chamomile into my bag, and then took his hand in mine and we fell into effortless step with each other. "She was laughing at me because she knew I was delusional to think I could be anything but head over heels in love with you."

"Ah, good to know I'm in love with a crazy person."

286

I squeezed his hand and laughed. "I'd have to be to fall for an old guy like you."

Something in him stilled. It was so slight I might have imagined it if it hadn't been for his words. "Connor and I have been talking."

"That's dangerous."

"Indeed." I loved the wry tone in his voice and wished he would stop there. "What if the cell stasis could be reversed? The porphyria neutralized?"

"What if? You'd do it in a heartbeat, right?"

"But what if it's like you? The clock stops whenever you're outside your native time, but resets to where it should be all at once when you get back."

"You mean, what if you pull a Buffy the Vampire Slayer and go "poof" in a million dusty pieces right before my eyes?"

"What's Buffy the Vampire Slayer?"

"She's a badass blonde who goes around killing every vampire she meets. It helps that they're basically demons inhabiting high school kids' bodies. The dusty poof was a practical device so she didn't have to bury, like, twenty bodies an episode."

"TV?"

"You never saw it? Come on, you mean you don't troll for every vampire movie and TV show you can find?"

He made a sound of distaste. "That thing you have about stories that break time travel rules? I have the same aversion to anything about vampires." He chuckled. "Nice change of subject, by the way."

"You liked that? Pretty much a guarantee when you start bringing up the idea of poofing."

He chuckled again. I wasn't kidding. I could pretty much deal with anything – a cure, no cure, human, Vampire – whatever. But dealing with him going up in a cloud of dust as if he'd never been there at all? I didn't have that coping mechanism in my repertoire, and had no plans to add it.

I caught the edge of some shimmery business off to my right, and then Connor stepped out from behind a tree. "Do you have my clothes?"

I think he startled Valerie, who tactfully pretended not to have heard our conversation, but she kept her gasp in the silent range. The rest of us were getting used to his Shifting. Archer tossed him his clothes, and a minute later he was beside us.

"What did you find?"

"The main encampments of English soldiers are on both sides of the river. The city walls are easier to breach on the inland side since there's only a small garrison near one of the city gates. The sewers are unguarded, and there are some excellent climbing trees with clear shots to the wall that guards seem to overlook on their rounds."

"Did you spot anything that looks like a decent place to Clock from?" We weren't whispering now, and everyone had gathered around us to hear the news.

Connor nodded. "There's an old mill on a tributary just a bit further upriver, west of the camps. It's abandoned now, and looks like it's been that way for years."

Archer clapped Connor on the shoulder. "Excellent. Thank you, my friend. Any trouble between here and the mill?"

"None that I sensed. The English camps were obviously much bigger around the city when it was under siege, but I could see evidence of the leading edge, and it's far enough away to keep the roaming soldiers out of range."

I sighed. "That's right. The English won this skirmish so they're just protecting their interests here at this point. When we go back, it'll be a full-on siege."

Connor grinned. "Trust me; I've played enough D&D in my life to understand battle tactics."

"D&D?" Valerie asked. The game had been a fixture in the high school I went to in L.A., and I'd always been a little jealous of the guys huddled around their dice, creating their fantasy characters and taking them into made-up battles.

"Dungeons and Dragons. It's a game."

"Explain." Ringo had an anticipatory smile on his face. I knew he and Connor would talk rules and strategy for hours. We fell into step behind the two of them, and I listened in as Connor described the different classes and races of characters one could choose. I thought Ringo would be attracted to the Rogues, with their thieves, assassins and tricksters. But he surprised me by asking about the Druids, who could communicate with animals and even shapeshift for a brief time.

Valerie watched the guys fondly. "I wish my Henry had had friends such as yours."

"I don't really know him. What's he like?" I asked.

Fondness colored her voice as she spoke. "Until he was sixteen, he was small for his age and very athletic. When he finally reached his height it took about three months for his coordination to catch up, so he became the comedian among his peers to account for his stumbles and falls." I could hear the smile on her face. "I remember one day he came home with a bloody lip and the biggest grin I had ever seen. I asked him what had happened, and he replied that he had tripped over a loose brick and had flailed spectacularly as he fell. He somehow managed to convince his laughing compatriots that he was rehearsing a new dance step, and within half an hour had them all practicing the Swan Dive."

I sensed that talking about her son was relieving some of her fears. "What else, besides sports, is he good at?"

"Henry is good at people. He understands them, enjoys them, and knows how to make them laugh. He has the natural confidence of the very intelligent, but with a sly sense of humor that completely disarms people's resistance to associating with those who can best them." A sigh accompanied the smile this time. "And he is tremendously charming toward young ladies."

That fit with the Henry I'd met in the Clocker Tower of St. Brigid's in 1554, and Archer covered his snort by clearing his throat. Valerie noticed, and her tone was wry as she continued.

"I have been terrified that I would one day find an irate father on my doorstep demanding my son do the honorable thing and marry his daughter."

She sighed again, but with the tolerance of a mother for her son. "To be fair, he has not been dishonorable, at least so far as I know. But I can imagine that more than one young lady has fallen in love with his smile and the way he looks at them as if they are the loveliest flower. I have hopes Henry will see past the pretty flowers to the striking willow who lives next door to our Sussex manor. Alas, thus far, he hasn't seen in Penelope more than the childhood friend with whom he once climbed trees."

She lapsed into the silence of her memories, and I found myself wishing Henry and Penelope a long and happy life together.

Connor led us up the small tributary, where we literally almost stumbled upon the old stone mill, hidden in overgrowth along its banks. The building was definitely ramshackle, and from the plant growth around it, I doubted it had been recently abandoned. The water wheel was broken, and moss grew thick on the splintered wood. The broken flagstones that had tripped me looked like they'd been hewn by hand, and even in all the eerie emptiness, the mill looked peaceful. Like it was a place of refuge.

Ringo and Charlie immediately went inside the structure to see if it could be made safe for Archer's daytime sleep, while Archer and Connor circled the perimeter of the property. Valerie and I had an unspoken mission to find a good spot for a spiral.

"I admit to being truly amazed that you are able to create the spirals we travel through." Valerie's tone was admiring.

"I didn't know other Clockers couldn't do the same thing. Then again, I basically don't know other Clockers. You and Henry are the first ones I ever met outside my own family."

I pushed aside some heavy overgrowth behind the house and discovered a sturdy wood door. There was some rot damage in the latch, but not enough to weaken it, and after a couple of tries we were able to get it open.

Inside the door was a secret garden. Probably not so secret when the mill was functioning, but vines covered walls that had been built to keep animals out of the vegetables, and there was a severe overgrowth of everything that thrives on neglect. It was the feral cousin to my mom's overgrown garden at Elian Manor.

The walls were mostly intact, and the place was definitely hidden from casual view. Rotten tomatoes hung from opportunistic vines, and a clump of carrot tops revealed small, perfect orange carrots that Valerie brushed off and put in my satchel. Clearly, even the vegetable production had remained undisturbed by humans.

I tugged at some vines on a mostly unbroken section of the wall, and they came away with only a token resistance. The stone beneath was smooth enough I could probably draw the spiral I needed instead of taking the time to carve it. I took another look around the garden, where moonlight played across the leaves of overgrown plants, and the walls formed a layer of protection against wildlife and wandering humans. My eyes found Valerie's and I nodded.

"Here."

"Tonight?"

I thought about that. There were probably five hours of darkness left – enough time for Archer to either scout and come back to rest, or make it inside the city and find shelter there.

"Let's see what the others say, but yeah, I'm up for going tonight."

"Will you draw the spiral now or wait until we go?"

"I have to wait. The minute I draw, it takes me."

She looked around the walled garden and nodded. "It's a good place. A serene refuge that will feed us and keep us safe while we wait for you."

"You're okay with that? Staying back with Charlie?"

She smiled. "Unlike you, I am quite content to avoid conflicts. I am only sorry that it is my son who has helped to create them."

I took her hand as we picked our way past the overgrowth and back outside the garden. "I hope he's okay." I tried for a reassuring tone.

Her voice sounded sad. "As do I."

Everyone agreed it was better to spend the rest of the night acclimatizing to the war zone than sitting in this time stream wondering and waiting for another day. Archer and Connor had found no evidence of human interaction with the mill for what looked like several years, so we were fairly confident it would still be deserted when we landed a couple months earlier.

We planned to arrive the night of May 6th because Valerie explained that the true history had recorded that Joan of Arc detonated the blast that turned the tide of the siege on May 7th, 1429. I had learned from my deadly mistake with Mary Kelly in 1888 that the calendar date started at midnight, but that still gave us several hours, or as long as a full day, to do what we needed to do.

And then Connor surprised me more than I thought possible when he whipped one of my fat markers out of his satchel. "You never know when you might need a spiral," he said mischievously.

The grin on his face turned to a grimace when I kissed him on the cheek. I was pretty sure kisses were still mortifying to a fourteen-year-old boy. "You're awesome – thank you."

"I was kind of hoping you might teach me how to make stencils someday." He sounded oddly shy all of a sudden, and I realized I only ever thought of Connor as a tech geek and scientist.

"Anytime, Wolf."

Archer and Ringo were pleased with the secret garden location for the spiral, and in a couple of minutes, everyone was arrayed around me. Charlie stood on one side of me, with Ringo on one hand and Valerie on the other. Valerie had Connor's hand, and he held onto my free left hand. Archer was on the other side of me with his arm wrapped around my waist so I could use my right hand to draw. Valerie was quite nervous about the number of people I was Clocking, but I thought that with Charlie's help as a conduit it shouldn't be too bad.

I took a steadying breath. "Hold on, guys." The marker was like an old friend, and the ink lay down perfectly. When the first spiral was done, I started to feel the buzzing. It wasn't just in my head, it ran through my body, and by the time the third spiral was done I could feel the pressure of Ringo's hand holding Charlie's, her hand clutching Valerie's, Connor's hands on both of ours, and Archer around my waist. It was like a chain with every link conducted through me and boosted through Charlie.

I held the picture of the secret garden in my mind, but I focused my thoughts on the date. May 6th, 1429. May 6th, 1429. May 6th ...

The sensation of *between* was like a pause between breaths. Peaceful and calm, with only the echo of the thrum and roil I was used to. Maybe it was just the short hop, or maybe it was Charlie's amplification of my Clocking ability, but when we landed in the same spot we left, I was barely dizzy.

Valerie looked at me in awe. "Impossible."

I was running a visual check on everyone, and only Connor seemed to be green around the gills. Everyone else was doing okay. I squeezed his hand. "You okay?"

"Yeah. Just feeling a little roller-coaster-ish."

I grinned at him, then felt Archer's arm tighten around me. He spoke quietly in my ear. "Talk to Valerie."

She was still staring at me like I was an exotic bug or alien species.

"That was easier than it usually is, but since Charlie started Clocking with me, there's been a lot less puking."

"I travel with a conduit nearly every time, and I have never experienced such peace between times."

"When I Clocked with my mom, I felt like all the sensations were going through her and I only got the echoes. Maybe with Charlie and me doing the actual Clocking, we were the filters and you got to just ride along." I smiled at her and looked over at Ringo. "You guys okay?"

Our voices were pitched low, just in case anyone was lurking outside the garden, but Archer was already moving toward the garden door, and Connor was right behind him.

"We're fine."

"I do wish we had a Seer with us." Valerie looked around nervously.

"We do." I went after Archer, who had just slipped through the garden door.

I found him outside packing Connor's clothes and boots into his satchel. He looked up as I approached. "Connor's going to Shift and do a quick scout before we all split up."

I grabbed Connor's arm before he pulled off his trousers. "Hey. Be careful and stay safe, okay?"

He gave me a grin that was as much Wolf as it was boy. "What you didn't know about me is my D&D avatar is an Eldritch Knight Warrior. He's a super-fighter with magical skills on his side."

"Dude, that's supposed to make me feel better? That's a game."

"It's a state of mind, Saira. And I can't believe you just duded me." His grin was huge. The kid was having fun, and despite the fact that the prospect of what we were all about to step into gave me stomach cramps of the food-poisoning variety, I could appreciate that he was finally acting like a fourteen-year-old boy.

So I decided not to say out loud that if anything happened to him I didn't want to be the one to tell his mom and Mr. Shaw. Reminders of what waited for us at home would not be helpful at this moment. So I just squeezed his arm and let him go. He stripped off the last of his clothes and Shifted almost immediately. I wished I had learned to control my beast like he could, because there was something really spectacular about what he did.

I turned to Archer as he gathered the rest of Connor's clothes and shoved them into his bag. "Any chance you can try to look with your Sight?"

He winced. "You know it's never worked like that for me."

"Maybe not when you were awake. But I asked you to See Ringo once when you were sleeping, and it worked then."

That startled him a little. I guessed he hadn't really thought that through. He held his hand out to me and I grabbed it. "I can try, but maybe you should ask me for what you want to see."

"You think that had something to do with it?"

He smiled. "I can't deny you anything, and perhaps my gift knows it too."

I went a little gooey inside, but firmly told myself to get it together. There'd be time for that later. And if I said that loud and often enough, I might even believe it.

Connor's Wolf nudged my leg, and I reached down to ruffle the fur at his neck. He must have been able to smell the wave of fear that washed over me, so he gave me his understanding before he took off to scout the area. I closed my eyes against the nerves, and then opened them to stare into Archer's concerned gaze.

"Are you okay?"

I nodded, and then shook my head. I closed my eyes again, took a breath, and dug deep for the conviction in my question. "Show me that you'll be okay."

His eyes were locked on mine for another heartbeat, and then he finally nodded and closed them. I watched his face for a moment. He was so beautiful to me. Almost black hair, fair skin that hadn't seen sunlight in more than a century, eyes I knew were practically indigo, high cheekbones, the jaw of a superhero, and expressive lips that were usually quirked in a smile when he looked at me. I needed to know he'd survive this. I needed more time with him. Time to know what it felt like to relax into love, to feel effortlessly safe and cared for, to understand the way my body responded to him. Time to know him like I was beginning to know myself.

I finally closed my own eyes, and when the darkness behind my eyelids grew light, I knew he could See, and I could See through him.

The visions came in flashes. Running through the woods with a Wolf. Scaling city walls. Watching Jehanne and her war council from a distance. Archer and the Wolf surrounded by French soldiers. A big man I recognized as Gilles de Rais consulting with Jehanne. Archer pushing de Rais in heated anger. De Rais coming at him with his sword in hand and a look of rage on his face.

I gasped and the vision disappeared. My eyes flew open, and I stared at Archer.

"You can't engage de Rais! You can't kill him on this time stream."

There was grim determination in his voice. "Can't I?"

"Archer, no. Please don't. It's not worth it."

"Not worth hundreds of children's lives? Really, Saira? You can look me in the eye ... no, you can look *yourself* in the eye and say you wouldn't do the same thing if given the chance?"

"But the time stream ..." My voice came out in a strangled whisper.

"Yeah, the time stream." He sounded angry and resigned.

"We have to fix it, Archer."

"Let me ask you something, Saira. If you were in a room with Adolph Hitler in 1933, and you had a gun, would you pull the trigger?"

"How can you ask me that?" This suddenly wasn't just about the time stream. This was fear and responsibility and everything else being here, in this time, risked. De Rais was dangerous, and according to history, he was supposed to live. What if Archer took him on and time stream inertia made sure de Rais lived. What would happen to Archer? The tears started then, and the anger on Archer's face suddenly dissolved. He pulled me roughly into his arms and held me to his chest.

"I'm sorry," he whispered into my hair. "Don't cry."

"I need you to live, Archer. I need you next to me when we face Wilder. And I want to go home and be normal with you for longer than five minutes."

"I will, Saira. I will always be with you."

I pulled back and looked into his eyes. "You promise?"

He wiped the wet streaks off my cheeks. "I promise."

My nose was running and I rubbed it on my own shoulder.

"Nice," he smirked, and I choked out a laugh.

"Then don't make me cry."

He pulled me in close and kissed the tears away from my eyes.

Just then, Connor's Wolf returned from his scout and gave a short bark to get Archer's attention. The Wolf looked him in the eyes, then turned away and looked back with a "let's get moving" bark. Ringo came out of the garden with Charlie and Valerie right behind him.

"Everythin' alrigh' out 'ere?"

The way he searched my face when I turned to smile told me he saw the tears. "Connor says the coast is clear, so they're going to take off."

"Findin' Jehanne, and then what?"

Archer stepped back to adjust the extra weight of Connor's clothes in his pack. "Try to get close enough to see who's with her, make sure Henry Grayson's not part of her retinue, and discover as much about her plans as we can."

"Sounds vague and dangerous." I tried for a normal tone.

"Not any more dangerous than what you two are heading into."

Archer clasped Ringo to him in a quick guy-hug. "Take care of yourself and each other."

Ringo looked back and forth between the impatient Wolf and Archer. "Ye, too. And quit makin' yer woman cry."

He pulled me in for a tight hug. "I promise." Then Archer kissed me. It wasn't a good-bye kiss. It was a "next time you'll be lucky if you remember how to breathe when I'm done kissing you" kiss.

"Be careful." Archer whispered into my ear.

"You, too." I whispered back.

He smiled at Valerie and Charlie, and then he was gone. Connor's Wolf ran at top speed, and Archer was right behind him. A moment later I couldn't even hear them in the woods.

I wiped the last vestiges of tears off my face with my sleeve in a distinctly twelve-year-old-boy move, took a breath, and nodded at Ringo. "Shall we?"

"Ye 'ave the look on yer face like 'e always gets when ye go runnin' somewhere."

"I do?"

He nodded. "And then 'e takes a deep breath, reminds 'imself 'ow capable ye are, and gets on with whatever needs doin'."

I smiled in spite of the pain that had wrapped itself around my heart. "Thanks, Ringo."

He gave a teasing scoff. "Ye'll get my bill later." He turned to Charlie and Valerie. "Now, let's get ye settled in the mill before we go after yer 'Enry."

Ringo and I left the ladies with whatever supplies they'd need to feed themselves for a few days, though to be honest, they probably had it easier than us with whatever they could harvest from the walled garden. I left them my sword because I was better with my daggers, and Valerie revealed the small boot dagger she carried at her ankle.

I told Valerie what I'd seen in Archer's visions, and the tone of her voice was as concerned as I felt. "My only true experience with altering the time stream is what Henry has caused. I cannot honestly say what would happen if this Baron de Rais were to be killed now."

Charlie looked up from the cabinet she was exploring. "Two hundred children would live."

"That's what's so terrifying, though. What if one of those kids turns out to do something extraordinary and changes history as we know it?" It was hard to get past the fear in my own voice.

"So? What if he killed an artist or a musician or a dancer? Would the world be better for never having experienced their art?" Charlie's eyes flashed fiercely, and I looked away. Valerie touched my arm gently.

"Tell Henry I love him, please."

"Of course, I will."

She pulled me in for a quick hug, then turned to busy herself rearranging the contents of her bag. Ringo kissed Charlie's forehead and whispered something to her before he met my eyes and nodded.

"If anyone comes, hide. We'll be back by tomorrow, or the next day at the latest, and then I'll take you home." I was looking at Valerie, and she met my eyes with the shadow of a smile.

"Charlotte and I will anticipate your return."

I gave Charlie a little wave as Ringo and I left the mill. We paused outside to tighten the straps on our satchels and turn the bag to our backs.

"You ready?" I said.

He nodded. "Let's run."

It wasn't hard to follow the little tributary the mill was built on back to the Loire River, and after about ten minutes of running west along its banks we were nearing signs of human habitation. The landscape began clearing, and we slowed to a walk at the edge of the wood.

The view across the open field toward the walled city of Orléans was pretty spectacular, even at night. The moon shone on the top of the walls, and the shadows that slashed down the face of it were eerie and magical. The defenses around Orléans were a feat of engineering I hadn't expected, though when I thought about it, the Tower of London had probably been built earlier and was even more impressive.

There were camps set up all around the perimeter, about three hundred yards back from the walls, presumably out of range of the bowmen. The horses were tied to trees even farther back, at the line of the forest. Fires dotted the fields, and bundles that I assumed were soldiers were arrayed around them. There were also a few pavilion-type tents dotting the field, and I figured that's where the head honchos probably slept.

"Do you think they would put Henry with the guys running the show, or would he be part of a small sabotage unit?" My voice was just a fraction louder than a breath, and Ringo answered in the same tone.

"The She-Wolf stopped gettin' 'er visions after the bridge didn't blow."

"That's what she said."

"Well, let's find the bridge and see if 'Enry shows up to scout it."

I nodded, and by silent agreement we set off, skirting the edge of the camp in the woods. We moved more slowly, since silence was everything. Ringo was a good partner in the silent running game, which is what it became so neither of us overloaded with the inherent tension of the situation. We'd take turns picking the route and challenging the other to step exactly where we'd stepped. Our strides were almost evenly matched, and I thought Ringo had grown even since I picked him up from 1889.

"Hey, when's your birthday?" We had stopped to plan the next silent route, and my voice didn't even hit whisper level.

He shrugged. "Dunno. Spring, sometime."

"Spring, sometime." I snorted. "You should have a birthday."

"Clearly I do. Just don't know which day."

"Well, pick one."

He obviously had never really considered that he could, and it made me sad that celebrating his birthday wasn't part of his world. "All right. I like May. It's warm, and things are bloomin'. And I was fifteen when I met ye. So, May 15th."

My heart melted at the idea that meeting me had mattered so much to him, but I didn't say anything because just then we had to pick our way past a group of tethered horses. They nickered softly as we went by, but none of them raised an alarm.

We made it back down to the banks of the river and found campfires lit all along the beach. I almost suggested we swim past them and downriver to the city bridge, but Ringo couldn't swim – a fact I hadn't known in 1554 when I'd jumped into the Thames and got him captured by Tower guards.

So instead, we sat on a mossy patch of ground with our backs against a big tree set far enough back from the beach we couldn't be overheard, but close enough to see movement from the soldiers when they woke.

"Have you learned to swim in the last couple of months?" I was watching the river flow past our hiding place.

"Nay. I smelled ye after the dunk in the Thames. Didn't want the same stench in my flat, and the river's the only option in London."

"This river seems clean."

Ringo grinned. "Ye thinkin' to teach me t'swim tonight?"

"Well, if you knew how, we wouldn't be sitting here right now."

"Hmph. Good point. Teach me to swim when we're done 'ere, then?"

"Deal."

The silence between us was comfortable as we watched the flickering lights of dying campfires in the distance.

"Valerie told me she wants to ask Charlie to go back to 1554 with her."

"She did ask." Ringo's voice was neutral, but his calm surprised me.

"What does Charlie think?"

"She's considerin' it."

"Really? I mean, I thought she'd want to stay with you."

He looked me in the eyes, and his voice lost its neutrality. "Saira, I'm only just sixteen. On May 15th, if ye can believe it." He gave a quick smile, but then got serious again. "We're both young, and there's some life I need t'live before I'm man enough for a wife. Would I miss 'er? Yeah, with every bit o' my soul. But I wouldn't stop lovin' 'er. She lives in my 'eart and I live in 'ers. If she went with Lady Grayson, I'd 'ave to get to know 'er again, and she'd 'ave to learn me, too. And if we still love the people we've become, then we're better for it, because there'd be so much *more* to love 'bout each other. And if we didn't much care for the people we'd become, well, that'd be good to know, too."

I looked at him a long time, until he finally took his gaze away and stared back out at the river. "How'd you get so smart?"

He smirked, but didn't take his eyes off the view. "Watchin' my two best friends."

I hooked my hand around his elbow and rested my head on his shoulder. There had been a few times since I'd known him that he felt like the grown up, and this was one of them.

"Love you, Ringo."

"Love ye, too, Saira." He kissed the top of my head. "Sleep for a bit. I'll keep watch."

So I did.

HENRY

Ringo woke me at dawn. The soldiers on the beach were starting to move around, and I sat up to get a better look.

"I think my arm's asleep, ye lug." He grinned at me as he worked his shoulder, so of course I stuck my tongue out like the cranky two-year-old I was.

I ran my fingers through the knots in my hair. The good thing about the chin-length cut was it was easier to manage, but I hadn't looked in a mirror in weeks. At this point I'd lost all attachment to the idea of long hair and was looking forward to playing with it.

Washing it would have been a nice start.

Ringo got up to stretch. "Be right back."

I used his absence to go find a private bush. I still envied the guys their ability to just turn their backs to pee, but that just wasn't an option for me. Besides being physically improbable, I truly didn't relish the idea of missing the ground and hitting a shoe. Ick.

When we met back up, the soldiers were moving off the beach toward the higher ground of the field beneath the city walls.

"Do we go now, before full light, and risk the stragglers? Or do we wait until they've all left the beach?" Ringo surveyed the English army as they put on their domed metal helmets.

"It looks like they might all leave the beach. What do you think?"

"I think they look like a swarm of ants crawlin' all over that field. And if they're ants, they may set themselves up around the queen – or in this case, whoever's stayin' in that tent over there."

It was easy to see which tent he meant. It was a huge pavilion, with five tent poles holding the roof up, and the side walls were actual striped canvas. The thing was straight out of a Renaissance Faire, and I wondered if there were rugs and proper furniture inside.

We watched the soldiers empty off the beach and report to the tent for work. If I was their commander, I would station look-outs over the river to prevent a surprise attack from the rear, and I said as much to Ringo. The bridge that crossed the Loire ended in a tall structure that seemed to be made of stone. It was definitely manned, but it almost seemed like a gateway, barring traders and travelers from entering the city from the south. The bridge spanned from the tower, across an island, to the city, and most of it used suspension construction. There seemed to be people working on it even now.

"They'll 'ave some sort o' signal fire to alert the army if there's trouble." He scanned the beach again. "They won't be lookin' for one or two bodies on the beach, though."

"You say that like you know war."

"Nay, I know street. The playin' field's bigger 'ere, but the tactics are the same."

I exhaled. "Right. So we just walk down there across the beach like we belong?"

He shrugged. "It'd be better if we 'ad some 'elmets to blend in, but yeah, that's the idea."

I grinned. "I know where we can find some."

His eyes narrowed for a second, and I could practically see the mental replay. Then they widened and he smiled, too. "Right. The 'orses."

There had been packs on a couple of the horses we'd walked past last night. I wiggled my fingers suggestively. "I'll trade swimming lessons for thieving ones."

He grinned. "Bargain."

It wasn't far back to where the horses had been tethered, and I remembered something that could make the job easier. Ringo looked at me oddly when I stopped to root around in my satchel, but when my hand came up with the carrots Valerie had tucked in there from the secret garden, he was impressed.

I handed him some, and we broke them in half so there were enough for horse bribes. The soft nickering when we approached the horses didn't have time to turn fearful, because once the closest horses got their carrots, the others were too interested in getting their share to bother raising an alarm.

I crooned softly to them as I fed them. I'd watched Archer with horses enough to recognize that soothing confidence was the most effective way to approach them. He told me the smartest horses were like ten-year-old children – just wise enough to learn caution, but still naïve enough to trust until they learned otherwise. So I kept the horses entertained while Ringo found the ones with packs and rifled through them.

There weren't any helmets in the packs, but he did pull out a couple of tunics like the ones we'd seen the English soldiers wearing – red with a white cross on the chest. They made us look like a giant target, but if we wanted to blend in with the soldiers long enough to get past them, it was the way to go.

"The English lost this battle, just remember that," I whispered to Ringo.

He grimaced. We were definitely playing with the wrong team.

I gave a sorrel horse closest to me the last of the carrots and rubbed its forehead for luck as we slipped back into the woods to make our way to the beach.

I studied the suspension bridge as we walked. If I was going to send a boat full of explosives out to blow it up, I'd go where the biggest concentration of soldiers were. And the more I saw of the movements of red tunics, I thought we might be on the wrong side of the river.

I stopped Ringo before we left the cover of the woods. "Look at the tower again." I pointed across the river. "There are red tunic troops gathering there, and in the last fifteen minutes the numbers have gotten significantly bigger."

The English soldiers had been arriving on the bluffs in groups of three or four at a time, but now they started forming into blocks of men, and suddenly I realized the troops on the city side of the river were just an advance unit. The main body of the English soldiers was on the south bank.

"She's not going to try to blow this side. It's too close to the city walls. She's going to cut them off from the main army at the tower. That's what I'd do."

Ringo nodded. "Most of the trade must come from the south, so that's been their main siege point. Which means," he surveyed the troops massing on the field near the walls, "these soldiers have been sent to soften the resistance. They're not cannon fodder, they're skilled fighters."

"But is Henry over here, or is he with the main troops?" I wasn't feeling too good about being surrounded by a bunch of commandos.

"Depends if 'e revealed himself to the blokes in charge."

"Well, crap. We might have to go across that bridge."

He looked at me with a wry grin. "Ye are one for runnin' 'eadlong into a 'ornet's nest, aren't ye? Today's the day it all goes wrong, isn't it? Maybe we just wait and see what the Frenchies are about. It might inspire somethin' better than becomin' ducks for the shootin' barrel."

"Part of me wants to go running down the beach yelling for Henry Grayson, but then I remember he's not necessarily going to be too happy to see us. He thinks he's doing something good here."

"And we can assume they didn't send kids with 'im. Not for somethin' worth a prophecy."

"You're right. The Seer is probably an enforcer or bodyguard type."

"Ye'd be right about that." The deep voice behind us practically growled, and we leapt to our feet in the space of a heartbeat.

About ten roundheads stood arrayed behind us, and their leader, the one who had spoken, wore a sneer on his face straight out of a Monger manual.

It made me bold for some reason. Probably because the guy looked like a bully preparing to launch his attack. I don't do well with bullies.

"So, you're Henry's Seer, huh? Or are you part Monger, too?" I knew he wasn't. I couldn't feel any Mongers around us, but I was baiting him. His eyes narrowed at me.

"Ye talk funny, and ye know Henry. There's two reasons to take ye down. Third one's if ye run."

Something about the Seer guy reminded me of a big, snarling junkyard dog, or maybe a pirate. I saw a glint of gold in one ear and remembered a story I'd heard about pirates wearing gold earrings to pay for their funeral if they washed up on shore somewhere. So he became Jack, either for Black Jack or for Jack Sparrow, I wasn't really sure. I looked at Ringo. Clearly we were going to run, but he'd seen the same things I had. The commandos with Jack either had hands on their swords or on the longbows slung over their shoulders. Everyone looked far too casual to not be twitchy with their weapons. The swords we could outrun, but we were going to have to split up and run patterns to avoid the arrows.

That silent conversation passed between us about a millisecond before I smiled at Jack and said, "Strike three."

And then we were off.

I figured Jack expected it. I didn't figure he'd planned for it. Two commandos in their red tunics, looking remarkably like Thing One and Thing Two, stepped out of the woods in front of me and took to their knees. Their bows were strung with arrows in less than a second, and I had to fight the fierceness of my drop-and-cover-my-head instinct. Ringo had already veered off to the left to draw as many soldiers off me as he could, but we both knew I was heading for that bridge.

So, instead of veering toward the right, I plowed straight ahead. Thing One's bow faltered slightly. He clearly hadn't been expecting me to run right at them. But Thing Two held steady, and I knew he was going to drop me like a charging boar. So I dropped first. Just as the arrow left the bow I fell forward into a summersault to keep my forward momentum. And then I barreled right into Thing Two, who had just stood up to try to get out of my way.

His timing was off on both counts. I felt the arrow slice the air above my back, and before he could dodge me, I took him out at the knees.

It hurt. A lot. Thing One got over his initial surprise pretty quickly and was already lifting his bow and turning to take aim again. I leapt to my feet, stumbled over Thing Two, and kept running.

An arrow whizzed past my shoulder, and I knew I wasn't going to get that lucky again. So I dove again, over a felled tree, and when I popped back up I'd already changed my trajectory.

Some of the commandos were yelling behind me. Some were calling to each other farther away. They were the ones on Ringo's trail, and I wondered when and how he was going to double back to catch up with me again. I swerved again, just as another arrow nearly clipped my satchel as it flew away from my body on the turn. I hadn't heard fabric tear, so I hoped I wouldn't be dropping my things like breadcrumbs behind me.

I launched off a rock on the small cliff and hit the river beach below with another tumble. An arrow stuck into the sand in the spot where I began my roll. The next one was going to hit me unless I shook things up. Jack barked something at the commandos that sounded like "aim ahead of 'er." He was running along the top of the cliff and was beginning to gain on me. He was on solid ground, and the sand was slowing me down.

I heard another arrow fly from a longbow. and I changed direction again – this time I aimed straight for the river. The sand at the water's edge was packed harder, and I was able to pick up speed again. I was also further away from the cliff and was seriously toying with the idea of jumping in and swimming for the river island, or even for the far shore. But I would have had to drop my satchel, and there were just enough time-anomalous objects in there that my Clocker identity would be revealed right away. I also didn't like the idea of leaving Ringo here on this shore just because he couldn't swim.

The bridge was getting closer, and my flight had gotten some attention up near the city walls. Jack was yelling at other commandos to get in on the chase, and one or two actually did scramble down to the beach. The red tunics were starting to close in around me, and I felt like every little move that had avoided an arrow just added one more to the guaranteed hit list.

My breath came hard and fast, and my focus had narrowed down to my feet, the sand, and listening for arrows cutting the wind behind me. Even the shouts of English soldiers blended into background noise in the interest of staying alive.

My focus shifted, and my eyes locked onto the bridge in front of me. There were narrow steps carved into the sandstone, and a rope hung down as a guide to get to the top of the steep embankment. A red tunic had begun the climb down from the bridge, presumably to intersect me, and Jack's voice became audible again.

"Don't let 'er climb!"

Yeah, we'd see about that.

The bridge was suspended from heavy cabled rope and thick planks of wood. It seemed to be anchored into the hillside with metal pikes buried deep in the ground and then supported on a crisscrossed structure of wood beams. The structure was my goal, and I just hoped the crisscrossed wood was enough cover to keep the long-bowmen from turning me into Swiss cheese. The guy coming down the embankment was almost down, and my attention was split between him and whatever arrows I heard slicing the air around me. My Shifter hearing was giving me just enough warning to dodge before they hit, but it required more focus than I had at the moment.

I was almost to the bridge.

The roundhead was almost to the beach.

And Jack wanted me hurt or dead. It didn't seem to matter, as long as I was stopped.

An arrow nicked my foot but hit the sole of my boot as I kicked out in a dead sprint.

The roundhead had a sword, and I debated going for my daggers. I was ten feet away from the tower when another arrow hit my satchel and stuck.

Crap!

Roundhead was ugly and smiling. It wasn't a kind smile. He suddenly stepped in front of me and swung his sword. I anticipated the move though, and leapt sideways into the river. It sucked getting my boots wet, but getting his sword wet would have sucked more. The sideways jump had stopped my forward momentum, so I used it. I kicked as much water and mud as I could send flying at Roundhead's face. His eyes were open when a big splat of mud hit them, and he screamed.

So I ran. Five strides later I was climbing the back side of the tower, using it to protect as much of my body from archers on both sides of the bridge as it could. Jack was yelling again, but I couldn't hear the words over the nose of clanking. Wait, clanking? I got halfway up the structure before Roundhead had the mud clear and could see me, but even he couldn't hear what Jack was yelling.

The clanking had a distinct metal on metal sound, and I suddenly pictured a big chain with heavy weights on it turning a wheel. That's what it sounded like. Then the sound of running feet overhead on the bridge confirmed it. The portcullis – the big metal gate that protected the city of Orléans from invaders – had just opened.

I scrambled to the top of the support tower and then crawled along a truss on the underside of the bridge. Down on the beach it looked like Roundhead wasn't worried about where I was anymore, which was both a good and bad thing. Good because I was tired of all the shish-kebab threats, bad because that meant there was something worse than me coming.

The running feet had stopped overhead, and more shouting in something that sounded vaguely English filled the air. An arrow thunked into the strut next to my head. If I hadn't paused to listen, it would have drilled my neck. I didn't look to see who was shooting; I knew. If Jack wasn't actually aiming the arrow, he was directing someone to do it.

Someone with very good aim.

I flattened myself behind a long beam and considered my options. The bowman only had to change position and I'd be exposed again, so I couldn't hide indefinitely. I was uncomfortable, exhausted, my lungs burned, my boots were wet, and I had an arrow stuck into who-knows-what in my satchel. I had no idea where Ringo was, but I hoped his commandos were less committed to murder since they didn't have Jack driving the charge.

None of my previous experience with Seers had involved me running from them, so Jack's ferocity was an unwelcome surprise. I probably should have expected it though, considering he *was* a Seer, and we *were* here to thwart Henry's plan.

The footsteps overhead on the bridge changed from frantic running to organized marching. Wood dust and dirt showered down on me through the slats, and I could see what looked like a big troop of soldiers leave the protection of the city and head across the river toward the tower.

The tower. La Tourelle. Jehanne had said something about losing it when they should have won. Could that be happening today?

I peeked my head above the beam that hid me from the archer. When no arrow came to hit me between the eyes I tried a full position change. Still no arrow. A good sign.

I scrambled across the trusses toward the bank, and when my feet hit dirt without another airborne attack, I got cocky. Roundhead had disappeared, and I wasn't being shot at, so I climbed around to the other side of the bridge and slipped out from under the wooden trusses.

"Ye'll not be moving if ye'd like to keep yer head on yer shoulders." Jack's snarl in my ear made every muscle in my body lock up tight. He was suddenly right behind me, as if he'd known exactly where I would materialize. Duh. He probably did.

I went for a dagger, but Jack was there before my hand even hit the holster. A steel blade in his other hand was already pressed to my throat. Jack's hand, holding my dagger, snaked up my thigh and brushed uncomfortably close to the proof I was female. Every muscle in my body clenched in revulsion at his touch. He seemed to know it, and the knife at my throat bit into my skin just as I was about to go for the other dagger.

My hand froze, and I debated screaming, but all he had to do to stop the noise would be cut my windpipe. A move he seemed to be inclined toward anyway. I wanted to bite him, kick him in the nuts, and slam my foot down on his insole, but he seemed to know every possibility that ran through my head because the blade of the knife turned to slice deeper into the skin at my throat, and his foul breath crawled across my face.

He tossed my first dagger out of reach. He took his time feeling around my thighs before he finally slid the second one out of its holster. When his hand, holding my dagger, was finally out from under my tunic, he dragged it across my body again, lingering at my chest. Then he pulled me tight against him and growled in my ear.

"Ye'll be just as much good to me dead as living since I can take my piece of ye in either condition. It's no matter to me, long as the body's still warm. Of course I'll want to know who betrayed me first."

Ugh. My stomach roiled and I was going to vomit.

Tiny drops of blood slipped down from the slice at my neck, and the scent of copper mixed with whatever had died in Jack's mouth made my knees buckle.

"So, who was it? That poncey headmaster, or did Henry finally find his conscience?"

I was going down, and the blade bit deeper into my throat as I sank.

I couldn't believe this idiot was going to kill me.

It was just too dumb.

Jack must've realized I was going to end up cutting my own throat on his blade, so he turned it flat again and clutched me tighter. "Who betrayed me?"

Indignation flared like a little pissed-off spark in my head. There was no part of dying this way that didn't suck, and after everything I'd already gone through, my death had better mean something.

I found enough muscle twitch left in my legs to lock my knees against their downward trajectory, and I reached back with a hand that was remarkably untethered.

I took a chance that a man's instinct was to push away the thing that grabbed his balls and twisted.

Testicles are remarkably fragile-feeling, considering that my intent was to crush the slippery little things like grapes.

Oddly, the thought that ran through my head was that all that boat-rowing we'd done to get here had paid off in a remarkably strong grip.

Jack shrieked, which was lovely. And pushed me away from him, which would have been even lovelier except that his blade was still at my throat, and mine was held across my chest. Lucky for me he was mostly just committed to getting me off him, so there was no real commitment to cutting my throat at that moment.

Probably wise, considering my muscles would probably have convulsed as I died, and who knows what kind of damage that would have caused to his little nutsack.

When I released my grip and managed to twist my way out range of his blade, I turned to defend myself. But Jack was doubled over, gasping for breath, his dagger hanging limply from one hand while the other dropped my dagger and curled protectively around his groin.

And much as he deserved a knife between the shoulder blades for even thinking about the kind of violations he'd threatened, I wasn't going to deliver him from the misery of his mean little mind. I was, however, going to inflict a little more because I was mad. Mad he'd scared me so badly, and mad because for a moment, I'd been totally powerless.

So I kicked his knife away with a sweep of one foot, and then I threw a knee. I connected with his nose in a satisfying bone-on-bone crunch fueled by a fierce snarl. "Touch me again and I'll kill you."

I didn't stick around to see if he was actually incapacitated, because if he wasn't I might have to do more, and frankly, I didn't have it in me. I swept my daggers up and replaced them in their holsters. The shaking started as I pulled myself up the steep embankment level with the top of the bridge. I made it to the top, but only because my body went on autopilot. I could feel the edges of conscious thought start to curl in protectively, and I forced myself to keep a clear head.

I stayed tucked in next to the bridge tower and finally opened my brain to accept what my eyes saw in the late afternoon daylight. The French army was marching out of Orléans. They were peasants and merchants, townspeople of all ages, mixed in with the soldiers that must have come with Jehanne from the king. Everyone carried a weapon of some kind – swords and longbows were most common, but some of the townspeople carried pikes and cleavers, and I even saw some wooden clubs among the crowd.

The English commandos on this side of the river were staying back at the field, away from the city walls. They were in loose formation and at ease, and I wondered if their commanders were going to have them close ranks on the French once they'd emptied the city of its defenders.

To be honest, I didn't really care who won this war. I didn't have a personal stake in the game, except that this history was supposed to happen a particular way, and some Renaissance Clockers had decided to go mucking around with time.

That's why I was here, trying not to break down in post-trauma tears, looking for a needle in a field of haystacks.

Something tugged at my satchel, and I whipped my dagger out as I spun to face whoever was behind me.

"Christ, Saira. What happened to ye?"

The look of horror on Ringo's face brought something between tears and laughter bubbling to the surface, and I flung myself into his arms before I could dissolve into anything hysterical.

I clutched him harder than I meant to because I felt him stiffen reflexively. I tried to loosen my grip, but my muscles wouldn't let go, and he must have known it because he smoothed my hair like he was petting me to calm me down.

I didn't have enough breath in my lungs to speak until I finally got a deep, shuddering gasp in. "Don't leave me alone, okay?"

He held me away from him so he could look at my face. "What happened?"

I just shook my head and wiped my eyes. "Later."

Ringo held up the arrow he'd tugged out of my satchel. "Are ye hurt?" His eyes suddenly widened and he tilted my chin to one side to see my neck.

"I'm fine." I backed away. "I'll be fine."

I don't know why I was keeping the truth from Ringo. I think maybe I didn't want him to worry or feel like he needed to go kill Jack, who was hopefully still knocked out on the embankment below us.

"Come on. Let's try to blend in with the townspeople and get across the bridge."

His eyes were still pools of worry. I had to look away so I didn't completely lose it right there. I didn't have time to break down. We still had a job to do.

Suddenly, my eyes were caught by a dark, curly head across the crowd. There were about twenty or thirty people between us, but I could distinctly see the civilian tunic over his shoulders.

"No, he didn't!" I was staring and Ringo must have thought I'd gone completely nuts.

"Who didn't do what?"

"Henry Grayson. He's not with the English; he's with the French."

I was already starting to move toward him, but the crowd of French soldiers was crushing. Ringo's eyes followed my gaze, even as he began pushing people out of my way.

"Why was his Seer with the English commandos?" I asked.

Ringo's voice held a shrug. "Protection? Insurance? Point is, 'e knew 'Enry was 'eadin' across the bridge today. That's why 'e 'ad to stop us." Ringo looked behind us at the city walls and surrounding fields. "Where is the Seer, anyway? I'd think 'e'd still be on us."

I didn't take my eyes from Henry's head. "He won't be on anyone for a while."

Ringo shot me a sharp look but said nothing, just used his particular thief's skills to move people away from me without alerting them to the fact they'd been touched. We were getting closer, and I almost called his name, but I wasn't sure who his Clocker support was and really didn't have it in me for another fight.

The townspeople we moved between looked tired and gaunt. They'd been under siege a long time, and desperation tinged a lot of expressions. This battle might be the last one they could rally for, and there was pain and fear mixed in with the determination I saw in most faces.

The glimpses I got of Henry's profile showed the same determination, but without the desperation. Acceptance into the ranks of adult Clockers was at stake for Henry Grayson. Lives and freedom were at stake for the people of Orléans.

I slipped between two uniformed French soldiers right behind Henry. Almost no time had passed for him since I'd stumbled upon him in his Clocker Tower bedroom at St. Brigid's School in 1554, and yet I felt like a whole lifetime had gone by for me. Then, I'd thought he was interesting and intriguing enough that I'd had to look away from his shirtless chest. Now, I studied him dispassionately. His eyes had the excitement and determination of a kid who hadn't experienced the cost of his choices yet.

I used to have that same look in my eyes. That same innocence.

Not anymore.

"Hi, Henry."

THE BRIDGE

I pitched my voice low and directly into Henry's ear, away from Jehanne's soldiers.

The excitement fled his eyes as he whipped his head around to see who'd spoken. It took him a minute to recognize me, but I saw realization gradually fill his eyes.

"You're the Clocker girl who woke me up at St. Brigid's."

"Give the man a prize," I whispered under my breath. He looked confused for a second, and then shook it off as unimportant. Smart guy.

"Why did they send you? I have everything in hand here."

Ho boy. "Henry, we need to talk – away from ..." I tossed my head at the soldiers.

He studied my face for a moment. He still hadn't noticed Ringo, who had slipped up behind him. Ringo scanned the crowd to see if anyone else had an interest in our conversation, then gave me a quick nod to say we were okay.

"We'll attract more attention if we stop. We can part company from them when we get to the south bank." Henry looked away for just a second, but it was enough to betray the lie.

Yeah, you'd like that, I thought. A support tower was just ahead of us, which meant we were about to cross over one of the river islands, and when I looked down I realized we were suspended only about ten feet above the water.

I shot Ringo a quick look, then grabbed Henry's arm and jumped off the bridge. Ringo must've seen my intention because I didn't have to pull hard. We hit the chilly water of the Loire River a moment later.

"Merde!" Henry came up sputtering. At least he had the presence of mind to swear in French. I kept a tight hold on his arm in case he couldn't swim, but he shook me off and started for the island with powerful strokes. I dove back under to follow closely behind.

When he hit the shore, he was mad. Really mad. He charged at me like he was going to swing, but stopped himself just in time. "What the bloody hell was that for?" He growled low enough not to draw even more attention from bridge-crossers above us.

The last of the sun's heat was gone, and I shivered in my wet tunic. Ringo dropped down from the bridge behind Henry. He spoke quietly, but I could hear the menace in his calm voice. "Ye got a problem with Saira, mate, ye take it up with me."

Just then another figure dropped to the ground from the other side of the bridge.

"Archer," I breathed. I didn't realize how quickly the daylight had faded, or how much I'd missed him until he crossed the distance to stand on the other side of Henry.

"God's teeth." Henry was still mad, but the fact he was so outnumbered had also registered in his brain. "What do you want?"

There were a lot of things I wanted to yell at him because, well, he was going to screw up. But he hadn't yet, and he didn't know it was wrong. So I took a breath and stepped carefully.

"Your mother is here."

His eyes widened, and his head whipped around.

"She's in this time, right now, about a twenty minute walk downriver. She wants to see you."

The surprise melted from Henry's face and turned into something harder. "There is a thing I must do. I will see her when I have completed my task."

"That's the thing. You can't do it."

His gaze narrowed, and I saw stubbornness set into his jaw. Just what I'd been hoping to avoid.

317

"Who are you to tell me what I can and cannot do?" His eyes took all three of us in, and I could tell he was assessing his chances against us. I had to admire the guy's commitment, even if it was misguided.

"I'm a Clocker, just like you. But I've seen the future you're going to cause, and it's not the one that's supposed to happen."

The scowl on his face cleared. "So, I succeed then? That's brilliant."

"No, it's actually not. You change history and cause a new time stream."

He waved a hand dismissively. "That means nothing to me. This mission is what I was meant to do. It will guarantee a place for me at the council when I go back."

"That's just it, you don't *go* back. Your mom came to find me because you change things, and then you disappear."

"Why're we even talkin' t 'im? Let's just take 'im to 'is mum and 'ave done with it." Ringo sounded bored, but he was standing alert, like he expected trouble to come at us from every direction. Archer had the same wary stance, and his eyes met mine from behind Henry.

"We can't do that though." Archer gave a little nod and glanced quickly at Henry. I turned my gaze to the Clocker standing so calm and confident between us. He was certain this would happen – so certain it made me nervous. "He has a back-up plan in case something happens to him. That's what the others are for – the Seer, and the conduit. If he fails, one of them will still carry out the plan."

My eyes shot to Ringo. "Crap. I left Jack at the embankment on the other side of the bridge."

Ringo didn't blink at the name. "In what condition?"

"Doubled-over with a broken nose and … twisted testicles."

He winced, and his eyes narrowed. "Right. I'll go find 'im."

"Be careful, Ringo. He was going to kill me."

Ringo scrambled up the support tower to the bridge and disappeared overhead a moment later. Archer moved closer to

318

Henry in case he had the idea that we were any less formidable minus Ringo.

"Who is Jack?"

I nodded toward Henry. "His Seer. The guy's a brute force of one, and he controls the English commandos on the north bank."

Henry looked a little startled. "You encountered Markus?"

I lifted my chin to show him the line that had scabbed across my throat. "Charming guy, Markus. He wanted to do more than this to me, and didn't care if I was alive or dead while he did it."

Every muscle in Archer's body tensed, although he didn't move an inch. Henry flinched, and I was glad to see he had some standards for acceptable combat behavior.

"He's a strong Seer though." I was speaking to Archer. Warning him. "He knew who we were and expected us. He also seemed to know exactly how I was planning to get away, so he Sees in almost real time. Kind of like Tom did when he was sword-fighting with Wilder." I actually said Tom's name without choking on it.

"Where is the conduit who was with you?" Archer spoke quietly to Henry. There was something dark in his voice, and Henry heard it.

"She died."

That startled me. "How?"

"Doesn't matter."

It did matter though. I could see it on Henry's face, and there was something else, something defiant there, like he knew something we didn't.

"Who else is with you?"

"Obviously, I stand alone." He indicated the space around him as if I was an idiot. Archer didn't like this guy, and he had pretty much had enough. He stepped up next to Henry and said, in a voice that practically bled the threat, "You forget, your lady mother is our guest. You are very clearly *not* alone here."

I knew Archer would never hurt Valerie. Henry did not, and the threat shook him. It was good to know he actually cared about his mother at least.

"We have a native."

"A native what?" Nothing about those words made sense to my brain.

"Someone from this time. My father arranged for him."

"When?"

"Last year. When it became clear I was destined to fulfill this mission."

I was filing that piece of information away. Clockers recruiting natives to help them change history. I wasn't going to sleep well for a long time.

"Who?"

"He's with the French witch. If I fail, he will kill her."

"His name."

Henry glared at Archer, whose expression remained chiseled in stone. Archer's tone of voice, however, said everything his face didn't.

"His. Name."

Henry swallowed. "Gilles de Montmorency-Laval, the Baron de Rais."

The hole in the pit of my stomach had just filled with acid. Of course. Nothing ever wrapped up nicely in a pretty red bow. No matter what happened now, we would change history. The only reason de Rais hadn't killed Jehanne before was that Henry had obviously succeeded and split time. But if he didn't, and Jehanne won the battle of Orléans, de Rais would find a way to kill her before she helped put Charles VII on the French throne, and time would split anyway. And if we took de Rais out of the equation, that could split time, too, because of all the children he *wouldn't* get to kill – who might go on to become *someone* in history.

"Awesome." It wasn't meant for anyone's ears, but Henry smiled.

"It is, rather."

I wanted to slap him. And his father.

There was a scrambling overhead, and my hands went to my daggers. Archer shook his head though, and I knew why a second later when Ringo dropped down next to us. Ringo looked at me.

"Gone."

I should have killed Jack. I couldn't call him Markus in my head – that sounded too civilized.

But I didn't want to kill anyone. I didn't want to be a killer.

"He's with the English. He has to go into battle to get close to Jehanne, because she'll be in the middle of it." Archer spoke absently, and I could see his brain churning, trying to form a strategy. I was so happy we were back together.

"Wait – where's Connor?" I asked.

"With Jehanne."

"How?"

Archer shot a look at Henry. "Later."

'With Jehanne,' meant Connor was directly in the line of fire between an English killer and a French psychopath. If he tried to protect her from either of them, he was dead.

We needed a plan.

I turned to Henry. "You were going to take out the boat, right?"

His eyebrows crunched up. "You have a very odd way of speaking. Is that how everyone speaks in the seventeenth century?"

"Huh? I don't know. I've never been there … then."

He shook his head. "Of course not. Otherwise how could you …" He stared at me. "How could you have Clocked to 1554 *and* to 1429? Unless … you didn't Clock to 1554, and you are actually a foreigner, native to my time. That is the game! You are part of a conspiracy to see my family name disgraced and my own contribution erased from the Clocker histories. You have come here to sabotage my efforts."

"Quit with the conspiracy theories. I'm not from 1554, and you don't know everything there is to know about Clocking, so shut it. You were going to stop the boat from blowing up the bridge, yes or no?" I was about ready to tie Henry up and let Valerie deal with him.

He was still staring at me, but Ringo and Archer had taken another step closer. He scowled. "Yes."

"What else is there to the plan?"

321

"I told you. I succeed or Markus kills the witch."

"That's all? Nothing else?"

"My mission is an adjustment, not a wholesale war."

"An adjustment? That's how they sold it to you? Like something's just a little *off* and you're here to *adjust* it? Henry, you're messing with people's lives. You didn't adjust time, you split it. Do you know what that means?"

I was starting to ramp up, and agitation made me louder than I should have been. His eyes had narrowed at me again, like he was assessing how much truth was in my words. I glared at him.

"Two months from now little kids are dying in Paris because Jehanne isn't with her king fighting battles. And for what? So a couple English landowners in your time can keep their French vacation homes?"

"The balance of power—"

"—The balance of power never goes to Clockers. Not even after you do this. Clockers are an endangered species, Henry, and *missions* are why. You don't make it home after you do this. You're just another missing Clocker, like all the other idiots in our Family who get lost in time.

I was so mad I was close to tears, which pissed me off even more. I had to take a couple deep breaths so my voice didn't crack, but when I looked at Archer, the expression of pure pride on his face calmed me down enough to turn back to Henry.

"Just walk away with us, Henry. We'll figure out what to do about your Seer and de Rais, but you don't have to be part of the insanity if you choose not to."

Henry's gaze flicked to Ringo and Archer and then settled back on me. "My father—"

I was officially disgusted with Mr. Grayson, whoever he was. "Your father contracted a serial killer to work with you. And I'm not even talking about Markus. History knows de Rais as Bluebeard. He killed hundreds of children, Henry. Is that really who you want on your team?"

"I will be dead to my father if I do not complete this mission. He aspires to be the Head of our Family one day, and I would betray him if I left it undone."

"I've got news for you, buster. You're dead to him whether or not you do it. But your mom, she's awesome. She came to find you – to bring you home. You're not dead to her yet, and you don't have to be if you choose something different."

My disgust and annoyance were evaporating at the scared kid I saw looking out of Henry's eyes. Archer must have seen it too, because the sharp edge I thought I'd hear in his voice was gentle. "My father's expectations of me were crushing. In my heart I knew it was because he wanted something great for me, something better than what he had achieved. But all I knew was his disappointment at my failures. Know this, Henry: the only failure that cannot be excused is the failure to act on an injustice or to right a wrong. Those are the failures history shuns because the people who stand by and allow evil to occur are very nearly as bad as the evil-doers themselves."

Archer had gotten to him. Henry's eyes weren't narrowed suspiciously anymore.

I had a different card to play.

"Henry?" I made my voice quiet and soft, so he had to lean in closer to hear me. "We're from the twenty-first century."

His eyes widened. Good. Got him.

"I am next in line to be the Clocker Head." His eyes widened even further. "And I've never seen your name in our Family history books."

His mouth fell open a little. "But …"

"The time I come from has the wrong history, Henry. Joan of Arc is a footnote in my time. And I promise you, France will be its own undoing. It doesn't need your help. Do the right thing, and I'll make sure it's recorded in our history. I'll make sure your choice to preserve the truth is known and that you are recognized for it."

His voice was almost a whisper. "I suddenly find I do not particularly care how history sees me."

"What about your lady mother? How she sees you? She misses you, Henry. She misses the little boy you were. She misses your antics, like the Swan Dive, and the way you always made people laugh." His eyes opened wide at that. "She wants you and Penelope to fall in love and give her grandchildren, Henry, and she is *proud* of you. Proud of the man you've become, and the man you will yet be."

His eyes were locked on mine, and I felt like he finally believed me. "Take me to her?" His voice was almost a whisper, and I thought he might be close to tears.

I reached out to take his hand.

"Saira!" Archer leapt forward to push Henry out of the way. But he was too late.

The arrow, shot from the bridge by the light of a nearly full moon, pierced the soft flesh of Henry's neck.

He opened his mouth to say something, or maybe scream, but no sound came out. His knees gave out, but Archer caught him. I rushed to help Archer pull Henry under the bridge, away from the line of sight of his killer.

Ringo was already halfway up the tower when Archer laid Henry down, half on me, so I could try to stop the blood. It was affecting Archer too much, and he took a step backward.

"Take him to Valerie, Saira. Right now. Take him."

I nodded, mute with horror, and started tracing a spiral in the dirt with the hand that wasn't clutching the hole in Henry's neck. Archer's eyes were locked on mine as the buzzing started, and I had to scrape under the horror to find the focus to picture the secret garden in my head.

At the last minute I looked down into Henry's eyes. They were clear and terrified, and my heart hurt so badly for him I could barely breathe.

"I'm so sorry, Henry. I'm so sorry." I think I whispered the words out loud, but they were a scream in my head as we slipped *between.*

Valerie's horrified shriek sent birds scattering into the air.

Hands pulled Henry from me, and other hands helped me move out of the way. Valerie held her son tightly to her chest, and her keening moan made goose bumps rise on my skin.

"Talk to him, Valerie. He's still there. Talk to him."

Somehow my words penetrated the fog of her despair and she looked into his face. His eyes were beginning to dim, and the wound in his throat bubbled.

"Oh, my love. My beautiful, perfect boy." Her voice was choked with tears, but she cleared her throat so he could hear her words. "I love you with all of my heart, Henry Grayson. You are my son, my hopes, my dreams. I will hold you in my heart for the rest of my days."

Her tears were falling on his face – running into his eyes – clearing the pain and horror from them. When the last light finally dimmed in them, they were wide and innocent and pure, and so very, very young.

I didn't realize I was sobbing until Charlie wrapped her thin arms around my shoulders. I touched one in thanks, and then crawled to Valerie. She rocked her dead son in her arms as if he were the baby she remembered, and I closed his eyelids. He looked like he was sleeping, and Valerie cradled him to her chest as she keened.

I don't know how long we stayed like that, but the stub of a candle they'd used for light had gone out, and a chill had settled into all of us.

Strong hands finally lifted me out of my stupor as I was pulled to my feet. "Go inside," Archer said to me. "Take Valerie and Charlie with you. We'll bury him."

"Here." Valerie's voice was hoarse from keening and tears. "I want him buried in our secret garden, away from my husband and the council who wasted his life."

Ringo was helping her to her feet, and Charlie tightened Valerie's cloak around her as if she was the child. I put my arms around her, and Charlie and I led her out of the walled garden.

Connor stood in the open doorway, his expression so sad the tears welled up in my own eyes again. I reached a silent hand out to him and he clasped it briefly, and then closed the door behind us as we left the garden.

My body was stiff from the cold, and from not moving for so long. I realized the guys had gone to find Connor, and then came back on foot. I could hear the sound of a shovel hitting dry earth inside the garden, and I felt the hole in the pit of my stomach widen.

Charlie and I got Valerie into the old mill, and between us were able to clean up most of the blood and get some wine into her. Although she managed to thank us for the attention, nothing that hinted of warmth or life came into Valerie's voice and eyes. Charlie watched her mentor sadly, ready to jump up at the slightest indication of need or desire.

When Ringo appeared at the door, dirty and disheveled, Charlie ran to him. He stroked her hair tenderly as he spoke to Valerie. "It is done."

She met his eyes and nodded, then closed herself back up again like a fan.

I slipped past Ringo and Charlie and out into the night. I found Archer down by the river, washing the dirt from his hands and face.

"Thank you."

He looked up at me from where he crouched by the water. "She got to say goodbye?"

I nodded and took a deep, ragged breath.

"Did you find who did it?"

Archer looked grim. "The French troops retreated when Jehanne took an arrow to the shoulder. There was no sign of Markus, and I don't believe de Rais would have left Jehanne's side for that."

"Is Jehanne going to be okay?"

"Connor said she pulled the damn thing out herself."

"Of course she did." I couldn't help the grumble in my voice. That chick annoyed me more than seemed humanly possible, but she was also tougher and more confident in her purpose than anyone I knew.

"You don't think Markus shot her, too?"

Archer shook his head. "Connor said it happened right around the same time, on a different part of the river."

I inhaled deeply, the scent of something flowery, like honeysuckle, gave the air a sweetness I didn't feel. "We were supposed to make things right."

He stood and dried off his hands, then held me close to his body.

I felt broken, like there were cracks all over me – the kind that leaked tears and oozed guilt. Breathing took effort, and even the warm spice scent of Archer's skin did little to quell the rising anxiety. "First Tom and now Henry. How many more people are going to die while we trip around in time pretending to know what we're doing?"

"If not us, then who?" The rumble of his voice was filled with an emotion I couldn't identify, and I pulled back from his chest to look at him.

"What is it? What's wrong?"

He wiped his eyes with the heels of his hands. "Nothing. Everything. It doesn't matter."

"Everything matters, Archer."

He pulled me into his chest again. His arms were like a barrier against everything painful, and I closed my eyes and sank into him. "You faced death today. Twice. If Markus had aimed for you, it would be your body in that garden grave."

I wasn't so certain he hadn't been aiming for me. After the way I'd assaulted him, I'd have expected the first arrow to have my name on it.

He watched me for a while before he finally spoke again. "When I hear you question any part of our purpose, I know I have to put away my fear and be strong for you. It is perhaps the reason I was put on this earth, because I am clearly useless at protecting you."

I gave a short bark of humorless laughter. "I don't claim to have access to a divine plan, but I'm pretty sure if there's one for you, it's bigger than being a bodyguard."

I touched his face gently. "What Markus did to Henry — that kind of danger is almost like getting hit by a bus. You'll just never see it coming, so there's no point in freaking out about it."

He scowled. "Before that, I was asleep while a murderer held a knife to your throat."

I gave him my best king cobra eyes, the ones he couldn't look away from. "While you were sleeping, I did a dumb thing and let myself get separated from Ringo. I put myself in a bad situation, and yeah, it sucked not having help to get out of it. But that happens sometimes. And the only shouldas, couldas, or wouldas about that situation are on me. Nothing worse than a scratch and a scare happened because I had the luck and timing to be stronger than my fear. Am I safer when I'm with you? Absolutely I am. But I have to feel safe when I'm alone, too. I have to be able to trust that I can do whatever's necessary to stay alive, and I do trust that. *Especially* after what happened today."

The fear and anger in Archer's eyes brightened and became something that looked like pride. His voice was gruff when he finally spoke. "It's insane how much I love you."

And because I needed to feel alive, I said, "Really? Show me."

He crushed my mouth with his, and with every beat of my heart, the fear and the pain receded behind pure heat and need. Archer's lips on mine, his body pressed against me, his arms protecting me, felt clean and right and real.

I don't know how long we kissed. It was long past the time when need built into ache and desire, and still, we only kissed. My mouth felt bruised and raw, but my heart had refilled with blood and heat, instead of the cold blackness that had slithered in with a killer's words. And I realized that Archer had given me back the power to want.

"Thank you," I whispered against his mouth.

"Nichts zu danken," he whispered back.

Valerie had finally fallen asleep, and when we came in, Charlie got up to join us.

"How is she?" I whispered to Charlie.

"Like glass. I'll stay with 'er as long as she needs." There was a tenderness I hadn't expected in Charlie's voice, almost like an adult child who realizes they need to be the parent for a bit. I also knew Charlie wasn't just talking about the time we had left in France.

I gave her a hug and whispered in her hair. "You're a good daughter."

Her eyes were wet, and she went to Ringo's side. Connor came to the door with our satchels, and Archer and I slipped outside while Ringo said goodbye. None of us was ready to return to the battle, but Henry's death hadn't halted the plan he'd set in motion. And so we were going back.

Connor handed me my bag. "The arrow got stuck in our book."

Our book. It was my book when it had to be carried, but it was our book now.

He smirked at me. "Good thing it's such a heavy book. The last chapters didn't even tear."

"Yeah, good thing the book's still intact. Skin can be stitched up, but books ..." I teased him, and felt lighter than I had for days.

Ringo joined us outside, and we quietly picked our way past the millhouse. Before we could leave the property though, I veered toward the secret garden. My heart clenched at the idea of seeing freshly dug earth, but I felt like I needed to see it was done. The guys had taken real care to mark the grave in a way that honored Henry, and maybe more importantly, Valerie. They had found a piece of flat sandstone, and had chiseled *Henry Grayson, Beloved Son* into it, then surrounded the grave with other, decorative stones. They had placed it so it could be seen from the spiral. Maybe Valerie would come and visit it, though maybe she had enough of him in her heart that she wouldn't need a burial place to feel close to him.

I looked at the guys, each so solemnly arrayed behind me. "Thank you."

We left the garden, and then by unspoken agreement, we ran.

TOM – AUGUST, 1429

Killing Wilder had been too easy.

He came into my tower room expecting a corpse. The one that greeted him had surprised him so much that slitting his throat with a shard of broken glass had been anti-climactic, and completely unsatisfying.

I drained Wilder, of course. Blood lust was a real thing, and it hurt like hell. Wilder's blood had tasted like something stale and moldy, and when I'd drained him completely I tore the head from his slashed neck, and then burned his body for good measure.

That bastard wasn't coming back.

I left the tower room to get away from the stink of burning flesh. It was a sickening smell, but now the air was full of smells. I felt like I had an animal's senses. I could see in the dark, my hearing was so acute I could tell when a person walked by outside because of their heartbeat, and scents layered the air like watercolors on paper.

I was strong. Anything I asked my body to do, it did. I wanted to run on rooftops, because the idea of falling didn't paralyze me anymore. What's the worst that could happen? It would hurt, but pain and I had long since become friends. And I would heal. I had healed from all the quill tracks and blood loss, and the Vampire blood I'd consumed felt like rocket fuel in my veins.

I also felt skilled. The Monger in me was much stronger, but it felt like a beast with a leash I had firmly in hand. I could feel the Seer respond to every action I took, so my short-Sight skill – the one that found the right hand and footholds when I climbed, or knew the railing would pull from the wall if I held on too tight — that was intact. I wondered if Wilder had recognized that he had my short-Sight, or if he had only been looking for long-term visions.

I didn't have those, but somehow I wasn't surprised by that.

I found the Clocker spiral in the annex just outside my tower room, and I wondered if Wilder's blood — no, Saira's mother's Clocker blood — was part of my legacy. I had Clocked with Saira, once by accident, once to escape, and suddenly it made sense that I couldn't see a future for myself here. Maybe there was none. If I could leave this time ... go where Léon's screams didn't echo in my head ...

I had to clean the blood off first though. There was no running water, of course. Léon had brought it in from a pump in the courtyard. Thoughts of him were as automatic as breathing, and more painful than dying had been.

Every cell in my body had stopped — stopped growing, stopped dying, just stopped, according to the science of Vampires. But it felt like each cell had been torn in half, with a million nerve-endings on fire for each one. I thought it was impossible to feel more pain than that, until I murdered the one friend who had made my life worth fighting for.

I would do anything, anything to take it back.

The night was warm and clear, and there was a scent of jasmine on the air from a garden nearby. I had not been outside the Hôtel de Sens since Wilder had brought me here. And not even then, because he had Clocked directly into the room next to my prison. Stepping outside the stone mansion felt like a gift I didn't deserve.

The cobblestone courtyard was empty, and I stripped off the filthy, bloody rags I still wore. I should have burned them upstairs, but nothing would get me back in that tower room now. I stood naked at the pump, splashing freezing cold water every place I could reach. Months of grime and filth were embedded in my skin, and no amount of splashing was enough.

I could hear a fountain nearby, but I couldn't see it. I was still naked, but I couldn't find it in me to care, so I climbed to the top of the courtyard wall and followed the noise of water.

A small garden stood between my wall and the next door house, and in it was a wall fountain with a deep trough. I jumped down, completely unconcerned about who might live there, and climbed into the trough.

The water cooled some of the fire left in my cells from my rocket fuel diet of stale Wilder blood, and I ducked my head under and closed my eyes.

The sound of water overhead amplified in my ears until it was finally louder than the echo of Léon's screams in my head. I tried to breathe the water so I'd never have to come up again, but my body wouldn't let me. My survival instinct had become stronger than my will. The despair of knowing I couldn't even kill myself to atone for Léon's murder was an intense stabbing pain, but the longer I stayed in that fountain, mostly underwater until the grime had no choice but to lift off my skin and float away, the more calm I became.

I finally pulled myself out of the fountain and startled a cat in the middle of its feast of rat. I debated stealing the rat for myself – the smell of its blood was an enticement I could scarcely resist, but the cat stood its ground, hissing and spitting at me, protecting its kill with an impressive ferocity. It was enough to break the blood-spell, and I took a step back.

"Bon appétit, petit chat." My voice sounded strange in my ears – deeper, with more resonance. I saluted the cat and climbed back up the wall to drop down on the other side.

Morning was coming. I could feel myself start to weaken. I thought about staying outside to burn in the sun, but realized the futility of suicide attempts while my body was so much stronger than my mind. I made my way back to the tower annex and pulled on the long, linen shirt and pants Léon had brought me before blood loss had robbed me of both strength and will. I was still barefoot and had wet hair, but I was finally dirt-free. I knew I'd never be really clean again, so this was as good as it got.

I needed a tunic, and Léon had hung his outside my tower door before entering. It was the habit of a butcher's son, he once told me, because bloodstains are difficult to clean. The irony was not lost on me when I pulled it from the peg, as if his ghost would suddenly rip it from my unworthy hands, then slid it on over my shirt. The smells of soap and herbs drifted from the folds of cloth, and I closed my eyes. I would not cry. I did not deserve the release of pain the tears would bring. But I would give myself his scent to wear, both as torture and as punishment. Something crackled in the tunic, and I pulled a creased and folded paper from the pocket. I had the vague thought that the paper seemed familiar, but I was certain I'd never seen the drawing that made the air leave my lungs and my throat close wetly.

It was Léon. His face, nearly profile, concentrated so hard on something that I almost looked over my shoulder to find whatever it was. His bones were sharp and looked like they could cut their way through his skin. It was angular and harsh and almost as beautiful as its model.

I didn't remember placing the drawing inside my shirt. I just knew it was the only source of a beating heart my body had. My hand reached into the other pocket for the black knight he kept there, but I couldn't make myself touch it. I had no right.

I stumbled into the annex and over to the spiral. My hand shook so badly I had to hold my wrist and force myself to trace the grooves.

The blood in my body began to hum to the frequency of the spiral. It was too loud, too much, and I tried to muffle my own brain to keep my head from spinning. The instant I quieted the noise in my head, Léon's screams came back. They seemed to echo in time with the thrum that pulled from deep inside as I unconsciously traced the third spiral. I couldn't undo what I'd done to Léon. The Vampire I'd become wasn't the horrific part of surviving. Living in a world where Léon did not, was.

The nothingness of *between* was like being underwater, where the thrum and throb of noise was louder than the screams.

But *between* didn't want me either, and it spit me back out on the stone floor of the annex. One hand went automatically to the drawing in my shirt, and the other clutched at the chess piece in my pocket. I took a halting step, not feeling the cold I expected from the stone floor, and looked inside my tower prison.

The bed I'd slept on for months was made and clean, and the room held no evidence of my torture. Heavy drapes were pulled across the windows, and the shelves were empty of the ever-present bottles. I didn't know when I was, and I didn't really care. I just knew I needed to sleep.

When I crawled into the bed and pulled the covers over my head, I breathed a small sigh of relief. They didn't stink of the blood and sweat and horror of my last days. The sheets smelled like sunshine and clotheslines, and my last thought before darkness consumed me was that they might be the last bit of sun I ever knew.

 ## Battles

The French soldiers were slipping out of the city in pairs and small groups under the cover of darkness. The English commandos seemed to be camped around the field exactly as they'd been the night before, without any clue what the French were planning.

I found myself scanning the riverbank as we ran, looking for boats. Apparently, Ringo was doing the same thing because he suddenly stopped running and turned down a steep embankment to the water.

I heard splashing, and then his quiet voice calling to us.

"'Ere. I found us a boat to get us past the commandos."

We scrambled down the weedy embankment and found him in a tiny rowboat, oars in hand, grinning proudly.

"Will it hold us?" I asked.

"It better. The river's the only way past the English camps, and I can't swim."

Connor shook his head. "It'll sink with all four of us. Take my clothes – I'll meet you under the bridge."

I waded out to the boat and climbed in while Connor Shifted. Naked boys had no power to shock me anymore. At this point, I had lived with these guys for weeks. I'd probably even forgive them an open bathroom door.

The boat sank considerably under my weight, but the water still didn't slosh inside. Archer didn't look so confident though, and he started stripping down, too.

"What are you doing?"

For all my unshockability by naked boys, naked Archer was an entirely different deal. He had pulled off everything but the tight trousers he wore under the tunic, and under the moonlight, the sculpted muscles in his chest and shoulders looked like something carved in marble.

"I don't feel the cold like you do. I'll swim." He handed me his clothes and caught me staring. Because I was ... staring. He was beautiful, and every time I saw his body like that it startled me how much I approved.

Seriously? Now was not the time to be indulging in eye candy. But there was a glint in Archer's eyes that told me he enjoyed my approval. Then he smiled and I scowled, at myself mostly, and he laughed and dove into the water.

We made good time on the river, even when we had to run silently. When we got close to the English riverside camps, Ringo pulled the oars into the boat, then reached into his pocket and handed something to me.

"'Ere. Ye might want this for what's comin'."

I took it, and instantly wanted to drop it into the river. Only common sense gave me enough control to hand the Shifter bone back to Ringo.

I wiped my hands and the chill on my skin subsided a little. "Why do you have that? I thought you left it at home." I was whispering, and there was a shiver in my voice.

"It seemed a useful thing for ye, and it'd be a shame to need it and not 'ave it."

"I will never need that thing." I spat like the words were frogs.

"Never say never, Saira."

Archer was pushing the boat forward, and I didn't know if he'd heard the conversation. I debated getting into the water with him to wash the feeling of the bone off my skin, but I didn't feel like shivering for the rest of the night.

I pushed the chill out of my mind as we floated the rest of the way in. We decided to land on the furthest island from the city, and Connor's Wolf was already there.

A small group of French soldiers crossed the bridge just after we hid the boat under some bushes where it couldn't be seen from above. The men were armed with proper swords, and they wore heavy plate armor over their chests. Their arms and legs moved freely, so they could walk without clanking, but I had the definite sense that they were done messing around. Tonight they were going to war.

Archer and Connor dressed quickly and silently while Ringo and I kept watch. The moonlight was strong enough to cast shadows, so we kept to the darkest parts of the island beneath the bridge.

"Do we split up again?" Connor's voice was pitched low as he and Archer joined us under the bridge.

I had just opened my mouth to answer and saw Archer do the same, but Ringo beat both of us. "No. We stay together. Markus will go for the boat, and de Rais will go for Jehanne. Our targets will converge at some point."

Connor nodded. "You guys can keep me from throttling Jehanne when we see her, then."

"Is it something specific, or just general disgust?" I smiled at the sour-taste expression on his face.

"She's convinced her visions are a gift from God, even though it's the same God the English currently worship, and despite the fact she's never led soldiers in battle before, she comes up with idiotic plans that somehow, ridiculously work. And because the crazy-town light is going full-blast behind her eyes, the mosquitos swarm to it."

I grinned at his disgust. "Thought about this much?"

He tried to hide his own smile, and failed. "Maybe."

"You guys haven't met in this time, right?"

"Not officially. I hooked onto one of her civilian mosquito units, and I move around enough that nobody remembers who I am."

Archer crouched down to draw in the dirt with a stick. "Here's the bridge ... from the Tourelle, which is controlled by the English, across the island, to the city, which is controlled by the French. If I were going to blow the bridge to do the most damage, I would set up a distraction over here …" He pointed to the fields where the English commandos had their camps, "and then draw a big unit of English onto the bridge. Then I'd blockade the far side, and when the soldiers were trapped, I'd blow the bridge here …" Archer pointed to the connection of bridge to land on the south bank of the river.

A smooth, deep voice spoke from above us. "Or even better, I'll catch the culprits trying to set the charge here. Ye'll be killed resisting arrest, and the witch dies next, before the boat's ever been launched." Jack was perched in the support tower aiming a weapon that looked distinctly like a seventeenth century matchlock pistol – at me.

I guessed that was logical. Threaten to take out the chick and all the guys drop to their knees to save her. Chivalry was alive and well in pretty much every other time but my own, and one quick glance at my boy, Connor, told me everything that was about to go down.

One. Shimmer.

Two. Dive.

Three. Shift.

Yup, it pretty much happened like that. Clothes disintegrated from Connor's body as he Shifted. He was in motion and already out of range of any projectile by the time the Wolf emerged.

And because Connor leapt, so did I. I don't like weapons pointed at me. So I became a moving target. Ringo and Archer were exactly a tenth of a second behind me in motion. I heard the shot fire, but knew without a doubt we were all way out of range.

And matchlock pistols made me happy, because they were absurdly hard to reload. More effective to use as a club than a gun after the first shot.

Ringo and Archer were headed up the tower scaffold to get to Jack, and Connor's Wolf was already sniffing around the base of the tower, presumably looking for any sign of explosives. I scanned the area overhead, looking for Jehanne's soldiers, when a thought hit me so hard it almost knocked me over.

What if the only way to ensure the bridge was blown was to set the charge ourselves?

We had a boat. We knew an unfortunate amount about incendiary devices. And we could probably steal the resources from the English camp. But then the bigger question – did I really want to be directly responsible for the deaths of English soldiers in a crazy girl's war?

And the answer was a resounding, no, I did not.

Overhead, Archer and Ringo had taken their battle with Jack to the bridge, which effectively snapped me out of my head and back to the tasks at hand.

I couldn't see much, but the clang of swords clashing gave me hope that Archer might actually get a fair fight with the other Seer. Except there would be nothing fair about a fight with this Seer.

I spun to find Connor's Wolf nosing around the base of the tower. "I'm going up," I told him. He did something that looked like a wolf-smile before padding to another section of brush to continue his search.

I had just reached the top of the support tower when Archer suddenly leapt backwards and almost ran into me. I put my hands out to protect myself from being hurtled from the tower and actually connected with Archer's thigh. He looked back in surprise at the unexpected support.

"Good. You're here. Got your daggers?"

He rushed forward again to force Jack backward with his sword. The two men were pretty evenly matched in sword skills, and the thing was, Archer was really good. I didn't spot Ringo at first, because I was looking for him at Archer's side. He was about twenty feet down the bridge, trying to hold off four English commandos from joining in the fight.

Okay, disable Jack and it would be three against four. Those were odds I could deal with. I drew the blades from their sheaths and took a breath to center myself. Jack's fighting style was aggressive and athletic, and he almost never left himself open. I looked for a weakness or a tell – anything I could use to anticipate his next move.

Jack spotted me then, and the look of concentration broke into a sickening grin. He suddenly spun away and switched directions, aiming his sword straight at me.

I threw my dagger reflexively, and the second it left my hand I knew it was a mistake. Too high and too slow. He laughed and knocked it out of the air with his blade. Archer lunged for his back, and he spun again to defend himself.

And then I saw it. Jack leaned to his left very slightly just before he did his spin moves, as if favoring something on the other side. Like maybe a testicle?

Jack slashed at Archer, who leapt backwards again almost faster than I could track. But with every lunge Archer made, Jack was a fraction faster. Because he anticipated everything. His Sight gave him the same advantage Tom had had when he'd fought with Wilder under the Tower of London. The difference was, Jack had skill, too.

Archer didn't jump back far enough on the next slash, and a line of blood appeared at his collarbone. I couldn't look at him; I had to keep my eyes locked on Jack's form. I had one dagger left. I couldn't miss.

There. The lean. I hurtled the dagger at the spot I thought he'd spin into.

Thunk.

The wet sound of a knife in meat made my gut roil for a second, but that was short-lived. A flash of pure rage, almost like a hazy red cloud, surrounded the man, and I staggered in fear. I'd stuck my dagger deep in the bicep of his sword arm, and he stared at it in disbelief. Then his gaze turned toward me, and I understood what fear tasted and smelled like, too. This time when he ran at me, Archer stepped forward with his own sword raised to stop him. But Jack's weapon clattered to the bridge, dropped by his useless arm. He growled in rage and yanked my dagger from his bicep and threw it at me.

Archer's sword batted the dagger out of the air.

And then imbedded itself into Jack's neck when he lunged at me.

Jack's eyes were locked on mine, and the rage in them terrified me. Archer stepped back. He hadn't meant to stab Jack, but there was no shock on the Seer's face. Just pure violence.

Jack swatted the sword away from his neck, and arterial blood sprayed the bridge. I barely unlocked my muscles in time to dodge his dive for me, but it was enough. Momentum carried him over the side of the bridge, and the thud of his body landing on the island was like a sandbag hitting concrete.

I looked over automatically and saw Connor's Wolf approach the sprawled and bleeding body. He leaned in, smelled something, and then growled ferociously before turning his back and walking away.

Markus the Seer was dead.

I shuddered and looked at Archer. He was already moving down the bridge to where Ringo still stood, sword raised, blocking the commandos from joining the fight. They looked as stunned as I felt, and Archer spoke to them in what I assumed was English.

They seemed wary, but one of them nodded brusquely, and after a few more words were exchanged, they turned and left.

Archer and Ringo had a brief discussion on their way back to where I stood, now finally all the way on the bridge. Archer picked up my dagger and was about to wipe the blood off on his clothes, but I stopped him. "No, don't. You'll be smelling his blood all night."

Archer cringed. "I'm smelling mine already."

I held my hand out for my dagger. "I'll deal with it. Thanks."

Ringo found the other dagger where it had fallen between planks. I put that one back into its sheath on my thigh. The bloody one I dropped down to the island after making sure Connor's Wolf was out of range. It landed, blade down, in the sand at the base of the tower, and I climbed back down the support structure to retrieve it.

Connor's Wolf came out of the river and shook himself off right next to me as I washed the blade of my dagger clean in the water. "Hey!"

He did his wolfish grin thing and stood next to me, panting.

341

"I have an extra shirt if you want to Shift back." That was the bummer about having helped save my life. He'd exploded his clothes.

Ringo dropped down to the beach, with Archer right behind. "I can pull the trousers off the Seer if ye want 'em."

Connor's Wolf sneezed and shook his head. Ringo laughed. "Yeah, ye're right. Corpses shite themselves and they probably stink."

I shuddered. "Do you think we should deal with him? I mean, I don't really feel like burying the guy, but he's not from this time."

Archer leaned over and searched Jack's clothes, but then backed away quickly. "Sorry, I can't …"

I stood up. "The scent of blood. I'll do it."

Archer looked relieved and annoyed at himself at the same time.

"Ye sure? I can do it, too." Ringo didn't want to do it any more than I did.

"I'm a big girl. I can deal."

I wasn't exactly sure why I felt the need to be such a grown-up about searching a dead body. But when I moved over to where Jack had fallen and stared down at his blood-splattered face, I knew.

He was big, and very strong. He was skilled with weapons, and skilled with Sight. He hated me, and probably had a thing about females in general. And he had scared me. Badly. I'd thought I was going to die with my own dagger in my windpipe, and the pleasure he'd seemed to take at describing it had been almost worse than if he had just done it and said nothing.

And now, standing over his dead body, I realized it wasn't because he was a man, or a big man, or a stranger, or a pirate, or a Seer that I'd been afraid. It was *this* guy, and *his* brain that had threatened to kill me. And the brain that could even think of those things had flatlined when he hit the ground, so I could let the fear it inspired flatline, too.

I took a shallow breath because Ringo was right, he did stink. I'd always read that bodies let go of their bowels when they die, and

342

yeah, based on the smell, I'd say that's pretty much what happened. So, here was this big, scary guy who had just pooped himself.

I struggled to hold back giggles.

Ringo appeared at my side and spoke quietly. "'E scared ye, didn't 'e." It wasn't a question.

I nodded, the urge to giggle wiped out by his solemn tone.

"Kick 'im."

I turned to stare at Ringo. His pose was casual, with arms crossed in front of his chest, but the look in his eyes told me he knew.

"I'm not going to kick him."

"Then drop wind on 'im and walk away."

I was still staring, but the giggles bubbled up again. "You want me to fart on him?"

"Sure, why not? 'E won't notice, not with that stink 'e's got goin' on, but it'll make ye feel better."

I did burst out laughing then, and Connor's Wolf raised his head to stare at me.

Ringo shrugged. "I say, some graves should be spat on, or shat on. Keeps the nightmares away."

I shook my head, still laughing, and walked away from Jack's poopy corpse.

LA TOURELLE

Dawn was approaching, and we still hadn't seen Jehanne. Wherever she was, de Rais would be, too. I rationalized that we could tie him up or turn him over to the English to get him out of the way long enough for Jehanne to blow up the bridge. Then, whatever happened could happen and we wouldn't have been responsible for the death of someone historically prominent.

Connor's Wolf nudged my hand in agreement, but Archer and Ringo said nothing, and their silence worried me.

"We can't kill him, guys."

I didn't matter what I said. They didn't respond. I was pretty sure Archer was still pissed at de Rais' future self for his potshot at me, but I thought Ringo's reaction might be about the kids de Rais would kill. His comment about nightmares and spitting on graves felt personal.

We had retreated to the Orléans side of the bridge, and were hanging out at the base of the support tower. Connor had stayed Wolf and swam across the river. The rest of us took the bridge. We left the little boat where it was hidden in the reeds since it couldn't hold more than two people anyway.

Connor's Wolf and Ringo were sitting off to one side of the tower base. Ringo didn't need to talk and Connor's Wolf couldn't, so they seemed content to stare out into the night.

I leaned back into Archer's body and his arms supported my sides. It felt protective, but not like I needed protection, and I was glad the poopy corpse laughter had chased the boogeyman away.

"What are you looking forward to most about getting back home?" Archer's deep voice rumbled against my back. I leaned my head back onto his shoulder.

"It feels so far away, almost like I can't let myself dream about it because of what's still between us and home."

"I wouldn't mind going away with you somewhere."

I chuckled. "Is there any place Mongers won't go?"

"I might have a couple of hideouts they probably don't know about."

I turned to face him, suddenly serious. "Then let's go. As soon as we're done and Mr. Shaw is safe, let's take a break from the insanity."

He tucked an errant hair behind my ear and smiled. "I would take you right now if I thought you'd actually go."

I winced. "I know. Sorry."

"Don't ever apologize for making hard choices, Saira. You know I will follow you to the ends of the earth, and across time – wherever and whenever you want to go."

The glow his words inspired was snuffed out by an outburst of yelling and the hissing of arrows that filled the air. We were on our feet and climbing up the tower support structure instantly, but Connor's Wolf beat us to the top of the embankment and took off across the field.

"Connor!" I shouldn't have yelled, but it wouldn't take much for one of those arrows to be aimed at a big gray Wolf running among the soldiers. The Wolf didn't even look back, and my heart thumped in fear for him.

Ringo took off after him, and Archer and I were right behind.

It looked like a melee on the field between French and English armored soldiers, with French townspeople lobbing rocks into the fight from above. The archery was apparently a one-time thing because now there were young French kids running among the fighting soldiers, trying to retrieve the arrows.

Here and there I caught a flash of gray Wolf among the fighters, darting in and out of the crowd. "He's looking for Jehanne," Archer said in my ear.

Of course he was. Connor had taken her on as his responsibility and nemesis, and I should never have brought him into something so dangerous and volatile.

"There's de Rais!" I pointed to the large, black-bearded man in full armor, about to swing a huge broadsword at the backs of two English commandos. I almost shrieked at them to watch their backs. They were parrying with some French soldiers when de Rais' sword cut them in half.

"Look for Jehanne." Archer's voice was grim in my ear.

Someone, a civilian maybe, flung a fist-sized rock down at us. I pushed Archer out of the way, and then promptly tripped over him. We landed up against the city walls of Orléans, and I suddenly wanted to go home so badly I almost cried.

But then I spotted the Wolf. He was surrounded by French soldiers with long pikes, and I saw, rather than heard, the snarling growls as he lunged at them, looking for signs of weakness to break free. Archer saw him too, and the next moment we were running.

It was the most dangerous free run I'd ever done. Every raised sword, every armored body was a moving obstacle. The rocks still rained, and clubs swung. We leapt over fallen fighters, dove under thrusts and parries, spun around armored soldiers looking for their next opponent. And the straightest line to a snarling Wolf was the only thought in my head.

A soldier raised his pike to throw like a spear. The Wolf couldn't see it, and his flank was exposed. I opened my mouth to yell because I wasn't going to make it. But then an armored man fell in front of me, and another dropped to his knees behind him. I used them like steps, their bodies giving only a little under the armor, to launch at the soldier with the pike.

The flight was high so the landing was hard. The armor was even harder and pointy in places that hit me badly. But I slammed into him as the pike left his hand, knocking it off course. The soldier and I took out two others like dominos, and the Wolf had his opening.

He leapt over us and bolted toward the city walls. For a second I watched him go and hoped he could make it inside, away from all the deadly weapons. But then he stopped, looked skyward, sniffed, and took off toward the bridge.

If Connor survived this night, I might have to kill him myself.

Archer's hands under my arms pulled me to my feet, and the soldier I'd taken out actually smiled, as if happy to have me off him. I was running hurt now, but I didn't think I was bleeding from any of the dents the armor had made in me when I landed on it. I scanned the battlefield for de Rais as we headed back toward the river, but his big figure wasn't obvious among the fighters.

Ringo met up with us near the city gates. "'The Wolf's swimmin' across. It's faster if we take the bridge."

"Not on top." I shook my head. The foot traffic was all headed toward us, and spoiling for a fight. "Across the struts."

Archer scanned the water as it ambled past. "Have you seen a boat?"

Ringo shook his head. "Nothin' that we're lookin' for besides a twitchy Wolf."

We dodged armored Englishmen to climb down the embankment to the trusses under the bridge, but Archer put his hand on my arm and stopped me before I could crawl onto it.

"No, wait, the fight will be here."

And suddenly I Saw what he could See. The bridge exploding. Jehanne and her fighters back on this side, poised to take out any English who escaped the blast. And the Baron de Rais behind her, swinging his sword.

"Crap." Connor was going to end up on the wrong side.

I ran down the embankment to the river. I debated screaming Connor's name, but Ringo beat me to it with a whistle worthy of a construction worker. I stared across the river, trying to decipher movement on either of the two islands in the dark.

The bridge was full of armored English soldiers now, and I had the thought that Ringo's whistle might have made them move a little faster across to our side.

And might have saved some lives.

BOOM!

The flash of light across the river reminded me of the white phosphorus explosions we'd caused at the Tower of London. It came from the base of the final support tower, and the groans of disintegrating wood shivered through the entire bridge.

But it was the screams of men that made my ears feel like they were bleeding.

Heavy armor splashed down into the water – fifty, maybe a hundred bodies fell from the crumbling bridge. The men screamed as they fell, and I could almost hear the water swallow the sound when they hit.

"My God, they're drowning!" I almost ran into the river then, but Archer yanked me back by my tunic.

"There's Connor." He pointed downriver, where a shaggy, wet Wolf crawled up the bank and collapsed onto the sand.

I took off running down the beach and made it to the Wolf just as the air around him began to shimmer. Connor was panting as hard as his Wolf had been, and he curled himself up in a sitting position, his arms wrapped around his knees. He was wet and shivering, and I draped my cloak around his body.

He looked up as I dropped beside him. "They used our boat."

I swore in a most un-ladylike way. "We're messing with time just by being here."

He shrugged. "I don't know what difference it really makes whether it's an English or a French king on the throne here right now. I just want to go home."

I hugged him to my side and was surprised at how hard he was shivering. "Did you see anyone send the boat out?"

He shook his head. "It was already set when I got there."

The trembling started to calm, and I don't think it was totally from the cold of the water. "I'm glad you got away before it went off."

He looked at me with haunted eyes. "But they didn't. The screams were so loud …"

"I know." My voice was a whisper, and he shut his eyes. The echoes of men's screams seemed to hang in the air, and I shivered.

Connor inhaled sharply. "I need pants."

I squeezed his shoulders and stood up. "Yeah, you do. Not sure where we're going to get them though."

He grimaced and struggled to keep the cloak wrapped around him as he stood.

The sound of clanging steel was suddenly louder than the fading screams, and it was coming from the spot where I'd left Ringo and Archer. I took off across the beach, not even waiting to see if Connor was behind me.

Three French soldiers were battling Archer and Ringo. The two on Archer were good, but not as good as he was, and they'd already taken some damage. The third was slight but strong, and when he turned, I gasped.

It was Jehanne. And she was going after Ringo with the very clear intent to end his life. I was about to dive into the mix when Connor grabbed me from behind. "De Rais."

I looked at the place he nodded to and realized that de Rais stood in the shadows of the bridge tower, casually leaning against a beam with his arms crossed in front of him. His eyes glittered at me as if he was delighted to have caught my attention.

He called out in French, and Connor translated for me. "If you go in to assist, so does he."

I wasn't sure it was possible to despise a man more than I hated that one. De Rais was just waiting to see if we were going to do his dirty work for him by taking Jehanne out of the equation, and I didn't want to risk changing history if any of us fought him.

Jehanne lunged at Ringo and nicked him in the shoulder with her sword. He didn't flinch, but he was bleeding, and the two soldiers on Archer were keeping him too busy to help.

"Yell to her. Tell her he's French." I spoke in a low voice to Connor. She didn't need to hear English conversation coming from us.

Connor called out to her, and she shot him a quick glance and then yelled something back. "She said I speak French with the accent of an English dog, so when she's done with him, I'm next."

"Awesome."

Archer got a decent stab in on one of the soldiers, hobbling him with a slice to the back of the knee. He was out, but his friend fought even more desperately after he limped away.

Jehanne's sword-thrusts were fierce and angry, and I knew Ringo was holding back so he didn't accidentally kill her. But it's hard to pull punches and not get your butt kicked, and she was definitely gaining the upper hand on him.

"Can you back her Wolf down?" I was getting desperate for her to stop fighting so neither of them got more hurt.

"I don't know. I'm not dominant to her until I beat her in a fight, and that hasn't happened yet."

Damn, he was right. That dominance fight he won was in the future. "Tell her we know she caused the explosion, and if she and her men let us go, she will be at Reims to crown Charles VII on July, 17th. But if she kills us, that vision won't come true."

He called out what I'd said in French, and then spoke to me quietly. "How do you know she had a vision about that?"

"I don't. I'm bluffing."

She shot us a very quick look, and I nodded at her. Then her gaze went to Archer, who had just knocked the sword out of his fighter's hand. "Here we go," Connor whispered.

Jehanne leapt back from Ringo and let her sword point drop to the ground. Ringo had been about to lunge at her, but stopped himself mid-thrust.

The sudden stillness was almost jarring, until de Rais pushed himself off the wooden beam and stepped forward with his sword raised. It looked like he was going to go for Archer, but instead he strode over to Jehanne like she made him tired. He raised his sword, and swung.

Nooo!

Ringo practically flew forward, hefting his sword as he went, to put himself between Jehanne and de Rais' sword. Connor Shifted beside me, and a second later had darted into the fray. But Archer was a half second ahead of all of them. He threw his body forward to shield Jehanne from the blow. His body, not his sword.

The sword slashed down on Archer instead of Jehanne, and as he was hitting the ground, Ringo was lunging at de Rais, and Connor flew at him to fasten his teeth on the monster's throat.

He was a monster. Charlie had called him that and it was true. I could see the Otherworlder looking through de Rais' eyes as he tried to raise his sword to bring it down on Connor's Wolf. But I couldn't see anything else. I was racing to Archer. He was down, and blood began to seep into the sand under him.

He rolled over under his own power and stared up at me, an odd confusion on his face. "It hurts."

I crouched next to him to see his wound. It was a slash that had opened his tunic at his chest, and a deep cut marked his skin across his ribs. For a few seconds, the skin of his entire ribcage was mottled with horrible bruises. The night was dark, so I wondered if my eyes told the truth, and when the bruises faded right before my eyes and the slice across his ribs began to seal closed, I had to rub my eyes.

Archer looked down at himself and took a breath like he was testing his ability to. The snarl of a Wolf dragged me back to the world outside of Archer. Connor's Wolf stood over de Rais, teeth bared and mouth bloody. Ringo stood on the other side of de Rais with his sword held ready. But it was Jehanne who held my attention. She glared at de Rais, her eyes glittering with rage. She spat something at him in French, and I caught the words "dog" and "dead."

De Rais was badly wounded, but it didn't look fatal. Jehanne's anger did though. She strode over to him with her sword raised, ready to plunge it into his belly.

"Wait! Jehannne! No!"

She shot me a sideways glance, and I realized she didn't know I knew her name. Or maybe it was that I spoke to her in English.

"Saira, we don't get a say in this." Archer's voice was pitched low and meant only for my ears.

"But history—"

"—will be what it is."

Jehanne was speaking to de Rais, her sword still raised above her head. The big man had a lazy smile on his face, but I could see the effort it cost him to keep it there. Neither Connor's Wolf nor Ringo had moved.

"God visited my dream last night and showed me death at your hand." Archer was translating the words Jehanne snarled at de Rais. "This is a war against tyranny. It is a war against the fear that the English have brought with them to France. I am not afraid to die, de Rais, but I will do so looking forward at the vanquishing of my enemy, not behind at the treachery of my friend." Her voice became a fierce growl, and I could hear her Wolf very near the surface. "I will not spend my days in fear."

I started to leap forward as the sword descended, but Archer grabbed my arm. "Don't."

Jehanne's sword plunged into the soft part of de Rais' belly, and I thought I saw a moment of panic in the Otherworlder's eyes when he realized she was actually killing him.

He tried to get up, but the sword had skewered him to the sand. I spun away and fell to my knees. Bile hit the back of my throat like acid, but I forced it down with great, gulping breaths. Archer's hand was on my back, and the only thing I could see when I looked at him was the place where the slashed skin of his chest had knitted itself together.

My eyes finally found his. "I want to go."

The air around Connor shimmered, but Ringo stayed where he was, sword still raised. Jehanne watched Connor warily, and when he'd become his human self, she spoke to him.

"You are like me."

Connor looked at the sword in de Rais' belly, then back to Jehanne. His voice was tired, and he wiped his hands across his face. "I am nothing like you."

They spoke in French, but it was simple enough for me to understand their words. "But you are a Wolf." She spoke as if that was everything.

Ringo tossed Connor his cloak, and when he'd put it on, he faced Jehanne with the last of his energy. "I'm a guy who becomes a Wolf. You're a Wolf in a girl's skin."

It was strange to see a man's eyes in Connor's face when he turned his back on Jehanne – strange, but not surprising. "Let's get out of here."

TOM – APRIL, 1429

Hunger consumed me. It woke me from a dead sleep like a slap to the face, and I was on my feet the next instant. My eyes adjusted immediately to the darkness in the room where I'd woken. It hadn't been a dream, then. The spiral was there on the wall of the annex, and I was in the bed where I'd slept. Would sleep? Did sleep?

I had no idea when I was.

And I was ravenous.

I was wearing Léon's tunic and the shirt and pants I'd pulled from the tower before I Clocked, but I had no shoes. I needed to eat, and I needed shoes, and I felt like something out of a twisted Dickens story.

Thoughts skipped around my brain with no order or logic, and they felt skittish and opaque. I couldn't hold onto any idea long enough to look at it because the hunger draped across everything like a heavy curtain.

The spectre of Léon sat heavily on my heart, riding around like a ghost I carried in my body. I patted the drawing at my chest and then clutched the chess piece in my pocket. Neither action did anything to lessen the guilt that pricked at my skin like a pervasive chill, and worse, the tower held all my memories of him. I made my way out of the house just to have something else to think about.

I wasn't prepared for the scents and sounds of nighttime Paris. The air was crisp, and the cobbles under my feet would have sucked the heat out of them if there'd been any to begin with. I noticed the pain of pebbles distantly, like the memory of stubbed toes, and a summer of barefoot cousins playing in the sun slid through my brain, too vague to hold onto.

A little girl ran in front of me. She tripped on a cobble and burst into tears, and I stared at her like I couldn't remember how to comfort someone. The scrape on her knee began to ooze blood and the hunger boiled up in me like a beast about to roar. I squeezed my eyes shut, but I could still smell the coppery tang in the air, and if I didn't leave, I would need to taste it.

The little girl's cries echoed in my head as I ran.

The scent of blood coated the air down every alley, and lay especially thick in the market squares. I was like a moth to a flame. I couldn't help seeking it even as I resisted taking it. The streets got narrower and the alleys more twisted as I followed the blood. The heaviest scent was concentrated on one street, and the closed butcher shops were to me like candy stores to a little kid.

It took almost nothing to pop the barred door open. The rocket fuel feeling of Wilder's blood had faded, but the things it left behind surprised me. Theoretically, I knew a Sucker was stronger and faster than a regular person, because I'd seen Archer in action. I didn't feel particularly strong or fast until I actually used those muscles, and then I surprised the hell out of myself. I could pull my body over things I used to have to climb, and jump things I would have fallen down in my real life.

My real life. A very different time and place than now. This wasn't real. Nothing since the moment I'd begged Saira to take me and the Seer cuff with her had been real life. That was the miserable thing – I'd begged her to take me. Begged. My dad was a right nob, so what? He had nothing on Wilder. I had a rubbish social life, and my cousins were practically my only friends. Big deal. I just murdered the only other person who thought I was worth a damn. There'd be no hiding the truth of my turning, either. The fading track marks on my arms and Sucker's blood in my veins told a very particular story.

The shop was clean, cleaner than I expected with such a strong blood-smell. I prowled around the front room looking for anything with blood. There were knives hanging from hooks on the walls that smelled of it, but the smell wouldn't feed the hunger.

My bare feet were silent on the dirt floor as I padded to the back of the shop. A short, dark hallway led to the back courtyard of the building, and that door was unlocked. The smell was strongest from there, and I couldn't stop myself from opening the door.

Lamplight flickered in a small, open shed in the courtyard where someone was butchering a cow. The scent of blood was overwhelming, and I suddenly found myself right in front of the side of beef with no memory of walking across the yard.

My eyes were fixed on the pan beneath the hanging carcass. It was full of steaming blood that still ran in rivulets from the beast and dripped in a mesmerizing pattern. I barely registered the gasps of surprise from the worker, and was on my knees in front of the pan, ready to dip my head in and drink.

"A cup, sir?" A whisper and then a shaking hand held a crude metal cup in front of me. I still hadn't seen the speaker because my eyes were fixated on the blood, but at least the voice registered. He spoke accented French, and I recognized the voice with some part of my brain. I finally realized that I was about to lap up a panful of blood like a dog. I took the cup as gently and patiently as I could, dipped it into the blood, and drank.

It was metallic and coppery, thick and warm, and it was right foul. But nothing in the world could have stopped me from drinking it.

A voice said, "There is more," and my world spun. I looked up, and for the first time since I'd stumbled outside in search of blood, I could see clearly. Léon had taken a step forward. He was afraid of me; that was clear. And there was no recognition in his eyes.

"Léon." My voice broke wetly.

He took a step backward – from the crazy tosser kneeling over a pan full of cow's blood. I would have, too – stepped backward, away from the monster I'd become. Unfortunately, the Sucker in me wasn't quite so suicidal with all this blood available.

I scrubbed my eyes with the heels of my hands. "I'm sorry." The French came automatically, like muscle memory, when I spoke with him.

"Do you need help?" Léon's voice was tentative.

I let my gaze find his again. He was so real and alive, and all I could see was the fear and pain I'd put in his eyes when I'd murdered him. I stood so suddenly I stumbled backward, and Léon almost reached out to steady me. I saw his hand twitch, even as common sense must have told him to stay away from me. I wanted that touch more than anything in the world at that moment. I wanted to know he lived, to feel his pulse and believe what my eyes told me was true.

"What is the date today?"

My question surprised Léon, who answered. "April 11th, year of our Lord 1429."

I went cold. April 11th, 1554 was the date history recorded Thomas Wyatt's execution. It was the date Wilder had taken me from the Tower of London. It was the date we had Clocked to Paris.

I didn't know much about Clockers, only what Saira had told me a lifetime ago. But I remembered that Clockers couldn't be in the same time as themselves. I must have slipped back to just before Wilder and had I arrived in this time, just before we made the simple jump back a hundred and twenty-five years.

What that meant for me now, I had no idea. If history repeated itself, the Tom Landers who arrived in Paris tonight was the one who would eventually kill his best friend.

Unless …

"I know I'm a stranger to you now, but you will know me, Léon, and when you do see me – even if I look weak and sick and like I'm dying – you need to kill me."

The horror on his face took me right back to the last expressions I saw before I drained him of his blood. He took another step back and I didn't blame him, but I did stop him. My hand reached out and gripped his forearm. He was terrified of me, but the warmth of his skin under my hand took me beyond caring.

"I will kill you if you don't, Léon. I am your murderer, and the only chance you have is if you do it first. Don't wait until I'm weaker, because we'll be friends then and it'll be harder to do." I took a ragged breath. "I am a monster, and the only way for you to survive knowing me is to kill me first."

"Who are you?" I wanted to hold on to every one of his words, even the terrified whispers.

"I'm your friend, and your friendship is more important to me than life. Please …" I had to try twice to get the word out. "Please, put a pillow over my face while I sleep, or cut my throat, I don't care. Just do it, and then run. Hide on your island for a while."

His eyes, already huge in his face, widened even further at the idea that I knew about their island.

I decided to pull out the big guns so maybe he'd take me seriously. I knew he thought I was crazy, and that wouldn't help my case unless I made him afraid of me, too.

"I know you, Léon. I know your grandmother makes medicinal ointments. I know you are worried about your father's business, which is why you help him even though you'd rather be making up songs to sing. And I know your voice is just about the best one I've ever heard, especially when you sing the nightmares away." I pulled the black knight from my pocket. "This is your favorite piece because you only have one."

He stared at it in my hand. "It is from my father's set. You could not possibly …" He pulled the black knight from his own pocket and held it next to the one in my hand. They were identical. I dropped mine into his palm. "Now they are together."

"How do you know me? We are friends, you said." I dropped my hand and backed away, shaking my head.

"A friend would not do what I've done to you."

The terror in his eyes had begun to fade into something different. "Who but a friend would warn me against danger?"

I was still shaking my head, still backing away, and my voice caught in my throat. "No, Léon. You have to kill me."

"Should I pick up one of those knives and do it now?" His tone of voice was almost scoffing.

"I wish you could. But now it's too late. I'm too strong." I made my voice hard, gathered fierceness into it. "Your father and your grandmother are vulnerable. I've killed you. I could kill them, too, far too easily. How can I make you see? If you don't kill me, I will murder your family."

The bravado fled his eyes, and I felt sick. "You have to do it when I'm weak. Kill me before I hurt you and your family any more than I already have." I was close to tears again and I turned to leave.

His voice was full of fear. "I will do it, if I must, to save my family, and then I will pray the Lord will forgive me my sin against you."

I took a deep breath against the stuttering of my heartbeat, but I didn't look back at him. "Thank you." For everything I couldn't say out loud, or even think to myself. For looking at me as a person with value. For being my friend. The words tumbled around in my brain, but my whole life had been spent *not* saying things. I couldn't get past the roadblocks put there by a lifetime of shutting up.

I stumbled outside, never allowing myself the luxury of a last look. I was like Orpheus. If I looked back at Léon, the spirits of death would drag him down to Hades with no second chance to live. So I just had to trust he had heard my plea and would do what needed to be done to save his life.

I made my way back to the Hôtel de Sens, barely even conscious of directions or landmarks. I just knew I had to get back to the spiral, and all the words I hadn't said to Léon were choking the air from my throat as I ran. The cavernous stone rooms were just as empty as when I'd left, but I knew Wilder would come, dragging my sorry self with him. If I could have stayed to kill him, I would have, but the laws of Time wouldn't let me.

I bent to blow out the candle I'd lit when I came in and accidentally brushed against the spiral. The buzzing started instantly, and I felt compelled to trace the design. I couldn't *not* do it, and my fingers glided over the engraved design with a will of their own. With the buzzing sound in my ears and the thrum of a stretched rubber band running through my body came the knowledge that I had the power to end this.

I may not be able to take my own life, but I could Clock, courtesy of Wilder and Saira's mum. If I didn't give myself any coordinates, if I deliberately envisioned the black nothingness of *between*, maybe, just maybe, I could lose myself there forever.

With that thought came peace; maybe the first peace I'd known since I'd begun this whole bloody journey.

I was almost through the fourth spiral, and the hum in my body had taken over for breath. I emptied my mind and closed my eyes, determined to finish the spiral by touch alone. Without sight I could hold the blackness in my mind. The hum and stretch of Clocking began to fill every cell, and I could feel myself losing contact with the stones under my feet. The complete absence of all sight, sound, and sensation except the frigid cold was a blissful relief after the torture of being inside the ravenous monster that was my body. My self-preservation instinct kicked in and wanted me to fight, but I willed my brain back to nothingness, and I let it claim me. I didn't take breaths, my heart didn't beat, I heard nothing and felt nothing and thought … nothing.

PARIS

Our journey back to Paris was instantaneous. We'd gathered Valerie and Charlie from the secret garden and then Clocked to the island in the Seine where we could leave them in safety. Archer, Ringo, and I convinced Connor to stay behind with them, more for his protection than theirs. He was done – emotionally wrung out, and there was a vacancy in his eyes I didn't like. I was glad to see his Wolf when he Shifted and lay outside the door to the small shelter. I thought his Wolf might find the experiences we'd had a little less PTSD-inducing than the boy did.

I used my marker to draw a quick spiral inside the lean-to. If something happened to me, Valerie could get everyone back to 1554, where I knew she'd take care of them. I didn't say any of that out loud, but I caught Valerie's eye when I was done. She nodded once before turning away.

I had never seen Ringo just hold Charlie like he did when we left the island. He spoke quietly to her as Archer and I stood far enough away to give them privacy, and she had tears in her eyes when she ran back to Valerie. His expression was set into something impenetrable, and Archer clasped his arm with a quick show of support as we stepped into the small boat.

We were mostly silent on our way across the river and through the quiet streets to the Hôtel de Sens. Jehanne had been in full Joan of Arc battle mode when we left Orléans, so we wouldn't be running into her wolves, and the only thing in front of us was the uncertainty of Wilder.

We stopped just before we entered the Marais.

"Weapons?" Archer said out loud what I'd been thinking. What were our assets against a Vampire?

I lifted the hem of my tunic to display my daggers strapped in their holsters to my upper thighs. I'd barely managed to retrieve them a couple of times, but they felt like old friends now.

Ringo lifted his sword from its scabbard, but didn't remove it. There are cultures where a drawn blade has to be blooded, and I was feeling superstitious enough just then to be glad he hadn't pulled it out all the way. Archer showed his own sword and a dagger at his belt, his eyes searching ours.

"Every weapon at our disposal." There was no question mark at the end. We were down to the three of us and whatever steel we wielded, and it had to be enough.

I didn't like going in at night, but it was the only way to have Archer next to me. Wilder was his nemesis even more than he was mine. And Ringo – he was in no matter what. He'd been wearing a grim expression since Archer was injured, and the scene with Charlie on the island wasn't helping his mood. We were all exhausted, and the prospect of more violence was not something any of us looked forward to.

The street in front of the Hôtel de Sens was deserted, and the air was so still it felt like the city was holding its breath. The heavy wooden door was predictably locked, but Ringo looked up at the windows above us, flexed his fingers, and was up a wall before I could whisper the words he already knew.

"Be careful."

I knew from the set of his mouth he heard me, and I knew he would be careful. I'd only said it to feel like I could somehow make a difference in his safety. Archer and I melted back into the shadows to wait, and he pulled my body in front of him so his voice was at my ear.

"Let me do this." It hadn't been more than a whisper, but his tone made me shiver. He meant Wilder, and Wilder was strong.

I nodded. "Let me back you up, though."

He didn't hesitate with his return nod, and it made me feel like he believed I was strong and capable enough to be at his back. That trust shot the smallest ray of light through my very heavy heart, and I pressed myself back against him. His arms came around me, and I closed my eyes for a second – just long enough to memorize the instant of contentment.

"Chhhttt!" Ringo's whispered sound snapped us out of our moment of peace, and we both moved toward it instantly. A moment later we were inside the main hall of the Hôtel de Sens.

The space was huge and very gothic, with pointed spires and carved stone. It was completely devoid of the signs of habitation, though. No furniture or fixtures, just the built-in decorations of stone and plaster. Gargoyles looked down on us from the corners of the ceiling, and I seriously would not have been surprised if one of them had suddenly left its perch and climbed down the walls. A massive stone staircase spiraled up from the hall.

"Towers and bedrooms are upstairs. Public rooms down. Where do you want to search first?" Ringo spoke with authority, and I believed him.

"The towers." I didn't know why I was so certain, but Archer and Ringo didn't question it.

"Let's go."

We took the stone steps two at a time, but our rubber soles stayed silent as we crept toward the closest corner of the mansion. The guys had fallen in line on either side of me, and because I felt like a bundle of twitchy nerves, I didn't mind being in the middle.

The first tower room was empty of everything but a big carved crucifix hanging on the wall. The Jesus figure was practically as tall as me, and I suddenly got a really bad feeling seeing him hanging from that cross. I usually just looked at religious iconography as art, but this one landed with me differently, somehow. Like a sign of death instead of rebirth. I spun away from it and left the tower before Archer or Ringo could even ask about the look on my face.

I was halfway down the hall toward the other tower before they caught up with me, and Archer could tell something was off because he put a hand out to stop me.

"Wait. Use your spidey sense. Wilder's a Monger, remember?"

My gut sense for Mongers had barely prickled the whole time we'd been in the fifteenth century, and considering we'd just been in a war, that was strange enough to seriously contemplate when we got home. But it meant I had stopped using it as an early warning signal, and Archer was right. If Wilder was around, I'd feel him like the onset of food poisoning. Uncomfortable for me, but almost certainly fatal for all of us if we walked in unaware.

Archer's use of a superhero term for it lifted a fraction of my unease. I knew it was calculated to, and that made it even better. I closed my eyes and concentrated on the tendril of instinct that knew Mongers. I imagined it unfurling and reaching out like a tentacle, past the guys next to me, ahead into the closest rooms of the mansion.

I didn't know if my sense worked like wifi – if thick walls blocked it – but I didn't get anything at first. Then slowly, the beginnings of nausea began to curl around my guts, and with each step forward, it got stronger.

I looked at Archer and Ringo watching me intently, and I nodded. "Ahead of us."

"Better than behind us, I guess." Ringo mumbled it under his breath, but I knew the feeling.

The prickling in my guts got stronger, and I suddenly knew my daggers wouldn't be enough. The swords that Archer and Ringo carried at their backs wouldn't be enough. My father, Will Shaw, and his massive Lion, hadn't been enough. Bishop Wilder was a tricky, vicious, break-all-the-rules Monger underneath the almost-impossible-to-kill Vampire. He was strong, intelligent, and calculating. And I was going in without all my weapons.

I turned to Ringo. "I need the Shifter bone."

Neither of the guys moved for a second, as if even their breathing had stopped. Then Ringo reached under his shirt and pulled the leather cord over his head. The few glimpses I'd had of the ancient carved pendant had made my insides twist in fear and guilt, but I knew it wasn't the bone that I was afraid of.

I hesitated just a fraction of a second, and I saw the smallest tremor in my hand as I reached for the necklace. Archer let out a breath as I pulled it on over my head and looked him in the eye.

"Every weapon at our disposal."

"Can you control her?" I knew Archer's worry was for me, not because he was afraid of my Cat.

"I don't know. Hopefully I don't have to find out."

He nodded brusquely and we continued down the hall. Ringo gripped my shoulder lightly for a moment as he leaned in to whisper.

"I like yer Cat. I wouldn't be sorry to see 'er."

His words of support helped lighten a little of the dread I carried at the idea of unleashing the Cougar again. Losing control of her was almost inevitable, and I had come to accept I was a proper control freak.

The door to the main tower room was unlocked, but I stopped Archer before he could open it all the way. The Monger-induced nausea had gotten worse, and I signaled that to the guys. They nodded understanding, and with battlefield sign language we worked out our positions going through the door.

Archer held up fingers – one, two, three – then burst through the tower door with me right behind and Ringo at my back.

We were in a small, dark annex that opened up to a bigger, high-ceilinged room. My first thought was that we'd entered Dr. Frankenstein's weird kitchen. Instant flashes of glass beakers partly filled with blood, a goose carcass, partially plucked and hanging upside down over a pot, and a giant, walk-in-sized fireplace crackling with a fire hit my brain at the same moment as I saw someone bent over a body across the vast room.

The guy across the room straightened at our entrance. He looked terrified. There was a pillow in one hand and a butcher knife in the other. He had just lifted the pillow from the head of the bed.

I was halfway across the room before I recognized Léon, the butcher from the island, and I almost stopped in my tracks. Almost.

Until I saw the boots on the floor by the bed, which was occupied.

I knew those boots. Doc Martens.

No. The word went flat in my brain. And then it spiked with understanding and I shouted, "No!"

Léon stared, wild-eyed and panicked, as I slammed past him to get to Tom.

Tom Landers stared up at me from the bed, his eyes wide and sightless.

"Tom! No … Tom." I shook Tom, and then started pumping his heart with compression force as I pleaded with him to live.

"You can't die. I just found you; you can't die now. Tom!"

"WHAT HAVE YOU DONE!"

Wilder's bellow sent my whole body into fight or flight, but I kept my hands pumping firmly on Tom's heart and locked my knees so I couldn't give in to instinct and run.

I didn't turn around. I couldn't look at Wilder. I barely saw Léon run. My eyes were locked on Tom's, and I willed him to live. I bent down to give him mouth-to-mouth, pinching his nose and tilting back his chin like I'd been taught.

But his skin was already starting to cool, and there was no air coming from his nose and mouth. I put my ear directly on his heart. There was silence.

"I'm sorry, Tom. I'm so sorry."

I felt the Cat inside me growl.

Rage poured into me like water in an empty vessel. The Cougar fed on it, used it to move and grow in strength. It was by the barest will I held my human form, even as the Cat inside me scented Archer and Léon's terror.

Kill the butcher who did this. The Cat was growling and pacing under my human skin. She wanted blood. She wanted to wrap her teeth around necks and feel them snap like chicken bones. The rage that fueled her became a laser that I dialed down to a pinpoint beam of anger and hate, which I aimed at the true butcher, Bishop Wilder.

Everything in my brain slowed down as I turned to face the focus of my rage. Wilder must have grabbed Léon as he bolted for the door, because he was still in the annex holding the struggling young man in his hands. The fury on Wilder's face when he looked at me hit me like a blow. His eyes were locked on mine when he broke Léon's neck and threw his body away from him like a limp doll.

The body slid up against the far wall, and my brain registered something that looked like part of a spiral hiding in its shadows. An escape hatch for us, and for Wilder. No matter how much I hated the idea of killing Wilder, this had to end here – tonight.

"Hey! Silverback! You think you're pretty badass with Seer and Clocker blood in you? But you didn't See this, did you?" I taunted Wilder with my nastiest tone, the one mean girls saved for the kids they tormented.

Archer and Ringo had swords out and ready, and I went for my daggers. I needed Wilder to come into the tower. To not go for the spiral and Clock away.

"You know you want my Shifter blood. Why don't you come and get me?"

He watched me through wary, glittering eyes. "Why? Why offer yourself up to me?" Wilder's voice was pure menace, and my survival instincts were screaming at me to run.

"Because I don't want you to leave."

I could hear Archer's exhale, but he stayed quiet and let me do my thing. I put my hands in the air and took a step forward from Tom's body.

"Come to me," Wilder hissed.

"I'm tired, not stupid."

Wilder's eyes flicked to Archer and his sword, then back to me. "Neither am I."

"Right. Okay, tell you what. I'll put a little of my blood in this flask over here. If you come in, you can have it. If you leave, I'll give it to Archer."

This time it was Archer who hissed, but I didn't look at him. My eyes were locked on Wilder's, and I could tell the idea that Archer could have what he wanted chapped him.

"What do you gain by giving me your blood?"

"A shot at killing you."

A grin sliced his face. "You can't kill me."

"Fine, they'll kill you. I just want it done now. I'm sick of chasing you all over time. Here, look." I took one of my daggers out and sliced into a little vein in my wrist. A sense of calm certainty settled around me, and I trusted my instincts.

"Saira! Don't!" Archer's tone sounded a little panicky, and I remembered it had been a couple of days since he'd been able to refuel. The sight of my blood must have made him a little nuts.

I held my wrist over one of the empty beakers and let the blood drip down into it. I mouthed "sorry" to Archer, and then turned my attention back to Wilder. His gaze was trapped by the blood, and he actually licked his lips. Gross.

A second later he was moving toward me, and then everything happened at once. Archer and Ringo thrust swords at Wilder, who dodged them both with too much ease. He was still coming at me, so I hurled my dagger at his chest. Wilder looked excited when he caught it in mid-air. It was an impossible catch, and I realized he had already fed on Tom's blood and was using Tom's fugue Sight to See the strikes a moment before they happened.

Archer knew it, too. "Get back!" Archer shouted at me. He lunged at Wilder's back, forcing him to spin and face the attack. My dagger in Wilder's hand was enough to block Archer's blade and keep it from descending on him. The two Vampires were locked, face-to-face, by their weapons.

Ringo dove forward suddenly and buried his sword in Wilder's femoral artery, skewering it from behind with so much force that the blade emerged from the front. Wilder roared, but he didn't drop the dagger, and the next moment he swung his thigh up and embedded the sword point in Archer's stomach.

The wound was deep, and Archer paled instantly. He staggered back, off the blade, and for a fraction of a second his body looked like it was riddled with gashes and cuts, his skin blue with bruises. It was as if every wound from his Tower of London fall and from the battle with de Rais appeared for a moment and then faded as the gash closed.

Wilder stared at Archer, as stunned as I was, for the space of a breath, and then he ripped Ringo's sword out of his thigh and lunged again. Archer was barely able to spin out of range, and I could see his chest rise and fall with the effort.

The Cat screamed at me to let her out, let her protect her mate, but her rage was so fierce I was terrified I'd never get her back under control. My hands were already headed toward my remaining dagger when Ringo shouted at me.

"Saira! Move!" I dove to the side as Wilder changed direction and launched directly at me. I flung a dagger at him before I hit the floor, and miraculously, it stuck in his arm. I staggered back with the flash of awareness I suddenly had that Wilder's soul was completely without light. He paused, and for just a second, I saw the blood from his thigh wound bloom again. Then he yanked the dagger out, and whipped it at Archer in a move that surprised us both. My last dagger stuck in Archer's collarbone, and I heard a sharp crack.

Archer stumbled back again with the same flash of wound memory. He had to drop his sword to reach up and pull my dagger out, and Wilder changed direction again to lunge at him.

"No!" Ringo flung two glass beakers in rapid succession, hitting Wilder in the head with the first one. He batted the second one away with a growl.

"I'm going to break you next, boy." The menace in his voice sent a bolt of horror through me. Not only the threat against Ringo, but the fact that his plan for violence seemed focused on Archer first.

Wilder picked up his sword, and in two strides was in front of Archer. He plunged the sword into Archer's stomach, and I screamed. My legs felt frozen for one horrible second as Archer's eyes widened and every single wound I'd ever seen him sustain, and even some I hadn't seen, bloomed on his body. The sword was stuck so deep it had gone through him and pinned him to the wood paneling of the wall.

Before I had even taken one step, Ringo was flying at Wilder with a glass carafe in each hand. He smashed one against Wilder's head, but it didn't break – the glass was too thick. It knocked Wilder back for a second though, just enough time for Ringo to crash the bottle against the stone floor, break the end off it, and shove it into Wilder's neck.

Wilder instantly paled, and the wounds in his thigh and arm began to bleed again. He stumbled when Ringo twisted the bottle, and I used that distraction to race to Archer. I needed both hands to pull the sword out of his gut, and every injury I'd ever seen him take still blazed on his face and body until the sword was out.

Archer fell back against the wall, and slowly the old wounds began to seal themselves closed. But it wasn't happening fast enough, and too much blood was still pouring out of the hole in his middle. His eyes had gone glassy.

"Archer!"

He didn't respond, and suddenly Ringo went flying backwards to hit the far wall with a CRACK. Wilder stalked past us, intent on getting to Ringo. I tried to get the sword up to stop him, but he barely even looked at me as he ripped the sword out of my hand and flung it across the room.

I turned back to Archer, frantic now. "He's going to kill Ringo."

The blood from his guts began to pool under him, and I realized if he bled out, he wouldn't be able to heal at all. He needed blood, and in a moment of pure instinct, I put my still-oozing wrist up to his mouth. "Drink!"

He tried to turn his head but I forced it back so he could see my eyes. "Drink, damn it! Ringo and I need you!"

"Not from you!" He was so angry that it came out somewhere between a shout and a growl. "I can't … contaminate you." There was a silent plea in his eyes, but I wasn't letting this go. I grabbed the beaker I'd dripped my blood into and held it up to his mouth. The blood rolled thickly down the sides and touched his closed mouth before some instinct made him open his lips.

I looked up then, terrified to see what was happening to Ringo. It was worse than I could have imagined. Ringo was nearly unconscious from being thrown against the wall, and Wilder had picked him up with one arm. He was either going to throw him again and kill him, or he was going to drink from him and kill him.

"Hey! I thought you wanted Shifter blood!" My voice was hoarse from all the tears I was going to cry if we made it past this night.

And then the Cat exploded. *Let go of me*!

So, I did.

My Cougar bounded across the room and rammed into Wilder with full force. He staggered and didn't go down, but he did drop Ringo. *He's mine!* She was so angry that Wilder had dared hurt one of her people, she trembled with rage.

Wilder was steady again, and he'd grabbed a sword. There was a manic gleam in his eyes, and he looked at me like my Cat was the prize he'd been waiting for.

"I should have tasted your father when he was the Lion. It would have made this a proper hunt."

If I could have spoken the words out loud, I would have told him exactly into which dark cavity that idea could be inserted.

He advanced on my Cat, gripping the sword in one hand and holding the other out as if he wanted to catch her by the collar. *Take him down. Make him sorry he hurt my people*. I felt a surge of strength and realized *I* was calling the shots. My Cat was urging, but she wasn't the driving force anymore. I could see Archer beginning to move again, and I needed to get Wilder away from both him and Ringo. So I pushed back to make her retreat further into the room.

What are you doing? She was growling at me, and I could feel her will pushing at mine. I dug deep under her stubbornness and found my own will to defy her. We can't use our teeth on him, I told her. And claws aren't enough to kill him. The most we can do is distract him while Archer gets Ringo out of the way. We need another Vampire to take him down.

I need no help to kill. She sounded like a know-it-all brat, so I laughed at her, even as I made her leap up to the top of the book case as Archer picked Ringo up and moved him. I could feel her confusion at my laughter, but I wasn't going to argue anymore. Wilder was getting ready to hurl the sword at me like a spear, and I

371

had to choose my landing. I had maybe a half second to plan my move.

The sword left Wilder's hand, and I jumped.

I could feel the hilt of the weapon pass under me as I rebounded off the heavy wooden arms of the big chandelier. The mid-air trajectory change was the only move he hadn't expected, and it gave me the chance to throw my weight at his side before we both tumbled to the ground.

Nice move. The Cat sounded impressed, and I had the tiniest moment of pride that I'd surprised her. But Wilder was up a second later, totally pissed I'd caught him off-guard.

"You will pay for that!"

The Cat and I both slunk backwards at the venom in his voice. I knew Archer would be back, and the only way we were going to take Wilder down was by surprise, so I drew him back into the annex to make the surprise quicker. I didn't expect the leap though. Wilder moved so fast I couldn't get out of the way, and his fingers dug into my sides with a vise grip.

"Now you're mine." His growl was feral, and for the first time in all my acquaintance with Vampires, I saw fangs.

Descending.

At. Me.

Crap.

BAM! CRASH!

Two explosions happened at once. Archer hurtled into the annex with the power and speed of an angry bull ... and something came crashing out of the spiral behind me?

Archer slammed into me and I hit the wall with a bone-breaking snap. My Cat retreated instantly. The shimmer of Shifting left behind prickly pain, but I couldn't take my eyes off the scene in front of me.

Archer and Wilder were in a tangle on the stone floor. There was rage in Wilder's eyes and fury in Archer's. But it was pure hatred that lit Tom Landers from the inside.

Tom.

I looked over at the bed where Tom's suffocated body had lain only a few minutes ago.

It was gone.

And he was here.

Barefoot?

The brain in shock is a fascinating thing. That Tom's bare feet registered at all would have made me question sanity in anyone else, but in that moment, it seemed like the oddest part of the whole scene.

In a glance, Tom took in the scene. Wilder and Archer were the biggest things in the room, then he found me, and finally, his eyes landed on Léon. He must have tripped over the body as he came through the spiral.

Wait. What?

Tom came through the spiral.

Tom could Clock.

With a primal cry of Léon's name, he launched himself into the mass of limbs that was the battling Vampires. I tried desperately, and failed completely, to follow the trade of blows and bites, punches and kicks that were being rained down in that tangle of men.

It became clear, though, that Tom was the freshest. He came back from hits like they meant nothing and healed from blows that would have crippled me. Wilder was slower to heal, and Archer was holding himself defensively – staying away from the worst of the battering, but still getting some heavy hits in on Wilder.

Archer and Tom began to work together. Tom was fueled by something filled with pain and hatred, and he seemed unaware of his own injuries. Archer was clearly the more experienced fighter, and he conserved his strength for the blows that would do the most damage.

But none of them had blades, or were close enough to get one, and a beating was not going to stop Wilder forever.

My body hurt. A lot. But the searing agony was layered under pure fear. I knew I was naked from Shifting, but that had about as much importance in the scheme of things as Tom's bare feet did.

The only vulnerability I felt about being nude was it would be easier for flying Vampire blood to hit one of my open gashes. But for this to end, I needed to find a blade, and I had to do it without making myself a target for Wilder.

My eyes scanned the annex looking for anything sharp enough to slice, but all the weapons were scattered in the main room. Finally, I spotted Léon's butcher knife, partially hidden under his fallen body. The knife had been in his hand when he smothered Tom with the pillow. I didn't have the energy to wonder about any of it.

I dragged myself around the edge of the room to where Léon's body lay in an odd, twisted heap. Whatever his future might have been was wiped out in a night of encounters with people who shouldn't have been in this time or this place. I thought I might have felt bad for Léon once, but now I couldn't feel anything that wasn't fear or hate or love.

If it wasn't primal, I didn't feel it.

I reached under Léon's body for the knife, but suddenly Tom was there, panting angrily. "Don't touch him!"

I flinched from the fierceness of his tone, but I reached the butcher knife and pulled it out from under Léon. "Here."

Tom's glare would have been a worrying thing if I'd had any capacity left for worry. He snatched it out of my hand and turned to charge back into combat. But Wilder was headed right for us, and his eyes were locked on the spiral.

"Don't let him go!"

Tom moved in front of the wall, and Wilder stared at him like he was only just now realizing who Tom was.

"You were dead. The worthless Jew killed you." Wilder's gaze flicked to the dead boy on the floor. I saw what looked like a smile crack the corner of Tom's mouth before it disappeared in his rage.

"I'm going to kill you for what you did to him."

Wilder suddenly tried to push Tom out of the way, but Tom seemed to anticipate his exact move. He blocked the hand with one arm, and then brought the other one around in a backhanded sweep. That was the hand with the knife, and in that one motion,

Wilder's head went from connected to, to just resting on his shoulders.

His eyes widened, and his knees buckled.

I turned away as Wilder's body fell.

 DONE

Wilder's head rolled to a stop near my foot, and I was saved from indulging my urge to kick it by Tom, who grabbed it by the hair and hurled it into the massive fireplace. The last image I saw of Bishop John Wilder was satisfyingly horrific. The Monger/Vampire who had tried to murder the people I love more times than I could count – his face grinning in the fire would be forever burned into my memory.

"'E's a right ugly bastard, isn't 'e." Ringo stood in the open doorway, and a sob caught in my throat. He reached a hand down for me and carefully helped me to my feet. His expression was guarded, and he looked away. Probably because I was naked. His eyes took in the scene around us, and narrowed when he recognized Tom.

The next moment, Archer was in front of me enfolding me in his discarded cloak. His own shirt was just tatters of bloody strips of linen, but the skin beneath the shredded fabric looked whole and beautiful. I stopped him from pulling me into his arms.

"Wait." I tore the remains of his shirt off and let my hands do the quick examination my eyes needed to believe. The scars were there, but they looked old and well-healed, even the sword wound that had entered his torso just to the left of his navel. My fingers traced the edges of that, and he inhaled at my touch.

"We need to leave this place, Saira." Archer's voice was low and filled with something primal. My urge to touch him was definitely echoed in his tone, and he seemed to be holding himself back with effort. My hands on his skin felt like a survivor's need –

376

to feel the things that told me I was alive, that I'd survived the horror and violence and could now keep on with the business of living.

I wrapped my arms around his waist and pressed my body into his. My heart nearly exploded with awareness of his skin, the warm, spicy scent of him, and the feeling of trembling muscles wherever I touched. He shuddered with the same need I felt, and drew me to his side with a strong arm.

Ringo couldn't look at us when he spoke. "We promised the Wolf some clothes. I'll find some for ye while I'm at it." He limped when he left the room, and I wondered how badly he was hurt.

Tom had hauled Wilder's body to the fireplace but hadn't yet burned it. I was grateful for that. I didn't think I could stand the smell. His expression was grim as he stepped past us to where Léon's body still lay on the floor. He didn't look at us, didn't make eye contact at all as he picked up the body with more ease than a guy his size should have managed and carried it into the tower room.

Tom laid Léon out on the same bed where I'd seen Léon kill him, and he arranged the body so it looked like Léon was sleeping. His self-control seemed to give way, and he dropped to his knees beside the bed and took Léon's hands into his. He bowed his head and could have been praying, except the shaking in his back said he was crying.

"Tom." I stepped forward, and Archer supported me as we entered the main room.

"Go away, Saira." His voice was full of anguish. All the time I'd known Tom, even after his dad basically disowned him for being the half-Monger son of another man, I'd never seen him cry. And he wasn't even trying to do the guy thing and hide it. He was obviously in too much pain to care what anyone thought.

"What can we do?" I wasn't leaving him there like that, and I think he knew it, because he finally looked me in the eyes.

"Help me bury him."

We took Léon to his island. Connor met us there with the news that Charlie and Valerie had gone back to 1554. Valerie had claimed she couldn't bear it if one of us was killed by Wilder, and she had Family political business to attend to. She also hoped we'd give her at least a year with Charlie.

Ringo closed his eyes and said nothing. His face was expressionless, but he took a breath when his gaze found Archer's. A moment of understanding passed between them, and then we got down to the business of burying Léon.

We all took turns with the shovels to dig Léon's grave, and it was almost dawn by the time the last stone had been placed on top of the fresh dirt.

Archer looked at Tom for permission to speak. He nodded, and Archer spoke directly to him.

"I will not insult you by trying to tell you that one day you'll forget. I know as well as you do that you will not. I can only hope that one day you will not remember as fiercely as you do now, and I pray that that day comes soon enough to give you some peace."

Tom met Archer's eyes. His voice was tight and hard. "I will never forget."

Archer studied him a long moment. There was so much that Tom wasn't saying. So much he had never said. "Never is a long time for us, my brother."

Tom looked away again and wouldn't speak as the rising sun forced Archer and Tom to retreat into the cabin. I thought if Tom's body had let him, he would have stayed out in the sun just to feel the physical pain his soul was in. Connor followed them into the cabin, as bone-weary as all of us were. It would take a long time before any of us felt properly rested again.

Ringo stayed outside with me, by the grave under the big tree watching the sunrise.

"He loved him." My voice and my heart broke for Tom.

"'Tis why 'e won't come back with us."

"What do you mean? Why wouldn't he? That's his home."

Ringo looked at the white stones ringing Léon's grave. "No, this is. At least as long as the guilt eats 'im up. Ye realize, if 'e 'adn't

378

gone back and told Léon to kill 'im, Tom, the boy, would still exist because we would have rescued him, and worse, Léon would, too."

Tom had told us everything while we dug the grave. From Wilder's torture of him, to his own murder of Léon. Waves of my own guilt crashed into me when I realized how close we had been to him then, and we might have changed everything if we'd just entered the Hôtel de Sens before going to Orléans.

We had also discussed at length our theories about why his oblivion attempt *between* had failed. Tom hadn't known, for example, that when I took Elizabeth Tudor's place on the scaffold and then Clocked out from under the executioner's ax, I skipped forward to the moment just after I'd gone from that time. He agreed it felt like *between* had spit him out, and the mystery of where his dead human body had gone wasn't something any of us was touching.

It made me wonder if Clockers actually could be lost *between*, or if they'd just be sent tumbling out to the next moment they didn't already occupy. I added it to the list of things to ask my mom.

I sighed. "He has to come back. He's a Clocker now. There's so much to learn."

"'E's a Vampire first, Saira. Do ye really believe Adam's going to 'old 'is arms out to 'im now?"

"Ava will." I knew he was right, though.

"And ye will, and Archer, and me, and likely Miss Simpson. But not many others. Can ye not feel 'ow alone 'e's been? And not just since Wilder took 'im. Did none of ye know?"

I shook my head. "He was always Adam's wingman." I said, lamely. I'd been clueless.

"Can ye imagine 'ow it made 'im feel? The secrets Tom 'eld must've eaten 'im alive. 'Ere, give me yer book." He held his hand out expectantly for the battered paperback that had been passed around our group of travelers so many times it was only *my* book when someone had to carry it.

The arrow slice had fused the first half together, and it took some unsticking before Ringo flipped to a dog-eared page he must have marked. "Yer man's talkin' about copin' with pain. 'E says there are four doors to the mind: first is sleep – it's the retreat from pain; second is forgetting – when the pain's just too deep. Then 'ere's the third ..." Ringo found his place and started reading. "*Third is the door of madness. There are times when the mind is dealt such a blow it 'ides itself in insanity. While this may not seem beneficial, it is. There are times when reality is nothin' but pain, and to escape that pain the mind must leave reality behind.*"

He looked up at me. "That's where I think Tom went, because of Wilder first, and then when 'e killed the one person who understood the truth of 'im."

I held his gaze until I could find the right words. "Madness scares me, Ringo. I don't know how to bring someone back from it, or even find them inside it." My eyes went to the shack where Tom slept. "What's the fourth door?"

Ringo read. "*Last is the door of death. The final resort. Nothin' can 'urt us after we are dead, or so we have been told.*" His eyes found mine. "'E's not comin' back with us, Saira."

The tears came then. "We can't just leave him here."

"I don't see as ye 'ave much say in the matter." The sigh at the end of that told me Ringo wasn't just talking about Tom anymore, and I rested my head on his shoulder.

"Should we go get Charlie before we go home?"

I could feel him shake his head, and my heart broke a little more for my friends. "She's not ready yet. She 'as some life to live first."

"What about you? What do you want to do?" I looked into his eyes and he smiled.

"Miss Simpson offered me a place at St. Brigid's. I think it's time I went to school, don't ye?"

I smiled then. It had been too long since my last smile, and I felt out of practice, but for that I could smile. "It's about time you learned something."

He snorted as he stood and helped me to my feet. "If I've learned anythin', it's that ye're a pain in my arse. Go to yer man and good riddance to ye."

He kissed me on each cheek and then turned me toward the cabin door, and I stumbled inside. Connor was curled in a tight ball just inside the door, and Tom had fallen asleep against the back wall. Archer was on one of the beds, and there was just enough space for me to crawl in next to him and press my body against his before I slipped into a coma of sleep.

HOME

Tom was gone when we woke up.

Archer was pissed, Ringo expected it, and I was just sad.

Archer wanted to go search for him. He hated the idea of an untrained, guilt-ridden, angry Vampire on the loose in 1429. He worried about the integrity of the time stream, and about the fact that Tom could Clock now. I wasn't so sure Tom had much control over his Clocking ability, and his attempts to get lost in time had been an epic fail. It wasn't that I didn't agree with Archer; I definitely didn't think Tom was safe or even necessarily sane right now. I was just tired of searching for people who didn't want to be found, and I wanted to go home.

We left at first dark, and even without Charlie, it was one of the simplest Clocks I'd ever done. Maybe because I wanted to be back in my mom's kitchen garden so badly I could almost smell the herbs in the air. Maybe because I needed to make sure everyone I loved was safe. Or maybe the little bit of my blood Archer had tasted had brought another Clocker into my world. I wasn't touching that thought yet, but it was there, in the background, waiting to be brought out into the light and acknowledged.

Something in Connor seemed to have scabbed over during his time alone on the island, and I was glad he hadn't been with us at the Hôtel de Sens. I thought it would be a long time before I didn't flinch at the sight of blood, and although his Wolf would probably have been really helpful as we battled Wilder, I was glad he didn't have to add the scenes in the tower room to his nightmares.

The kitchen garden at Elian Manor was so peaceful I almost cried when I dropped to my knees in a bed of creeping thyme. Archer's arm had been around me as we Clocked. For that matter, he hadn't let go much in the past twelve hours, and I almost didn't want to put on the clothes Ringo had acquired for me and Connor, just because it would mean there was something separating me from his skin.

I could feel the Cat just below the surface. Her approval at Archer's touch was as disconcerting as it was encouraging. I didn't know that I was emotionally ready for what she inspired in me physically, but I wasn't necessarily *not* ready either. I knew I would have to be the one to make the physical moves though, so I only had my own desires and insecurities to battle.

And right now, the only desire I had was to be held close by the man who loved me.

"Spidey sense," Archer whispered to me before we left the safety of the walled garden. He was right – we didn't know what we might be walking into, and after the weeks we'd had, a Monger ambush was the very last thing on a long list of things we didn't need.

I reached out with my senses, and for the first time I felt my Cat underneath them, propelling my intuition and instinct forward. So that's why I could sense Mongers – they were predators like she was, and her instinct was to stay safe and away from trouble.

"Want me to Shift?" Connor's voice was low, but I could hear a little bit of boyish excitement back in it. I smiled at him.

"I think we're good. I'm not getting anything."

I led the way out of the garden, and we made our way to the kitchen door. Before I could root around for the spare key, the door was flung wide open, and light and warmth flooded us from the room inside. Sanda stood there with a gruff expression.

"Took ye long 'nuff."

One second of surprised hesitation later, I flung my arms around her and practically knocked her over with my hug. She sniffed loudly, and I expected the glare when she finally looked at me. "Now see what ye've done? I 'aven't cried in years."

I kissed her cheek and stepped inside the kitchen while she grabbed Archer for the same rough hug. I knew both Ringo and Connor were next, and it was exactly the homecoming we all needed.

What I didn't expect was a kitchen full of people. Ava barreled into me first thing. She whispered "welcome home" in my ear, and then spun lightly away to greet the others. My mom and Millicent sat at the big kitchen table nursing mugs of tea; Miss Simpson was serving Jeeves a slice of pie; the Armans were standing in a corner with Adam; Connor's mom was refilling the teapot; and Mr. Shaw looked like he had just stood up.

It was to him I ran.

Mr. Shaw picked me up in the biggest bear hug I've ever received in my life, and I felt a piece of darkness lift from my heart. "You're safe," he whispered into my hair.

"You're here."

"They only held me for questioning, and these two" – he indicated my mom and his sister – "worked together to ask some very uncomfortable questions that Rothchild couldn't answer without revealing all their Family secrets."

"Do other people know about the Monger ring?"

"It was part of the deal. We'd keep their secret so long as they backed away. We're at a bit of a stand-off with them at the moment, and they know they overplayed their hand by taking me. I don't doubt they'll regroup and come back stronger, though hopefully we'll have a bit more understanding of their game when they make their next play."

My mom held her arms out to me, and I was held in a tight hug. There were a lot of embraces and back slaps all around the room, but for a moment, I was only conscious of being my mother's daughter. Her heartbeat grounded mine, and I could feel that she was totally there.

I searched her face. "How long did it take?"

"To shake off the effects of the ring? Longer than I like. Jeeves and Elizabeth were instrumental in pulling us both out of the fog in which the ring left us. There were a lot of very honest and forthright conversations had, and in the end, truth was the thing we couldn't ignore. It was the thing that lifted the fog."

"I'm so sorry I wasn't there to help you."

My mom looked sad. "Oh Saira, I'm sorry I couldn't help *you*. You have had to do so much on your own."

"I was never alone. I've always had family with me." I looked around the room full of people I cared about. Like me, Connor was in his mom's arms, and there was a Bush Baby perched on his shoulder, while his uncle hovered right behind them. And Ringo and Archer were talking to Miss Simpson and the Armans while Sanda fussed over them. I imagined the Seers had Seen us come home, which was why we had such a great welcoming committee. Jeeves winked at me from across the room, and then my eyes met Archer's. He came to my side and kissed my mom on both cheeks.

"Thank you for keeping her safe, Archer." I loved that my mom and Archer genuinely liked each other.

"We keep each other safe, Claire." His arm snaked around my waist, and I felt like I was truly home. "You should know that Bishop Wilder is dead."

My mom gasped quietly, and her eyes filled with tears. "Thank you," she whispered.

Mr. Shaw must have sensed my mom was upset, because his arm went around her protectively. The gesture made my heart jump in my chest, and the smile she gave him through her tears was even better. "I'm okay, Bob. Just ... so glad they're home."

Mr. Shaw growled at Archer in a voice filled with emotion. "Since you made her cry, Devereux, I'm going to need some more blood."

Archer looked at me quickly, and I nodded. "That could be interesting ..." The two men broke off to speak quietly in a corner of the warm kitchen, while Mom and I smiled at each other.

"So you're ..." We started to speak at the same time, but I finished. "...together?"

"Yes." There was a content look on Mom's face as she watched Mr. Shaw.

"Good." I really meant it. Mr. Shaw was as much a father to me as I'd ever known, and usually much more.

"And you, Saira? Are you happy?"

"Happy? That doesn't feel solid enough, somehow. Like it's fleeting or transient, and whenever something crappy happens, it's gone in a puff of smoke." My eyes caught Archer's for a moment and he smiled in a way that warmed me all the way to my toes. "I'm in love with someone I want to spend my life getting to know. He makes me feel safe and trusted and strong and beautiful, and all the things that give me validation that who I am is someone worth knowing. I guess it feels more bliss than happiness."

Mom pulled me in for another hug. "Bliss is good."

I smiled at Archer's laughter across the room. "Yeah, it is."

Adam came over and gave me a big hug. "I'm glad you're here," I whispered into his shoulder.

"Are you kidding? Ava Saw you guys first, then Miss Simpson called my parents, and next thing I knew we were all in a car racing to get here."

Something about Adam had changed in the past couple of months. He'd gotten more serious since I'd come back from the Tower of London without his cousin. And now I was going to add to that. "We found Tom."

There was no spark of hope in his eyes. I knew he assumed the worst, though I wasn't really sure what the worst actually was for Adam. "He was turned."

There was the spark. "Wait, he's not dead?"

I shook my head mutely. It was such a huge conversation, and I knew we'd be having it with everyone soon enough. Adam's eyes lit up, and he pulled me in for another hug. "Thank God!"

I couldn't stand the idea of crushing that light back out, but I had to be honest with him. "I don't know if he'll come back here, though."

His eyes held mine for a long moment. "The fact that he might is enough."

Mr. and Mrs. Arman joined us then, and after Adam told them the news about Tom, I asked the question that had been weighing on me since I saw them. "Has anyone heard from Daisy or the other missing people?"

Adam answered. "Alex got a letter from Daisy. She said she was doing some work in Wales and she'd be back in a couple of weeks." His voice didn't sound right though.

"But you don't believe the letter."

"No, neither does Alex. There's a friend of Olivia's called Tam. He went missing after you left, and his family got a letter, too. They've confirmed the handwriting is right, but the letter just feels ... wrong. Scotland Yard has people working on it now because the letters have tied some of the missing people together."

"The Mongers made a mistake with those letters. They might be getting nervous."

Archer came over and joined us. "Nervous Mongers are a dangerous thing. I anticipate things will get worse before they get better."

As Archer and the Armans greeted each other, Millicent raised her voice in an imperious tone. "If everyone would please sit, we can feed these poor children and get to bed."

Mom and I shared a look and a secret smile across the room, but we all did as Millicent had commanded.

A sudden thought occurred to me. "Hey, Millicent?"

She turned to face me with a very slight smile on her usually haughty face. "Yes, dear."

Dear? That was new. I guess she had missed me. "What can you tell me about Joan of Arc?" Archer's, Ringo's, and Connor's attention swiveled to our exchange. The success or failure of our "mission" of the past couple of weeks pretty much depended on whether Jehanne's accomplishments at Orléans and after that had been important enough to make it into the history books.

Millicent looked confused and my heart sank.

"The Maid of Orléans?"

I dared to hope. "You know her?"

Millicent shot me her version of a smirk. "Not personally, no. But of course I've heard of her. Saint Joan, who was burned at the stake."

Instantly, my own knowledge of Joan of Arc was exactly that. Connor looked at me incredulously. "*Saint* Joan?" he mouthed. Yeah, no kidding.

Millicent hadn't seen our reactions because she had continued. "Joan of Arc had visions she was to help defeat the English, and then joined with Charles VII and was instrumental in his coronation as King of France. She was later burned at the stake. I believe the actual charge leveled against her had to do with dressing in men's clothes." Millicent cast a disparaging eye over my own wardrobe, and then cracked a completely out-of-character smile.

Despite the surprise of Joan's sainthood and the manner of her demise, a thousand pounds of tension lifted off my chest. Archer's shoulders relaxed, Ringo grinned, and even Connor allowed himself a small smile. I could see the conflict in him, though. I knew how he felt about the aggressive, vindictive, righteous mixed-blood who had made his life hell for weeks.

"Must've been a Seer, right Jane?" It was weird to hear Mr. Shaw address Miss Simpson by her first name.

Miss Simpson smiled at me. "Perhaps Saira and her friends know the answer to that?"

Hours later, a vat of shepherd's pie had been demolished, every story had been recounted, and nearly everyone had stumbled off to a bedroom somewhere in the vast manor. Apparently, Jeeves had moved Connor's mom and the kids into his big flat over the garage so he could keep an eye on their safety. He slept in the butler's rooms in the manor, but from the way they kept stealing looks at each other, I wondered how long that arrangement would last.

Archer and I slipped out and headed to the walled garden to finally be alone. We rounded a corner, and I nearly ran right into my cousin Doran.

I almost punched him. Just on principle.

"Hello, Cousin. Sucker." He nodded to each of us genially, as if it wasn't exceptionally strange to meet around a dark corner just before dawn.

"I just got home. Unless it's life or death, I don't want to talk to you." I growled at him. I think even my Cat growled at him, but he just looked vaguely amused.

"My, you're awfully feline tonight. I just stopped by to say well done on removing the skill-collector from among your variables."

I stared at him, and I could feel Archer tensing at my back. "Among my variables? Are you insane?"

"Not usually, no, though I might have phrased that badly. What I meant to say was thank you. That time stream split would have been simple enough to leave alone, but you saw the problem and you didn't just look away. Thank you for choosing what was right instead of what was easy."

I narrowed my eyes. "What's your game, Doran? Why am I doing all the heavy lifting when you can clearly see what's happening, *and* you can Clock to fix the problems."

He gave me a dazzling smile. "Aren't you the Child in Aislin's prophecy?"

And then he exploded into a huge, black, shimmery Raven and flew away.

Wait, what?

I spun to stare at Archer, and his eyes were as bugged out as mine were.

"Did Doran just ... Shift?" Archer sounded completely flummoxed.

"I'm going to kill him. It's official. Doran will be my one and only murder victim. My Cat is going to hunt his fricking Bird, and all that's going to be left are guts for someone to step in."

Archer struggled not to smile. And failed.

"Come on." He held his hand out to me. "I think drastic measures are in order."

"What kind? Oh, I know, maybe you should teach me to shoot a hunting rifle next, or something high-powered with a scope." I scowled. "Except then I'd be tempted to just start shooting random ravens, and they'd arrest me for animal cruelty or hunting the territorial bird of the Yukon – did you know Ravens are the territorial bird of the—"

Archer kissed me to shut me up.

As ways to shut me up went, it didn't suck.

When I had sufficiently calmed down from my Doran-induced murder fantasies and we had settled ourselves on the garden bench, I leaned my back against his chest and stared up at the constellation of Orion over our heads.

"You know the scorpion still chases Orion across the sky?"

Archer's reply at my ear made me shiver in a way that had nothing to do with cold. "Does the scorpion chase him, or does he hunt the scorpion?"

"Does it matter? In the end, someone's always running. I'm so tired of running."

"Let me be the place you rest, then."

I turned to face him and draped my legs over his where he straddled the bench. "You are everything to me, Archer." I took his face in my hands and kissed him with all the passion that went with those words.

When the kiss ended, and my heartbeat still slammed in my chest, Archer ran his hand lightly over my arm. "Saira?"

"When someone says your name and you're right in front of them, either you're in trouble, or they are." I joked to cover up the nerves that suddenly fluttered through me.

Archer smiled at that. "I guess it's me who's in trouble."

"Why?"

"Because of everything that happened in that tower room – all the violence, the horror, and the bloodshed – the only thing I can seem to think about is the way your skin felt when it was pressed to mine."

My answering smile was slow and probably very feline, because my Cat preened and stretched languorously inside me. I leaned in close to him and whispered, just before I kissed him.

"Yeah, you're in trouble."

The End

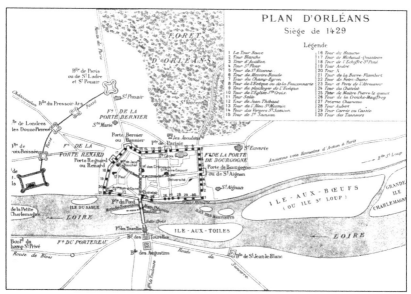

Map of Orléans in 1429 – Courtesy of the Gutenberg Project

AUTHOR'S NOTE ABOUT THE HISTORY

Thank you for forgiving the liberties I've taken with history. This was not a time period I knew very much about before a very interesting fact presented itself during the writing of *Tempting Fate*. 1429 was a perfect one-ring jump back in time from April, 1554, and a search for historical events of note at that time revealed Joan of Arc's decisive role in ending the Siege of Orléans.

With that, I had the setting for *Changing Nature*.

The real Joan of Arc was quite remarkable in her pure conviction and her surprisingly effective battle tactics. Jehanne d'Arc, as she was known then, was an illiterate peasant who managed, at age seventeen, to convince Charles VII of France that her visions of his ascension to the French throne and her role in putting him there were divine directives from God. Even historians who doubt her sanity, much less her role as God's interpreter, don't deny that Joan of Arc turned a dynastic squabble for French royal inheritance into a popular war of national liberation.

391

On May 7th, 1429, under the command of Joan of Arc, a boat set with explosives collapsed part of the bridge that crossed the Loire River at Orléans. An estimated five hundred English soldiers, in full armor, fell into the river and drowned. It was a deciding factor in ending the Siege of Orléans.

In Orléans, Joan of Arc worked side-by-side with military-commander-turned-national-hero, Gilles, Baron de Rais. On October 26th, 1440, nine years after Joan of Arc's death, de Rais was tried and convicted for the murder of between seventy and two hundred children. He is reputed to have been the inspiration behind the legend of Bluebeard.

Two years after the Siege of Orléans, Joan of Arc was burned at the stake by the English, convicted on a technicality related to a biblical clothing law. In prison, while on trial for heresy, she had worn male clothing, which allowed her to fasten hosen, boots, and tunic together into one piece as a deterrent to rape. Twenty-nine years after her death, a retrial overturned the conviction and declared Joan of Arc unjustly executed.

The Wolves of Paris were a real threat in 1450. That winter was remarkably harsh, and the city walls had deteriorated so much that the wolves, led by a tawny-colored alpha the Parisians called Courtaud, were able to enter through breaks in them. Forty people died before the citizens of Paris finally cornered the wolves on the steps of Notre Dame and slaughtered them with pikes and swords.

The Hôtel de Sens in the Marais district is one of the last medieval buildings still standing in Paris. It was built in 1475 as the primary city residence for the Archbishops of Sens, and currently houses the Bibliothèque Forney. The Île Saint-Louis, one of two Parisian islands in the Seine River, actually was grazing pasture for cattle before the seventeenth century, the eels under the bridge in Melun were famously fat from the flour mill, and the Saint-Séverin Abbey in Château-Landon, though currently a rest home for seniors, remains one of the most striking medieval churches in France.

As you can see, there are liberal sprinklings of historical events throughout *Changing Nature*. The details are as accurate as I could make them, but liberties were taken with dates in order to weave them through my plot. The fifteenth century produced some fascinating people doing extraordinary things, and I feel very privileged to live and write in an age of internet research, Wikipedia translator, soap, and toilet paper.

And finally...

Thank you so much for reading *Changing Nature*. If you enjoyed this book, your review on Amazon or Goodreads would be very appreciated. You can find more information and my blog at www.aprilwhitebooks.blogspot.com.

I sincerely appreciate hearing from readers, and thank you, again, for joining Saira, Archer, and Ringo on their adventures in time.

~April White

Thank You

Changing Nature happened because I have extraordinary children. They have encouraged and supported me every step of the way in the plotting and writing of this book. They've helped define characters, fill holes, and create elements, and our long dog walks always began with the question, "So, what'd you write today, Mom?" They are amazing boys with fantastic imaginations, and I am the luckiest mother in the world.

My husband, with whom I share our unbelievably cool offspring, is the love of my life, the man of my dreams, and the reason I can write action scenes. He is the most visual storyteller I know, and he inspires me to *show* him what Saira, Archer, and Ringo do. It just makes him nervous that I don't always know what they're going to do next.

I treasure the collaboration I have with my editor, whose patience, knowledge, and understanding make everything better. We became friends through books, and it was she who introduced me to my favorite fantasy novel, *The Name of the Wind*, by Patrick Rothfuss. This is the book that Saira carries with her on the journey to 1429, and the passages she and Ringo read out loud are courtesy of its very generous author. So, very special thanks to Angela Houle and Patrick Rothfuss – it's such a pleasure to put both names in the same sentence.

Strong, generous, lovely women surround me, and their support has kept me sane, reasonably interesting, and able to laugh. My mothers, my sisters, girls I knew when we were finding our way, women I met when I'd grown up – whether we're bound by DNA, marriage, history, proximity, shared interest, or books – you are the family I choose, and I thank you with all of my heart for choosing me.

And to the readers who have discovered the Immortal Descendants – who have read the books, recommended them, left reviews, written me notes – THANK YOU! Your generosity and kindness have been overwhelming, and I am so honored that you've chosen these stories to read.

Printed in Great Britain
by Amazon

81204552R00231